WORSTVILLE

a community crime

Ford Preston Weber

Author/Publishing Ford Preston Weber
2916 Barrington Drive
Toledo, Ohio 43606
www.worstville.com

Publisher's Note: This is a work of fiction. Names, characters, places, and incidents are a product of the author's imagination. Locales and public names are sometimes used for atmospheric purposes. Any resemblance to actual people, living or dead, or to businesses, companies, events, institutions, or locales is completely coincidental.

Book Layout ©2017 BookDesignTemplates.com

Ordering Information:
Quantity sales. Special discounts are available on quantity purchases by corporations, associations, and others. For details, contact the "Special Sales Department" at the address above.

Worstviile/Ford Preston Weber -- 1st ed.
ISBN 978-0-9600079-1-2 (Print)

This book is dedicated to my loving wife Cyndy and our daughters Jennifer and Sarah for bearing with me, to my parents for modeling voluntarism and civic engagement, to everyone with whom I've had the pleasure of working throughout my career for all your contributions to society and for letting me absorb a fraction of your collective knowledge, and to everyone who devotes some measure of their life toward the betterment of the world in which they live.

Contents

Preface

The opening sentence of Jane Jacobs's introduction to *The Death and Life of Great American Cities*, written in 1960, reads: "This book is an attack on current city planning and rebuilding." She goes on to state that her book, probably the most influential and insightful urban planning book ever written, is "mostly an attempt to introduce new principles of planning and rebuilding, different and even opposite from those now taught in everything from schools of architecture and planning to the Sunday supplements and women's magazines."

In boldly quoting one of my intellectual heroines, I do not mean to imply that anything I write is worthy of mention alongside her masterpiece. However, I do think that if someone is so compelled to share his thoughts that he takes the time to write a book, well then, he ought to plant a flag in the ground and clearly state his motive and purpose for doing so. While some local governments, such as Dayton, Ohio where I currently serve, do an outstanding job of aligning city programs and initiatives with community needs and visions under extremely difficult conditions, many cities are failing to do so. And so I hereby state that this book is meant to be a practical novel whose story gradually reveals much of what is wrong with many local governments today—particularly as seen through the lens of urban revitalization in a struggling city. And since we live in a democratic republic, we are culpable for the systemic sins of our government. Moreover, local government is generally the "proving ground" for state and federal officials. It is at the local level that many career politicians first learn either the art of service-oriented public leadership or of obfuscation and kicking the can down the road—to name just a few tricks of the trade.

1

This book doesn't propose revolutionary solutions that will improve the functioning of government and enhance the quality of our elected leadership. I'm not certain that it is possible to accomplish that directly by legal and regulatory reform. However, I *do* hope to wake up the overwhelming majority of the public—a public that ignores the actions and policies of government and in so doing shrugs off the responsibilities that accompany the liberties bestowed by democratic government. Frankly, most of us stumble through the process of self-government in a collective narcotic trance of sorts, only occasionally rousing ourselves like groundhogs waking from hibernation to really get involved, and then only for the briefest periods of time. Hopefully, people will read this book and get more involved in government. Not just physically involved by voting, volunteering, and advocating, but also thoughtfully engaged in exploring the issues and asking probing, challenging questions.

As I write this book, I am aware that some people may use it as an argument for severely limiting local government. They may in effect say, "Government is so bad, we should have as little of it as possible," which may in fact turn out to be not merely less government than is optimal but less government than a healthy society requires. I say this because while the thoughts of these "governmental minimalists" may be appealing to some, local government performs a vital role—particularly in urban areas. We are no longer a nation of subsistence farmers in which each family is largely self-sufficient in its own right. In that era, government could have been and was much smaller. Today we are primarily residents of metropolitan areas in which we are all interdependent for the food, water, and other commodities we need to live and to enjoy life—and for the economic prosperity that makes it all affordable. Our actions impact each other in ways that never happened on the rural, self-sufficient/self-contained farms of a bygone era. Moreover, how the owner of one property in an urban metro area chooses to use, maintain, and invest in that property affects the value and utility of nearby properties, and vice versa. So it is that for the vast majority of the population, our financial prosperity and our living environs are interdependent.

Local government plays a critical role in providing the infrastructure, safety forces, and educational opportunities that are essential in this interdependent world. Local government also has provided the mechanism for enforcing building, zoning, and property maintenance codes. It also plays a major role in shaping the physical character of a city through its planning processes and the ways it chooses to invest in its various neighborhoods, including downtown. Most importantly, this role in shaping the local character of a community is absolutely vital because it is fundamental to creating environments in which people thrive and to which they become emotionally attached.

Creating great urban places is absolutely essential to any city's prosperity. Millennials and empty nesters increasingly prefer urban living. Businesses cannot succeed without good employees, and as the existing talent pool continues to be unable to meet the needs of the job market, the ability to attract and retain skilled workers is of paramount strategic performance. As former Pittsburgh mayor Tom Murphy has repeatedly stated, cities must strive for excellence and cannot afford to adopt a "that'll do" mentality. When "good" no longer guarantees success, "pretty good" is failure.

For these reasons and others, local government's role is not likely to diminish or even remain unchanged. On the contrary, it is very likely to increase. Therefore, it is imperative that citizens actively engage in governing. Furthermore, it is quite likely that successful communities will (1) utilize advanced information technologies to broaden public input in local decision making and (2) increasingly utilize more comprehensive approaches to delivering services and tackling complex issues through expanded partnerships with other public, private, and not-for-profit entities.

Therefore, rather than constrain and "starve" local government, the better response is to shoulder our burden as *governing* citizens and become more actively and deeply engaged. As we do so, we must bear in mind the difference between merely asking our government to manage itself better (i.e., to become more efficient) and demanding that our government have visionary, principled leadership. In many communities the political discourse is generally limited to questions of efficiency—to the question of providing better basic services like paving streets, patching potholes, fixing leaking waterlines, collecting trash, and providing better police and fire protection. In most communities there is almost no conversation about envisioning the city's future as a location where people thrive and to which they become deeply attached. A city where all of its neighborhoods nurture children with the expectation that they will flourish. A city that competes globally by developing, attracting, and retaining talent.

This does not have to be an "us versus them" confrontation. An engaged citizenry can be extremely helpful to public servants, because the direction and feedback the engaged citizenry provides gives the elected official or administrator "political cover" to stand up to powerful special interests that might pressure the government to support self-serving or misguided projects and programs. I have personally witnessed mayors and city council members state that they are supporting or opposing a project or issue because they know that the public engagement process with their constituents recommended a particular course of action. In the absence of such engagement, it is difficult to *guestimate* where the people stand and to marshal the courage to take a difficult position.

Engaging the citizenry requires the sustained effort of elected officials and the public they serve. The elected officials must inform the public of the relevant facts, possibly provide potential alternative courses of action, afford the public ample opportunity to investigate the issue and express opinions, and then respect the public's input and follow through in a manner that is consistent with that engagement. Too often local government finds it easier or preferable to not engage the local population in planning processes and, more importantly, fails to encourage the community's sustained engagement by actively following through on their direction. In communities where this level of citizen engagement and follow-through is not occurring, the electorate needs to demand that it start happening and hold the elected officials accountable. This is not to say that there are no local leadership bright spots from time to time across America without public involvement, but these upticks are generally aberrations resulting from a particularly charismatic, principled, and effective leader. Rarely, if ever, are they the result of sustained diverse local leadership derived from an engaged populace. Consequently, these bright spots are usually short-lived flares rather than boilers fueling the steam engines of sustained progress.

This book is about the failures of local leadership—particularly local government—throughout the United States. It is also relevant at the state and federal levels. It is most likely applicable beyond the borders of the United States.

The fictional city of Westville is a vehicle for talking about these failures, and all of the characters are purely fictional. And while some cities have either turned the corner or appear to be on the right path, most cities have substantially or even grossly underperformed over the past eighty years or so. Broadly speaking, the failures of Westville are the failures of governments across the entire nation and beyond.

The appendices at the back of the book provide some information that readers may find helpful as they read:

Appendix A is an essay by Dr. Harold Hearst on the topic of cities as having life-like characteristics.

Appendix B is a complete list of Dr. Harold Hearst's emails to Frank Clark written as he was mentoring Frank.

Appendix C is the final approved WIN proposal.

Appendix D is a list of the characters and their titles or roles.

Appendix E is a timeline of the main events in the story.

CHAPTER 1

"The Mayor will see you now, Mr. Clark." Joan, the Mayor's Executive Assistant had a tough job: partly the kind but firm gatekeeper, and partly the friendly, concerned face of City administration. Joan excelled at both, although with perhaps a uniform air of formality that should have been slightly less formal for people like Frank Clark whom she knew well. As with the rest of the Mayor's senior staff, it was always "coat and tie" with Joan, never the business-casual approach that permeated the rest of Westville. Her officiousness was delivered with such genuine sincerity that it made Frank wish she would let her hair down a little. Somewhere beneath her professional barriers there must have been some, possibly suppressed, laughter that would have made for a little friendly office banter. Nonetheless, she was a bright spot in an inner sanctum that would have benefited from an injection of genuine camaraderie and a little bleeding off of excess self-importance.

It was a beautiful day in early August of 2000, and Frank was in the foyer of the Mayor's office waiting to see him about an exciting new redevelopment initiative Westville had launched. Westville was a declining Midwest "rust-belt" city that had seen its population decrease by about twenty percent in the past thirty years. It was an incredibly generic community with a proliferation of chain restaurants, drugstores, and gas station/carryouts that were haphazardly thrown about. It had some outstanding institutional anchors, but instead of connecting with their immediate neighborhoods, they remained isolated and frequently undertook large

7

expansion projects that usurped private property and split once-vibrant urban neighborhoods into scattered fragments. No one seemed to notice that as locally-owned businesses that provided neighborhood amenities gave way to institutional healthcare facilities (as was generally the case) that Westville's neighborhoods, and the city along with them, lost their sense of place – their fundamental reason for being. Westville's civic and political leadership liked to boast about its affordable cost of housing and lack of traffic, but these advantages were actually symptoms of its decline: a steadily decreasing population had resulted in depressed housing prices and a lessening of traffic. It also led to budget crises as a declining and less affluent population was supporting a larger network of public infrastructure and a growing demand to fund social services and address urban blight. Nonetheless, the out-of-touch political, civic, and business leadership turned a blind eye and boasted about the outstanding qualities of a community that growing numbers of young people had referred to as "Worstville" for at least thirty years.

Mayor Charles "Red" Paley was a career politician who had been reelected to a second four-year term as Mayor of Westville the previous November. He had had a tumultuous first term and was not expected to win his bid for reelection. By campaigning hard through Election Day on the theme of a "city in constant motion" and simultaneously promising the world to everyone, he eked out a stunning victory by five-tenths of a percentage point. Perhaps most importantly, he had the support of organized labor.

When the dust had settled and the city had caught its breath, the *Westville Wire & Telegraph,* which had endorsed his opponent, ran the following editorial:

A Reprieve from the Electorate

Mayor Paley has won a stunning victory in this week's election, a testimony to the energy he brings to his roles as mayor and, more particularly, candidate. His theme of a "city in constant motion" obviously appealed to a narrow majority of voters. We wish him and our city all the best, but we are neither impressed nor encouraged. During the first four years of his tenure we have witnessed more commotion than motion, more platitudes than progress, and more turmoil than triumph.

Westville continues to be among the national leaders in too many of the wrong categories: functional illiteracy, infant mortality, poverty, the percentage of people receiving some form of government assistance. We could go on and on. The list would be monotonous if weren't so tragic that a community with the promise of Westville is doing so badly.

While we acknowledge that these problems require long-term strategies, the current administration has offered little if anything in the way of solutions. Simply navigating from one crisis to another is neither a vision nor an implementation plan. Perhaps the greatest indicator of Westville's failure to achieve its potential is the fact that for thirty years, we have steadily lost population. Last Tuesday, Westvillians voted at the polls. *For three decades they have been voting with their feet.*

Nonetheless, we can always hope that Mr. Paley will grow into the job and focus his energies on lifting

Westville out of the economic and social morass that led us to endorse his more capable opponent. (In all candor, it is more likely than not that he won't elevate his game; but that prospect would be yet another blow this community should not have to suffer.)

On the optimistic side, we are pleased that Mr. Paley promoted Roderick Campbell to the position of Chief of Staff eighteen months into his administration and that he has added Byron Swift as his Senior Director of Strategy. As these men continue to develop in their roles (it would be nice to see a woman in an equal position), perhaps they will be able to assist Mr. Paley in the fine art of governing. Of course, no matter how able they are, their effectiveness will be limited by Mr. Paley's degree of interest in focusing himself on furthering Westville's revitalization. Given Mr. Paley's penchant for moving up the political ladder, we are not optimistic that Westville's prosperity, rather than winning the Governor's office, is his top priority. If our suspicions are correct, then Mr. Paley owes the community an enormous apology.

Westville desperately needed some new strategies if it was going to reverse its thirty-year decline, and Frank Clark was optimistic that this opportunity could play a key role. The Mayor and he were about to meet to talk about the next steps in implementing a brand-new community revitalization strategy, and Frank was champing at the bit. Frank had been with the City for only a year and had learned a lot in his short tenure. He was about to learn a great deal more.

*****

Frank Clark came to the City in August of 1999 as a senior attorney with thirteen years' experience in both the public and private sectors. He had practiced three years in the County Prosecutor's office and then more than five years in a corporation's legal section before trying his hand in private practice. Frank liked being part of a cross-functional team working on a longer-term basis advancing organizational objectives. He preferred this to the life of a legal "hired gun" generally asked to deal with crises that could have been easily avoided with better planning and counsel.

More important to Frank, his intervention as an attorney was episodic—he was called in as necessary to deal with a problem and had no connection to long-term strategies and their overall success. Even at the City he was brought in only as necessary. This frustrated him even more because he was already on the payroll which meant his services came free of charge to the administrators and departments he served.

As a senior attorney, Frank reported directly to Law Director Karen Jones. Karen had an incredible ability to remain calm in the midst of even the most violent storm—and there were many. Like Frank, she had had considerable experience in private practice, and she always told everyone that the Mayor was her client. During her career she had had some good and some not-so-good clients. The Mayor was just another client. (The difference, which Frank never expressed, was that now the Mayor was her *primary* client, and he could make her life, and the life of everyone else, miserable.)

January 2000

It seemed as if there were always multiple "crises of the day" in Westville City Hall, and the morning of January 3, 2000, wasn't any different. Frank had been on the job about five months, and at 8:15 he was called into Karen's office. Fortunately, the crisis wasn't too serious, but Frank found the way it was handled to be very revealing.

He entered Karen's office to find Chief of Staff Roderick Campbell and Senior Director of Strategy Byron Swift there as well. Under some circumstances, that combination could be pretty ominous, but it was obvious that today they were just in a collective problem-solving mode.

Karen was sitting behind her desk and leaning forward, fully engaged. Seeing Frank enter the doorway, she spoke up with a calm but energized voice. "Have a seat, Frank." Three chairs arced in a semicircle in front of her desk, and she motioned him to sit in the empty chair closest to the door. Roderick and Byron sat in the other chairs.

Karen began, "Frank, we need to make some modifications to your memo on the City's potential liability for the Jonesboro Trucking Warehouse. I didn't want to do it without having you in on the discussion."

"Thanks," Frank said. "What's wrong with it?"

"Legally it's fine," Karen said reassuringly. "But it's a little too technical for us to send to the Mayor. He will probably misinterpret it, and it could generate a lot of questions and meetings that wouldn't be productive. We really can't afford that."

"That's for sure!" The smile on Frank's face made it clear he wasn't too upset about having to reword his memo. However, he was more than a little interested in hearing what had to be changed and why. He had served as corporate counsel for a number of years in private industry and thought he was pretty good at translating legalese into plain English.

"So where's the problem?" Frank asked.

Karen continued: "You do a really good job of laying out the background of the warehouse, how it's been a vacant, dilapidated eyesore that the City finally took title to through tax foreclosure. And the Mayor will eat that up, because the D2 [Derelict Demolition Program] is his baby, and this advances that program. But he won't understand the part about the City having potential environmental liability when we transfer the warehouse to a new owner."

"I thought I put it pretty plainly. Until the state enacts the new Clean Hands Slum and Blight Redevelopment Bill, the City could have some legal exposure if it is determined that it either directly caused some contamination or indirectly caused it by failing to keep the property properly secured from illegal dumping."

"Right," Karen said. "And believe me, the memo is a perfectly fine outline of the law. Roderick or Byron, maybe it's time for one of you to jump in here for minute."

Roderick took the baton. "Sure. Byron and I both read this yesterday afternoon and then talked it over. After sleeping on it overnight, we called Karen this morning. Here's the problem, and, like Karen said, I'm sure your memo is legally correct. And it would be more than satisfactory if it was only going to me, but it's not. The Mayor requested a memo on the potential liability, so the memo is going to him. And even though he doesn't read much, we are sure he will read it."

Frank acknowledged their thinking with a nod.

"Either or both of two things are likely to happen. First, he will go off half-cocked on a rant about the idiocy of the current law. I can hear it now: "How can we have any liability for some dirtball coming in and illegally dumping, yada, yada, yada." None of us have time for that bull. Second, he will probably want a second memorandum further detailing the law, and that will probably lead to a third and maybe even a fourth memo."

"And at the end of the day, he'll be cursing the law, our legal department, and the entire legal profession," Karen interjected with a slight smile.

"So you want me to cut out the last paragraph about the potential liability until the Clean Hands Bill gets enacted and simply say that the City's legal exposure should be minimal?" said Frank with only a little concern that he wasn't being quite as informative as he believed an attorney should be.

"Yes." The simultaneous voices of Karen, Roderick, and Byron came in perfect harmony.

"I guess that's easy enough to do." And then directing his comment to Karen, Frank added, "I will have the revision for you in a few minutes."

"Thank you, Frank," Karen replied.

Then Roderick added, "Karen, if you don't have any objection it would be good if Frank joined us for the Mayor's staff meeting tomorrow morning. That way, if and when this subject comes up, he can be part of the discussion. He can leave after that."

"I have no objection at all. That's a good idea," Karen replied.

Frank told them he would be sure to be there, and he left Karen's office with the three of them expressing their appreciation and with Frank thinking about how much time and effort were wasted managing the Mayor's idiosyncrasies. "If this is what happens on a little item like this, what happens on the really important stuff?" he wondered.

CHAPTER 2

The Mayor's staff meetings were supersized and legendary. The supersizing had two dimensions. First they lasted up to six or seven hours. Second, the staff meetings were regularly attended by about forty of the City's most senior staff, which led one department director to quip that it reminded her of a Hollywood party in which celebrities invited five hundred of their closest friends. After all, how many senior staff could a city of 300,000 people have?

That said, there was certainly no question that the Mayor's Chief of Staff and Senior Director of Strategy *were* senior staff. Both were African American men, but that was about the only thing they had in common.

Introducing Roderick J. Campbell

Roderick J. Campbell had been the Mayor's Chief of Staff for the past two and a half years. He was brought on midway during the Mayor's second year in office. Publicly, the Mayor had stubbornly insisted he didn't need a Chief of Staff because he wanted to maintain an open-door policy where the dozen or so directors could have direct access to him, and vice versa. In reality, he wasn't a very trusting or trustworthy individual, and he was concerned that empowering a Chief of Staff would necessarily disempower him. Privately, most insiders figured he was naturally suspicious of others and simply didn't want a layer of reporting authority between his department heads and him. To him that would bode trouble, as alliances could form that would circumvent his initiatives or fail to disclose necessary

17

information. However, the utter chaos of the Mayor's first year in office left him no choice but to reorganize, and bringing in Roderick was his first move.

Roderick proudly and understandably viewed himself as a self-made man. Roderick's father left Roderick's mother when Roderick was only four years old. Roderick and his mother wouldn't be alone for long, for not only did his father walk out on them; he walked out on the twin daughters his wife was carrying at the time. Being raised by a single black mother in Westville's depressed Creekside neighborhood, Roderick was forced to grow up in a hurry. From the time he was eight years old, he brought in money by doing odd jobs for families in the neighborhood and by helping an older boy with his paper route, eventually buying the route when he was eleven. As a teenager, he kept the paper route and also stocked shelves and bagged groceries in Elmer's Market, the neighborhood grocery.

These responsibilities taught Roderick how to manage his time and get things done, and he quickly translated that skill into making sure his younger sisters pulled their weight. First he made sure they picked up their toys and put their clothes where they belonged. As the girls got older, they graduated to cleaning house, doing laundry, helping do the dishes, and carrying out the trash. And always, schoolwork and Sunday church were top priorities. Playtime came afterward.

Somehow Roderick found time to excel academically and also play football. His leadership abilities and six-foot, three-inch athletic frame enabled him to become co-captain of the high school football team even though it was unusual for a defensive end to have that role. Elmer Schmidt, the owner of Elmer's Market, allowed him to have a flexible work schedule to accommodate his football and academics, something a large chain store probably wouldn't have done.

Roderick's grades and athletic talents coupled with his work experience were enough to earn him a scholarship to the University of Westville. Going to college on a scholarship was the easiest thing Roderick ever did. He earned dual bachelor's degrees in public administration and political science with honors and earned another scholarship which enabled him to get his Master's in Public Administration, during which time he also served as a teaching assistant.

Roderick had made tremendous sacrifices to get where he was in life, and one of the things he seemed to have sacrificed along the way was any sense of real enjoyment. His stone was one that rolled through life without gathering any true joy or moss. A career bachelor, he had few personal friends and no deep friendships. Even his younger sisters didn't know what Roderick did to really have a good time. Everyone agreed they had never seen him cut loose to even the slightest extent. As part of a "Who's Who in Westville" profile, he told a reporter that he enjoyed drinking coffee and reading the Sunday paper and an occasional political biography or good mystery. One thing about Roderick: his mind was always working, even when he was seemingly at leisure.

Having taken charge of his own life and helped raise his sisters, Roderick was a natural at running the City government. He had served for a number of years as Director of Public Service, having meritoriously worked his way up through the ranks from an entry-level supervisor position. At the weekly staff meeting he usually had the first thirty minutes with the team before the Mayor came in to take the helm. Roderick knew how to take advantage of that time and make his thirty minutes count.

It was just before 8:00 Wednesday morning in early January 2000 when forty of Westville's senior staff filed into the large conference room on the twenty-second floor of the Regional Government Building. People were exchanging brief pleasantries, asking how they had enjoyed the holidays and which stores had the best sales, and talking about the usual release of holiday movies and the plethora of NFL playoff and college bowl games. Several of the more junior men were yucking it up about the Rose Bowl, which had come down to a particularly controversial play. The more senior men and women were noticeably more reserved. There was always a certain latent tension at the top of the City hierarchy, and those who had been around long enough always remained a little guarded. The conference room was arranged with a closed rectangle of tables with additional chairs along the wall for midlevel managers to sit on. The directors and the Mayor's staff always sat at the tables, with the Mayor and his senior people sitting directly opposite the door to the conference room. Along the back wall were a large coffee urn, pitchers of water, and a modest supply of fresh fruit, and yogurt. You could stay caffeinated, hydrated, and fortified for the meeting marathon.

At exactly 8:00 Roderick entered the room and began walking to the opposite end where he would take his customary seat immediately to the right of the center seat. The center seat was always reserved for the Mayor, and Roderick—being his right-hand man—always sat to the Mayor's immediate right. Chief of Strategy Byron Swift always sat to the Mayor's immediate left. On the way to his seat, Roderick briefly chatted with the HR Director, and everyone else promptly sat down as if on cue.

Roderick sat down and began speaking:

"Welcome back. I trust everyone had a safe, enjoyable, and relaxing holiday. I'm sure the Mayor will ask you to share stories about your various festivities, so let's get down to business.

"Bill, I think your crews did a good job of handling the snowfall on New Year's Eve and New Year's Day. The Mayor has also expressed that opinion, so please pass that along to the troops."

"Thank you. I will do that. They had to work some overtime which took them away from their families for a few hours each day, but they really pulled together. We also got a nice assist from the Water and Forestry departments with their conversion plows."

Bill Zawodny was a seasoned veteran of the Department of Public Service whom Roderick had promoted last year to Director of the department, and he knew that a few compliments to his colleagues could go a long way to ensuring future cooperation. Plus he was truly sincere in expressing his appreciation. It took teamwork to clear Westville's streets, and seven inches of powder over a holiday was nothing to sneeze at. He was a true professional, and Westville was darn lucky to have him.

Roderick continued:

"Good. Very well done, everyone. Get me a report on the OT expense by the close of business Friday and verify that we aren't burning through our overtime budget or our salt and deicer too quickly."

"We won't have the official payroll numbers for that period until the following week, but I can get you a good estimate on the labor expense as well as our inventories of salt and deicer."

"Okay. Get the best info you can by Friday and the final figures as soon as they are available. I want to stay ahead of the media and City Council on any budget and supply issues."

"Moving right along, Chief McNally, my phone was pretty quiet over the holidays, so it looks like your team must have kept a pretty good lid on things."

Chief McNally had come to Westville a year earlier from Middleburgh. It was a big move going from Chief of Police in a city of 40,000 people to Westville with its 300,000 population. He knew this was a tough community with a difficult political situation given the Mayor's personality and the impending reelection campaign, but he felt it was a career opportunity that he simply couldn't turn down. He replied quickly and professionally: "Thank you, sir. Our guys have been pretty successful on a couple of raids, so I think that knocked some of the gangs on their backs a little. I'm not sure how long that will be the case, but we're cranking on it."

"So when the media asks, I shouldn't say the drop in crime was due to the cold and snow?" Roderick said with a bit of a knowing smirk.

"That may have been part of it, but I think we can take a little credit."

"I agree. Your officers have a tough job, and they're handling it well. Let's make sure we don't let up."

As Chief McNally was concurring with Roderick's comments, a young clerical woman walked in, handed Roderick a file, and quickly whispered to him. Roderick immediately continued addressing the staff.

"All right. So the Mayor is going to be here a little earlier than usual. I want to take a few minutes to express some thoughts that the Mayor may echo. If he does, a little reinforcement of this message won't be a bad thing."

Roderick began speaking in a very measured but not overly dramatic voice, making sure everyone clearly heard and understood him. He didn't have to tell them how important his message was.

"So we put the election behind us two months ago, and now the holidays are behind us as well. The Mayor may be a lame duck as far as this office goes, but he isn't resting on his laurels and neither are any of us. I'm not going to tolerate any postholiday hibernating. And anyone who thinks a lame duck isn't going to care about the next four years is going to be a dead duck.

"We all worked very hard last year to deliver really good services and help the Mayor win a campaign that frankly most people thought he was bound to lose. All of you played a big role in that, and I know the Mayor appreciates it. But remember, it is also your job to hustle and make sure this city delivers. So this year we are going to look for new initiatives that can be game changers and legacy builders for the Mayor. And we need to do that without slacking off on our delivery of basic services. I know we had to tap into our financial reserves last year, but we cannot slack off. If we do, the Mayor's critics will have their point proven—that he robbed from the future to further his own reelection." Roderick raised his voice slightly and increased his firmness. "That's not going to happen!

"So I want each of you to come up with some strategic ideas your department can implement. I want this to be ongoing this year, but all of you are to bring me at least one idea for your department by two weeks from today. Lay out the strategy, the cost in City resources, the timeline for implementation, the benefit to our citizens, how you can accomplish it without negatively impacting City services, any return on investment it can provide to the City Treasury, and anything else you think is pertinent. We're going to have the ideas vetted in this meeting in front of your colleagues, so don't bring me garbage. These need to be big-picture game changers, but they don't necessarily have to require lots of resources. If they are low-budget strategies based on us becoming more nimble and responsive, so much the better."

Introducing Red Paley

Mayor Charles "Red" Paley was sixty-four years old, five feet, nine inches tall, and of average build. He was a hard-drinking man who had earned the nickname "Red" from his red hair which he continued to maintain by having it professionally dyed on a regular basis. He was too short to be a stellar football player—his childhood dream was to be a star quarterback—and too tall to have the stereotypical Napoleonic complex. This combination led to many heated debates among the amateur psychologists in the community and on his staff, for whom analyzing the Mayor was a major hobby. If it was possible to be a driven, self-absorbed, superficial but charismatic asshole, well, . . . that was Red Paley.

Red Paley strolled into the conference room with his executive secretary Joan trailing behind him and sat down next to Roderick Campbell. He was beaming and high energy.

"Good morning team. I'll tell you I had a great holiday down in Naples. Low 80s every day. Nothing but sunshine and blue skies. Stayed with Wilfred and Susie Richardson at their seaside home overlooking the gulf. I think their place must be 10,000 square feet. Cost a mint, but it's a drop in the bucket to Willy. I'm sure it was cheap compared to his divorce from Helen. And let me tell you, he's living it up now with the trophy wife in his seaside castle. I told him he had the TC2—Trophy in the Castle on the Coast."

The Mayor chuckled, and a weak sycophantic chuckle echoed from the staff, particularly from the men.

"He also has a beautiful cabin cruiser that we took out into the gulf. Willie let me take the helm for awhile, which I thought was very thoughtful and generous of him."

Red paused briefly and then continued.

"Two things I want to share. First, Joan, before I forget. I went into a Costco store for the first time ever. They had all kinds of free samples, the best of which was a seared pork dish called 'hot caliente.' I want you to call the El Casa de Mexico and see if you can get me a takeout order for lunch today."

Joan looked puzzled. "Mayor, what is that dish called again?"

"Hot caliente. I tell you it's great! Seared pork, had some onions and peppers cooked with it. Loved it!"

"Hot caliente what?" Joan inquired.

"Hot caliente!"

Just then Valeria Rodriguez, the HR director interjected. "Mayor, 'caliente' is the Spanish word for 'hot.' The dish they were sampling wasn't hot caliente. 'Hot caliente' was just a bilingual caution sign that the cooking element and the food were hot and might burn you."

"What!? Are you sure?"

"Trust me. It's true sir."

Mayor Paley looked around the room searching for supportive eyes. Not finding any, he quickly recovered. "All right. Joan, call Costco and find out what they were sampling and get me something like it."

Mayor Paley then stood up, confidently restoring his presiding presence over the staff.

"Now here's the other thing, and it's far better and infinitely more important than food. So the rage down in Naples seems to be these fancy hubcap devices on cars that keep spinning forward even though the car has stopped at a traffic light or stop sign. At first I thought the car was still moving, but that's just an optical illusion.

"I was thinking this was pretty stupid and frivolous, but I couldn't get the image of the wheels spinning out of my mind. 'The wheels keep spinning.' I kept repeating that thought quietly to myself. 'The wheels keep spinning. The wheels keep moving.' And, thinking of things that don't stop, I remembered F. Lee Bailey's famous book *The Defense Never Rests*. And that's when it struck me. The light bulb clicked on in my head. The City never rests. Hell, this City, *my* City, never sleeps. So yesterday afternoon I outfitted my Escalade with some of those wheels. And Zawodny, I want you to do the same for all City vehicles. Because I want everyone in Westville to know this City never stops! Red Paley won't let it stop!"

Moving along, the Mayor then began interrogating each of his sixteen department heads regarding matters they were working on. This took approximately four hours, with the Mayor chiding and encouraging his staff as he felt necessary. The biggest cheer was for Zawodny and his team for their excellent snow plowing, with the Mayor actually "ordering up" a standing ovation for Zawodny. At the opposite end of the spectrum, the Mayor berated the Law Director for "allowing" a major evidentiary hearing to be scheduled in conflict with his weekly staff meeting. In the Mayor's opinion, Karen had asked the judge to deliberately schedule it so that she could be excused from the staff meeting. Frank's memo on the Jonesboro Trucking warehouse barely made a ripple, which is exactly what everyone was hoping. When the topic came up, Karen pointed out that Frank had the lead on the matter. The Mayor looked directly at Frank and said, "Franklin Jefferson Clark. I'm glad you're handling this matter and on our team. Everyone keep an eye on this guy. He's going places!"

At the conclusion of the staff meeting, Frank was the brunt of a couple of good-natured, brown-nosing comments from his colleagues. Fortunately, that was cut short by Roderick Campbell's directive for Bill Zawodny and Art Hill, Director of Finance, to meet him in his office.

*****

Roderick's office was in the Mayor's suite immediately adjacent to the large conference room. Bill and Art reloaded their coffee cups and walked into the office. On the way they passed Joan's desk. She had her phone to her ear. "Yes. That's right. I would like to know what grilled pork dishes you have on your menu."

When they entered the office, Roderick was already seated behind his desk. "Shut the door and have a seat," he directed them.

Bill quickly spoke up as Art shut the door: "Listen, I'll get those overtime estimates on the snow plowing to you as quickly as I can. I know it's important."

"I know you will. This isn't about that," Roderick replied. He continued:

"When I promoted you two last year, this situation—being able to respond to and manage what happened during the Mayor's staff meeting—is exactly what I had in mind. Now what we are about to discuss is completely confidential and doesn't leave this room until I tell you it does. Do you read me?"

"Yes sir." Bill and Art responded simultaneously and leaned in closer. Bill spoke up: "But what exactly are we responding to and managing?"

"The fucking hubcaps!" Roderick said it as earnestly and forcefully as he could without risking the sound of his voice penetrating the office walls. "I don't know what he was drinking in Florida, but this is the most ludicrous idea I've heard yet. It's not only stupid; it's expensive. And that's where you two are going to quietly help me build my case. Understand?"

Bill and Art once again nodded their heads and uttered their concurrence. Roderick continued:

"Now we aren't going to flat out tell him we shouldn't do it. He'll only dig his heels in and blast us to the moon. And at the end of the day, he will get his way, and all we will have to show for it are the scars on our backs. No . . . we are going to have to subtly prepare him to make the right decision—and it will be *his* decision.

"Here's what we are going to do. Bill, you need to personally take a look at the inventory of vehicles that your guys in Fleet Maintenance keep. Take that list and scratch any vehicle that has an operational routine that would probably result in quick damage to those damn hubcaps. Garbage trucks, construction equipment, fire trucks, police cruisers, dump trucks, snowplows—scratch all the heavy-duty shit first."

"Got it." Bill replied.

"Good. Then take the balance of the vehicle inventory and figure out a ballpark figure on what new wheels are going to cost. Now, understand this: you must do this personally and secretly. Call some shop and pretend you're just a private consumer. Get a quote and figure out some type of twenty-five percent fleet discount and multiply it by the number of vehicles that remain on the inventory. Okay?"

"Yes."

"Art. In the meantime, you look at some of the budget items that got eliminated or sharply cut in the annual budget process we just completed last month. Find some of the ones the Mayor cared about the most. When Bill gets us his budget estimate, we can compare that expense with some of the Mayor's top priorities. If we lay this out right, and I handle him the right way, he just may agree that this is not a prudent thing to do."

"Got it," Art replied.

"Good. Now it's getting close to 1:30. Fortunately, this wasn't one of the Mayor's six-hour specials. The three of us are meeting back here at 4:00. Bill, you will have your fleet inventory and a rough estimate of the cost of putting spinning caps on the light-duty vehicles. Art, you will have a range of priority budget items that got cut. We need to move on this before the Mayor shoots his mouth off to too many people or the media gets hold of this. Time is against us, so get going."

Bill and Art scurried out of the office, and Roderick walked over to Joan's desk. "Is the Mayor free for a drink at 5:30?" he asked Joan. "Right now his calendar is surprisingly free," she replied.

"Great! See if I can meet him at Lonnegan's. He's probably anxious to get over there after being out of town over the holidays."

"I'll make it happen," Joan replied with a wink.

CHAPTER 3

The adage "A lot of work gets done after work is over" has particular application to media and to government. The media is always looking for the next bit of news or gossip—the next buzz, so to speak. Public officials are always looking for feedback on programs, information on events of the day, ideas for potential new policies and initiatives, and basically ways to just stay in touch with constituents, particularly key stakeholders. And public officials like to occasionally schmooze with others in order to maintain good relations and see what they can learn. In Westville, much of that interaction took place at Lonnegan's.

Lonnegan's Irish Pub was Red Paley's favorite downtown watering hole. In fact, it was practically everyone's favorite bar. It was the perfect place to bend an elbow and to rub elbows. Its founder, Casey Lonnegan, emigrated from Dingle, Ireland, at the turn of the century as a sixteen-year-old with an itch to make something of himself. In 1915, after working in the railroad yards of Westville for twelve years, he had saved enough money to lease a small storefront and open what was initially an inconspicuous pub just two blocks from the County Courthouse. He and his pub managed to stay afloat during the Prohibition Era, generating legendary tales of bootleggers, gangsters, gambling, and loose women in the process. It was hard to tell how much of it was true, but pretty clearly Casey Lonnegan lived life on the edge, maybe even *over* the edge when his survival called for it. At any rate, he not only survived Prohibition, but he also did well enough to expand into an adjacent space in 1927 and then purchase the building outright in 1934 when the owner became a casualty of the Great Depression.

Lonnegan's had always been known as neutral ground where everyone was welcome regardless of their political affiliation or fidelity to societal norms. In many respects it was Westville's melting pot. And although Casey didn't exactly embrace people of color, he did book white jazz bands that were derived from African American blues and jazz. And after World War II he openly booked black acts and integrated his bar and wait staff. (The kitchen and cleanup areas had always been integrated.)

Casey Lonnegan died in 1961, having lived just long enough to witness John F. Kennedy's election, but the family kept the business up and was now in its third generation of managing ownership. The Lonnegans seemed to have a natural affinity for people and knew how to make people feel welcome. That plus good business sense, a knack for knowing what the public wanted, and the wealth of nostalgic memorabilia that permeated the pub made it a Westville landmark.

Roderick Campbell walked through the door at 5:25 and squinted toward the bar area as his eyes adjusted to the dim lighting filtered through numerous tiffany lampshades. He could hear Red Paley holding court with a few regulars at the corner of the bar, his voice easily carrying over the Fats Waller tune that was providing the quiet, yet provocative, ambience that was a Lonnegan's hallmark.

As Roderick approached the bar, the Mayor spotted him and cheerfully called out, "Roderick, get yourself a drink, I'm buying."

"Thank you, sir." Turning to the bartender he said, "I'll have a ginger ale."

"I said get yourself a *drink,* not a soda pop," Red said, smiling. He knew that Roderick rarely drank and wasn't likely to do so when he was there to talk business.

"Thanks, Mayor. Still got some work to do, and I'm worthless after I have a drink."

"I figured. Boys, if you'll excuse us, we had better grab a table where we can talk quietly."

The Mayor and his top lieutenant walked through the far end of the bar and into an overflow room that wasn't being utilized. The Mayor sat down at a booth as far from the door as possible and faced the doorway to keep an eye on things. Helping himself to the closed room was the Mayor's prerogative, and the Lonnegan's staff was flattered to give him a private area for his business. After all, political intrigue was part of what made Lonnegan's *Lonnegan's.*

Roderick began:

"Thanks, boss. I've just got a couple of things that I want to close the loop on while we are still early in the year."

Red Paley took a sip of his Jameson. "Good idea. Go right ahead."

"It's not major in the big scheme of things, but we have some discretionary budget requests from community groups that are still pending. It would probably be good if we got back to them before they either remind us or, worse yet, actually start spending money that they haven't got."

"I agree."

"So . . . here are some of the more significant requests we deferred. In no particular order, we've got the Urban Ministers' Justice Fund that wants $25,000 so they can expand the afterschool programming at their community center to include weekends."

"That's a good program, and I want to take care of the black ministers."

"Yes sir. There's also the St. Dominic Savio House for troubled youth. They requested $30,000 for some roof repairs and kitchen upgrades."

"Yes. I'd like to take care of Father Affonso. And I know the Bishop likes his program. He's a rising star in the Church."

"I think the third one of note is the Police Athletic League. PAL wants to partner with the Westville Public Teachers Union to offer tutoring as part of the athletic program. This would be a pilot program in the Creekside neighborhood. They're asking for about $30,000 to hire teachers to do some supplemental tutoring."

"Creekside. That's your old stomping grounds, right?"

"Yes sir. Still is."

"Good. Will the teachers be paid at union scale?"

"Yes sir. There's some cost involved, but in their defense, they already work a lot of hours and shell out personal money for classroom supplies."

"Hmm. All of these are good causes, and all of them have backing with political clout. They total what, about $85,000 if fully funded?"

"Yes sir. We've only got $60,000 of discretionary impact funds and a whole year that may bring new requests and opportunities."

Red Paley paused, grinding through various scenarios in his head. He took a little heavier sip and spoke.

"These are good causes, and I'm not going to pick winners and losers on this one. The black ministers will skewer me, the Bishop will be disappointed, and I've got union negotiations starting later this year. We're going to have to grow the pot."

"Yes sir. And there's something else that might go along with that."

"Wait a minute. I'm getting another drink. Do you want a refill?"

"That would be great. Thank you."

Red Paley got up and walked across the room and through the doorway to the main bar. As he saw him walk away, Roderick reflected on all the history that must have occurred in Lonnegan's. Red Paley's tenure as Mayor was a small matter in the big scheme of things, but it was part of the Lonnegan's aura nonetheless. He had no doubt that someday people would look back and say, "Yeah. I remember when Red Paley was here. Boy, did he know how to do old-school politics."

Red Paley continued to the bar. "Joe. Have someone bring another round to the back, would you? Roderick's just having a ginger ale. I've got to hit the head."

"Yes sir, Red!"

Closed room or not, a fresh round was on the table by the time the Mayor returned. Lonnegan's was smart enough not to let the regulars get too dry, and the Mayor was no ordinary regular.

"I'll tell you, I'm so busy I'd pay someone to take a piss for me if I could," the Mayor said as he slid back into the booth.

Roderick broke into a broad grin. "I bet you would, Mayor!"

"Anyway . . . back to business. And by the way, this is good, but it's better back there," he said tilting his head toward the bar.

"Thank you, sir. I just need a few more minutes, if I may."

"It's no problem. You never waste my time. I can't say the same about everyone on my staff."

Roderick acknowledged the Mayor's compliment with a smile. He knew that Red appreciated his hard work and his efforts at efficiently managing their communication. Now it was time for him to demonstrate another talent.

Roderick began: "Well, sir, I liked your thoughts on the spinning hubcaps and the City being in constant motion. . . ."

"Good!" Red interjected.

"But there is one issue that I think I have resolved. It's just a speed bump on the way to implementation, but I want to make sure I brief you and that I'm on the right page."

"What's that?" Red's mood became more somber.

"Well, we have about 2,000 vehicles in the City fleet, and your Escalade costs us $410 for parts, labor, and general overhead when everything is totaled up. That comes to over $800,000 for the entire fleet, but I'm sure we can back out some of the heavy-duty equipment and other vehicles."

"Of course. It would be silly to put that on a dump truck, plow, or front-end loader." The Mayor wasn't about to show that he had been caught unaware by the cost of the program; so, practicing the primary rule of improvisation, which is to "go with the flow," he followed right along.

"And then I'm thinking we could back out most of the emergency vehicles, because I just don't think the spinning hub caps are durable enough for the rigors of a police cruiser or fire truck."

"That sounds right. Go on."

"So let's say we bring it to the truly civilian vehicles like the directors, commissioners, inspectors, field supervisors, meter readers, and the vehicle pool. At that point we may be at a couple hundred vehicles. I'm guessing it would probably be less than $400 per vehicle because those aren't luxury cars, and we may get some volume discounts, etc."

Red perked up a little. "That sounds about right. Where are we now?"

"That brings us to something more like $60,000. Let's say $70,000 to be safe."

"That's almost as much as the requests for discretionary funds." The Mayor's political mind was clicking again.

"Yes sir, but I think we just might have the same thought in mind."

"Which is?"

"It was appropriate to start with your vehicle as the only one with the spinning wheels, because frankly, you're the Mayor and no one works harder or longer than you. Your vehicle *is* the flagship of our City fleet, so it *should* be the first to get the new wheels. Then, we have a performance-based contest among the other departments. The department that wins the contest gets recognized by the Mayor and gets the spinning wheels. We could do this annually and gradually convert more cars."

"I like the concept. But we still need to find the money even though it's a smaller project."

"Right. Now this may be a bit of a reach, but I'm thinking we could go to the business community and ask them to raise the money. After all, it will be a performance-based competition, which they all should be in favor of as part of a good-government approach. And we don't need to raise all the money at once."

Red thought for a second. "You know, that just may fly. The Republicans thought they were going to win this election, and wouldn't it look statesmanlike if I offered them an opportunity to promote City productivity?" Red winked, took a sip, and smiled. "Plus they would be helping *me* find some money for *my* projects."

"Yes sir. And maybe the same time they are raising money for that, they can also raise a little to take care of our three pending requests for Discretionary Impact Funds."

"Exactly. That's what I was thinking earlier, and now we just layer the spinning hubcaps on top of that. We'll put in $40,000 from my Mayor's Fund and ask them to raise the other $45,000. Plus they can raise another $10,000 for the hubcap competition—that ought to cover the winning department. You can run with that, Roderick. Get some of the staff together. Figure out the rules for the competition and a catchy name that plays with the public, especially businessmen. Get back to me tomorrow afternoon and let me know what you've come up with."

"Thank you, sir. I was hoping you would like it."

"I do. It's not done yet. But I *do* like it. Now . . . to the bar!" And with that, Red Paley stood up and made his way to his home away from home.

Not So Fast

Roderick headed to his car as Red Paley headed back to hold court at the bar. He drove to his Creekside townhome, poured a tall glass of tomato juice, sat down in his reading chair, and reflected on the day. Overall, it had been pretty good. Roderick was all about good management, and he had performed one of his primary functions, which was to make sure the Mayor didn't roam too far off the reservation—a job that increasingly consumed Roderick's time and energy. The hubcap idea could have made Red Paley a public laughingstock, but Roderick figured he had managed to put the genie back in the bottle before it had fully escaped. Knowing he couldn't get the Mayor to completely drop the idea, he had shrewdly guided him to a more sensible concept that had a chance of playing fairly well with the business community—or at least as well as an idea as crazy as installing spinning hubcaps on City vehicles *could* play. He might have sucked up a bit too much by designating the Mayor's vehicle as Westville's "flagship," but then again, desperate times call for desperate measures. And if the Mayor became a laughingstock, at least it would be limited to his flagship and not the entire City fleet.

What Roderick didn't know for sure, but certainly suspected, was that the City's gossip mill was already fast at work. Starting with the adjournment of the staff meeting and continuing through bowling and other after-work gatherings, the stories of spinning hubcaps and ordering hot caliente were circulating through the City staff and beyond.

At 7:30 Roderick's phone rang. Caller ID revealed it was Tom Folks, the political reporter for the *Westville Wire & Telegraph* (frequently referred to as the *Westville Waste of Time*). Roderick took a deep breath and answered the phone. "Hello."

"Hi, Roderick. This is Tom Folks. Do you have a minute?"

"I think I'd better," Roderick said in his most matter-of-fact manner. "What's up, Tom?"

"Well, I heard you had an interesting morning," Tom replied in an equally straightforward manner.

"How's that?" Roderick figured he'd play dumb and let Tom show his hand.

With slightly more levity, Tom obliged him. "Let's just say I hope I'm not interrupting your dinner. Tell me, is hot caliente on the menu?"

"Oh. You heard about that?" Roderick chuckled, hoping to make sure Tom realized he was treating this as just a humorous anecdote. This wasn't a bad situation. Embarrassing to be sure, but, unlike the spinning hubcaps, it didn't involve launching a ludicrous new City program.

Tom laughingly continued. "I'm just wondering how you like it prepared. Open flame-grilled, sautéed in a wok, maybe slowly cooked in a Crockpot. What do you think? I know I like mine with a dash of Tabasco and an assortment of chopped peppers and onions."

Roderick laughed. "Well, the Mayor may have been a little culturally challenged on that one."

"No doubt about that!" Tom chortled. "It takes way too much patience to ponder the meaning of hot caliente before leaping to a conclusion and pronouncing it publicly. Of course, I think the spinning hubcaps are even better."

Roderick's spirits dropped. He tried not to reveal it. "Yeah. I imagine that one is traveling pretty fast. "

"I tell you Roderick, this is so good I went over to Lonnegan's about 6:30 hoping to find Red. You know, I needed to hear about this firsthand. So he was at the bar having a whiskey and pretty much holding court like he always does. He sees me and shouts out, 'Hey Tom. I want you to see my car. I'm launching a new program for the City fleet, and as the City's flagship, my Escalade got it first. Come outside with me, and I'll show you.'

"So Red and I walk outside with a couple of other guys that were at the bar tagging along. And we get to his vehicle and I pretend I don't notice anything. So he says, 'Look at the wheels. I've got those spinning wheels on my vehicle.' So I egg him on a little more and say, 'The vehicle's parked. I don't see what you mean.' So Red naturally gets in the Escalade and does a lap around the parking lot before bringing it to an abrupt stop. And I see the hubcaps continuing to rotate, but this is too much fun. So I'm like 'Okay, but I don't get it.' And Red says, 'Don't you see. When the car stops, the wheels keep turning. That's because the City is always in motion. Just like a shark.' Then he says, 'You know, Tom, sharks need to keep moving or they die. Red Paley's Westville never stops!'

"So I asked him if I could quote him, and of course he obliged."

Tom had to stop for a moment because he was laughing too hard. Then he continued:

"So the upshot of it is that I wanted you to know we are going to be running a story in tomorrow morning's paper."

"Thanks for the heads-up, Tom. But you know, when the Mayor rolls the whole program out and puts it in context, I think it will make some sense. Did he tell you the plan?"

"Hell yes, he told me the plan. And it doesn't make any sense to me at all. Do you really think City departments are going to compete to get spinning wheels on their vehicles? I'd do everything I could to make sure I *didn't* win this competition. This just screams of comparisons to gerbil wheels, people running on treadmills, and stuck cars spinning their tires in the mud. All kinds of action and no results. Go ahead, tell me I'm wrong—I dare you!"

"I think the Mayor has a vision that clicks with him, and if people let him get his story out, explain the program, and give it a fair chance, it just might work." Roderick could practically feel his nose growing longer as he talked.

"I'll say one thing. You're definitely loyal to your boss. I hope Red appreciates that. Believe me, your own City staff is splitting a gut over this one. How the hell do you think I found out about it? Red's given all the media in this town enough material to keep us going for days! Hell, this may even go national!"

Roderick decided to throw a Hail Mary pass. "Nonetheless, I'm sure you've got bigger stories than this. I'll look for it on page 12, right?"

"That's your best one yet! This is either front page of the paper or front page, second section. It'll probably be above the fold. You know, Red asked me the same thing. Naturally, he wants it on the front page. Of course, he doesn't realize the angle I'm taking. At any rate, I don't think the editor has determined which page it will be on. One thing, Roderick: I'm not writing it maliciously. It's more in the nature of a human-interest story. You know, 'A Funny Thing Happened Today at City Hall.'"

"Sounds like a great musical comedy," Roderick deadpanned. "I appreciate that, I guess. Anyway, Tom, thanks for the heads-up."

"You're welcome, Roderick. Frankly, I've got to give credit to Red for something."

"What's that?" Roderick said curiously.

"I'm surprised he could come up with the hubcap idea *and* a competition to determine the winning department. After all, his idea of multitasking is to drink a whiskey *and* a beer," Tom chortled again, unable to contain his laughter at his own lame joke.

"That's a good one, Tom," Roderick replied dryly. "Have a good evening."

"Thanks. You too, Roderick."

Roderick hung up the phone feeling a little less smug about his day. And now the Chief of Staff of the City of Westville had more work to do. Picking the phone back up, Roderick dialed the City's Director of Public Relations. They would have to do some early morning damage control.

*****

The media had its fun with hot caliente and spinning hubcaps—both of which made a small splash on the late-night talk shows. Red Paley didn't seem to mind it at all. For the most part the media treatment was a blend of humor and bewilderment. The hot caliente was appropriately chalked up to Red's cultural ignorance and spontaneity. After all, it was *much too difficult* for him to quietly figure out what "hot caliente" meant before opening his mouth and praising its culinary attributes in front of forty staff members. Even the more serious hubcap issue resolved itself satisfactorily. After overcoming the shock of being totally dumbfounded, several businessmen actually came to the conclusion that modest sponsorship of an interdepartmental, good-government hubcap competition might be relatively harmless and generate some goodwill. Red publicly invited several suburbs to join the competition. Not surprisingly, all of them declined.

Naturally, Red called a press conference at which he chastised the suburbs as "sticks in the mud" and "cowards." He likened their fleets of vehicles to "horse-drawn buggies" as opposed to the "turbine-powered propellers of his mighty flagship." In turn, Mayor Pickett of the suburb of Greenfield retorted that Red's "flagship" was more like a "Worstville Death Star" and vowed to defend his community against the "evil empire's hegemony."

It mattered not at all that Mayor Pickett could not cite a single recent example of any attempt by Westville at anything approaching regional hegemony. (After all, Westville had been declining for decades.) The media, which already had plenty of material to work with from Red alone, now had an absolute bonanza. The *Westville Wire & Telegraph* ran a cartoon portraying Red as a modern-day Admiral Nelson commanding his mighty flagship *Westville Forever* against a flotilla of suburban sloops and dinghies. Meanwhile, the *Suburban Times Dispatch* (popularly referred to as the *Slanderous Times Dispatch* and other "STD" nicknames the reader will have no trouble imagining) ran a cartoon depicting Red as Darth Vader aboard the *Westville Death Star* (they were too polite to call it the *Worstville Death Star*) and Mayor Pickett as a lone Jedi knight defending the tiny asteroid of Greenfield.

Of course the best humor was shared at gathering places such as Lonnegan's, which actually concocted a Westville Death Star cocktail in honor of the brouhaha. It was essentially a double Manhattan with a dash of Napoleon brandy (with apologies to the Saratoga cocktail)—limit two per customer.

CHAPTER 4

A Flashback to May 1999 – the Recruiting of Byron Swift

The other leading member of Red's team was Byron Swift, Senior Director of Strategy. Red hired Byron in May of 1999, about six months before the November election that would determine whether he would serve two terms as Mayor or just one. His "recruitment" had come about the previous year in typical Red fashion.

In the spring of 1999 Red Paley's mind was consumed by two over-arching thoughts, each of which was steadily intensifying. First, as a professional politician, Red was consumed with the prospect that he might lose his bid for reelection. Red's standing among the African Americans and Latinos that predominantly populated Westville's central-city neighborhoods was very weak. During Red's first three years as Mayor, he had generated a lot of bombast, making a show of demolishing some buildings that were public eyesores and carrying out high-profile neighborhood cleanup projects, but none of these were changing the lives of the residents who were still mired in poverty and living in blighted neighborhoods that were experiencing a steady flight of people and jobs. The residents of those neighborhoods were still disconnected from economic opportunity, and Red had little support from them and even less credibility with them. Fortunately for Red, voter turnout in these precincts had historically been appallingly low. However, an opportunity nonetheless existed for a Republican to snatch victory in November.

Red's second headache was also of his making but of an entirely different nature. Despite his braggadocio and confident demeanor, Red Paley was extremely insecure. As he saw Roderick Campbell continuing to excel as his Chief of Staff, Red began feeling that his "supreme authority" was being threatened. It wasn't that Red didn't appreciate Roderick's devoted loyalty, tremendous competence, and unequaled work ethic. Red greatly appreciated all of those qualities and knew they contributed greatly to his success. Rather, it was because Roderick had been so successful — particularly in recruiting replacements for the senior administrators who had left Red's administration after its first three years—that Red felt a need to get someone else in as part of his inner sanctum. Adding a senior cabinet member who reported directly to him would create a competing base of power that would serve as a counterbalance to Roderick and inherently diminish his stature somewhat. Further, as an old-school politician, Red wanted to make sure everyone knew that they owed their jobs, and their loyalty, to him. Bringing in someone new to the team who was clearly *his* direct recruit would help reinforce the fact that he was unquestionably running the show.

And so, Red concluded that he needed to recruit an executive that would help him win neighborhood support and subtly offset Roderick's influence.

Therefore, the question in Red's mind wasn't whether to bring someone in, but *whom* to bring in. Red had a number of shortcomings, one of which was that he was an extremely linear thinker who was intellectually impatient. Whatever else Red was, his intellect was neither broad nor deep. These characteristics and others caused him to develop some simple criteria that led him to settle on Byron Swift as his nearly perfect candidate.

The first requirement was that his recruit would have to be an African American. A white candidate wouldn't improve his stature in the disadvantaged neighborhoods, and in any event Red wasn't willing to risk creating tension between a black senior executive and a white senior executive. In the process, Red rejected the opportunity to broaden his base and be more inclusive by recruiting someone from the Latino community, because he believed that as an Irish-Catholic, he already had the Catholic community in his camp.

His second requirement was that the recruit would be active in the African American church community, thereby further enhancing his political value to Red. Roderick did not actively participate as a member of any congregation, and Red believed a recruit with strong ties to the faith community would be of great benefit to him. Red's interest in this matter was derived from Red's belief in a cultural/ethnic paradigm that was deeply rooted in the 1950s and '60s, the era in which he began cutting his political teeth. More than one generation had come of age since then, but Red's view of the world hadn't changed. The strength of the African American community in Westville, Red believed, was not in producing professional executives. In his opinion, the strength of this community in Westville was evidenced in its churches and their collective ability to turn out people for rallies and elections—provided they were properly energized. This is what had made an indelible imprint on Red's consciousness in his first days of political activism; the African American community – primarily through its churches - could turn out masses of people, but not generate a large pool of executive talent. (In Red's mind, Roderick Campbell was the exception that proved the rule.)

Third, Red's recruit was going to be a man—no racial tension *and* no gender issues. Moreover, while Red's mindset had evolved enough to permit women of any race to hold high positions in his administration, he was much too chauvinistic to allow them to be part of his innermost circle. The good old boy network was still very much alive in Red's world of drinking, backslapping, and deal crafting. Female departmental directors such as Valeria Rodriguez of Human Resources and Karen Jones of Law were not afforded the opportunity to advance into the core. They and other women were relegated to simply being capable tools in his toolbox. They also doubled as proxies for his commitment to inclusiveness whenever he was so challenged. Nonetheless, their impact on strategic thinking was limited. The art of strategic design and deal cutting was left to the men.

Fourth, someone who came from outside of government would be preferred. In hiring such a person, Red figured he would show the private sector that he recognized the need to instill new practices and perspectives in City Hall. A further consideration in not wanting someone from government was that a person from the private or not-for-profit sectors could be given a reasonable transition period while still generating an immediate positive impact on the electorate and certain elements of the business and civic leadership.

Red had another shortcoming. Regardless of how little effort he put into forming an opinion or how sound that opinion was, Red was infamous for his inability to change his mind once he reached a conclusion. Among City staff, the joke was that Westville had a county morgue and Red's morgue, that crypt in Red's mind where ideas contrary to his were sentenced, locked up, and never heard from again. The phrase "Dead on Arrival" mutated within the City administration to "Dead on Red," or "D.O.R."

So it came to be that Red Paley's perspective produced an unwavering commitment to recruit an African American, churchgoing male from the private or not-for-profit sectors as a counterweight to the growing influence of his incredibly competent Chief of Staff. In order to have an immediate impact before the election, the candidate would have to be local. Since Red wanted to keep the whole thing confidential, he took it upon himself to find just such a man.

Unfortunately, Westville didn't offer a deep talent pool within those parameters. Westville had suffered a brain drain of talented young people for the past generation, and it was particularly acute among disadvantaged populations that were looking for more diverse, inclusive, growing communities where they had a better opportunity to prosper. Red also failed to account for the fact that the African American churches were hardly a unified force. Red knew this to be true, but somehow the truth of it hadn't penetrated his broad-brush paradigm. It didn't occur to Red that one of Roderick's assets was that he had sidestepped any charges of partiality by evading *all* of the African American congregations. His price for avoiding the politics and rivalries of the local churches was enduring the relatively mild complaint that was occasionally voiced by the African American community that he didn't attend *any* church. Red's handpicked, churchgoing Chief Director of Strategy wouldn't be able to do that.

Someone a little more patient and circumspect might have paused to reconsider the situation. Not Red. Any thoughts of selecting a woman or a white male, or of abandoning the concept entirely, were Dead on Red.

Red's search for a key player serendipitously coincided with the University of Westville's need to shake up its Athletic Department. For a mid-level Division I school, the men's football and basketball teams had had a good deal of success over the past ten or so years, with the football team twice cracking the top twenty-five, and the basketball team qualifying for four NCAA tournaments. However, a series of recruiting and academic scandals involving both squads dictated a change in direction. When the NCAA announced the results of its investigation, Red suspected that Byron Swift, as Assistant Athletic Director for Marketing, was vulnerable. Although nothing could be directly pinned on Byron, Red's instincts told him that anyone who had that much contact with well-heeled boosters was guilty by association. Plus, Red assumed that a new era most likely required a new profile. Red thought Byron could be the man for him, and he figured that if the University's leaders weren't thinking along those lines, he was just the guy to illuminate them.

Byron met all of Red's threshold criteria. He was a local African American, churchgoing male, well-known in the community. He was the upbeat, backslapping socializer the Mayor was looking for. He didn't come from government, so his newness to the situation could help explain away any errors he might make. He was tainted only by his proximity to the athletic scandals, and there were already some murmurs of potential backlash in the community among those who believed the University should protect him. These feelings were particularly strong among African Americans, and Red saw an opportunity to shore up his support by "doing justice for Byron" while simultaneously creating a scenario where it would be very awkward for Roderick to object to this expansion of the core team.

However, the informal rules of institutional protocol dictated that Red first broach the subject with the university's leadership. Plus he probably needed the university to nudge Byron in Red's direction. Red seized upon this as an opportunity not only to gain permission to recruit Byron but also to earn the university's gratitude for doing so.

Red made his gambit during a private lunch meeting with Quincy Dewberry, Chair of the Westville University Board of Regents, and Dr. Janice Carter, President of the University. Quincy Dewberry came from one of Westville's founding families. Born and raised as a genteel and cultured gentleman of wealth, he was ill prepared to deal with the public scandal that was now laid at his feet. He had not planned on this type of difficulty when he sought the stature of being the Chair of the Board of Regents, and he wanted as little to do with it as possible. President Janice Carter had earned her doctorate in art history, specializing in art of the Renaissance. She had little interest in athletics but appreciated the revenue it could generate almost as much as she appreciated the "Venus de Milo." And she knew that an athletic scandal and the loss of revenue it threatened could leave her just as powerless as the armless sculpture she so loved. She was hoping to find ways to fund a new cultural center at the university, and somehow she had to find a way for the university's athletic department to keep purring along.

Meeting amidst the rich mahogany of a private room at the iconic Westville Literary and Game Club, Dewberry and Carter were like deer caught in the headlights of Red Paley's Escalade. Red brought up his sympathy for the university's misfortunes and offered his assistance. He tactfully mentioned that they would probably want to make some personnel changes and noted that he was looking to make some moves himself. Then he moved in for the kill.

"Byron's well liked in the community, but my advice is that you ease him out. He doesn't appear to be culpable in the scandals, but he's *sooo* familiar as the face of the Athletic Department that you are going to have trouble changing the perception of the program if he's still there. He's got two kids in high school, and his wife has a good job here. Plus they both have family here, so I'm sure he doesn't want to relocate any time soon. Fortunately, it just so happens that if you feel a need to ease him out, I'd be glad to take him on as a senior member of my personal team. The last time his salary was publicly reported, he was earning about twenty grand a year more than I can pay him. But if you give him a separation package of that amount, say, $20,000 a year paid in annual installments for a few years, he can land softly at the City. He won't take a hit on his total income, and, best of all, he can remain in the state pension plan. He can't be too upset about that, and he may even be relieved not to have to deal anymore with the NCAA. You'll come off as more than reasonable, even generous. Byron and the community will thank you for it."

Quincy looked at Janice and said, "Well, what do you think? Seems like a clever solution to a predicament with Byron that I'm not sure we had thought enough about to realize we even had. I'll put it to you, Red. You're smart as a fox."

Dr. Carter didn't mind that Quincy had asked and answered the question for her. Like Quincy, she hadn't thought far enough down the path to realize they would have to do something (totally buying into Red's logic) with Byron. "I agree. $20,000 a year for five years as severance will make up the difference and let him work for the City for a few years."

Red was elated. He couldn't believe Dewberry and Carter were such pushovers. "Good. How soon can you talk to Byron? I think you want to act before anyone gets the impression you are reacting to public pressure. He's a popular, churchgoing family man, you know."

"Quincy, if you can speak with confidence for the Board, I will talk to Byron this afternoon," Dr. Carter replied.

"I believe I can," Quincy stated confidently with the air of a man who had just been given a judicial reprieve for a crime he didn't even know he had committed.

"Great!" Red practically shouted. "Let me know as soon as you have talked to Byron. I want to close the deal with Byron and get him on my squad!"

And with that, the deal was struck. Byron Swift had effectively been traded from the University of Westville to the City of Westville.

Extra Credit

Red Paley wore a smile as he drove back to City Hall. The meeting couldn't have gone better. Just as Red had figured, the blue-blood board chair and the intellectual president were totally out of their respective high-society and academic elements. They welcomed a solution to a problem they were too naive to discover for themselves. Once presented with the "Byron problem" and a way out of it, they were only too happy to follow Red out of the public relations maze. But Red now had two concerns on his mind.

First, it was important the entire transaction with Byron Swift be wrapped up before Quincy Dewberry and Janice Carter realized he had exaggerated the situation somewhat. He did not want them to change their minds about Byron's future. The Athletic Director and the head coaches had to go, but Byron was probably salvageable. Red was confident President Carter would meet with Byron that afternoon, so he didn't worry too much about the possibility that she would reverse her course. Coming fresh out of a meeting with her board chair with her marching orders in hand, President Carter wasn't likely to be dissuaded by anything Byron would say.

The second concern was to ensure that everyone knew that the transaction was his idea. In Red's mind this wasn't just to be presented as a win-win in which the university solved an image problem with a popular employee and Team Paley got a new star. There was a third "win" component: that this was Red Paley's idea, born out of his creative and magnanimous genius. Red needed to be publicly perceived as concerned both for the reputation of the University of Westville *and* for the welfare of Byron Swift. After all, Red was the one facing a difficult election day in less than six months. And so, when Red returned to City Hall, the first thing he did was place a call to Tom Folks.

A Matter of Timing

Roderick Campbell was a composed—but not happy—man when he walked into the Mayor's office with a copy of the *Westville Wire & Telegraph* in his hand the next morning and inquired, "Good morning, Mayor. Do you have a minute?"

"Sure, Roderick. Have a seat." Red Paley was still on cloud nine, flush with fleecing the university with his "acquisition" of Byron Swift.

Seeing Roderick opening the paper, Red interjected, "Oh, I bet you want to ask me why the paper quotes me as saying the University and the City are going to be making some big announcements."

"Yes sir. As you might guess, people are asking about it."

Red leaned back in his chair, put his feet on the desk, and clasped his hands behind his head. He was about as smug as Roderick had ever seen him. "This is very confidential, which is why I haven't told you," Red said smoothly. "I've been thinking we could use a 'Mr. Outside' on our team to complement you as our 'Mr. Inside.' So I met with Dewberry and Carter yesterday and arranged to add Bryon Swift to our team. We'll be helping them reorganize in the aftermath of the NCAA sanctions, *and* we'll be strengthening our lineup at the same time. It's a win-win for them and for us. Not too bad a plan, if I say so myself."

Roderick didn't like being left in the dark, and he didn't see where Byron would add much, if anything, of substance, but he remained stoical. "How's Byron feel about it?"

"Carter was going to speak with him following our meeting. He'll be more than pleased to be able to stay in Westville. They'll offer him a severance package that will cover the spread between what he earns now and what we can pay."

"What if . . . ," but before Roderick could finish his question, Joan, the Mayor's Executive Assistant, poked her head in the door and interrupted Roderick with, "Mayor, President Carter is on the phone for you."

Red immediately leaned forward and picked up the blinking extension on his phone. "Janice, how are you?" he beamed.

"Well, to be honest, things are a little awkward this morning. I picked up the paper and there's Tom Folks writing that he talked to you, and he's got it on authority from you that there's going to be some big announcements today."

"That's correct. I had a chance to talk with him at Lonnegan's last evening, and I figured he could use a bit of a scoop. Of course, I didn't give him any details. By the way, how did Byron react to his new opportunity?"

"That's just it, Red. I haven't been able to talk to Byron, or to my Athletic Director, or to my coaches. I forgot they were all in Indianapolis for the conference's spring meeting, and I wanted to talk to each of them personally, face-to-face. I planned on doing that this morning. Now they are hearing ominous rumors through the morning paper. I just wish you had checked with me before moving forward."

Red Paley didn't miss a beat. "You know what I'm looking at right now, Janice? I'm looking at a picture I keep on my desk of a great white shark knifing through the ocean."

Roderick found the conversation growing more and more interesting, because he could clearly see that there was no such picture of a shark. Red continued: "You know why I keep that picture, Janice? Because sharks die if they stop moving. They have to move in order to breathe. So that picture reminds me that things have to get done. That if you aren't getting better, you're getting worse. That's why I and my City have to keep moving, and it's why I talked to Tom Folks. It's too bad you haven't talked talk to your people, but they'll be fine."

"I understand, Red. But please . . . don't contact Byron until I have spoken with him."

Red's combination of chauvinistic paternalism and opportunism leapt to the fore. "Hey, I've got a better idea. How about if you set up the meeting, and I'll be there with you? That way, Byron will know immediately that he's being taken care of. If you set it up and give me thirty minutes' notice, I will break away from my meetings and get over to your office."

Janice Carter thought for a moment. She had some reservations because Red was, well . . . Red. But being caught up in the fast-moving current of events, she agreed. She figured she just might have to do a little swimming along with Red. "All right," Janice replied. "I'll let you know when I've set it up."

"Excellent!" Red replied.

Just as President Carter was beginning to mentally play back the freewheeling conversation she had just had with Red, her phone rang. Her Executive Assistant announced that Byron Swift was on the line. "Perfect timing!" Janice thought. "I'll be able to set up this meeting and get this mess under control." She quickly picked up the phone.

"Hello, Byron. I'm glad you called."

"Thank you, ma'am. I'm glad you want to talk. I've got a couple things on my mind, but maybe you should go first."

"Thank you, Byron. That's very considerate of you, as always. I've been thinking about the aftermath of the NCAA investigation and sanctions, and I'd like to have a very confidential conversation with you regarding your future."

"So what Tom Folks says is true?"

"Well, we haven't figured everything out yet regarding our realignment. I want to talk to you first and see what you think."

"I'm glad to hear that, because Tom just called me and said I was going over to the City."

"What!?" Janice couldn't believe that Red had done this to her.

"Tom said the Mayor invited him to meet him for a drink at Lonnegan's after work yesterday. According to Tom, the Mayor advised Mr. Dewberry and you to 'trade' me to the City. He said the Mayor said he was really excited—almost giddy—to add me to 'Team Paley.'"

"Byron, I'm very sorry you are hearing about it this way. I wanted to tell you personally yesterday, but I forgot you were in Indianapolis. Can you be in my office in an hour?"

"Yes ma'am."

"And Byron . . . ."

"Yes?"

"You're not being traded. This is an opportunity that you should feel perfectly free to turn down if it's not right for you."

"Thank you."

"And one more thing: "I'm going to try to have Mayor Paley here to tell you about the opportunity he has in mind for you."

"Thank you. I'll be over in an hour," Byron said somberly.

With that, Janice Carter, PhD, President of University of Westville, bowed her head into her hands. "My God! How far I've sunk," she thought. "I've allowed myself to get caught up in events. We've been treating Byron not as a human being but as a piece of property. How could I have been part of this?" Then, with a deep sigh she sat up and rallied herself for the task at hand.

Meanwhile, at City Hall, Red Paley and Roderick Campbell had resumed their conversation.

"Roderick, I think you were about to ask me a question when Dr. Carter so rudely interrupted us," Red said with a smile.

"I was just thinking, sir." Roderick paused for effect. "What if Byron doesn't want to be on our team?"

Red shot back without hesitation. "Nonsense. We are taking care of him. The University's going to give him an annual severance package that makes up the difference in salaries. He won't have to relocate his family, and he stays in the state pension plan. This works for him." To Red, it was cut-and-dried.

"Well, sir. People do have career goals and aspirations. This may not fit in with what he wants, where he sees himself going."

Red thought for a moment. It hadn't occurred to him that Byron might not want to come. After all, his economic and family needs were being met. And who wouldn't want to be on Team Paley? After a pause he replied, "I highly doubt that's going to happen. Besides, he doesn't need to be here forever. He can be a big help for a year or so. If after a while, he decides this isn't for him, he can move on."

"Do you have a position and responsibilities in mind?"

"Yes. He will be the Senior Director of Strategy and report directly to me. He may have an executive assistant, but other than that, probably no direct reports. He will help us in the community and pick up other duties as assigned. We'll sort of drive the car while we build it, if you know what I mean."

"Yes sir."

Just then Joan poked her head in the doorway. "Mayor, President Carter is on the phone. She wants to know if you can be in her office in an hour."

"Definitely!"

At the President's Office

Red Paley walked into President Carter's office and was greeted warmly by her Executive Assistant, a young man, much to Red's disappointment.

"Hello, Mr. Mayor. I'm Pierce, President Carter's Executive Assistant. President Carter is in her private conference room with Mr. Swift. She asked me to have you wait here for a moment. She wants to come out and speak with you briefly. Would you like any coffee or water?"

"No, thank you," Red replied.

The Executive Assistant walked into the conference room, which was just a few steps away. Red could hear his presence being announced and heard Dr. Carter say, "Thank you, Pierce. Byron, if you'll excuse me, I will be back in a minute with the Mayor."

President Carter came out of the room and Pierce gently closed the door behind her before resuming his seat at his desk. Dr. Carter walked up to Red and, extending her hand, quietly and slowly said, "I have spoken with Byron. He's not sure about this, and I want to be clear: if he isn't agreeable, it isn't going to happen. This University has principles, and they don't include treating people like cattle. It is up to you to make this happen if you so choose. Do you understand?"

Red was taken aback. He hadn't expected to lose the initiative in the chess game he had conceived. Ironically, but fortunately for Red, Roderick's concerns about Red's handling of the transaction helped the Mayor recover his balance. "I understand, Janice," Red said quietly. "I am sure I can sell him on this." And then he added a subtle reminder that the President potentially had a problem if this didn't work out. "If not, he's yours."

With that, they entered the conference room. President Carter took her seat at the head of the table, with Byron Swift sitting to her right. At President Carter's direction, Red sat to her left, opposite Byron. They exchanged brief pleasantries, and then President Carter got down to business.

"Red, Byron was just telling me that Tom Folks called him this morning and told him he was being traded to the City to play for Team Paley."

Red blurted, "I can't believe that sonofabitch did that!"

President Carter continued: "Funny, because I had a fairly similar reaction myself when Byron told me. Although my dismay and disappointment might have been directed a little differently," she said looking directly at Red.

Continuing her comments, President Carter moved the subject back to Byron's immediate employment status. "At any rate, I've told Byron about the University's interest in moving in a different direction and your offer to give him a senior position reporting directly to you. Red, would you like to address that?"

"Thank you, Dr. Carter. Byron, I'm sorry you heard about this first from Tom Folks. That isn't right. However, the important thing is I think very highly of you, and I want you on my team. I'm creating a new position of Senior Director of Strategy just for you. You will report directly to me. We'll make sure you are taken care of financially, and you won't have to relocate. How does that sound to you?"

"I appreciate both of your interests in looking after me, but I'm a college sports marketing professional. It's not just what I do. It's what I am. I don't know anything about city government and strategy. I never thought I'd be leaving athletics, and I'm pretty numb at the moment. I mean, I thought I'd be Athletic Director someday. If not here, *somewhere*."

Red Paley wasn't about to let his new star player slip out of his grasp. He jumped in at full throttle. "Trust me Byron, this politics stuff ain't that complicated. It's mostly about being well known and having people know you care about them. You're already well known, and I can tell you're a natural at the people-caring part of it. In fact, I can see you as Mayor when I'm done. We can put you up as a candidate in the midterm council election. You're popular, and you're made of Teflon. None of the bad stuff will stick to you—the buck stops with me. You'll be elected to council, and four years from now, when I'm term-limited, you will be elected Mayor. I can see it all. You can't miss!"

"Geez. I don't know, Mayor. I'm very appreciative, but I've never aspired to politics."

"That's only one path, but I think it's real. If you want to work for me and discreetly have your feelers out for a college post, that's fine with me as well. But believe me: I think you have a great future in Westville politics."

"It sounds a little overwhelming, but if I can keep my options open . . ."

"You can!" Red interjected. "President Carter, don't you agree? Byron's a natural."

Janice Carter had never contemplated anything remotely resembling Red Paley's prognosis, but she had a personnel problem—or at least a perceived problem—and a million more important issues. Concurrence was the path of least resistance. And so she took the plunge. "You know. It had never dawned on me, but it's obvious. The same charismatic qualities that make Byron so successful here are readily transferable to politics. Byron, I think this could work for you."

Continuing, Dr. Carter threw a bone to Byron. "Byron, this is absolutely your decision, but we will grant you a five-year severance package that makes up the difference between what Red can pay you and what you earn here, plus an additional ten percent for, shall we say, career discomfort? And I won't rule out the possibility of your returning here in a year or two when things have sorted themselves out. But frankly, I think I see Mayor of Westville on your future *curriculum vitae*.

Red continued pressing for the kill. "I know this is a big change, Byron, but since Tom Folks is leaking the story [Red didn't let the facts that it was he who leaked the story and that it was the press's duty to report the news get in the way of his sales pitch], I really need an answer now. We need to be able to effectively handle the media. If you need to call your wife quickly, that's understandable, but you're getting a raise and so forth, so I don't see any downside."

Byron thought for a moment and replied. "It's something I've never thought of doing, but it is becoming more interesting. Plus I get a net pay raise, and my kids can stay in place. This sounds bad, Mayor, but I need to ask you. What happens to me if you don't win the election in six months?"

Red immediately responded in the most gracious of manners. "I'm not offended at all. People say I'm the underdog, but I don't buy it. With your help, I'm going to win. Plus I'm sure the University has a marketing or public relations slot they can slide you into in the remote chance that becomes necessary."

President Carter quickly replied, "Um, yes. I'm sure there is something. Something is always turning up, and we can guarantee your salary will remain unchanged."

Byron paused, but only briefly. "My wife is traveling on business and unavailable. I don't like saying yes without talking it over, but since it's an increase in pay, and I have no real future at this time with the University, I'll do it."

"Hallelujah! You've made the right choice!" Red could hardly contain his enthusiasm.

President Carter then weighed in. "Byron, you are a true gentleman. You have performed a great service to this institution, and we appreciate your class. I will have the severance agreement drafted and see that the other paperwork is commenced."

"Could I have two weeks paid leave before starting at the City?"

Red quickly accepted. "I'm fine with that if you are, Doctor. I think that would be on your dime."

President Carter concurred, and with that, the deal was consummated. The three of them parted ways very amicably. It was agreed that the University and the City would issue a joint press release no later than 4:00 PM that day, in time for the evening news. Byron Swift was now part of Team Paley.

CHAPTER 5

Back to the Present - March 2000

Byron Swift had played a role in helping Red Paley win his reelection by a nose, and Roderick Campbell came to find him to be of some value as a member of the innermost management circle. But in the world of politics those events were in the distant past. In late March, nearly three months after Red's "spinning hubcap and hot caliente" staff meeting, the thought had gradually grown in Red's mind that it was time to again shake up his staff. A firm believer that the average person gravitated toward complacency, Red was concerned that his team was experiencing post-election lethargy. This was reinforced by the fact that the challenge he had issued to develop innovative programs had failed to generate any dramatic proposals. In his opinion he had thrown down the gauntlet only to pick it up himself, having concluded that his spinning hubcap idea was "far and away the best initiative."

The biggest of Red Paley's leadership changes was to be at the Department of Neighborhoods. And the biggest change of all was going to be for Frank Clark. Red was a man of action, but his programs really hadn't done much to make life better for the average Westville resident. He needed a new Director of the Department of Neighborhoods that could give him a honeymoon period with neighborhood-based groups that were growing impatient with Red's penchant for bombast. Byron Swift had bought him enough goodwill to help win the election, but Red had his eye on a bigger prize, and he couldn't afford to have the neighborhoods snapping at his heels. Most people in the more disadvantaged neighborhoods felt that Red's spinning hubcaps were a perfect metaphor for the Mayor: lots of talk and gyrations, but few real results.

Red had been impressed with Frank Clark, and he came with no history, no baggage. "How could the neighborhood groups be upset with someone as fresh and clean cut as Frank?" he reasoned to himself. They would need to come to know him before determining if they liked him or not. That should buy a little time. And if he had to make some budget cuts to community organizations, who better to have stick it to the people than a new face? Maybe the dirty work and its political consequences would both attach themselves to the newbie?

In a worst-case scenario, he could try to have Byron take the fall, but Red was still actively thinking of grooming him for local office. Red and Byron had not discussed it since that day nearly a year ago in President Carter's office (and Red had never mentioned it to Roderick), but Red was strategizing that if he became Governor, he could have a thankful Byron Swift as Mayor of Westville. Red's mentorship and political coattails should surely be worth some favors from Byron down the road.

And so it came to pass that one Monday morning in early April Frank once again arrived at the Law Department only to be called into Karen's office in the presence of Roderick Campbell and Byron Swift. Karen started out by stating that Roderick and Byron had something to talk about that was of the highest level of confidentiality. She then turned it over to Roderick.

"Frank, we've all been impressed with your performance—not only the quality of your work, but the way you get along with people and present yourself on behalf of the Mayor and the City. We also know you're a sharp guy, and we are interested in moving you into a new area of responsibility."

Frank gently nodded his head in appreciation, and Roderick continued.

"The Mayor needs to make some leadership changes in the organization. As you probably agree, we've got a pretty strong team, but 'pretty strong and pretty good' aren't good enough for the Mayor or this City. We're going to make a couple of changes, and hopefully one of them concerns you."

Frank nodded again.

"We've got some issues with the Department of Neighborhoods, and the Mayor thinks you are the right guy to step in as the new director. All of us agree. So this afternoon the Mayor is going to call you into his office and offer you the position. We hope you will accept it."

Frank had absolutely no idea this was going to happen and no burning desire to leave the Law Department. "This is quite a surprise. I'm very flattered, but it's going to be a big transition for me with a heck of a learning curve. What more can you tell me?"

"It's a large department with a lot of responsibility to deliver programs as well as manage federal funds. As you note, there will be a learning curve, but we are confident you will be a quick learner. And by the way, it will come with a nice increase in salary."

Byron Swift then chimed in: "The Mayor is counting on you, Frank. We know you are going to hit it out of the park."

Looking at Karen, Frank asked, "I assume you are okay with this?"

"Yes. We will miss you here, Frank, and you are always welcome to return if it doesn't work out."

"Well. It sounds like something I should accept. Let me give my wife a call, but I think I'll be saying yes."

Karen, Roderick, and Byron expressed their thanks and assured him it was the right move. Frank excused himself from Karen's office and made his phone call to his wife before returning to the contracts on his desk.

*****

That afternoon, Frank Clark was summoned into the Mayor's office, where they were joined by Roderick and Byron. Red Paley was at high energy, almost effusive, and he got right down to business.

"Frank, you're probably wondering why we are here talking in the *oval office*. Well, you're not in trouble. In fact, we are all very pleased with you, and I have a promotion in mind for you. I've got less than four years left as Mayor, and I want to see some progress in our central city neighborhoods. More importantly, that has to happen soon, because I've got neighborhood groups crawling up my ass. We need a fresh start, and you're just the guy to come in and give us a clean slate. So I want you to be my new Director of Neighborhoods.

Roderick and Byron, you agree that Frank is just the guy for the job, right?"

Byron normally deferred to Roderick's seniority and title, but he dove in headfirst. "Frank, you're just the man for this. You're going to be a huge success!"

Frank humbly stated his gratitude for their support and then added, "Can I ask what is going to happen with Bobby?"

Bobby Turkel was the current Director of Neighborhoods. A native of the Bronx, Bobby had a long career in community development, with stints in numerous cities beginning in New York and a series of progressively smaller cities thereafter. Red Paley had brought him to Westville as Director of Neighborhoods shortly after beginning his first term as Mayor.

It had long been Red's opinion that the community development industry in Westville was an incestuous, backstabbing mob, and he didn't trust anyone who came out of that cluster. This led him to bring in an outsider who, Red presumed, would be zealously loyal to him. Bobby Turkel was third on his candidate list, but when the two women ahead of him couldn't come to terms with Red, the selection defaulted to Bobby. Red was so anxious to bring in an outsider that he overlooked Bobby's less-than-stellar career path. Bobby in turn was more than eager to leave his last post before the heat caught up with him, for Bobby was, to put it mildly, a bullshit artist of the highest order, always trying to stay one step ahead of reality.

Bobby Turkel had served a wide range of roles in the other cities where he had been, but this was by far his best and longest gig. Most immediately, he had been the Manager of Community Revitalization in a small, declining industrial city for just over a year. When he came to Westville, he tried to compensate for his weaknesses with snappy dressing and fast talking. As he made his initial get-acquainted rounds through Westville's neighborhood associations, he introduced himself as Bobby "The Turk" Turkel, but within a few months he was widely referred to as "Jive Turkey" Turkel.

The fact that Jive Turkey Turkel had survived to the beginning of Paley's second term was primarily due to both Bobby and Red. On Bobby's part he wasn't marketable enough to jump ship and get as good a position somewhere else. On Red's part, no suitable replacement appeared to be available. In addition, both of the men enjoyed having a drink together at Lonnegan's from time to time, each finding the other to frequently be good entertainment. Now, with Byron Swift onboard and Frank Clark in the wings, Red felt he could pull the trigger.

Responding to Frank's mild inquiry about Bobby Turkel's status, Red Paley launched into a brief but sharp tirade.

"Turkel? That jive turkey's goose is cooked. He's been lying his way from one end of town to the other. And when I asked for innovative proposals a couple months ago, you know what he came up with? Zip. Not a goddamn thing. We'll buy him a one-way ticket to Indiana, 'cause that's the way he seems to be migrating."

Frank was half sorry he asked and was somewhat embarrassed that he was entertained—in a rather surreal way—by Red's staccato rant. "I see. Well, I've got to talk it over with Ellen tonight, but I'm pretty sure that if *you* think I'm your man, then I *am* your man."

"Attaboy! You're making the right move!" Red's energy was almost as high as when he was going off on Turkel a moment earlier. "Let me know first thing, so we can have a press release and handle Turkel's exodus. With your smarts and Byron's neighborhood connections, we'll be in great shape!"

Roderick had been silent until then, but he quietly affirmed Frank's decision. There was only so much oxygen in the room, and he was more than willing to let Red take most of it. With that, they all shook hands and left Red alone in his office. Frank went back to the Law Department and, poking his head in Karen's door, let her know that the conversation had occurred as expected with no surprises.

*****

That evening, as Frank Clark went home to talk about his eventful day with his wife, Ellen, Red Paley sat down at the head of the bar in Lonnegan's and enjoyed a Jameson on the rocks with a splash of water. He made eye contact with Bobby Turkel as he walked into the pub and waved him over. "Hi, Bobby, how the hell are you?" he said with a loud smile.

"I'm doing great, Red!" Bobby said as he took off his Brooks Brothers suit coat and carefully draped it on the back of the barstool. "Mind if I join you?"

"I'd mind more if you didn't!" Red said with a gleam. "I'll buy. Jack and soda as usual?"

"Nothing but," Bobby said with a grin.

"Hey, Joe, get us a Jack and soda when you can, will ya?"

"Sure thing, Red!" Joe O'Neil replied from the center of the bar.

"How's your day been, Bobby?" Red said calmly.

"You know me, Red. I follow your philosophy—every day's a great day." Bobby smiled broadly. "But today is even better than usual," he continued. "Today we got a commitment from Central Trust to loan $300,000 on the rehabilitation of the Crown Apartments and subordinate it to the primary financing. So it looks like the project, with forty refurbished units, is going forward."

"Fantastic!" Red said as Joe set a tall drink in front of Bobby. "Here's to you, Bobby!"

With that, Red Paley (otherwise known as "he who was about to fire the Jive Turkey") and Bobby Turkel (aka Jive Turkey, and otherwise known as "he who was about to be fired by Red Paley") drank to Bobby's good news.

"I'll tell you, Bobby. You've had your detractors as you know, but I owe you a debt of gratitude. I'm just beginning my second term, and you have been here almost the entire time. Not many can say that."

"You're welcome, Red. It's been a roller coaster of a ride, but with Crown Apartments in place, I think we start knocking out the projects like dominoes."

"I think you're right, Bobby. It's going to be a good four years." Red said with a grin. "Are there any HOME funds involved?"

"No. This is all market-rate housing. The downtown rental market should be able to handle it."

"Market rate? That's good news," Red said as he took another sip.

"Yes, I've been steering clear of using the HOME funds as you know," Bobby replied. Then he added, "But eventually we will have to open the dam a little and let the money flow again."

"Yes, I know," Red replied. "But let's talk about other things, today."

Red and Bobby stayed at Lonnegan's and enjoyed a second drink while listening to the classic jazz and blues and telling stories. Then they parted ways without Red having given any indication that he was about to rock Bobby's world.

Meanwhile, Frank Clark arrived home and gave Ellen a warm hug and a kiss. They each simultaneously asked the other about their day. With a smile Frank said, "You go first, Ellen. We know mine is going to take awhile."

"Yes. And I can't wait to hear about your big meeting with the Mayor. I opened a bottle of cabernet to let it breathe. The kids are at practice, and I swapped our carpool duties for tomorrow, so we don't have to go anywhere. Let's kick back on the porch."

Relaxing on the porch, Ellen briefly talked about her rather uneventful day at work and said their two children had pretty typical days as well. And then, "So tell me how the meeting went. I'm just a little curious about your big career move, you know."

Frank recounted the meeting in full detail, and they both were a bit taken aback by Red's blistering attack on Jive Turkey Turkel. Frank added, "I hope he lands on his feet, but then again I guess he always has."

"So you're going to take the job, right?" Ellen asked knowingly.

"Yes. I think I should, don't you? This will give me an opportunity to really impact the community and hopefully get Westville back on track. Plus it's a ten percent pay raise when the City hasn't been very generous, and Karen says she'll take me back in the Law Department if it doesn't work out."

"Yes, Frank. I think you should and *need* to take it—for your professional fulfillment even more than the money."

And with that, Franklin Jefferson Clark's professional adventure was about to begin.

CHAPTER 6

The next morning Roderick arrived at the office and immediately called Jack Barnes, the Director of Information Technology.

"Jack, this is Roderick."

"Hello, sir. What can I do for you?"

"We're going to make a personnel change, and I need you to confidentially and personally lock Bobby Turkel out of the network. Make sure he can't access any files, email, calendar, etc. If he calls you, tell him it must be a technical issue, and you will get on it. You know the drill."

"Yes sir. It'll be done in a matter of seconds."

"Thank you. Let me know if there are any problems. I'm going to be talking to him in a few minutes, and you know what that means."

"Yes sir."

He then picked up the phone and called Bobby Turkel. His assistant answered and informed him that Bobby was at a meeting until 10:00 AM. Roderick checked his calendar and saw that he had a meeting he could reschedule without too much trouble. "Have him come up then, Ann."

Shortly after 10:00 Bobby Turkel was shown in to Roderick's office. Roderick greeted him and gently closed the door. Roderick motioned Bobby to have a seat facing him and took his customary seat behind his desk. Roderick was at his most emotionally detached level of professionalism and began speaking as if reading an obituary.

"Bobby. I've got some bad news for you. We are doing some realigning of our team, and I'm afraid it entails having to part ways with you. Your employment with the City is terminated as of now. This isn't a for-cause termination. We won't contest your claim for unemployment compensation, and we aren't going to embarrass you with a showy escort out of the building. Valeria is waiting for you in her office down in HR to review your vacation and sick pay. You will give her your keys, ID badge, etc. She will provide you with a neutral letter of recommendation as well. IT has frozen your access to your computer and the network. You'll have until noon to clean out your office, and then I will meet you at your office. I will tell people we are going to lunch. I know I can count on you to be a professional."

Bobby was floored and considered fighting the issue. "This is #$*! bullshit. I don't even get another position in the City? After all I've done, I'm gone just like that?"

Roderick remained calm but extremely firm. "We don't have any suitable management vacancies to slide you into. The Mayor created a position when he hired Byron, and he can't afford to do that again. And frankly, Bobby, I wasn't going to bring it up, but we've been more than fair in carrying you this long."

Bobby saw the writing on the wall and countered with a feeble protest. "But I saw Red at Lonnegan's last night, and everything was fine. We had drinks and talked about plans for the coming years."

Roderick remained completely stoical. "Surely you don't expect him to fire you at a bar. Whiskey and employment terminations don't exactly go well together, do they? Now head down to Valeria's office, and I will see you in your office at noon."

Bobby started for the door and then paused. "Who's taking my place?"

"That won't be public until this afternoon." Then he added firmly, "I'll see you in awhile."

Bobby opened the door and walked out of the office. Roderick stared blankly at his calendar for a few moments. Letting people go was never pleasant, even when they were underperformers like Bobby. That's why it was always best to get straight to the point and then move the person along to the next step. No good could come from wallowing in the process.

*****

The exiting process went smoothly, and that afternoon Roderick, Byron, and Frank met the Mayor in his office. Red Paley was in high energy and good spirits, glad to see that his plans were coming together.

"So Bobby Turkel left without incident?" Red asked rhetorically. "That's good. It's hard to soar with the eagles when you've got a turkey on your team!" Red laughed at his own joke, and the others chuckled obligingly. "Or, as my grandfather who liked to play the ponies used to say, 'There's no use in having the jockey whip a lame horse.' And Bobby's as lame as they get.

"But let's get down to business. The reason we are here is to talk about what this change means." Red was interrupted by Joan's voice at the door. "Mayor, Councilwoman Streeter is returning your call."

"Put it through. You gentlemen can stay put. It won't take me long to handle this."

The phone rang, and Red picked it up. "Hello, Dorothy. How are you today? I hope you're baking some of your famous sweet potato pie." There was a short pause and then, "Oh, I'm sorry to hear that. Well, please put me on your list the next time you get to do some baking." Then about sixty to ninety seconds elapsed during which all anyone could hear were an occasional "hmm" from Red and one "I'm sorry you feel that way." During the course of that time, Red's mood changed from condescending, to sympathetic, to serious, and then to inflamed. Finally, Red erupted.

"Listen. If you think you're going to try that shit with me, you've got another thing coming. I've got more ammunition on you than Fort Knox. So you better think twice about that, Tootsie!" And with that, Red brusquely hung up the phone.

"I'll tell you. All these people think they can threaten me. I've got more cards up my sleeve than Houdini. There isn't a damn one of them down in City Council with any backbone. All they can do is slink around and try to sting you like some gooey jellyfish. Well, . . . *I've* got backbone. They think they know what MADD is, but I'm the one who knows M-A-D-D like nobody's business. They don't have a clue what they're up against!"

Byron spoke up. "MADD sir? Are we in a battle with the Mothers Against Drunk Driving?"

"No. MADD is the cold-war strategy of 'Mutual Assured Double Destruction.' Neither the US nor the Soviets could launch a nuclear attack against the other, because each power had enough capacity to destroy the other. That's how we preserved peace in a nuclear age. If a war broke out, they would both be devastated. And those wannabes in City Council don't have a clue what's in my arsenal. Not a clue at all."

Frank spoke up. "That's interesting sir, but MAD only has one 'D' in it. It stands for 'Mutual Assured Destruction'—not 'Mutual Assured Double Destruction.'"

"Like hell it does!" Red was still red-hot. "Believe me, I lived through the heyday of the Cold War. It's double destruction because both countries get destroyed." He paused for a moment and then continued. "Let me break it down for you youngsters. *Mutual* means that both sides know it is *Assured* they will *both* be destroyed, as in *Double Destroyed,* as in *blown to hell.* Do you understand now?"

"Yes sir." Frank answered for all of them. There was no upside to continuing this end of the conversation.

Roderick brought them back to point. "So, Byron and Frank, the Mayor has some thoughts on how we can move forward in Community Development."

Red Paley righted his ship *and* his composure. "Yes. Byron and Frank, you are going to form the perfect team. Byron, you are here because everyone likes you, and Frank, you're here for your brains."

Roderick interjected: "Now obviously that doesn't mean you're stupid, Byron, or you're unpopular, Frank."

Red wasn't in a mood to be assisted by the ever-able Mr. Campbell. "Do you mind??" he said sternly. "*I* am the Mayor and this is *my* meeting if that's all right with you."

"Yes sir."

"All right, then. Now, Byron and Frank, Roderick is absolutely correct. But once in awhile I would like people to give me a chance to get to my next point. I was just emphasizing your strongest qualities. Byron, you are going to use your popularity to buy us time in the community. Frank, you are going to use the time Byron buys to come up with a strategy that appeases the neighborhoods (he could have added, 'and makes me look good'). Everyone understand?"

Byron and Frank indicated they understood the orders, and Red continued. "Now, I asked all my directors to come up with ideas a couple of months ago, and I've gotten next to nothing. And that overstuffed jive turkey came up with zip. He went from Mr. Know-It-All to Mr. Know-Nothing. So, Byron, it will be easy for a while for you to hold them at bay because Turkel set the bar so low. Frank, you come up with something good."

Then Red walked behind his desk. Picking up the phone, he dismissed them as he got his assistant Joan on the phone. "Joan, get me that cute intern I like. What's her name, Kayleigh, I think? I've got an assignment for her."

A History Lesson

At the next morning's staff meeting, Red Paley walked in as usual and sat down next to Roderick Campbell. Clearing his throat, he opened: "I'm sure Roderick has filled you in on our change with Frank replacing Bobby. I just want to say that Bobby wasn't terminated for cause. He didn't do anything illegal. Frankly, he just didn't do enough that was good. This is a first-class ship of state, and we can't have anyone on it who isn't first class. Understood?" There being no dissent, Red continued.

"I expected everyone to get me some innovative ideas, and Bobby generated nothing. There are only so many grains of sand in the hourglass, and his ran dry. Frankly, it ran dry long ago, and I'm a sap for keeping him on as long as I did. But I had to act strategically, and now I have—like a cobra. But a good cobra, a good cop—not a bad cobra, not a bad cop. Together, Frank with some help from Byron, is going to have us far ahead. And soon, not in the long run. If not, well, . . . I won't be as patient next time.

"Now. Moving along, I've asked our graduate intern, the lovely Kayleigh, to give us an update on something that came up in yesterday's conversations. Kayleigh, stand up over here next to me and share your research with Team Paley."

Fully blushing bright pink, Kayleigh came up from the far end of the room and stood next to Red, who had nudged Roderick over slightly to make room. She began to speak. "MAD is a theory that developed during the Cold War to avoid the outbreak of a catastrophic nuclear war. The idea was that both the United States and the Soviet Union had sufficient nuclear arsenals to inflict unacceptable losses on the other even if a surprise first strike by the other did significant damage. In other words, no side could truly win a nuclear war no matter how clever or devious it was."

Red loved it. "Now. Tell them what MADD stands for," he said with a confident gleam.

"Yes sir. MAD, M-A-D, stands for Mutual Assured Destruction." Red cringed, and Kayleigh, standing to his side and, therefore, not being able to see his reaction, continued, growing in confidence as her knowledgeable recitation further distanced her from Red's embarrassing introduction. "The term arose because *mutual* meaning 'two' implies that both sides were assured of being destroyed. Would you like me to continue with the theory of the triad of the nuclear delivery systems, Mayor? It emphasized a combination of land-based ICBMs as well as nuclear weapons delivered by or fired from bombers and submarines."

"No, Kayleigh. That is fine, thank you."

Kayleigh went back to her seat, and Red took a moment to visibly admire her long scarlet locks before continuing. "You may be wondering why I looked Kayleigh into this. I mean why I had Kayleigh look into this. Well, we're playing hardball with City Council, and I want all of you to rest assured that no one plays hardball like me. I can assure you my balls are hard, and I've got your backs covered as we go to battle on the budget, programs, deals—you name it. That collection of clueless cowards doesn't know what they're up against."

The staff meeting continued for another four hours, but nothing of interest or importance occurred.

CHAPTER 7

When the news broke that Frank had been named Director of Neighborhoods, Joe Schwartz, a senior litigator who was nearing retirement, asked him if he wanted to grab lunch. Joe was one of the most respected and best-liked attorneys in the department, and Frank quickly took him up on it.

They had lunch at Maury's, a local delicatessen located just a block and half from City Hall that was a long-standing "institution" for downtown workers, particularly attorneys and government employees. Between bites of his Reuben, Joe asked Frank why he had accepted a demanding position that also meant that his career path was taking a revolutionary turn. Frank told him that while he appreciated the helpfulness of all the attorneys on the staff, including Joe, he felt that he really wasn't doing enough to help Westville—his hometown. Frank also told Joe that he wanted to be on the leading edge of projects rather than the draftsman in the backroom who created legal documents furthering ideas and initiatives that he had little or no part in helping formulate. In essence, Frank told Joe that he was relishing the chance to help lift Westville out of its decades-long downspin.

Still chomping on his sandwich, Joe asked, "What happens when you are part of a team that isn't moving the City in the right direction? Or when your ideas are vetoed by the administration or council?"

With little hesitation Frank responded. "I realize that there will be some political considerations along the way that might result in a few detours or wrong turns, but I'm guessing that doesn't happen too often. And, after all, all I can do is advance good ideas and figure that some of them are going to take root."

Like a good trial attorney, Joe delved a little deeper. "So what makes you think there won't be too many political decisions or detours, so to speak?"

"Well, . . . it seems to me that any elected official ought to be able to win reelection if they have a strong record of accomplishments. Naturally they would lose if they have a weak record. So I'm thinking that while politics, favors, and patronage have a role, it can't be that big. I'm guessing it's maybe 85 percent good government and 15 percent not so good. I mean at some point, they wouldn't be able to get reelected if it got much worse than that."

Joe responded with such animation that it was a good thing he had swallowed the mouthful he had been chewing or Frank would have been sprayed with a partially masticated combination of Thousand Island, corned beef, rye, Swiss, and sauerkraut. "You've got to be kidding!" he exclaimed. Trying to lower his voice so that he wouldn't be overheard in his excitement, he proceeded to give Frank a free "senior counsel's" lesson.

"Listen. These guys are always thinking politics. And it's always really short-term thinking. And believe me, it's *front and center* in their minds. Most of them are career politicians, and they don't let anything get in the way of their reelection, because once you lose, you are a *loser*. Even the ones that don't aspire to anything higher than City Council know that getting elected and perpetually reelected is their mission, and the stakes are too high for them to take any serious risks. They don't want to do anything controversial. Controversy is like radioactivity to them, so you always see the can being kicked down the road. The result is a bunch of people who lack the balls to tackle even the most obvious critical issues. We just muddle through, delay action, and watch things get worse. Kicking the can down the road isn't just a short-term tactic. It's a long-term strategy. Sometimes it takes the form of announcing a study or launching a planning process. Sometimes, they simply say the data is inconclusive, that we have to wait and see."

Frank sat numb as Joe continued the lesson.

"If it's a development project, they may arrange for a friendly developer to express interest and take out a long-term option to purchase a property during which time the developer is supposedly doing their due diligence. But it isn't real: they are just accomplices helping the elected officials stall for time by creating the illusion that progress is being made. When the option expires, they simply say they have chosen to pursue other opportunities. Moreover, the smart politicians always know who they are going to blame if they run out of time and nothing's happened. In fact, my experience is that most of them seem to spend more time thinking about how to manage the fallout from failure than they do trying to succeed. For them, slick exit strategies are more important than victory parades. Sometimes I swear they care more about having a parachute than they do about having the plane make a safe landing.

"One last thing: most of these politicians aren't smart enough or articulate enough to translate a good government track record into votes. Don't believe President Carter or any of the other blowhards at the University of Westville when they proclaim that this is a college town. This is a shot-and-a-beer town, and it's hard to tell a working stiff that you had to lay off a few cops because the City had to update a computer system that is so old no one will service it. Fred and Ethel can see a cop, even if he's at the diner or the donut shop. They can't see a new computer system or an extra clerk in purchasing or accounting—the subsurface things that are needed to keep government functional. And they sure as hell don't want to see any more attorneys like us!" he added with a chuckle.

"I guess that's why Westville is doing so well." Frank said with understated sarcasm.

"You can say that again," Joe replied wryly. And then, calming down, he added, "I guess that's why so many people call it Worstville. In fact, my daughter who's working on her Master's says there's a college bar that has a Tuesday "Worstville" happy hour special featuring bottom-shelf liquor. But hey, it's still not a bad place to earn a steady paycheck with benefits. It's not great pay, but you can get by and retire with a pension. It's just that nobody is up there trying to turn this ship around. They're just living from election to election."

A few uncomfortable minutes passed while they quietly ate their lunch. Frank was feeling a bit deflated, and Joe felt a little bad about being the cause of it. But Joe was worried Red was going to exploit Frank for his own ends, and he didn't want him to get too badly damaged if that was the case. He had one more thought to somberly add: "You are leaving the Law Department, a position as a senior attorney with a good deal of respect and job security, to leap into the frying pan of neighborhood development—something of which you, as bright as you are, know nothing about. You may want to quietly develop an exit strategy of your own. Karen will take you back."

Frank thought for a moment. Joe cared enough about him and his future to take the time to deliver this warning. As excited as he was about his new promotion, he had to honor Joe's sage advice. "I appreciate that Joe. I think your advice is good. While I kind of want to burn my ships like Cortes and not look back, I need to protect myself and my family. I'll keep that in mind."

"I'm sorry to bring you down, but I've been around a long time, and I've seen a lot of good people get burned."

"I understand," Frank said trying to cover his concern.

As they finished lunch and turned the conversation to sports and their respective plans for the weekend, Frank kept thinking of what Joe said. However long or short, Frank hoped he would have a successful tenure with the City that would really help reverse Westville's course—something much more than just a gig with a paycheck. He wanted to be part of something significant in his hometown. To have something good to look back on with pride. Something meaningful to show his children and grandchildren, whatever it may turn out to be. But would he have that opportunity?

CHAPTER 8

With Joe's warning still ringing in his ears, Frank started his new job as Director of the Department of Neighborhoods the Monday morning following the announcement. He needed a couple of days to transition out of the Law Department, and there wasn't anything earth-pressing in the Department of Neighborhoods that the remaining management couldn't handle or at least triage for him. He began his first morning by calling all eighty employees of his new department together and addressed them briefly in a large open area between the cubicles and the elevators.

"Good morning. My name is Frank Clark, and it is my honor and privilege to be your new director. I know this department is right in the line of fire given our condition as a declining rust-belt city. Well, we can't do anything to change Westville's condition this very day, but we can do a lot to make sure it isn't in this condition in the future. All of us have something special in common—we have the good fortune of being paid to make our community better, and that's what I think we are really all about. Whether we are citing people for failing to maintain their property, providing funding for affordable housing, demolishing dilapidated buildings, or even processing paperwork in the backroom, we are all here making Westville a little bit better day by day. Not many people can truly answer their phone or the knock on their door by saying, 'I give at the office,' but each of you gives every day. And you have every right to be proud of that fact.

"I don't want to keep you much longer, but I'm guessing you want to know something about your new director. I can tell you a little bit,

93

and then I think you will slowly learn the rest as we work with each other. You know I'm an attorney. What you probably don't know is I want to be here because I think with your help I can make a bigger difference in my hometown—our town—by being here. Second, I'm not a micromanager. Heck, I don't know enough about your jobs *to* micromanage you. What I want you to do is work hard and work smart. I trust that you are all passionate about the opportunity each of you has to make Westville better, but at a minimum I want you to work hard *and* smart.

"I'll be making the rounds to meet with our different programming staffs, and you can ask me questions then. But are there any questions now about the department as a whole?"

There were a couple of general questions about general work policies as well as a couple of unsolicited voices of welcome. All told, the group meeting was over in about five minutes.

Orientation Begins

Frank then touched Walter Sage on the shoulder and asked him if he had a few minutes to chat.

The two entered Frank's new office and sat down at the small conference table within the office. Frank closed the door, and the two of them struck up a conversation. Walter managed the department's finances and contractual obligations, and they knew each other fairly well from a couple of contracts they had worked on together. This made for a fairly casual conversation between the new director and his veteran lieutenant.

Frank confided the obvious, which was that he didn't know much about the department's workings or the rules, mostly federal, by which it was regulated. He asked Walter for some candid advice on his transition.

Walter trusted Frank, and he appreciated that Frank had tabbed him for this conversation. Plus he had about thirty-five years of service with the City and was fully vested in the public pension. This combination of circumstances enabled him to be forthright and relaxed during their conversation. Walter's advice was simple and straightforward: echoing Joe Schwartz, he told Frank, "This is a precarious position, so be yourself, and don't be afraid to openly acknowledge that you are on a steep learning curve. We can advise you of the necessary regulations in the meantime. Essentially it could be summed up as 'You are in a high-profile, demanding position, but on a honeymoon with your staff. So don't pontificate about your strengths and their weaknesses. Own up to your mistakes and rely on them—you have a grace period.'"

Frank acknowledged the soundness of Walter's advice, which encouraged Walter to volunteer a little more information about his former boss—information he had not previously disclosed because he felt obligated to remain loyal to Bobby Turkel as long as he was the director.

"Bobby didn't do any of these things. Let me tell you how Bobby got the nickname Jive Turkey." When Bobby first came here, this was the biggest job he'd ever held. He wasn't up to the task, and he tried to cover for it by going around and promising funding for projects that he didn't have the authority to fund. Some of the projects weren't even eligible for funding. He also went around boasting about accomplishments in his prior positions that turned out to be greatly exaggerated. I don't think he realized how easy it was for people to research his background on the internet.

"About six weeks into the job, he had to meet with the board of the Abyssinian Progress Association and backtrack from a promised grant of $250,000 for the credit union they were establishing. Apparently, he fed them a story that was so contrived, the director cut him off.

"The director told Bobby that he thought his excuse was ridiculous. He also told him that some of the board members and he had checked his background and discovered that his employment track record was filled with tales of broken promises and commitments that weren't honored. He flat out called Bobby a 'jive turkey.' Deacon Wilkens said, 'Amen to that,' and that was the birth of Jive Turkey Turkel."

"You're kidding me!" Frank was flabbergasted that such an incompetent and unethical individual could be hired for—and then occupy—a critical position for so long.

"Not at all," Walter calmly replied. Frankly, the Bobby Turkel story wasn't that shocking to him after so many years of city employment. Not that he had been totally desensitized to these types of personnel decisions, but dysfunction in Community Development had become a bit of a business-as-usual situation at the City.

Walter proceeded to recite the next chapter of Bobby's history. "So the jive turkey incident caused Bobby to devolve from being insecure to being a bit paranoid. Are you familiar with *The Caine Mutiny*?"

"Yes. I read the book twice in school and saw the movie with Humphrey Bogart as Captain Queeg."

"Good. That will make it easier. You remember the famous strawberry incident, right?"

"Sure. That's when Captain Queeg summoned the officers of the ship because he was convinced someone had eaten a quart of strawberries, in the process depriving him of a midnight snack. He basically launched the equivalent of the Spanish Inquisition to ascertain the guilty party."

"Right. So in this case, Bobby was so paranoid he launched a major inquisition to figure out who stole the charger for his mobile phone."

"What?"

"So it was a couple of weeks after, his Jive Turkey nickname was born. And everyone was laughing about it behind Bobby's back, but he knew what was going on and it was really getting under his skin. So one Friday afternoon at 4:30 he called all six managers and administrators into the conference room for an emergency meeting. He told us he had just noticed that the charger that was always plugged into the outlet by his desk was missing, and he needed to take it home for the weekend."

"And . . . ?"

"He told each of us we had to immediately ask each member of our staffs whether they had stolen it. And I had the added duty of calling the custodial crew chief to see what she knew, and of course half of her team doesn't even speak good English. We had to drop everything, even the reports we preparing for the Mayor's weekend reading, so that we could track down Bobby's 'strawberries.'"

"What happened?"

"Nobody found it, so Bobby stormed out of here in a rampage that would make Red proud. Strange thing is, it showed up in Bobby's office first thing Monday morning."

"How did that happen?" Frank's curiosity had reached about a ten on the "Curiosity Richter Scale."

"Aisha, who used to be Bobby's secretary, was working flextime late that Sunday afternoon following church. Bobby came in to supposedly grab a couple of files he wanted to review and left. When she went into his office to put a couple of things in his in box, she saw the charger plugged into the wall where it always was."

"So he came in and returned it himself," Frank asked rhetorically.

"And announced on Monday morning that the guilty party had obviously returned it anonymously, and that he was going to graciously drop the entire matter. Aisha swears Bobby had to have returned it himself because it wasn't there when she went into Bobby's office earlier that Sunday afternoon."

"That's incredible. So why did Red keep him onboard so long?" Frank asked incredulously.

Walter got up, opened the door, and took a peek around before closing it again and sitting down.

"I don't know for sure, but here's what most of us think. Just before the midterm City Council elections two and a half years ago, there was a strong rumor that Red was going to can Bobby. At the same time, Bobby and Red were making a big push to announce some neighborhood investments that would help their friends on Council win the election. Bobby had lined up three meetings with developers who wanted to do affordable housing projects. In preparation for the meetings, I reviewed our budget with Bobby and told him we only had about $200,000 available for new projects. Well, Bobby went ahead with the meetings and promised a total of $550,000 in assistance to the three developers.

"The next thing I knew, Bobby and Red were holding three press conferences on consecutive days announcing the three separate projects and promising $550,000 in subsidies. I was on vacation at that time, but there is a pretty credible rumor that Bobby got Red's approval to go ahead and overcommit the City's funds. A couple of Bobby's buddies at Lonnegan's heard him say that according to Red, 'The chickens wouldn't come home to roost until after the election.' Frankly, I think it's a true story, and it helps explain why Red didn't let Bobby go."

Frank was more than curious, particularly given Joe Schwartz's admonition about being used by Red. "And now enough time has passed, most importantly Red's reelection, that Red figures Bobby is expendable despite the fact he might spill the beans?"

Walter nodded. "That certainly appears to be the case. Most likely Red has promised to help him find another job. That might buy Red a little time. Plus Bobby may not want to reveal his own lack of honesty by attacking Red publicly."

"Another case of Mutual Assured Double Destruction," Frank said with a grin, and they both shared a chuckle. "So which project got the funding, and why didn't the other projects pitch a fit?"

"Abyssinian had a new rental housing project; that's the one that got funded. The other two projects were from out-of-town developers. They weren't as politically important, and they didn't get funded. Red was right about one thing. The story is that he told Bobby the other projects would proceed anyway because by the time they found out that the City couldn't deliver on the funding, they would be too deep into their projects to turn back. And that's exactly what happened. Of course those are two good affordable housing developers that aren't ever going to do business here again."

Frank thought for a moment. "And I suppose the City had the usual disclaimers that the funds weren't really committed until City Council authorized them?"

"You got it. The developers did it all on the basis of a handshake and a press conference."

"But they still could have called the City out on it?" Frank was still puzzled at the story of how Red and Bobby ran the operation (or scheme, as appeared to be the case).

"Sure they could have. And what are you going to do when you don't get your building permit on time or the snowplow never seems to come down your block? Why shoot yourself in the foot?"

Frank was stunned but remained even-keeled, not wanting to appear totally naive *and* unknowledgeable of the department's workings. "Geez. I hadn't thought about that, but I guess you're right. So what does Roderick think of all this?"

"I don't know. He was pretty new as the Chief of Staff back then, and Red might have frozen him out of the conversation. At any rate, I've never heard him mention it, and I certainly haven't brought it up. The funny thing is, we now are sitting on a two-year backlog of about $3.5 million of HOME funds from the US Department of Housing and Urban Development. We are in danger of losing about half of that funding in another sixteen months or so if we don't commit it to projects."

"How can that be? I thought Red and Bobby wanted to spend the money for political reasons, let alone actually do some needed reinvesting in our neighborhoods."

"I don't know. I'm guessing they got too close to the flame and are afraid of getting burned this time. One thing's for sure—the money has to be spent. There will be front-page headlines if we have to give it back to the Feds."

"That's for sure!" Frank figured this was likely to be his first of many challenges as the new Director.

The conversation wrapped up, and Frank sat behind his desk. He had a pile of paperwork to wade through and try to make sense of, but his mind was somewhere else. "Will I get stuck in the middle of these kinds of unethical shenanigans?" he worried. "Is this what I am going to be in for? Was Joe Schwartz's warning prophetic?"

After a couple of minutes, an anxious Frank got back up and walked over to Walter's office. He tapped on the slightly closed door and walked in to find Walter at his desk reviewing a spreadsheet. "Thanks for your advice a minute ago. I forgot to ask you if there is anyone I should talk to who could give me a leg up on my learning curve."

Without hesitation Walter replied, "Probably the best place to start is with Dr. Harold Hearst. He's Chair of the Planning Department at the University. He used to be on the planning commission, and he can tell you the lay of the land as well as share some thoughts on what the City should do."

"Thanks!" And with that, Frank returned to his office and placed a call to Harold Hearst.

CHAPTER 9

That Thursday afternoon at 4:00 PM Frank Clark entered the office of Harold Hearst, PhD Chair of the Planning Department at the University of Westville. Dr. Hearst had been a member of the faculty for twenty-seven years and Chair of the Department for the past ten. He was a native of Brooklyn and had an accent to prove it. With his beard and slightly mussed gray hair, he looked every part the professional academic.

Their conversation began very casually, with Frank primarily expressing his appreciation for the professor's time and the professor in turn asking some questions that were geared to ascertain Frank's background, motivation, and open-mindedness. In response to Frank's question regarding why he settled in Westville when he obviously loved more intense urban cities, Dr. Hearst replied that his wife was from here and wanted to stay near her family—several of whom had disabilities and periodically required her assistance. On his part, when Dr. Hearst was duly convinced that Frank knew nothing about urban planning and revitalization, was truly interested in learning for the purpose of improving Westville, and was coming to him as a malleable blank slate, he decided to probe the subject matter.

"So you mentioned a few minutes ago that you spent a couple of days in Manhattan when you were in high school and really enjoyed it. What did you most like about it?"

Frank's eyes gleamed. "Just taking in the whole experience. I was fifteen years old, and we were staying with a young couple that lived in a small apartment on Broadway. We had an entire weekday to kill while they both went to work, so we just started walking down Broadway. We didn't know enough about New York to have anything particular in mind—we were just checking out the city on a warm July day. I couldn't believe how many people there were and how different they all were. That, plus all the shops and street vendors. There was a really exciting hustle and bustle I'd never experienced before. And we weren't even anywhere near Times Square."

Dr. Hearst nodded slightly. "Tell me about the people. What did you see?"

"There were tons of them. Some of them seemed pretty far out on the edge and struck me as weird. But mostly there were just a lot of people." Frank thought a moment and then added, "The other thing is, they were there for different reasons."

"What do you mean by that?" Dr. Hearst inquired.

"It was obvious that some of them lived nearby and were running their daily errands—buying groceries, going to the post office or the bank, things like that. It was in the middle of the week, and a lot of them worked in the area. Some of them, like us, were just visitors and tourists."

Clearly enjoying the conversation, Dr. Hearst smiled and said, "The leading book on urban revitalization is *The Death and Life of Great American Cities*, written by Jane Jacobs forty years ago. It's on the bookshelf behind me. Jane was a self-educated studier of urban life in Manhattan and noted four requirements for having vibrant cities. In your recollections of your visit to Manhattan, you've referenced two of the four essential requirements for having a vibrant urban neighborhood."

"Really?" Frank replied. "What are those?"

"You have to have population density because the large numbers of people need goods and services, which means their sheer number creates business opportunities. That's pretty obvious, don't you think?"

"Yes," said Frank leaning forward. "What's the second requirement?"

Dr. Hearst took a drink of his herbal tea before replying. "The second is a bit more subtle. A vibrant neighborhood needs a variety of primary uses."

Frank had never heard that term, "primary uses." "What does that mean?" he asked.

"It means the neighborhood can't be just residential or just commercial. It requires a mixture of uses in order to be vibrant. Unfortunately, zoning rules that most communities adopted in the early 1900s mandated the creation of single-use districts, districts that were purely residential, purely commercial, or purely industrial."

"That's interesting," Frank said. "Tell me more."

Dr. Hearst gladly obliged.

"If it is nothing but office buildings, everyone goes home at 5:00 or 6:00, and it becomes vacant. Restaurants have to make all their money at lunchtime, because no one is there at dinnertime—the area has been vacated. One of the best examples of the problem is government buildings. In most cities, they have all been built close together in a governmental and judicial/criminal-justice complex, under the theory that the governmental entities can operate more efficiently if they are in close proximity to each other. I don't think the savings from grouping government buildings close together amount to much of anything. On the other hand, as a consequence of grouping all these similar uses together, half a dozen or more critical blocks of prime downtown real estate shut down at 5:00 every workday and never even open on Saturday and Sunday. Suddenly there is a temporary ghost town in what is supposed to be the most vibrant part of any city. It's impossible to have a vibrant area under those circumstances, but virtually every city in America has done that. This really damages downtown vitality because all of these cities have a large area in the heart of their city that contributes nothing to the nightlife and is totally dead on the weekends. It is the exact opposite of vibrancy.

Dr. Hearst continued his introductory lesson.

"On the other hand, if an area has nothing but housing, there's nothing to do. There are no jobs, no entertainment, and no retail. It results in a different kind of dullness. Vibrant neighborhoods must have a variety of uses, including restaurants, retail, residences, and so forth. These elements combine to create vibrancy, which in turn attracts other people to the neighborhood who may work there, shop there, or dine there. In that way, there is a flow of people through the neighborhood at varying times of day. All of these people who are in the neighborhood for a wide range of activities are potential customers of the neighborhood businesses. Plus they populate the sidewalks, which makes for a safer and more interesting environment. As the shops and restaurants attract patrons, a self-reinforcing cycle of vibrancy emerges."

Frank was intrigued by such a commonsense approach to urban vitality. "That's really interesting. I've heard the phrase 'live, work, learn, and play.' Is that part of it?"

"Yes. The idea is that a really good and healthy neighborhood offers many different elements of living. The most vibrant neighborhoods or districts can be enjoyed even if you are simply passing the time with no particular purpose, as you were doing during your stroll down Broadway years ago. These are the places you can tell visitors to go to if they want a good opportunity to simply explore the city. I call them 'no-agenda districts,' because you don't have to have a specific reason—a checklist, if you will—to go there. You can simply wander the district. And while the districts have entertainment venues, they are not entertainment districts. They offer much more than just an opportunity for a pub crawl. They are perfect if you have out-of-town visitors and you need to be a bad host and go to work for a few hours. You can simply tell them to go to that area and enjoy themselves. You experienced that while you were exploring New York on that summer day so many years ago.

"We don't have any districts like that in Westville. We have some interesting things to do like the art museum and the zoo, but we have to give people a specific agenda of what to do in order to enjoy their stay. We don't have an interesting area that they can simply explore and see what comes up. Even Victorian Village is a pure residential neighborhood. It is not a true village where you can shop and in addition have access to various personal and professional services. It doesn't even have a coffee shop. It's not a place you can explore except during its annual architectural festival."

"That's an interesting point," said Frank. "It helps explain why so many young people call Westville *Worstville.*"

Dr. Hearst chuckled. "It's a major shortcoming of Westville, because at the end of the day vibrant neighborhoods and districts are what make a great city. My students have been complaining about the dullness of Westville for as long as I can remember. Vacancy and dullness, the opposite of active and vibrant, are the principal enemies of a healthy urban environment."

"What about crime?" Frank asked.

"Crime is primarily a symptom of the first two. Where you have people—eyes on the street—you are much less likely to have crime. Places that are vacant and dull inherently don't have many people, so the people who do happen to be there are much more vulnerable to criminals. And of course the buildings get tagged with graffiti and even fall victim to arson."

Frank was eagerly exploring the opportunity to learn and hopefully develop some conceptual strategies. "That's an interesting point. So what does Westville have to do to improve? How do we convert it from Worstville to something better?"

Dr. Hearst smiled wryly. "Here's where weak market cities like Westville are particularly challenged. Most of the citizens are clamoring for better public services and more police. They want streets to be maintained and plowed, trash to be collected, and a bigger police presence. So that's what the elected officials almost exclusively focus on. Unfortunately, that's a big problem."

"How is that?" Frank was puzzled, because he thought that was what people wanted government to do—basically take care of running an efficient operation.

"It's a problem, because none of those things create an active, vibrant place. If a city isn't designed and built in a manner that instills vibrancy, spending all the money in the world to better maintain it won't create an interesting place where people want to be. Neither will providing better trash collection and improving safety. *Well-managed sterility is still dull.* People with opportunities, with options and choices, choose to live in places that are great places to be, places that are themselves alive and where people believe they can realize their dreams. To achieve this, Westville needs to reinvent many of its neighborhoods, not simply do a better job of maintaining and servicing them.

"This isn't to say that maintaining a neighborhood, delivering good services, and providing safety forces isn't important—it is, and the community demands it. But that's just the threshold criteria, the ante for getting into the game. No one with real freedom of choice affirmatively chooses to move into a neighborhood *simply* because it is safe and the city has efficient operations. Even parents of school-aged children frequently want a *good neighborhood* in addition to a good school system. If it's a boring place that doesn't quite click, they aren't going to choose to live there. On the other hand, if a neighborhood doesn't meet an individual's requirements for safety, that individual will move out immediately if he or she can. So merely providing good safety forces and public services isn't sufficient to enable Westville and communities like it to rebuild their populations. It's valuable because it can slow the exodus and possibly create a threshold foundation for rebuilding the neighborhood. But it takes vibrant neighborhoods that click to attract people who say, 'I have choices of neighborhoods in which I want to live, and I believe this is the right neighborhood for me.'"

Frank was struck by the logic of what Dr. Hearst was saying. "So I'm picturing neighborhoods as being like buckets, and the people are like water. If a city doesn't provide good services, and if there isn't a certain level of safety, the bucket leaks water out the bottom. Fixing the leaks by providing better services and improving safety might stop or slow the leak, but it won't pump new water—new people— into the bucket. The only way to replenish the water, that is, the population, is to create a great place. Is that right?"

"Perfect!" Dr. Hearst exclaimed. "Creating a great place is the spigot or tap that enables new people to flow into the bucket or neighborhood."

Frank was following the logic. "So what does a city have to do to create an environment where people thrive and want to be?"

Dr. Hearst laughed and said, "Now that's a good question with a long answer." Reaching behind himself, he pulled a book off the shelf. "Here's my copy of *The Death and Life of Great American Cities*. How about if you read that, and we meet again in a couple of weeks?"

"I'll be sure to. Thank you!" Frank said as he graciously accepted it from Dr. Hearst.

"Also, I'll send you an email summarizing some of the key points of our discussion. That will help both of us keep track of what we've covered. We can update it as we cover more ground."

"That would be very helpful! Thank you!" Then, after a moment's thought, Frank added, "Let me give you my personal email address— no sense creating a public record since this is as much about my personal development as it is City-related."

"Good idea!" Dr. Hearst said heartily.

With that, their mentoring session ended and Frank departed. As he looked out his window at the academic quad, flush with the full greenness of spring, Dr. Hearst contemplated his new project. "Frank Clark has promise," he thought to himself. "The key will be the extent to which he reads, comprehends, and embraces the teachings in *The Death and Life of Great American Cities*. If he doesn't read it, this project ends quickly and is simply an extended meet-and-greet. If he reads it but doesn't get it, we will have a slow sunset. But if he reads it, gets it, and embraces it, well, . . . then we have something." Then, as he prepared to leave for his home, he said out loud, "Only time will tell."

That evening Frank received the following email from Dr. Hearst:

> Frank, it was a pleasure meeting with you this afternoon.
> I can tell the City is fortunate to have you. Here are some
> basic principles that we touched on as well as one that I
> am adding, but which I don't think you will have any
> difficulty comprehending:
>
> *1. Cities need to be vibrant in order to be
>   successful—vacancy and dullness are the primary
>   enemies of any urban neighborhood.*

2. *Two of the four essential requirements for a vibrant neighborhood are population density and a variety of primary uses (e.g., housing, retail, offices, restaurants, institutions, etc.).*

3. *Single-purpose neighborhoods and districts such as housing-only neighborhoods and government/judicial complexes are fatally dull.*

4. *The best urban neighborhoods and districts can be enjoyed aimlessly. They don't require an agenda of things to do.*

5. *Providing better city services and beefing up safety forces can help a declining city slow its population exodus, but they are not sufficient to enable a city to **replenish** its population. Doing that requires the development of vibrant neighborhoods that offer an appealing quality of life to people who have the wherewithal to choose where they are going to live.*

6. My last point, which we did not discuss, is this: *Urban projects need to be designed and planned by people who have three qualities/characteristics.* First, they must have a basic knowledge of how great urban areas function for the benefit of people (how the Built Realm best furthers the Human Realm). Second, they must have an urban mindset. Suburban thinkers can't design and plan great urban places, because they simply aren't capable of sufficiently

adapting their thought patterns to urban environments. Third, the designers and planners must have a passion for urban living. They must design places as if they themselves might actually live in them or utilize them, and they must view the potential spaces from the perspectives of a diverse range of people who may live in or utilize them. Too often, powerful executives who might have good intentions drive projects forward that simply don't create great urban places. In most instances, these executives lack all three of these characteristics.

I've also attached a brief essay I wrote a year ago describing cities as essentially having many of the characteristics of living entities and urban redevelopment as being a form of urban medicine. You may find it interesting.

CHAPTER 10

It's a Matter of Trust

Two days later Frank walked into his neighborhood coffee shop at 8:30 AM. He had received a phone call from a local consultant on organizational development, Dr. Camilla Johnson, who, having heard about his promotion, wanted to volunteer some free advice to a new department head (and perhaps lay the groundwork for doing some paid consulting). Frank took her up on her offer and suggested that Saturday morning would work well while his daughters were at swim practice and Ellen was running the family errands.

On Saturday, looking around at the patrons in the coffee shop, he made eye contact with a woman who, like himself, was signaling that she had an appointment to meet a stranger.

Walking over, Frank began, "Dr. Johnson, I presume?"

"Yes, but please call me Camilla." Dr. Johnson stood and extended her hand. She was a tall, svelte African American woman perhaps a few years younger than Frank.

"Thank you for taking the time to meet with me, particularly on a Saturday morning."

"You're welcome. Like you, my boys will soon be heading off to soccer practice. My husband can handle that," she said with a smile.

They each proceeded to briefly summarize their respective backgrounds. Camilla was impressed that Frank seemed serious about trying to turn Westville around, and Frank appreciated that Camilla, as a lifelong resident, was, like himself, tired of seeing her hometown struggle. They quickly established a good rapport, and Frank casually mentioned that a couple of people had questioned his judgment in accepting the position, even suggesting that others might be setting him up.

Camilla had planned to talk about the department's activities and perhaps suggest some techniques for performance-based management. But she sensed that although Frank had only casually mentioned the question of trust, the issue carried greater weight than he was letting on.

"So there is a question about whether you can trust the people you are working most closely with and report to. That doesn't make for a fun first week on the new job."

"No. But it's probably nothing." Frank didn't want to let anything diminish his optimism, let alone admit that he had leapt into perilous waters.

Camilla wasn't ready to leave the topic. "That's probably true, but it's very interesting. Some of them, particularly the Mayor, may be exploiting you and your reputation for their own advantage. And you aren't paranoid. You've been independently warned about this possibility by what, two or three unrelated individuals?"

"Yes."

"Are these people who are in the Mayor's office and would be in the know, or are they people more or less at your level in the organization?"

"More or less peers of mine, but with a long tenure at the City. One is an attorney, and the other is one of my new direct reports in the Department of Neighborhoods."

"Very well. So they have seen a lot in their careers, and they are concerned for your welfare—concerned enough to speak about it to you. This complicates a situation that is already very complicated. You have to learn how your new department operates, and the subject matter over which it has sway. Meanwhile, this trust issue has impact on your immediate job security and success as well as for the success of any initiatives you may conceive. I think a deeper discussion of trust is warranted. Do you agree?"

"Yes."

"Okay. Trust is an interesting topic because it is hard to know what one means when one talks about trust. I think we can quickly agree that there are six to seven dimensions to trust, maybe more that we don't think of right now."

Frank nodded to indicate that he wanted Dr. Johnson to continue. "Let me rattle off a few with you:

1. One meaning of trust is that I expect you to be truthful or honest.

2. Another is that I expect you to keep confidences confidential.

3. I think we can agree that trust means that not only will you keep my confidences confidential; you won't exploit them to your advantage.

4. This is similar to the previous, but trust also means that not only will you not exploit my confidences to your advantage, but that you won't take my confidences and use them against me.

5. If I trust you, I expect you to do what you say you are going to do. That I can rely on you to do something.

6. Similarly, that I can depend on you to carry out activities competently. To not only do what you say you are going to do, but to do it properly.

7. That I can trust you to act in alignment with the organization's goals and objectives. I can't force you to agree with where we are going, but I *can* demand that you execute directives and policies accordingly."

"It didn't occur to me that such a simple word could have so many dimensions."

"Yes. And there may be more, but I think we have cited enough to identify your challenge."

"Which is?" Frank was anxious to hear more.

"Well, . . . first, Stephen Covey says, 'In order to gain the trust of others *we* must first be trustworthy ourselves.'"

"That makes sense. After all, why should I be honest with you if you are not fundamentally honest yourself?"

"Right. Now, establishing that you are trustworthy takes time. It takes repeated acts of demonstrated trustworthiness without intervening acts that demonstrate untrustworthiness. It is reputational, and reputations take time to earn. But, Frank, I get the sense that you can do that fairly quickly."

"Thank you. I hope so."

"But you have a larger problem that is largely beyond your control. Whereas *you* may be able to demonstrate trustworthiness, the organization as an entity may not be able to do so. Are the Mayor and his senior team trustworthy? Is the City Council? I think not, because I haven't seen them consistently demonstrate that they are. Moreover, an intervening act of untrustworthiness is extremely damaging— sometimes fatal. In fact, it appears to me as an outside observer that there have been more occasions of exploitation for political gain or expedience than otherwise, so I would say that on the trustworthiness scale they are in negative territory. Yes, there have been times when they have acted in the public's best interest but usually that has been when the public's best interest has coincided with *their* best interest."

Frank sighed quietly. "So we have people practicing medicine who don't even know they are practicing medicine and who most likely would be violating the Hippocratic Oath even if they knew they were practicing medicine?"

"I don't follow you," Camilla said with a puzzled look.

"I'm sorry. Doctor Hearst at the University of Westville shared an essay he wrote explaining that since cities are composed of living human beings, they must themselves be treated as if they were living organisms, or at least as if they were lifelike themselves. Continuing that train of thought, our land-use decisions, investments in infrastructure, economic development incentives, housing subsidies, demolitions, etc., constitute the act of practicing medicine on a living organism—the city. But as city leaders and as a broader community, we don't realize that we are practicing medicine. Moreover, according to what you just said, and I pretty much agree with you, we wouldn't act much differently, because we wouldn't care that we are practicing medicine—we don't have the patient's best interests in mind."

Dr. Johnson considered what she had just heard for a moment and then responded.

"That's outside of my realm of expertise, but it sounds like a plausible and distressing analogy. Here's something else to consider Frank. You aren't the CEO of your own company, so your ability to change the City's corporate culture is severely limited. Corporate culture is set from the top down, and there is little you as a departmental director can do to offset the actions of the Mayor's administration and City Council. Let's assume that you are trustworthy and that you can establish a level of trust between you and your team. Even then, that level of trust will be marginal."

"Why is that?" Frank asked.

"You have to be loyal to the chain of command, so there will be times when you will be required to order your staff to execute directives that violate one or more of the dimensions of trust. Each time you do that, the line between your personal trustworthiness and the City's lack of trustworthiness will become more blurred. You will become guilty by association. Eventually, people will have trouble distinguishing your character from the City leadership's character. As a result, your perceived trustworthiness in the eyes of your staff and everyone you interact with or impact will quickly be eroded. Inevitably, your reputation is almost certain to be tarnished as a result of your role with the City."

"What do I do?"

"For a while, you should be able to earn and maintain the personal trust of the people that work closest with you, the people who report directly to you. You will be able to do this by maintaining their confidences and being truthful with them. But they won't buy into the element of professional trust that relates to organizational alignment. As you direct them to carry out orders that they know are simply politically motivated and self-serving for the people you report to, they will come to believe that you, like so many others above you, do not have the City's best interests at heart."

"Will I be able to have any success at all?"

"It's possible. To a great extent it depends on the Mayor and his key leadership team. Your window of opportunity is not indefinite. It might be a couple of years; it might be much shorter. External factors that are outside of your control could slam it shut at any time."

Frank spoke softly, somberly, but with a degree of determination. "So I've got to get my feet under me, learn what this job is all about, and try to do something impactful as quickly as possible."

"Yes. If the winds of fortune are favorable, you may have sufficient time. But every time the Mayor carries out a political maneuver or pursues some other crass opportunity, there is the possibility it will impact you. And of course it doesn't help that everyone knows he wants to run for higher office, probably Governor."

Frank swallowed hard and concurred. "I'm afraid I have to agree with you," he said grimly.

"I know you have a lot on your plate," Camilla said respectfully. "But I'm guessing that as a lawyer you do a lot of reading, and I have a suggestion, for what it's worth."

"What's that?" Frank replied.

"If you haven't read *Good to Great*[1] by Jim Collins, I suggest you do so. Its subject matter is excellence in the corporate world, but I think you will find that it can be adapted to the public sector. The discussion of Level 5 Leadership will be particularly interesting."

"Thank you. I received a copy of it as a Christmas gift, but I haven't read it yet. I will be sure to do so."

They chatted for a while longer, and Frank thanked Dr. Johnson for her time. In turn she offered to meet periodically to check in as Frank thought necessary. She also mentioned that she had some organizational management thoughts she would like to share;

---

[1] *Good to Great* was published in 2001. I am exercising artistic license in advancing its publication date.

however, they both agreed that those would be better left for another day.

CHAPTER 11

Two weeks later on Thursday afternoon, Frank Clark arrived promptly at Dr. Harold Hearst's office for his second session with his mentor. After a quick exchange of pleasantries, Dr. Hearst quickly launched into the lesson with enthusiasm.

"I'm afraid I have to be a little abrupt this afternoon. We are on spring break next week, and I need to wrap up a few things. Tell me, how did you like your homework assignment?"

"I enjoyed it quite a bit," Frank responded with equal enthusiasm. "It's very interesting!"

"Good! How much did you read?"

"I read the first twelve chapters of the book, as well as your essay."

Dr. Hearst was pleased. "That's a quick pace. If you read it too quickly, you may not be able to adequately reflect on what you have just read. This gives us more than enough to talk about."

"Good. I would have read a little more, but Saturday morning I had a meeting with an expert on organizational development that took up some time and diverted my thinking a little."

"Hmm, . . . how so?" Dr. Hearst had failed to account for the fact that Frank had to learn how his new department functioned as well what constituted good urban development. He suddenly appreciated the multiple dimensions to Frank's transition and was concerned about the "diversion" of Frank's thinking.

"Dr. Camilla Johnson contacted me and . . . ."

"Oh yes. I'm familiar with Camilla, but she might not recall me. She did some consulting for the University a couple of years ago, and as a Department Chair I was able to participate in a couple of focus group discussions. She did a very good job as far as I could tell."

"She called and offered some free assistance, and I took her up on it. I think she's very good."

"You said she diverted your thinking somewhat," Dr. Hearst probed.

"I told her that two people have cautioned me that the Mayor may be exploiting me and that I had better keep my parachute handy in case things don't go well."

Dr. Hearst leaned back and stroked his chin briefly as he thought. "Hmm. Well, I must confess that the thought had occurred to me as well. But I didn't think I was close enough to the situation to form anything more than a faint suspicion."

Frank forced an ironic smile and said, "Well, now I've been cautioned three times about accepting the best job I've ever had. Or at least what I thought was going to be the best job I've ever had. But now that I'm here, I want to make the most of it."

"Good! We'll change the topic. When we left off, you were asking me what Westville needs to do to create vibrant neighborhoods where people thrive."

"Yes. We need to make that happen."

Dr. Hearst leaned back in his chair. "Based on what you've read so far, what do you think?"

Frank thought for a moment and then responded. "We have such long way to go that it's going to be an enormous challenge to recreate amenities like storefront shops with apartments overhead to generate really vibrant neighborhoods. I don't think we even have one in the City, and, as you pointed out, we certainly don't have any 'no-agenda neighborhoods' in Westville that you can simply enjoy exploring."

Dr. Hearst leaned forward. "Yes. That is a major hurdle. We aren't going to be able to do it across a very large geography. It will have to be done incrementally, maybe with a couple of pilot projects along a few blocks of neighborhood commercial corridors. Most of the City will remain unchanged. We are a weak housing market and are not going to see the necessary level of private investment to make rapid changes for a long time."

Frank nodded.

Dr. Hearst continued. "The best growth comes very gradually in a form of organic urban evolution. As you will see as you continue reading, Jane Jacobs discusses this later in her book. Small-scale investments in neighborhoods that prove to further the creation of healthy, people-oriented environment can be reinforced with subsequent complementary investments. Those investments and projects that don't enhance the neighborhood can be considered relatively inexpensive 'experiments' that didn't work out. They can be replaced with other projects much more easily than major capital investments that fail to strengthen the neighborhood. One of Westville's problems is that we just aren't seeing enough good quality investment, some neighborhoods aren't seeing any."

"I see," Frank said in concurrence.

"Good," Dr. Hearst said. "So as a result, we need to focus our limited resources on modest, but strategic projects. This is very difficult in Westville. Our elected officials are used to spreading community redevelopment resources evenly around the City. There's a fundamental fairness and political rationale for doing that, but it isn't strategic. It won't generate catalytic change. Convincing the City administration to focus resources will take some doing, but we have no choice. They must concentrate resources in order to have sufficient impact to generate synergy and spark reinvestment. As the saying goes, 'Spreading the peanut butter too thinly over the whole piece of bread makes it impossible to taste it.'"

"Can I ask you a quick question?" Frank asked.

"Certainly," Dr. Hearst replied, glad that his pupil was actively engaging the subject.

"I was thinking about the analogy of cities and neighborhoods to buckets that may or may not have leaks in the bottom and an opening for new inflow at the top. And I'm wondering why cities don't focus more on the opening? It seems like Westville focuses exclusively on the leaks."

Dr. Hearst's energy level increased, and he momentarily forgot that he was anxious to get going.

"That's a good observation. There are a number of factors, and we don't have time to explore all of them. But let's try this one on for size. Places like Westville, Toledo, Pittsburgh, Flint, and Dayton used to attract people on the basis of job opportunities, not quality of life. They had booming manufacturing plants that provided very good wages for semiskilled workers. They didn't have trouble getting blue-collar workers. They were also home to the headquarters of Fortune 500 companies that transferred employees in from other locations or had such good job opportunities that it facilitated their talent recruitment. As long as America cared only about suburbia and automobile-oriented development, and as long as people were more interested in a good job than an exciting community, they were able to do all right. They weren't weak markets back then; they were prosperous midmarket cities. Now that these midmarket cities have lost most of their manufacturing jobs, Fortune 500 headquarters, and local banks, they don't have as many attractive career paths to offer to aspiring young people. Plus they don't have the power to compel people to accept transfers here like a corporate HQ can do.

"Today these types of cities need to be able to adjust to a different game, to a different set of rules. The best career paths and the power of a corporate headquarters to compel upwardly mobile management talent to come to places like Westville are gone. Plus suburban living isn't the only game in town. Now, the people who care most about a city being a great place to be are people who are career-mobile. These are primarily young people, particularly those who are going on to some level of post–high school education, and young professionals. Those populations have the opportunity to choose where they are going to live—not just choosing among neighborhoods but choosing among entire communities. These highly talented young people are the primary source of what we keep hearing as brain drain. They are place-driven, choosing to live in communities that they believe are more vibrant and exciting—even if they don't have a job already lined up. They also believe these cities will offer greater opportunity in the long run.

"Unfortunately, for several decades, upwardly mobile young people have tended to avoid the weak market cities. These cities are no longer prosperous midmarket cities and have disproportionately aging populations that planted their roots long ago.

"To put it bluntly, these longtime residents aren't particularly interested in some grand scheme to spend *their tax dollars* to create new, vibrant neighborhoods for *other people* to live in—particularly when they don't have confidence that a major development project will pan out. With the loss of thousands of manufacturing jobs in these cities, many of the residents aren't doing as well financially as their parents did. They are left trying to make the best of a bad situation, and they want their cities to 'stick to their knitting' and provide good basic services. In their mind *that* is good government, and what *their* government needs to do for *them*.

"This situation worsens over time. Weak market cities get even weaker, because as the city becomes even less competitive as a great place to be, the brain drain accelerates. As a result, the population increasingly becomes culturally inbred and opposed to new ideas. The city lags behind other cities, which means it isn't offering enough opportunity. It becomes increasingly noncompetitive. In addition, fiscal issues become more serious as the city continues to decline.

"The general public's preference that government should just deliver basic services coupled with financial pressures generates an inertia that is virtually insurmountable. The community becomes extraordinarily cautious and avoids any type of bold, risk-taking investments. As a result, most successful politicians cater to that sentiment and focus on bragging about miles of roads that have been paved, number of police- and fire-recruiting classes, and services like snow and leaf removal. It becomes a focus on management, not visionary leadership. Without realizing it, they are concentrating solely on fixing leaks in the bucket and ignoring the opening in its top.

Dr. Hearst paused and then offered a final observation. "There's one more thing to remember and of which there can be no doubt: no matter how bad the status quo is, there are some people and organizations who benefit from it. They are not going to embrace anything revolutionary."

Then, feeling a bit rushed, Dr. Hearst closed with, "I am obviously painting with a very broad brush here. We can talk about this more deeply some other time."

Frank periodically nodded in agreement as Dr. Hearst spoke. When he finished, Frank said, "That's an interesting theory. I look forward to exploring it further with you." Standing he concluded, "Thank you again, Dr. Hearst, I really appreciate it! Have a great vacation!"

And with that, the meeting wrapped up and Frank Clark headed home to his family.

That evening Frank received his second email from Dr. Hearst.

Frank— Another good conversation with you this afternoon. Keep up the good work! Here is my summary of our session:

1. *Westville will need to concentrate limited resources on narrow target areas through pilot redevelopment projects in order to have enough impact to be transformational. This will be very difficult, because the elected officials prefer to spread resources evenly across the City. The transformation of weak market cities such as Westville takes a very long time, because, as weak markets, they do not experience high levels of private investment. As a result, neighborhoods tend to be relatively stagnant and slowly but steadily continue to age and devolve. On the other hand, the best urban growth comes about gradually and organically through urban evolution. In that way development that furthers a healthy people-oriented community slowly but steadily reinforces itself.*

2. *Weak market cities frequently don't focus enough on reinventing themselves as vibrant urban places (building an opening for the inflow of new people), because the majority of the population has suffered financially due to globalization and innovation and simply wants the city to efficiently and effectively provide good basic services.*

3. *No matter how bad the status quo is there are those who benefit from it and resist change.*

CHAPTER 12

The following Wednesday, during one of the Mayor's marathon staff meetings, Director of Finance Art Hill was called upon to make a presentation regarding the City's perpetual budget crisis. Red Paley had been traveling and hadn't been briefed in advance, so he asked Roderick Campbell to quickly set the stage, which Roderick did very tersely.

"The Mayor has asked Art to give us an overview of our budget projections. I simply want to say this is a very serious matter. I know all of you are tired of hearing that money is tight, but it is. And it's not going to get any better. So, Art, fill us in."

A small, portable lectern that was used for press conferences and ribbon cuttings was at the opposite end of the room from the head area where Red and Roderick always sat. Art walked up and began reciting his liturgy of financial doom and gloom. He reviewed the historic revenue and expenditure trends and pointed out that the City had a permanent "structural" budget problem that was going to generate annual deficits of $6 to $10 million for as many years into the future as anyone would care to project—ten years at a minimum. Art attributed this to relatively flat municipal income-tax collections and rising costs for healthcare, safety forces, and construction and maintenance of infrastructure. A significant portion of the infrastructure expenses were not technically for new infrastructure but substantially rebuilding aging infrastructure. For example, the City had to pave sixty lane-miles of roads a year in order to keep pace with normal wear and tear. It had been more than twenty years since

Westville had paved thirty or more lane-miles. And that didn't take into account hundreds of miles of shabby alleys that served about a third of the City.

Art concluded with the following pronouncement:

"Given the mandatory programming we have to do and the level of our nondiscretionary expenses, I think our only solution is to slash all discretionary spending beginning with cutting our economic development incentive pool from $1 million a year to $250,000."

Cuts this dramatic were totally unacceptable to any Mayor who was planning on running for Governor and wanted to continue making a splash, and Red Paley was no exception. He erupted.

"I'm sick and tired of your endless talk of financial Armageddon! You're like a broken record, always repeating the same message that the City is on the verge of financial collapse!"

Art tried to defend himself. "I'm sorry, Mayor, but I repeat myself each year because this is a recurring structural problem with our finances."

"Nonsense!" Red would have none of it. "You're nothing but a 'forecastropher' always forecasting financial catastrophe. Why, you have *mastered* the science of 'forecastrophology!'"

Karen Jones leaned over to Frank and whispered, "Last year the Mayor did the same thing, only he called Art a 'catastropher.' So I guess his vocabulary is expanding."

Frank smiled discreetly and said, "So I guess that would be the science of 'catastrophology.'"

Roderick attempted to calm the situation by suggesting that they form an internal task force to evaluate whether Art's forecast was too pessimistic and whether other cuts could be made if necessary.

That placated Red a little, but he rejoined with "The way to solve this is to grow our way out of it. We need more economic development projects to grow the base and more ribbon cuttings to make people feel better. Then they'll spend more money. Keep the green flowing, and you'll see what happens. Green money generates black ink—you'll see!"

As the meeting transitioned into other subjects and finally adjourned midafternoon, Frank was thinking about the structural deficit, particularly the fact that Art Hill didn't see a light at the end of the tunnel. The severity of the situation puzzled him, because in the past three years Westville had saved its largest manufacturing employer as well as the World Headquarters of a Fortune 500 corporation by providing incentives to help each company find a new, modern, competitive site in town. This problem seemed to be deeper than just a case of the incentives costing the City more money, thereby reducing the net tax revenue generated by the two companies. But why? Maybe Dr. Hearst could help provide some answers. Frank would be sure to bring it up at their next session.

Searching for Resources

About 3:30 that afternoon, Frank Clark placed a call to Michael Casey, Manager of Environmental Services for the City of Westville.

When Michael answered the phone, Frank began looking for resources.

"Hey, Mike, this is Frank Clark. How are you?"

"I'm doing fine, Frank. Congratulations on your new position. I've been meaning to give you a call or send an email, and I haven't gotten around to it."

"That's no problem. We're all pretty busy. Do you have a minute?"

"Sure."

"I was thinking of when we were working on the Jonesboro Trucking Warehouse a few months ago. I think you said we had some funds to do environmental assessments on brownfield[2] sites, right?"

"Yes. As a matter of fact we received a $400,000 grant from US EPA a year ago and still have about $350,000 left to spend on investigating properties to see if they are contaminated."

"Do you know what sites you are going to spend it on?"

"Not exactly. We have over a hundred brownfield sites and about a year and a half to spend the money. So we figured we would continue to let environmental engineering firms know we have the funds and see what projects they bring to us. The problem is that the

---

[2]Brownfields are vacant commercial and industrial sites such as factories, warehouses, gas stations, and dry cleaners that may have been impacted by environmental contamination.

economy is slowing down, and we aren't getting as much interest in the larger industrial sites. In the meantime we just received word from EPA that we are going to receive a $1 million RLF grant."

"Congratulations, but what is an RLF?"

"That's a brownfield Revolving Loan Fund that can make low-interest loans to fund remediation."

"Perfect! So now you can do investigations and help fund cleanups?" asked Frank, glad that at least someone seemed to have some uncommitted resources.
"Right."

"Would you mind if I met with you to learn more about the program? I may be able to come up with a couple of ideas, if you don't mind the input."

"Not at all. The last thing I want is to be stuck with funds I can't spend. Plus we are looking at applying for some additional brownfield remediation funds in about three months. Any thoughts on that may be helpful."

"Great! How does tomorrow afternoon, say, 4:00 work for you?"

"That works for me. Do you want to come my way? There are some maps of our brownfield sites that might be helpful."

"Sure. See you then!" Frank hung up the phone and thought to himself, "Well, now there may be some resources available to do something. We've got $3.5 million of HUD housing funds, a $1 million brownfield loan fund, and over $300,000 for brownfield investigations. I don't have an idea of what we should do, but when we figure that out, we've at least got something to work with."

Looking at his watch, he realized it was nearly time for him to meet with Pamela King, Executive Director of Creekside Community Development Corporation (CDC), a not-for-profit organization. Frank had met with Pamela very briefly a few months ago when he was reviewing an agreement by which the City was providing funding to Creekside CDC. The CDC's mission was to improve the Creekside neighborhood, primarily by rehabbing aging housing, constructing new housing, and supporting the small, struggling, local business corridor, and the City was a conduit through which funds from the United States Department of Housing and Urban Development (HUD) supported the organizations community revitalization work. Creekside was Roderick Campbell's neighborhood. He had suggested that Frank meet with Pamela as part of his orientation.

Welcome to Creekside

About fifteen minutes later, Frank Clark found himself pulling up on Elm Street in front of the office of Creekside CDC. As a sign of the times, there were only two other cars parked along the curb, which Frank assumed belonged to the staff. Frank parked behind them. The CDC's office was in an imposing cut-stone former bank building that probably dated back to the 1920s.

Frank walked up a short flight of steps and, thanks to Jane Jacobs, appreciated for the first time how the elevated entrance set the building back from the public realm of the sidewalk. Opening the heavy glass door, he stepped into the large lobby of the former bank. Pausing for a moment to get his bearings, he spotted Pamela King coming out from behind her desk. She extended her right hand with a bright smile.

"Hello, Mr. Clark. It's good to see you again."

"Thank you, Pamela. It's my pleasure, especially since I'm not wearing my city attorney's hat this time. I'm anxious to hear what you've been doing. And please, call me Frank."

"All right, then, Frank it is. Before we sit down and chat, how about if I take you on a short walking tour? There are some things within a few blocks of here that I'd like to show you."

For the next forty-five minutes or so, Pamela led Frank on a tour of the area immediately surrounding the building. They walked a couple of blocks down Elm Street. Frank was struck by the sheer emptiness of what once must have been a thriving neighborhood commercial node. The faded signs on the buildings revealed the street's downward spiral. Gone were the hardware store, both drugstores, and the neighborhood grocery. Pamela pointed out a vacant dry cleaner and an abandoned gas station, noting that each was likely environmentally contaminated. As Frank was looking at the buildings along their way, he stumbled over a large crack in the sidewalk and nearly fell.

"I'm sorry!" Pamela exclaimed. "I forgot to warn you that have to beware the cracks, holes, and heaves in the sidewalk. Sometimes it looks like a minor earthquake hit us."

Frank assured her it was his fault. As they continued walking, he thought about how it epitomized the dullness that Jane Jacobs said led to the inevitable decline of urban neighborhoods. Elm Street was absolutely desolate. There were no pedestrians, and the few automobiles that passed did so far in excess of the thirty-five-mph speed limit. Buildings were boarded up, some had been tagged with graffiti, and several had broken or cracked windows among other scars. More than uninviting, Elm Street seemed to be squawking, "Stay away!" It had truly become a place to leave.

And yet, not everyone *had* left. After two blocks they came to Creek Lane and headed down it to the right. Upon walking a few steps, they came to Ella's Styling Salon. Behind the large window they could see a woman, clearly beyond normal retirement age, tending to a customer while two other ladies sat opposite them in chairs, holding magazines and engaging in a conversation.

Pamela gave them a wave and headed toward the door. "Let's go in and say hello," she said, opening the door. "Ella Rickman is an institution here." Frank awkwardly but dutifully followed his docent into the beauty parlor.

"Hello, Ms. Rickman, good afternoon, ladies," said Pamela, trumpeting their entrance. "I hope you don't mind my intruding, but I'd like you to meet someone. This is Mr. Clark, the new Director of Neighborhoods for the City." In turn, Pamela quickly introduced Frank to Ella, Joyce, Carolyn, and Mavis. She then continued:

"Ella, you've been here what, fifty years or thereabouts?"

Ella stopped working for a moment and thought. "Let me see. I'm seventy-three, and I've been doing hair since I was nineteen, so I guess I've been in the neighborhood fifty-four years now. First, working for Mrs. Thomas, bless her soul, and in my own shop right here since I was thirty-five. So that makes it thirty-eight years now. My, how time has flown!"

Joyce, Carolyn, and Mavis signaled their concurrence, particularly with Ella's last comment, and Pamela continued:

"Ella's is one of the bedrocks of Creekside, along with the library and the churches, of course. When you want to know what's going on and what people are saying, these ladies will tell you. Won't you ladies?"

Once again, the ladies, including Ella, concurred. Mavis volunteered with a smile, "We've told you a thing from time to time, Pamela."

"That you have," replied Pamela good-naturedly. "And I'm darn glad you still do."

After exchanging a few pleasantries, including a parting invitation from Ella to come back anytime, the tour continued. They walked two more blocks along the residential side street passing a mixture of very old, wood-sided homes ranging in various stages of upkeep from well-maintained to several that were on the City's demolition list. They also passed about a half-dozen vacant lots where homes had already been demolished, as well as four homes that Pamela particularly called Frank's attention to—homes that the CDC had rehabilitated a few years ago with assistance from the City. Overgrown weeds revealed that several of the vacant lots and the yards of the dilapidated homes had yet to be mowed this year. Frank was impressed and somewhat puzzled that a few of the homeowners took such good care of their homes and yards in the midst of the surrounding blight and abandonment.

At the end of the two-block walk down Creek Lane, they came to Creekside Park, which was home to idle playground equipment, a basketball court, a couple of shelter houses, and eight or nine picnic tables embedded in concrete anchors. The park backed up to the creek that gave the neighborhood its name. The park was very clean and well-groomed, but no one was using it except a man who was sleeping on the furthermost picnic table.

"The park is looking as good as it will look all year," Pamela said. "We participated in the spring watershed cleanup this past weekend, and the City came through on Monday and mowed the park. Now if only we could get someone to enjoy it."

"Why doesn't anyone use the park?" Frank inquired.

"In the afternoons and evenings there are frequently gang members hanging out here dealing drugs. When they move on, a few homeless people drift in and bed down for the night. So parents don't feel safe, and they don't want their children here. The children don't feel safe either. The police are doing a little targeted enforcement right now in conjunction with the spring cleanup, but that's not enough to get families to use it. We'll have a picnic in a couple of weeks, but pretty soon it will slump back to what passes for normal."

Frank sighed in acknowledgment. "That's a damn shame," he murmured.

"Yes," Pamela replied. Then pointing to a the large rustic wood sign that identified it as Creekside Park, property of the City of Westville Department of Parks and Recreation, she said, "Next week that sign will read 'Worstville' instead of 'Westville.' Every spring we correct it, and almost immediately, some vandals come in here and white out 'Westville' and paint 'Worstville.' The young people here simply have no hope for a better future."

They walked back toward the CDC's office taking a different side street that unfortunately offered much the same scenery as Creek Lane: old homes in various stages of maintenance and disrepair, vacant lots, and a few homes that Creekside CDC had rehabbed. The entire route was traversed on sidewalks that needed to be repaired and roads that badly needed resurfacing. Frank was struck by the correctness of Dr. Hearst's point that providing better services (in this case, some demolitions and park maintenance) hadn't created a place where people *wanted to be*. Furthermore, doing some road and sidewalk maintenance wasn't going to cut the mustard either. The vandalized park sign accurately reflected the view of many of the neighborhood's residents -- for them this was definitely 'Worstville.'

Along the way, Frank asked Pamela what she thought could be done to help the neighborhood rebound.

Pamela didn't need to think long. She lived with this question daily.

"The problem is, we need everything. Creekside CDC's success has been with housing, but that hasn't made the impact we hoped for. Who wants to live near an empty commercial corridor and a park that serves only drug dealers and people who are too far gone to use a homeless shelter? On top of that, our whole infrastructure is crumbling. We need new streets and sidewalks—and I haven't even shown you the alleys. We will need a car, preferably an SUV, to do that. Even then, some of the alleys are impassable."

Pamela continued.

"That's just the physical dimension. Our residents need jobs, training, education, healthcare, better police protection, you name it. There isn't a magic pill that will solve our problems."

They reached Elm Street and walked a block to the office. They had been gone nearly an hour, and the traffic had picked up slightly as the afternoon faded into the evening rush hour. Otherwise, the street and sidewalks were as empty and foreboding as before.

When they entered the CDC building, Pam led Frank to the conference room and then disappeared briefly, returning with a couple of bottles of water. "I figured we could use these after our walk," she said.

"Thank you. I can definitely use some hydration," said Frank as he eagerly unscrewed the top and took a swig. "So what's the game plan for the neighborhood?"

"We did a strategic plan a couple of years ago. We've been having trouble implementing it. Here it is." Walking over to a shelf, Pamela pulled a large bound document from the top of a stack of about a dozen or so of the same. She opened it to a neighborhood diagram centered on the two blocks of Elm Street which they had just walked. "Our goal is to revitalize this commercial node while we continue to work on the housing conditions. Each of these should slowly reinforce the other. As we get a couple of businesses, it will be easier to get good residents to move into the housing stock. In turn, those residents will hopefully encourage more businesses to open, and so on."

Frank nodded. "It's going to be a heavy lift, isn't it?"

"Yes. Housing and the businesses that provide some neighborhood amenities and maybe a little job creation will be a help. But we need help with everything, and those probably aren't sufficient." Pamela was continuing to walk the talk, but it was clear she understood the reality of the situation.

"What agencies are the most helpful or could be the most helpful?" asked Frank, continuing to seek answers that could accelerate his career transition.

"Your department is the most helpful. In fact, in many ways we are an extension of your department. We need your HUD funds to continue rehabbing the housing, demolishing the homes that can't be saved, and hopefully renovating a couple of the buildings on Elm Street for new businesses. The City needs us to perform these functions and also build up a sense of neighborhood identity among the residents. So in addition to providing housing subsidies, you also fund some of our staff and other overhead. We, and the other community development corporations, are the neighborhood-development equivalent of police precincts. Unfortunately, the City hasn't put much federal HOME funding for housing subsidies into the neighborhoods the last couple of years."

"Yes. I just heard about that."

"Well, I don't know what they're saving the funds for, but we need the investment now. Do you know what's going on with that?"

"No, but I hope to find out soon and get the money flowing again," Frank said a tad uncomfortably. Moving the conversation to a safer point, he asked, "Who else is or can be helpful?" he asked.

"Other City departments should be more helpful. I've got my two brownfield sites—the gas station and the cleaners. Public Service needs to get on my streets, sidewalks, and alleys. Also, the Westville Schools could have an extended day program for our children. They need a safe place where they can relax and also get help with their homework. They don't get that at home. Most of them can't even count on getting a good meal and a bath at home."

"What would it take to generate a more holistic approach to your neighborhood and the other neighborhoods in Westville?"

"For starters, it would help if the leadership in this town would recognize the problem."

Frank was puzzled, something he was getting more accustomed to since coming to the City, and particularly now in his new role as Director of the Department of Neighborhoods. "How can they possibly not see the problem? It's obvious."

"They see it, but they don't recognize it. They refuse to acknowledge that we need to reinvent our central city."

"Who? The City government or the civic leadership?"

"Both. Don't you realize the elected officials in this town just kick the can down the road?"

"Yes. I heard something to that effect a couple of weeks ago," he said sardonically. "How about enlisting the business community and other civic leaders?"

"It's just as bad. My board chair and I called on the President of the Chamber of Commerce a year ago to try to enlist the support of the business community. He told us the business community was of little help. The few of them that think there is a problem believe the situation is too far gone to be salvaged."

"What about the majority?"

Pamela laughed. "Are you kidding me? I thought you were a native?"

Frank smiled and nodded for her to elaborate, a request which Pamela was only too willing to oblige.

"The business community doesn't have to be in the center city. And as you can see, they sure aren't in Creekside. They think everything is fine, that the center city's problems are the same as in every other city—that they are inevitable and are best off isolated. They seem to be in favor of what I think of as segregation by neglect. They think the only thing holding Westville back is the people who think Westville has significant problems that are handicapping it. To them, the only illness afflicting Westville is the naysayers who are calling attention to obvious problems while ignoring the positive. In their opinion, these naysayers are creating a negative undercurrent that holds us down. Hell, they even apply for national quality-of-life awards. Imagine that: a city that has been consistently declining for a generation entering various urban beauty pageants. It's unbelievable!"

Pamela was on a roll and Frank was all ears.

"Here's my take on the prevailing culture in the political and business circles. If Westville were a person visiting a physician for an annual physical exam, and the physician had the same mindset as that which permeates Westville's leadership, the physician would respond to Westville's symptoms of lethargy and depression by simply saying they should trash that negative attitude and get back to their daily routine. Oh, . . . and probably to work out so that they'd have more energy to do even more of the same old same old. Trust me—almost everyone, at least everyone who counts—is in complete denial that we have a serious problem."

Frank somewhat agreed with Pamela but didn't think it was wise to say so. Instead he played it safe and waffled. "Well, I haven't been in government for very long, but maybe Red will come up with something now that he's a lame duck?"

Pamela was beside herself. "You slay me! Red's part of the problem. He's not going to change his spots at this point in his career. If he does something big that is actually constructive, it'll be by accident. The only thing he cares about is his political career, just like the rest of them. Trust me, they all say how much they *loooove* Westville, but none of them care enough about this town to shed their own blood, to risk their own political capital to fight for what's best for Westville. They just pay lip service to loving this town and go with the flow."

Frank moved it along. The conversation was on another uncomfortable point—his boss—and that wasn't good for his job security. "I hope you are wrong. At any rate, maybe we can come up with something so good that Red will jump on it because it's good for the community *and* for his career," he said, forcing himself to stay upbeat.

"What would that be?" Pamela asked hopefully.

"I'm not sure. Let me think about it. In the meantime, I will look at your strategic plan. It's getting late, and as much as I appreciate this, I had better get home."

"Yes. It's a little after 6:00. I've enjoyed it as well." Pamela's sincerity was reflected in her smile.

"Thank you again. I will stay in touch."

CHAPTER 13

The following morning as Frank was doing a little managing by walking around, he poked his head into the office of Walter Sage, Senior Administrator of HUD Programming. Seeing Walter sitting at his desk, Frank said, "Good morning!" and then quickly inquired, "What's that you're reading?"

Walter looked up. "Good morning, Frank. This is last year's NOFA."

"What's a NOVA?"

"It's NOFA. It stands for Notice of Funding Availability. HUD issues it every year. It has about twenty different programs that communities can apply for. They cover a wide range of issues that impact cities, like lead-based paint, fair housing, home-ownership incentives, and so on. The new NOFA will be released pretty soon, and I thought I'd look at last year's in order to have a better idea of what we can expect this year."

Frank liked the idea that potentially, this could be another source of resources. "I'm sure we can always use more funding, so let me know if there's anything you think we should pursue."

"Definitely."

Frank continued. "Say, I've got a meeting with Michael Casey at Environmental Services at 4:00 this afternoon. He's going to educate me a little on their brownfield program. We've got over $1.3 million for investigations and cleanups. Would you like to join us?"

"Sounds interesting. Since the meeting's at 4:00, do you mind if we drive separately? I don't live too far from their office."

"That's fine. I'll see you there."

That afternoon Frank and Walter sat down with Michael Casey in a small conference room. Michael laid a map of Westville in front of them. It contained about a hundred red dots concentrated in Westville's older central city and industrial districts. Michael began explaining it to them:

"This map shows the locations of a hundred and three brownfield sites we've identified. As you can see, some of them are pretty large industrial sites. For example, this one along the West River is the old Edison coal plant that closed about six years ago. It sits on about thirty acres. On the other hand, we have a lot of smaller sites in the neighborhoods that are more compact. Some of them are really bad."

Walter joined in. "Yes. We've got sites that predate the automobile era. Those sites have housing immediately around them so that in the past, people could walk to work. They've become real sources of blight in many of our neighborhoods."

Michael piggy-backed on that theme. "These old sites . . . you know back then they just pretty much pitched everything out the back door or let it corrode in barrels out in the grounds or in a shed—sometimes even in an underutilized part of the main plant. They didn't know anything about environmental contamination, and they didn't care."

Frank's memory was jogged. "Yeah. I remember riding to the country dump in upper Michigan when I was a young child a couple of times. We would tie up our trash, go to the dump, and just toss everything down a hillside. There was a little creek at the bottom. I hate to think of what some of these old industrial sites must have done."

Michael shrugged slightly. "Yes. It's hard to believe, but back then they actually thought the creek would wash it away. There was a feeling that the planet was big enough to absorb it all."

Frank was intrigued and needed to better understand the problems Westville's neighborhoods confronted. "So if I wanted to drive by a couple of these to see what they are like, and how they are impacting neighborhoods, could you give me a couple addresses and some direction?"

"Sure. There's one not too far from here."

"Thanks. So you were saying on the phone that you've got some funding that you haven't committed. Could you fill Walter and me in on that?"

"Yes. We've got about $350,000 left on our $400,000 Brownfield Assessment Grant. We spent the balance of it on Phase I and Phase II assessments of the Jonesboro Trucking site as well as paying the University of Westville to inventory our sites and prepare the map we're looking at."

"What are Phase I and Phase II assessments?" Walter asked.

"Environmental Site Assessments, or ESA for short. A Phase I ESA looks at the historical use of the site and might include a quick tour of it to see if the past uses or current appearance reveal reasons to believe there might be contamination. For instance, there may be old insurance records showing that there was once a pretty intense industrial use or gas station. The tour may reveal some distressed vegetation that might indicate contamination.

"If Phase I concludes that further investigating is required, it will identify the types of concerns and the areas on the site that require physical investigation. That work is done pursuant to a Phase II ESA and would normally include some actual soil and/or groundwater sampling and analysis to see what the extent of the problem is. The results may require actual environmental remediation. That's where our other grant could come into play."

"That's some serious money. Tell us how that works," said Frank.

"Sure. We received a $1 million Brownfield Revolving Loan Fund Grant a week ago. You might have seen a small blurb in the paper. The grant can be used to make low-interest loans to help finance brownfield remediation. It can also make grants to not-for-profit entities like CDCs. There are some restrictions on that. For instance, only forty percent of the money can be used for grants. The other sixty percent has to be used for loans. That's because EPA wants us to have a permanent source of funds for remediation—hence the term Revolving Loan Fund."

Walter whistled softly. "That's a sweet piece of change, Michael!"

"Yes. There were only about twenty of those grants awarded nationally."

It was Frank's turn to be impressed. "Boy, that puts Westville in pretty good company!"

Michael smiled. "Thanks."

"So you've got a million dollars for environmental remediation, and theoretically $400,000 could be grants?" said Walter, seeking confirmation of the facts.

"Yes. I think each grant is capped at a maximum of $200,000."

"And you don't have a definite plan for spending these funds?" asked Frank.

"That's right. We thought we had a confidential project at the Edison site, but it looks like our prospect backed out."

As an attorney, Frank appreciated the importance of confidentiality, but he wanted a little more general information. "What kind of prospect was it?"

"It would have been a corporate division headquarters for a financial or insurance firm with a backroom processing/call-center component. I hear it might have brought around seven hundred jobs. I don't know the details, because the Mayor was handling it personally. I'm not sure why they backed off."

"And now you're back to the drawing board?" Walter asked.

"Yes."

"Do you have any possibilities?" Frank inquired.

"Not really. I mean, we've got some properties that we can do the assessments on and maybe run through the Mayor's Derelict Demolition Program like we did with Jonesboro, but nothing that's very exciting."

Frank continued mining for opportunities. "The Mayor wants us to come up with something that has a little pizzazz. What do you think?"

Michael took a deep breath and thought for a moment. "I wish I had something for you. Even with the Revolving Loan Fund grants, the market is pretty soft. I'm not sure what we can jump-start."

Then Michael's voice offered a slight opening. "Tell you what. US EPA Region V has its summer brownfields workshop in Detroit next month. Let me check—yes, it's June 12 and 13. Our grants provide funding to attend the workshop, and EPA expects its recipients to attend. Why don't you plan on attending? Between the two of us, maybe we will be able to come up with some intel."

"Thanks, Michael. That sounds like a good idea. I'll check with Roderick."

Meeting a Neighborhood Brownfield

With that, the meeting broke up. Walter continued home, and Frank drove by one of the nearby brownfield sites that Michael had mentioned. On the way there, he passed numerous buildings that graffiti artists had converted to canvasses for various expressions of "Worstville." In a like manner, the locals had converted numerous references on municipal signs from "City of Westville" to "City of

Worstville." Frank had never visited this neighborhood before – it had nothing of particular value to offer to non-residents – and he didn't realize how pervasive the "Worstville" sentiment was in Westville's distressed neighborhoods.

Frank drove down a blighted residential side street, very much like the ones he had walked with Pamela King in the Creekside neighborhood, and came to an abrupt stop where the street dead-ended into a T-intersection and stared in shock at an ominous three-story brick building. The site was overgrown with weeds that in some places had even managed to take root in cracks in the paving. As far as Frank could tell, every opening in the building was unsecured. Doors were flung open or missing altogether, and every window was shattered. There was a gaping hole in the roof of the main building, and one of the auxiliary buildings was imploding. Looking at the main building, he could see the faint traces of "Western Manufacturing Company" that had once proudly proclaimed the name of a company that used to provide a livelihood for hundreds of families. Now the entire eight-acre site screamed "Death!"—death of a factory, death of opportunity, death of community, death of hopes and dreams for so many people.

Frank was overwhelmed by how in your face the entire scene was. As Walter had said, the old sites were embedded in what used to be walkable neighborhoods. Consequently, they were barely set back from the streets and sidewalks. The Western Manufacturing site almost seemed to be reaching out, strangling the neighborhood with its tentacles of rust and blight, fueled by the demise of a bygone era. It projected its rot and despair down the streets and alleys, into the homes, parks, and schools. Approximately half of the homes were dilapidated, abandoned, or already demolished. Frank found himself looking at another place to leave—another area of Westville that people had either deserted or ended up being left behind. And yet, like Creekside, there was the occasional home that was immaculately maintained by people who had chosen to stay and push back against the seemingly irresistible force that the abandoned factory had morphed into.

After slowly driving the length of the narrow, snakelike site and up and down several side streets, Frank carefully drove two alleys. As he expected, they were even worse than the street views—garages were caving, weeds and even shrubbery were infringing on the right-of-way, and trash was everywhere. He even passed several abandoned appliances that appeared to have been rusting away for longer than anyone could probably recall.

At about 5:45 Frank cut his tour short and headed home. It was a pleasant, warm evening, and the remaining residents were enjoying it as they worked in their yards, fired up their grills, and chatted over the fence posts. It had gradually dawned on Frank that they might perceive him to be some kind of voyeur who had to come to the neighborhood to gawk at its blight. Respect for them and their neighborhood dictated that he move along.

CHAPTER 14

At 10:00 that evening, Roderick Campbell closed the financial report he had received from Art Hill and set it on the stack of paperwork he had reviewed over the past two hours. He got up from behind the desk in the spare bedroom that served as his home office and walked to the living room and put a CD in his sound system. He then sat down in a more comfortable upholstered chair and listened as the sound of Miles Davis's trumpet surrounded him.

Closing his eyes, Roderick thought about what he had just read. Despite Red's protests there was no doubt that Art Hill's conclusion that Westville had a severe financial problem was correct. Art's analysis was supported by a review by an independent accounting firm. There was no denying the fact that there was a permanent hole in the City's budget. Costs were rising faster than revenues, and about ninety-five percent of the costs were unavoidable—pension plans, healthcare, capital improvements that had been deferred for far too long, and even internal computer systems that were so old they were no longer serviced by their vendors. Worse yet, every indication from Washington signaled another major cut in the funding that cities receive from the federal government. Most important of these funds was the federal Community Development Block Grant (CDBG) allocation of about $10 million per year. It looked as if Westville was going to receive a ten percent annual cut of $1 million dollars. The City used about half of this money to pay the wages and salaries of some of the staff in the Department of Neighborhoods. Of the remaining half of the funding, some went to demolish vacant buildings, mow vacant lots, and help repair decaying public

161

infrastructure in central city neighborhoods. About $3 million funded twelve community development corporations, including Creekside and Abyssinian, and social-service organizations like various homeless shelters and the St. Dominic Savio House for troubled youth—the same charity for which he had scraped together funding as part of the hubcap compromise he had worked out with Red. "How ironic that we might now have to cut that organization's funding," Roderick thought to himself.

Roderick sighed deeply. He was going to have to give Red some bad news—if not tomorrow, then the next day. The sooner this was dealt with, the less painful it would become. Left alone, it would blow into a real financial crisis. Painful cuts would have to be made, cuts that even the jazz he so loved couldn't soothe.

*****

The following afternoon found Roderick, Byron, and Frank sitting in the Mayor's office. Knowing that Art Hill was a lightning rod for Red's frustration, Roderick had specifically excluded him from the meeting. Since strategies require resources, he felt it was appropriate to include Byron as the Senior Director of Strategy. Frank was included because Red had confidence in him and because his department would be severely impacted by both the proposed federal CDBG cuts and the City's larger general-fund revenue crisis.

Roderick opened the discussion: "Mayor, I wanted this opportunity to meet with you on a couple of serious matters that I want to make sure we stay out in front of. I asked Frank to join us because this first item has a major impact on the Department of Neighborhoods. As we feared, the Feds are cutting our annual CDBG allocation by about $1 million. We'll be going from just over $10 million to just over $9 million."

Red reacted quickly with energy but restrained composure: "Those bastards in Washington can't be trusted. We'll have to make the ten percent cuts and blame it on them. I can manage that. What's the second issue?"

"It's not good, sir. I've re-reviewed Art Hill's budget analysis. Mayor, as hard as I try, I can't fault his conclusions. I even had Bill Thompson's CPA firm conduct a confidential review. There's just no getting around the fact that we have a $6 million permanent deficit in our budget."

Red paused. He stood up and walked around the entire perimeter of the room. The others sat quietly, blood pressure slowly rising, expecting the inevitable volcanic explosion. Red surprised them. Roderick had been cagey enough to trust the budget review to one of Red's strongest political allies. Red couldn't denounce and dismiss Bill Thompson's conclusions as he had Art Hill's. After circling the room, he sat down and leaned toward the three men. Then he began speaking firmly but with complete control:

"All right. We're going to use the CDBG funds to pay for every possible position in Frank's department. We'll slash the funding we allocate to the community development corporations and social charities, homeless shelters, you name it. That will enable us to avoid laying off his staff.

"In addition, let's see what happens if we establish our own impound lot for towed vehicles. The Fraternal Order of Police proposed taking this away from the private sector and bringing it in-house in the last round of contract negotiations. They thought we could generate enough revenue to fund something like five or six cops. They had a little support for that from City Council. It shouldn't be too hard to resurrect that plan and see if it holds water.

"We'll have to cut the Economic Development Fund by $1 million. We can backfill it with our $1 million brownfield grant we just got. That's not exactly apples to apples, but it's something. We can still say we are budget-neutral, just not as flexible.

"Maybe if we do these things and don't fill any vacancies that pop up through retirements and resignations, we'll be okay. Roderick, see if we have anyone in the general fund that we can transfer to the Water Department and still borrow back, so to speak.

"Get back to me as soon as you can with an implementation plan."

"Thank you, sir." With that, Roderick led Byron and Frank out of the Mayor's office. When they had cleared the door, Frank asked Roderick if he had time for a quick question.

"Just a second," Roderick replied. "Say, Byron, can you call Chief McNally and see if he can dust off that tow-lot concept?"

"Sure will!" Byron replied as he headed into his office.

Roderick walked into his office with Frank in tow. "What's up, Frank?"

"It regards our brownfield funds. I met with Michael Casey, and he said the grant includes funding to attend a workshop in Detroit next month. Michael suggested I join him, and I think that's a good idea."

"As long as the grant pays for it, I agree. Red's expecting something big, and this conference should be beneficial."

"Thank you."

As Frank turned to leave, Roderick asked, "By the way. Did you meet with Pam King yet?"

"Yes. We had a very good meeting a couple days ago. We walked the neighborhood a little bit, and I got a copy of their strategic plan, which I've reviewed. They've got a challenging situation there."

"No doubt. It's my neighborhood, but I'm not sure if they've got a true vision or just a pipe dream."

"One more thing: she mentioned that we haven't put any HOME funds into projects in a couple of years. Walter Sage pointed that out to me as well."

Roderick thought for a moment before responding. "I hadn't thought much about that, but you're right. Bobby got into a jam a couple of years ago, and I think he got a little gun-shy. I'm an operations guy and had just assumed this role. My plate was full enough, so I never got that involved. The Mayor and he handled it."

"I can see that, but we are going to lose $1.75 million in HOME funds if we don't spend them." Frank didn't know how much Bobby had communicated, and he figured he'd better make sure Roderick knew about that.

Roderick was surprised. "How much time do we have?"

"I think until the end of next June. So we have some time, but we want to make sure we don't have a fire drill."

"I agree, stay on top of it," Roderick said calmly but firmly.

"I will. Getting back to Pamela, should I give her a heads up about the budget cuts?"

"No," Roderick quickly replied. "When we get the details worked out, we'll call the CDCs and social service groups together and announce it. But stay in contact with her. She's good people."

"Right," Frank concurred and excused himself from Roderick's office.

CHAPTER 15

The next morning the *Westville Wire & Telegraph* ran the following editorial regarding the federal government's cuts to the Community Development Block Grant (CDBG) funding:

An Assault on Cities

If our elected officials in Washington are wondering why the American electorate has such a low opinion of them, they need look no further than yesterday's authorization of a ten percent cut to the Community Development Block Grant (CDBG). CDBG provides critically important funding for urban revitalization, the elimination of slums and blight, and services for people of lesser financial means.

Westville currently receives $10 million from this program, which funds the demolition of over 200 dilapidated buildings, periodic mowing of over 1,000 vacant lots, maintenance of central-city roads and sidewalks, the salaries of several City Code Enforcement Inspectors, as well as a myriad of other vital activities. Not least among these other activities is $3 million of funding for programming and operating support to over two dozen nonprofit community development corporations (CDCs) and social service agencies that play a crucial role in stemming urban deterioration and maintaining the social safety net.

As an example of the local impact of these funds, try imagining what it must be like to be a battered woman and not having a healthy and safe emergency shelter available for you and your children. Well, apparently our representatives in DC either can't imagine what that is like or simply don't care.

While the City hasn't had an opportunity to determine how to manage this painful and inexcusable $1 million cut to its funding, in all likelihood it means a *pro rata* sacrifice across the board. This translates into a $300,000 cut for the nonprofit community. As a result, more of our Westville neighbors will go hungry, live in substandard housing, and be denied access to public health clinics and emergency shelters. If Congress and the current Administration still can't figure out why we're outraged, perhaps they will be able to interpret the message we can send at the polls—that seems to be the one language that is not impaired by their political dyslexia.

*****

The following Monday, Roderick, Byron, and Frank reconvened in the Mayor's office to brief Red on the details of their budget plan. This time Roderick had Art Hill join them. Now that Red was acknowledging the budget crisis, Roderick figured the advantages of having Art there to provide details more than outweighed the potential that Red would lash out at him.

It was a beautiful spring day in late May, and Red was in a fairly upbeat mood despite the negative nature of the subject matter. Roderick figured that perhaps it was a result of his coming to terms with the reality of the situation. "Perhaps," Roderick thought to himself, "Red had braced himself for the inevitable budget battle that was about to commence and was ready for the 'big game' to begin." Because for Red, despite the high stakes, it was a game, a game he played very seriously, but a game nonetheless. He enjoyed the drama of political maneuvering and the heat of battle.

Red opened the meeting: "So what do you have for me?"

Roderick controlled the flow of information once again: "I think we've got a viable budget solution. The two areas we want to particularly brief you on are the CDBG cuts to community organizations and the impact of the police impound lot for towed vehicles. Those are going to cause the most controversy, and I'm not sure we can count on being able to decouple them into two separate battles."

Red was unperturbed. "True. Go ahead."

Roderick continued: "So if we transfer as much of our personnel costs to the CDBG budget as the federal regs allow, the resulting costs to the CDCs and other nonprofit service agencies are going to be dramatic—probably a thirty-three percent cut for them resulting from only a ten percent cut in the CDBG funding."

Red remained calm. "All right. What's the deal with bringing the impound tow lot in-house?"

Byron interjected, "Mayor, I want to make sure you realize the CDCs are going to scream bloody murder! Some of them may end up going under as a result of these cuts." Byron had taken his role as Mr. Popular seriously, and he was concerned about the resulting loss of popularity for his boss *and* for himself.

Red got cross. "Do I look like I care about them? Two weeks ago I thought my directives made that clear! If a few of them go down, that's just that many fewer groups that can call a press conference and command a podium from which to denounce me. Besides, the other groups will be winners. It won't take them long to realize that a pie split among fewer groups leaves a larger percentage of it for them. They'll just wait for the budget to recover and lick their chops over the prospect of getting a bigger piece."

"Yes sir," Byron replied meekly.

"Good." Then, turning to Roderick, he said, "Now tell me about the tow lot."

Roderick picked up the story line. "We can bring the impound lot in-house and charge four police officers and two civilians to it. The current operator and the towing companies won't like it. They've got about $600,000 in positive cash flow coming out of there each year, and it's pretty stable revenue for them. Enforcement of the parking scofflaws and tows from accidents and DWI charges are pretty much recession-proof."

"Tough. They're making a fortune. It's a rip-off. In fact, instead of investigating predatory lending, we ought to be investigating predatory towing. They stake out parking lots after hours and tow cars without notice at the drop of a hat. They can go to hell for all I care!

"Convene your annual HUD briefing session with the community organizations like you always do and give them the news. Frank, as the Director of Neighborhoods that's your duty. Bobby had to do it, and now it's your turn in the barrel. Oh, and by the way, get me the latest performance-monitoring reports on all the CDCs. I'm going to need some ammunition."

The group nodded its concurrence, and the meeting dissolved. As they left the Mayor's office, Roderick herded them into a small conference room where he got right to the point. "Two things. Not a word about these cuts in advance of the briefing. Frank, you will have to do the math yourself. Art, you may be able to help him a little even though your forte is the general fund." Directing his comments back to Frank, Roderick continued: "You can bring Walter in the day of the briefing to confirm the numbers with you, but no other staff members are to have any idea this is going on. As soon as you get to your office, have Walter get you the monitoring reports the Mayor wants. Tell him they are for your own education—that's more than plausible. Then run them up here to the Mayor. Second, you will announce the cuts at the very end of the stakeholder meeting. If you do it earlier in the briefing, all hell will break loose, and you won't be able to present the other information about the application process and our funding priorities."

The trio concurred, and Roderick directed them to convene the stakeholder meeting the following week in order to minimize the possibility that the cuts would be leaked.

CHAPTER 16

It had been three weeks since Frank had met with his mentor, Dr. Hearst, and he was very much looking forward to this third session. In the intervening weeks he had finished *The Death and Life of Great American Cities*, had watched Red Paley go off on Art Hill only to subsequently acknowledge the existence of the budget crisis, had met with Pamela King and Michael Casey, and had done some substantial neighborhood exploring. All in all, he was slowly gaining an understanding of the urban issues his new directorship demanded he address. And although this appreciation deepened his understanding of the enormity of the challenges he confronted, he remained undaunted. He also refused to allow himself to be preoccupied by the possibility that Red was simply using him for his own advantage.

For his part, Dr. Harold Hearst was nearly as eager for this session as Frank. Having been on vacation for two weeks, Dr. Hearst was anxious to see how his "project's" urban education was progressing. He greeted Frank with a broad smile. "Hello, Frank, how have you been?"

"Good, Harold! How was your vacation?"

"It was exhilarating! We took our children to New York for a few days. It gave me a chance to visit friends and family. And of course we explored the city, particularly Jane Jacobs's old stomping grounds in the Village. Then we went to Boston for another urban adventure before spending a few days in the Adirondacks—that broke up some of the monotony of the drive home."

173

"That does sound like a great trip!" Frank imagined that Harold must have really enjoyed exploring two iconic American cities with his wife and children.

"It truly was. But enough on that subject. As always, I'm a little pressed for time, and I'm more than a little interested in hearing how you have been doing and what is on your mind."

"I've been pretty busy. I finished reading *The Death and Life of Great American Cities*, which is phenomenal. I've got some questions about applying it here. I found the chapter 'Gradual Money versus Cataclysmic Money' very interesting. It seems Westville and other cities are always looking for that major project that is going to magically turn a community around instead of rebuilding more slowly and organically. And because the projects don't incorporate the principles for vibrant neighborhoods that Jane Jacobs delineates, the massive influx of money actually harms, rather than benefits, the community.

Dr. Hearst concurred. "Ah, yes we always want to find the secret short cut to success. It inevitably fails, leaving us worse off than we were before. We lack the patience and understanding to do it the right way. Please continue, what else have you been up to?"

"I was also able to visit some of our older neighborhoods. Naturally those were real eye-openers. Plus I learned we have a budget crisis that is going to hit us pretty hard."

Dr. Hearst laughed sympathetically and said, "You certainly don't need any more excitement for a while. Speaking of the City's budget crisis, I heard about the federal cuts to the CDBG program. It's not good policy. Fortunately, our *friends* in Congress limited it to a ten percent cut."

Frank followed up: "It's compounded by our local budget problem. The City has determined that it also has a $6 million general-fund deficit."

Dr. Hearst paused. "Ooooh," he said slowly. "That isn't good."

"No. Confidentially, we've decided to transfer as many general-fund employees to the CDBG budget as possible. Since more of the employees will be paid out of the CDBG funds, the money being invested in neighborhoods for housing and other activities through the block-grant program is going to be cut by $1 million. I'm announcing it next week."

"Hmmm." Dr. Hearst thought for a moment. While he was thinking, Frank continued. "I can see why we are avoiding the layoffs. After all, we need inspectors to cover the neighborhoods and enforce the property-maintenance codes so we don't get overrun with nuisance properties. And, of course, we need administrative people in the office to run the program."

Dr. Hearst sat up straight in his chair and abruptly spoke: "Two things come to mind. The first is that you are seeing the influence of the public-employee unions. For the politicians, laying off the City's union employees is something they avoid at all costs. The Mayor is preemptively making that clear by tapping the CDBG budget. Now it may be that doing so is good policy; I'm not sure. What I *am* sure of is that the public-employee unions are the most important power whenever it comes to influencing the City's internal policies. So Red isn't daring to cross them, and the nonprofit groups are not likely to prevail if they fight it."

"How do you define internal policy? And if there's internal policy, what would *external* policy be?" Frank inquired.

"Good question. I think of internal policy as the City's compensation and benefits—its terms and conditions of employment and how it runs its operations, including operations in the community like police, fire, trash collection, etc. Also, what systems and equipment it chooses to invest in, like new computers, software, heavy equipment, infrastructure, and so forth. So I would estimate that about ninety-five percent of the City's budget and activities are internal. I would guess that about five percent of the City is external—that would be economic development and investments in neighborhoods, a lot of what your department does. In this case there is an overlap between internal policy—funding City positions that provide services to the neighborhoods—and the external policy of investing money in neighborhoods. The public-employee unions, or their perceived influence, are clearly and predictably overriding the external policy in this case."

"If the public-employee unions are the most dominant force on internal policy, who is the most dominant force on external policy?"

"The Building Trades Unions," Dr. Hearst replied without hesitation.

"Really?" Frank was barely aware of their impact.

"Yes. They are far and away the largest donor to the local Democratic Party. Plus like the public-employee unions, they can mobilize the manpower necessary to put up yard signs, go door-to-door, attend fundraising events, you name it."

"What's their agenda?"

"To make sure all the big construction projects are built exclusively with their union labor. And, to a lesser extent, to make sure all the relevant local policies and political stances are pro-labor. Now, I'm all in favor of good wages and safe working conditions, but there is no counterbalance to the building trades' clout. They are good people zealously advocating for their union and its members, and that's their job. But no one is looking out for the greater good of the community. The building trades advocate for union construction projects without considering the project's impact on the broader community, and especially whether the right project is being built at the right site. And while we can't expect the building trades to say, 'Hey, wait a minute. What about the greater good of the community?' we *can* expect that *someone* will represent the community's broader interests in ensuring that the right development occurs at the right place. But that just doesn't happen here. The plan commission doesn't have enough clout, and our citizenry isn't engaged. The building trades are like a good trial attorney advocating in the court of public opinion without any opposition, and they inevitably win. The good news for you is they don't get involved in neighborhood housing and other smaller projects because those projects generally aren't large enough to be constructed by their members. They focus on the larger commercial and industrial projects."

"I had no idea they were that powerful." Frank thought for a second and then continued. "So couldn't I potentially enlist their support? They would be a strong ally."

"No." Once again Dr. Hearst didn't hesitate.

"How can you be so sure?"

"Because, Frank, I've served on the Plan Commission—wait, on second thought, let's approach it this way. We agree that Westville is not a competitive urban center - that it needs to dramatically improve to become a place where people thrive, right?"

"Definitely."

"So if we thought of Westville as a student, we'd say its cumulative grade-point average is probably a C-minus. Is that fair?"

"Yes," said Frank playing along with Dr. Hearst's approach to explaining the problem. "Maybe more than fair."

Dr. Hearst continued. "So let's say Westville has to have an overall grade of B-plus to be a place where people want to be and have a chance to thrive."

"I'm with you," Frank earnestly volunteered.

"What kind of grades does Westville need to get in the future in order to achieve a B-plus average?"

Frank was incredulous. "To bring a C-minus grade point up to a B-plus or better? You'd pretty much need to earn straight As for a long time."

Dr. Hearst nodded. "Correct. Similarly, if Westville were a golfer who shot five over par on the first nine, it would need a bunch of birdies on the back nine, right?"

"Yes!" and then Frank added, "And you better not have any bogies."

Dr. Hearst smiled. "So returning to the real world, what kinds of projects does it take to convert a substandard community into a place where people thrive?"

"Obviously very high quality projects—filling up empty spaces with mediocrity isn't going to achieve excellence."

Dr. Hearst smiled again, pleased that his Socratic approach was leading to the right conclusions.

"Now, in order to get really good projects, the kinds of projects that can elevate and transform Westville. . . ." Dr. Hearst paused for emphasis. "The City, the entire community for that matter, is going to have to start saying no to a lot of projects, including most of the ones that would currently be accepted. As I noted in the essay I shared with you, some projects are simply bad and need to be completely vetoed, just like some medical procedures should never be done." Then he slowed his pace for emphasis. "*No amount of tweaking can make right that which is fundamentally wrong.*

"Unfortunately, we usually end up nibbling around the edges of bad projects to try to make them more palatable instead of simply terminating them. We add a little more landscaping or increase the amount of union construction labor until they are approved. I call it 'modify to mollify.' Westville needs to terminate bad projects so that they don't make it off the drawing board, and that is exactly why the building trades unions are *not* a potential ally."

"How so?"

Dr. Hearst feigned a sense of exaggerated disappointment. "You've forgotten. They care *only* about creating job opportunities for their members. As far as they're concerned, *any* construction project that employs union labor *is* a good project. They aren't going to tolerate people saying that a union project isn't good enough."

Frank concurred. "I see. Well, I guess it makes sense from their perspective."

Dr. Hearst immediately responded. "From their *shortsighted, myopic* perspective, it makes sense. I think they would be better off if Westville had a rising economic tide, and a more vibrant urban core would help make that happen. I'm sure that converting Westville from a weak market city to a strong, growing market would lift *their* boat." Then the tone of his voice became less energetic and more somber. "The really sad thing is the way developers insidiously exploit Westville's insecurities to get their way."

Frank was puzzled. "Westville's insecurities? What do you mean?"

Dr. Hearst indulged in a little more pontificating. "They play on our community's deeply rooted inferiority complex. The undercurrent here is that we are weak market, a second-rate city, and that we had better support every project we can because it will probably be a long time before another development plan comes along." He paused to emphasize an aside. "Surely you are aware of this sentiment." Then he continued the lesson. "And of course they don't mind suggesting that the next proposed project—when and if it finally comes along—might not be better than the one they are currently proposing and could even be worse. Essentially, they play to our mass psyche by implying that beggars can't be choosers. Doing so not only helps them get their way, but it perpetuates and reinforces our communal inferiority complex, because now you have an influential voice pronouncing it."

"Man, oh, man! I didn't realize it was *that* bad! Doesn't anyone think of the *community*?" Frank asked rhetorically.

"No, or at least very few." Dr. Hearst's response was quick and emphatic. "Lots of people say they love Westville, but cities are like infants. They are defenseless. Now, cities do have some resiliency just like children. And like children, strong and healthy cities are more resilient than weak cities, just as strong and healthy children are more resilient to afflictions than sickly and malnourished children. So just as to love a child is to nurture and protect it, so it is with loving a city. To love a city, you must be willing to fight for good development and against bad development. This is true even in some instances where the bad development is projected to generate significant tax revenue, because if you violate the planning principles that Jane Jacobs identifies, the collateral damage to the city will probably be too great to be offset by the increased revenue—the collateral damage will wound the city, thereby depriving it of the economic activity the damaged part could have generated. Plus the damaged part may become a source of cancerous dullness and eventually blight. That's part of what she was referring to in her discussion of cataclysmic money." Then Dr. Hearst sighed and added, "The passion to stand and fight for a vibrant city rarely occurs here, especially if powerful forces line up on the opposing side."

Frank just shook his head sadly and commented, "That's terrible."

"It is a real tragedy. Now, let's get back to the point I was making a few minutes ago. Since Westville is a weak market with poor self-esteem, the 'take it or leave it, beggars can't be choosers' development approach almost always prevails. In addition to their psychological attack, developers can quickly count on the support of construction workers, a city that's desperate for immediate tax revenue, and politicians that like ribbon cuttings."

Frank glumly concurred. "I imagine they can." He thought for a moment and then moved on. "You said you had a second thought that came to your mind?"

"Ah, yes. I forgot that we were talking about the budget cuts to the neighborhood-development organizations and social-service providers. The City is making the new Director of Neighborhoods tell the community groups he has to work with that he's slashing their funding. That's not good."

"Yes. That was Red's directive."

"Naturally," Dr. Hearst said bluntly.

Frank sloughed it off, trying to remain upbeat about the opportunity to do some good. "My understanding is that the Director of Neighborhoods always has a meeting where he tells the community groups about the process for applying for HUD funds from the City."

Dr. Hearst was not convinced. "That may be true, but there is a significant difference between having you *convene* a briefing on the process and making you the *bearer* of the bad news. People cautioned you that Red might be taking advantage of you. It sounds to me like that may be what we are seeing with Red putting you out in front on this."

"I think that might be true. But my question is 'How do we turn this place around without more resources?' That's what I'm most concerned with."

Dr. Hearst chuckled. "I appreciate your focus on the community, but this issue is also a problem for you. It could impair your effectiveness. To be frank, it could impact your employment. But let's focus on urban revitalization since that's my area of knowledge and your primary interest. Is anything else on your mind before we delve into this more deeply?"

"I'm thinking of the need for population density as Jane Jacobs talked about it. You need a lot of people to support the wide range of businesses and amenities that create a vibrant urban district. I see policies that move us in the opposite direction, and I don't know how we are going to achieve the necessary density."

Dr. Hearst quickly agreed. "Density is indispensable. What policies have you identified as impeding it?"

Frank thought for a moment to gather his thoughts. "I'm thinking the only way to get density is to promote more multistory apartment buildings and condominium projects. Those are the densest forms of housing. But everything I hear in the community is about home ownership. Plus the only condominium project we have in the core is downtown, and it's not doing well. I feel like I'm in high school trying to solve an algebra problem that is just too complicated. I'm puzzled and a little frustrated, but I haven't quit yet."

Dr. Hearst remained enthusiastic. He liked the fact that Frank was thoughtfully identifying significant issues. "Good! You should feel that way. Cities like home ownership because they falsely believe that only homeowners are good community stakeholders. Second, they believe that homeowners maintain their property better than landlords. While slumlords are certainly bad, not all rental properties are owned by slumlords. Moreover, there are lots of rundown properties that are owned and occupied by people who no longer have the means to properly maintain them. Then again, there are also a lot of rundown properties in our declining neighborhoods where the longtime owner has died, and no one can locate the heirs. So there's no simple answer to the problem of property maintenance."

Dr. Hearst continued. "Community Development Corporations generally share the same stereotype about homeownership versus rental properties when it comes to property maintenance and having committed stakeholders. In addition, many CDCs make money by building and rehabbing homes and selling them at a subsidized price. They also don't have the headaches of property management that come with rental properties."

"Yes. I've heard those thoughts recently," Frank replied.

"Pardon me, Frank. I forget the other observation about housing density that you mentioned."

"That our only condominium project—River Place in downtown—isn't doing well."

"Oh, yes. I think I know why that is, but it's just an educated guess. My thinking is that most people in Westville have never lived in a downtown before, neither here nor anywhere else. It's very difficult to ask them to make an equity investment as an owner of a downtown condominium when they don't know what they are getting in for. They are better off renting first. That gives them an opportunity to dip their toe in the water before diving into the pool. Also, rental properties are naturally more appealing for people whose career paths have them moving from city to city or from urban to suburban, particularly young people who may start families and begin looking for larger yards and better schools."

"I hadn't thought of that," Frank said. "It sounds logical."

"Like I said, I can't be certain, but I think that is the root cause of the weak condominium market in downtown—particularly when our downtown doesn't have that much to offer. It's still woefully lacking in amenities; we still roll up the sidewalks at 6:00 on most nights."

"I noticed another policy, but I don't think it's as important."

"Oh. What's that?"

"We are actively decreasing the population density of our older neighborhoods by taking vacant lots and basically giving them to the adjacent homeowners so long as they don't have any property-maintenance violations and are current in their taxes."

"You're right. That's a problem. It's a real predicament for the City. I sympathize with their position. They are trying to get rid of the vacant lots so that they don't have the obligation to mow them. In the process, they are creating larger lots which will eventually decrease the population density of the central city, in effect making it a little more suburban like. That never works. Cities don't become vibrant by becoming more suburban. And they can't succeed if they aren't vibrant. It's short-range thinking, and it's counterproductive. The homes that add the adjacent side lots aren't going to become more marketable if the area doesn't become more dynamic. This is not going to stabilize housing values because it isn't going to reinvigorate neighborhoods. Once again, they are only treating a symptom and not addressing the root causes."

"What could we be doing instead?"

"The City would have to undertake a combination of actions. In the areas you are talking about, where they are decreasing density by combining vacant lots with adjacent homes, they need to offset the impact of that by increasing the density of nearby areas, perhaps by constructing apartment buildings. That combination might possibly be enough to create the necessary population density for neighborhood vibrancy. But, in reality, you need much more than single-family residences in order to have the necessary density for vibrant, walkable commercial nodes.

"In some places there are several contiguous vacant lots. If you can consolidate them into one large development parcel, they can become a potential site for an apartment complex, urban agriculture, or even a small manufacturing facility. One problem will be the zoning code, because most of these traditional neighborhoods have been zoned for residential uses only—and many of them for only single-family residences, essentially homeownership. Consequently, the zoning code probably prohibits most of these uses. That's a problem with a lot of rust-belt communities. Instead of having policies that encourage people to do the things that have to be done to revive many of our blighted areas, we have codes that prohibit them. As a result, they are developing short-term ways of dealing with current symptoms and are creating greater problems in the process. At the risk of repeating myself, it's just another way of failing to tackle the fundamental problems that are causing these neighborhoods to be so undesirable."

Frank shrugged slightly. "Hopefully, you can see why I'm a bit overwhelmed. On the bright side, I was able to learn about our brownfield program. We have over $1.3 million in funding from US EPA, but no real plan for it."

"That's excellent!" Dr. Hearst's enthusiasm, which had diminished during the preceding minutes, rebounded. "We will need to be comprehensive, and brownfield sites must be addressed. They are the worst manifestations of blight and dullness. And who knows, we may be able to find some good uses for those funds."

"Yes. Say, I know it's getting late, but I have a question about the City's deficit. If we retained our manufacturing base and a corporate headquarters recently, why do you think we still have such a bad deficit? After all, we preserved a lot of our tax base. I've been wondering about that."

"Another good question. I'm going to be brief, because of time. I think it boils down to the fact that people spend their paycheck where they live, not where they work. Too many people have moved out of Westville, and they are spending their paychecks elsewhere. That means their money is circulating among stores and restaurants in the suburbs, thereby bolstering *their* tax bases. So while Westville is capturing the immediate income tax, it's not capturing the full economic impact, and maybe not even the majority of the economic impact. That would be an interesting study in economics.

"However, I am out of time. Let's meet again in a couple of weeks. At that time, I am sure we will have even more to talk about."

Once again Frank received an evening email from Dr. Hearst:

Frank, as always, it was good talking with you this afternoon. Walk carefully among the land mines that seem to be planted along your path. We need you to stick around!

1. *Weak market neighborhoods and cities need to do exceptionally high quality projects in order to elevate their overall quality of life and create a community where people thrive.* You don't improve from average to good by simply doing more of what got you there, just like a C student doesn't raise his or her grade to a B without earning mostly A grades.

2. *No amount of tweaking can make right that which is fundamentally wrong.* There are some buildings, roads, and other proposed uses of land that are simply critically flawed and need to be dropped or terminated altogether— not just modified to mollify. As Jane Jacobs points out, capital investment in the wrong project actually does more harm than good, and major capital projects that are erroneously carried out can be cataclysmic.

3. *To love a city, you must be willing to fight for good development and against bad development.* Cities in a way are like infants: they are defenseless. Now, cities do have

some resiliency just like children. And, like children, strong and healthy cities are more resilient than weak cities, just as strong and healthy children are more resilient to afflictions than sickly and malnourished children. So just as to love a child is to nurture and protect it, so it is with loving a city. Therefore, to love a city, you must be willing to fight for good development and against bad development.

4. Another thing we didn't discuss but which I once again believe you will have no trouble grasping is this. *The predicament for weak market neighborhoods and cities is: How do you do A-quality work when the developers believe the market can only bear the cost of C-quality work?"* The solution is to use strategic subsidies to prime the market until such time as the market becomes strong enough to support high-quality projects. This need for project subsidies usually leads to serious conflict in weak market cities because they are confronting a wide range of increasing needs and costs while simultaneously having fewer financial resources with which to address them. The funds that are necessary to bridge the quality gap in weak neighborhoods are direly needed to solve numerous other problems. The result can be an epic conflict over the "revitalization bucket"—how to fix the leaks while also generating a flow of water through the tap.

CHAPTER 17

On Tuesday afternoon of the following week, the time arrived for Frank to break the bad news to the not-for-profits. Frank convened the City's annual HUD allocation briefing session in the Westville City Council chambers. The room could hold about three hundred people; and even though fifty-some people from the not-for-profit sector were in attendance, it looked empty. The collection of staff, volunteers, and board members sat there totally unaware of the proposed budget cuts. Frank Clark welcomed them and thanked them for their service to the community. He stated the City's priorities for the uses of the various funds and turned the meeting over to his staff to discuss the details of the application process. Walter Sage and other staff from the Department of Neighborhoods explained the process for applying for Community Development Block Grant (CDBG) funding for urban revitalization, Emergency Solutions Grant (ESG) funding for homeless shelters and other programming for the homeless, and other HUD funds that passed through the City.

Forty-five minutes later, the information had been presented, and Frank walked back to the podium to conclude the formal presentation and open up a question-and-answer dialogue.

"As you prepare your applications for funding, I want you to be aware of our funding constraints. As Walter pointed out earlier, we are receiving a $1 million cut in our CDBG funding from HUD. Therefore, we have only $9 million in CDBG funds to work with instead of the customary $10 million. In addition, the City's midyear financial analysis reveals that we are projected to have a $6 million

191

general-fund deficit. As a consequence, we are not able to make as much money available to third-party service providers. For the past several years, we've been pretty steady at about $3 million in funding for outside agencies. At this time we are projecting that only $2 million will be available."

This announcement was immediately met by an outcry of protest. One of the protesters exclaimed, "How can you do this to us?" to which another responded, "It's not Frank. It's Red. He's sold us out again."

Several hands shot in the air, and Frank, seeking a voice that was likely to be civil, called on Father Affonso, Executive Director of the St. Dominic Savio House.

"Can you tell us how you intend to use the $1 million that you are taking away from us?" he asked with a troubled but calm voice.

Frank replied calmly, "Yes. As you know, about a third of the staff in the Department of Neighborhoods is currently paid out of the CDBG allocation. These funds will primarily be used to pay the wages of additional employees in the department that have previously been paid from the general fund. This will help us avoid or at least minimize any potential layoffs."

Father Affonso continued the dialogue. "Yes, but you may be requiring *us*," he motioned to make it clear that he was referring to the greater 'us' as well as his organization, "to lay off our staffs as a result."

Frank tersely and somberly acknowledged "That may be the unfortunate result."

Seeing Pamela King's hand raised, Frank acknowledged her (as another likely civil voice).

Pam was calm, but a little more challenging than Father Affonso. "So you are saying that it is more important to save a City worker's job than a nonprofit job?" The crowd's collective murmur confirmed her observation.

Frank remained calm and terse. "I'm not saying that. We have a difficult situation, and we have core functions that have to be performed. That requires personnel."

Frank then called on John Nowak, Executive Director of Ironton CDC.

John had a reputation for lecturing the City officials about their policy and programming decisions, and the tension continued to elevate. "So does the Mayor's office realize how unfair this is to us? You get a ten percent cut in CDBG funding and that translates into a thirty-three percent cut for us. What's fair about that? Do they realize what they are doing?"

Frank remained calm and sought to avoid a response that would launch a full-blown debate or worse. "I believe they can do the math on this." He then took some of the edge off his terse response by adding, "We realize this imposes a hardship, but we do not have any easy or painless solutions."

Then, after a brief pause, Frank concluded the session. "We will be letting you know the precise funding that will be available. This is an opportunity for you to get a head start on your proposals. Thank you."

With that, the meeting ended, and Frank could hear several of the CDC directors making plans to run over to Carmen's Bistro to commiserate and strategize. Frank walked straight to the elevator and headed up to his office. This was not the time for further conversations with an irate sector of the community that would end up putting him in the uncomfortable position of further defending the administration. "Let Red handle this," Frank thought to himself. "I've done my part."

Opposite Ends of the Pole

Thirty minutes later, the not-for-profit community development corporations were busy huddling at Carmen's Bistro. The CDCs met on their own, without the social-service providers. There was a philosophical and financial rift that prevented them from forming a united front against the proposed cuts. The CDCs believed that they were the most appropriate recipients of the federal Community Development Block Grant (CDBG) funds, because they were in the business of rebuilding neighborhoods. In their minds they were the cornerstones of community development in Westville. And, frankly, the high-performing CDCs could make a strong argument in defense of that position. On the other hand, they viewed the social-service agencies that operated programs such as homeless shelters and programs for various classes of disadvantaged persons as providers of necessary charitable services—but not builders of communities. This philosophical rift was amplified by the fact that they were all competitors for scarce resources. Further, the CDCs argued that the social-service providers should receive their funding from sources such as Health and Human Services.

Unfortunately, the CDCs were further fractured among themselves. Each viewed the other as a competitor for the limited pool of CDC funding. Each served a well-defined geographic neighborhood or district, and in private they frequently disparaged each other's neighborhoods and organizational effectiveness. Nonetheless, they were united in their opinion that the pool of funds for which they would compete among themselves could not be slashed. Moreover, they had an additional bone to pick with the City—the failure to make HOME funds available for housing projects had deprived the CDCs of needed subsidies for their housing projects and, in the process, had choked off a substantial source of their operating revenue.

They had been at Carmen's for only a few minutes, during which they had spent the time well (ranting about Red, pausing only to order appetizers and drinks), when John Nowak walked into the bar and up to their gathering. John was a tall Polish American, and he towered over them as he proudly announced, "I just got off the phone with the Mayor's office. He will meet with a delegation of us at 11:00 this Thursday morning. How's that for getting results?"

Pamela King quickly took some of the wind out of his sails. "It's one thing to get an audience with Red the Terrible. It's another thing to get real results, to preserve our budget." Then she quickly added, "Not that we aren't appreciative of your efforts, John, but this is going to be a *real* challenge."

"Geez, a lot of thanks I get," John rejoined sarcastically.

Bill Smith, Executive Director of North Towne CDC, came to his rescue. "Here, John, let me get you a beer for your efforts. I'm good at that. You guys start working on our plan of attack—you're better at that than I am. We don't have much time to get ready for our meeting with his Majesty the Mayor."

Over the next hour the CDCs developed an outline of their position and determined who would be in their delegation. By the time they finished, they were feeling pretty pleased with themselves.

Meanwhile, in the Mayor's office a different meeting was taking place. Roderick and Byron had been summoned to confer with Red. Stepping inside the office door, Roderick unexpectedly found the Mayor wrapping up a conversation on his flip phone. "Listen," Red said into the phone. "It hasn't even been sixty days. I told you I'd help, and I will. Trust me on this. I've got to run, we'll talk soon." And with that, the conversation ended and Red closed his flip phone.

Roderick apologized. "I'm sorry, Mayor. Joan said your line wasn't lit up, so I assumed it was all right for us to come in. You wanted to meet with Byron and me?"

"Yes. Come in, gentlemen, and have a seat." Red seemed to be in a peculiarly good mood given the phone call that had just concluded, not to mention the near-riot that had occurred in the Council chambers a few minutes earlier. "My wife and children have been trying to get me to use my cell phone. Be more modern, and all that stuff. Plus our esteemed Law Director tells me records of our phone calls are public records, but not my personal cell phone unless I violate some other legal mumbo jumbo. But anyway, yes, I wanted to see you."

Roderick spoke up. "Thank you. I've got some thoughts on potential strategies for dealing with the fallout from the CDCs."

"Fallout from the CDCs?!" Red was incredulous. "Why is everyone so concerned about them? They're not worthy of killing any brain cells. Joan got off the phone with John Nowak ten minutes ago. I'm going to meet with their delegation of bootlickers Thursday morning at 11:00."

"Oh, . . . I just figured—." Roderick couldn't finish his thought before Red cut him off.

"I didn't call you two in here to talk about the CDCs. Didn't I make it clear last week that they don't scare me in the least? Byron, surely you might remember my thoughts on the topic?" Red's sarcasm was a not-so-subtle reminder of his disappointment with Byron's level of concern.

Byron saw an opportunity to recover a little lost stature. "Yes sir. I believe you made it clear that you have it covered."

"Covered! I've buried them six feet under! Soon I'll be dancing on their grave and erecting a tombstone on the top as a testament to their ineptitude."

Roderick asked the obvious question: "So what is it you want to discuss, sir?"

"The hubcap prize! It's time to announce the winning department. I'm going to have a press conference at 10:30 Thursday morning. We're going to have a vehicle from the winning department parked in front of City Hall with the new hubcaps. All we have to do is decide who the winning department is. Byron, you're the Senior Director of

Strategy, and this is certainly a strategy. What department do you think should win?"

Byron was caught totally off guard by the topic and the question. Thinking of the bad afternoon Frank had just had, and figuring that Red liked Frank, he reflexively said, "How about Neighborhoods? They have a lot of light-duty vehicles for inspectors and program monitors, and they are out and about in the community. They'd be visible." As he said it, he began convincing himself that he had actually pulled a good answer out of his ass.

Red didn't like it. "No. Frank has gotten too much glory. I'm going to take him down a couple of notches before he gets too big for his britches." As Red reached into a jar of assorted hard candies on a coffee table that separated the three of them, Roderick and Byron looked at each other with mutual WTF expressions.

Having found a cinnamon candy, Red began unwrapping it and asked Roderick for his opinion.

"Well, sir. I still remember the excellent job Public Service did with that New Year's snowstorm. It might not be a bad idea to put that back in front of people now that the good weather is here."

"Why Roderick, are you suggesting I try to milk that untimely snowstorm for another PR hit?" Red asked with humorous sarcasm.

Before Roderick could reply, Red continued. "We'll give it to them. Their heavy equipment can't win the hubcaps, so it's only right that we make up for that circumstance and throw them a bone and make them the first winners." He then called out to Joan, "Get Bill Zawodny on the phone!"

A moment later Red was on the phone talking to his Director of Public Service.

"Congratulations, Bill. Public Service is the first winner of my hubcap competition. It'll be your Division of Street Maintenance. Have one of your SUVs hooked up with the hubcaps and parked in front of City Hall Thursday morning. I'm holding a press conference at 10:30 to present the honor to your department. Have as many of your personnel there as you can spare. It won't take up too much time." And then, after a pause in which he listened to Bill, he said, "You're very welcome, Bill. Your team deserves it. Now get on it right away; we don't have much time."

With that, Red hung up the phone and said, "Thank you, gentlemen."

Byron and Roderick left the Mayor's office and intuitively walked into Roderick's office without saying a word. Then Byron whispered, "Did you hear what I heard? He's holding the press conference at 10:30 to announce he's putting spinning hubcaps on City vehicles and then telling the CDCs at 11:00 to go to hell."

Roderick looked at him and quietly said, "Yep," and shrugged his shoulders. Then the conversation closed with "should be an interesting day."

As Byron left Roderick's office, he saw Red heading out the door and heard him tell Joan that he had a 4:30 meeting and would see her in the morning.

*****

When Frank got home from work, Ellen asked him how his day was.

"I've had better. The briefing on the budget cuts was pretty bad. They don't think it's fair for them to take a thirty-three percent cut when the City received only a ten percent cut from HUD."

Ellen continued preparing dinner, "Well, . . . we knew they wouldn't like that."

"I know. They might not like the news, but I think the cuts are at least somewhat defensible from a policy perspective. That's not what bothers me the most."

Ellen stopped her preparations for a moment. "Oh? What does?"

"Remember when I met with Dr. Johnson and she said I would eventually lose my credibility as a result of this job?"

"Yes."

"It looks like that began today."

"But you didn't make the decision—Red did," Ellen protested.

"That's true. And the groups realize that. I could hear them talking about it. But how long can you be the messenger and not be tarnished? I don't think my Teflon is that thick."

"I wouldn't worry too much about it. Everyone knows Red's a jerk, not you."

"Yeah, but some of them deliver more bang per buck than we do. And there's one more thing I have to deal with."

"What's that?"

"I was brought in to come up with some kind of magical neighborhood program. I'm less than sixty days into this job, and I'm already announcing budget cuts that harm the organizations and programs that are going to have to be a big part of that magic, whatever it turns out to be. I can't help hearing the *Mission Impossible* theme song beginning to play in the background."

Ellen smiled. "Somehow you'll figure it out," she said encouragingly.

CHAPTER 18

Wednesday was relatively quiet and routine. Roderick called Bill Zawodny first thing in the morning. "Hello, Z. I wanted to follow up on the Mayor's conversation with you regarding the hubcap honor."

"Yes sir."

"I know when I promoted you to succeed me as Director of Public Service, you didn't want to be in the spotlight, but your background in operations really pulled us through this past winter, and the Mayor appreciates that."

"Thank you. The team and the other departments that helped us out really pulled through."

"Yes. I don't know how the team feels about this award program, but as you know, this is a big deal for the Mayor. So I need you to have a good, enthusiastic turnout tomorrow morning."

"We will, but like you said, I think the guys think this thing is a joke."

"I know. Make sure your supervisors make it clear this is serious. If anyone screws up, I'm going to come down on them like a ton of bricks," said Roderick gravely.

"I'll make it clear, boss."

"I know you will. One other thing. Put some orange construction cones and those sawhorse barricades up in front of City Hall this evening. I want to make sure you can park the display vehicles there for the press event without any trouble. I'd get one or two pieces of heavy equipment as well. Even though they can't use the hubcaps, they make for a better show."

"Will do!"

"One last thing. Let me know if Fleet Management has any trouble getting one or two vehicles outfitted with the hubcaps. Frankly, if we have to pay an expediting fee, do so. Get it done before noon, so we are sure there aren't any snafus."

"I'm already on it."

"Thanks, Bill. Remember, whatever the rest of us think, Red *is* serious about this being a great program and a real honor for your crew."

"Yes sir."

The preparations for the recognition ceremony went smoothly, as did the rest of Roderick's day. Things changed dramatically on Thursday morning, as Roderick knew they would.

The CDC delegation met in the backroom of Maury's Delicatessen for coffee and final preparations before their 11:00 summit with Red Paley. Their delegation consisted of the executive directors of three CDCs, Pamela King, John Nowak, and Bill Smith; Deacon Wilkens, the pastoral power behind the Abyssinian Progress Association and a not-so-subtle reminder of the power of the central city churches; and

Quincy Dewberry, who served on the governing board of a CDC. John Nowak had urged having Quincy as a member of the delegation given his status as an elder statesman. John mistakenly believed that Quincy had exercised more leadership ability the previous year in transitioning Byron Swift from Westville University to the City than was actually the case.

They had plenty to talk about, for while the topic of drastic budget cuts was already fodder enough for their meeting, Red Paley had spiced it up with a heaping dose of hot sauce. John Nowak was particularly agitated:

"I can't believe what I'm reading here in the *Waste of Time*! Tom Folks has a lot of nerve attacking us in his column! He titles it 'Leaders or Leaches,' criticizes us for low housing production, and cites Red as questioning whether we are value-added enterprises; and further whether our time has come and gone. Doesn't he know Red is the one refusing to pass the HOME funds through to us that we need! And Tom Folks never talked to us to get our side of the story! The two of them are the leaches! They have formed some kind of unholy alliance!"

Deacon Wilkens spoke up. "What? Is that in today's paper? I haven't seen it."

Pamela King replied while John Nowak tried to regain his bearing. "Yes. Tom Folks must have gotten his information straight from Red. He says we haven't gotten any production the last year and a half, but he doesn't point out that the City has a backlog of $3 million in HOME funds that we need for subsidies in order to make the houses affordable. It's really off the hook."

John piled on. "It's a hatchet job on all of us. And there's Red, first choking off our funding and then saying we aren't producing. He ought to be hanged!"

"We were able to construct a thirty-unit elderly housing apartment complex with the funding we received a couple of years ago," said Deacon Wilkens in reference to the infamous project where Bobby Turkel had overpromised funds to three different developers. "Didn't the article mention that?"

"No," John replied.

"We don't count rental units as an asset here," added Pamela sarcastically.

Bill Smith, holding the paper in his hand, added, "Listen to this, it says: 'The CDCs that are charged with revitalizing Westville's most destitute neighborhoods are currently being subsidized to the tune of about $1.5 million a year to essentially simply lobby for more funding for their salaries, whereas $1.5 million could easily fund 200 or more housing demolitions.' You know what? I think he wants to take our funding to do more demolitions, because that way he can add a couple more City demolition crews and further bail out his budget."

"And cozy up even more with the public-employee unions," Pamela surmised.

"It just isn't right," Deacon Wilkens said softly with a tone of utter disgust. "You can't starve us, then misrepresent the facts and go for our throats. That's not right."

Then Quincy Dewberry added a thought of his own, "I think we should go to the paper after our meeting with the Mayor and demand a retraction or at least equal time."

"Hell no – let's sue them for libel!" exclaimed John.

A Best Practice, or Just Rubbing Salt in the Wounds

And so the conversation continued without much being accomplished until, noticing that it was 10:30, they decided that they had better head over to City Hall for the showdown with Red. As they walked out the door and rounded the corner, they spied a commotion of sorts in front of City Hall. Seeing a City dump truck and front-end loader along with orange cones and barricades, they at first thought it was a construction project. Then, seeing a gathering of people, they feared that an accident had occurred at their presumed construction site. Then, as they continued walking, they gradually realized that the City vehicles were on display and that an assembly of some type was going on. After a few more steps they realized that Red Paley was getting ready to address a group of reporters and camera crews. They stood in the back of the small gathering of about fifty City employees and members of the media to see what was going on. After all, they reasoned, they couldn't possibly be late to a meeting with the Mayor if the Mayor was right in front of them holding a press event.

The Mayor began his comments. Standing behind him were the President of the Westville Area Chamber of Commerce and Bill Zawodny, Director of Public Service. "Good morning. Today is a big event for Westville, a historic event for Westville. Today, we continue rolling out a program that will make waves across the state, across the country, probably around the globe. Like all cities, Westville has long sought ways to recognize City workers for exceptional performance. To achieve that goal, I started the Westville Exceptional Service Program earlier this year, in March, I believe. Today I am announcing the first winners of that goal: the Street Maintenance Division of the Department of Public Service. But before I present the honor to them, I want to explain what this program is and why it is so unique.

"First, many of our employees work very hard, but they can't be financially rewarded above and beyond the compensation set forth in their union contract or the City's pay ranges. *But*," said Red, pausing dramatically, "*But*, they can be *recognized*! The question, I said to myself, is how do we best recognize them?' And the answer is that the award should symbolize their hustle and quest for continuous improvement. Ladies and Gentlemen, I am here to proudly state that the spinning hubcaps you see on this City vehicle to my right do exactly that!"

With a gesture and a turn of his head, he drew the audience's attention to a Chevy Tahoe that had been jacked up about two feet so that none of its wheels were touching the ground. In what had to be a violation of every safety regulation known to mankind, an employee of the Division of Street Maintenance was sitting in the driver's seat. Red addressed him.

"Go ahead, Bob. Rev her up and hit the brake."

With that, Bob Sanders started up the Tahoe, revved it up to about twenty-five hundred RPMs, and applied the brakes. As the wheels came to a stop, the shining new hub caps continued spinning, glistening in the morning sun.

"Look at that!" Red exclaimed delightfully. "Those rims are still spinning. They are spinning because Red Paley's Westville never rests. Like a shark that dies if it stops moving, this City is always hustling, always doing more, never sleeping, *never* dying. These hubcaps are an honor that inspires the winners to keep up their great work and encourages others to aspire to greatness. Because of this, the Westville Exceptional Service Program will become a model for employee recognition. The winning division is having these installed on all of their non-heavy-duty vehicles.

"And now, drumroll, please," he said smiling. "I am presenting this award to Bill Zawodny, the Director of the Department of Public Service for the fine work the Division of Street Maintenance did, especially in response to last winter's holiday snowstorm."

With that, Bill shook Red's hand and received a framed proclamation naming the Division of Street Maintenance as the winner of the first award under the Westville Exceptional Service Program. Bill made a few humble comments, followed by the President of the Westville Area Chamber of Commerce who proceeded to awkwardly extol the merits of the program and the private sector's interest in promoting better public-sector efficiency and service.

The event was then opened up for questions. The first came from a local television reporter, Susan Keating.

"Mayor, did you just say that you started the program in March to motivate City workers through recognition of their performance, but that you are awarding it for something that Street Maintenance did over the New Year's holiday?"

"That's correct, Suzie. They did a super job plowing the streets. Really, all—or many—of the City departments came together on the holiday to plow snow and apply salt. They really did a superb job, one of the best snowplowing operations ever, anywhere."

Susan continued, "I know they did a good job." "*Great* job!" the Mayor interjected.

"Right, Mayor. But my point is how can this program be a motivator if in fact the performance it is rewarding occurred before anyone was aware of the program? In fact, before the program even existed?"

Red was caught off guard but recovered with an answer in typical Red Paley fashion. "Easily. First, if they hadn't done a good job mowing weeds and what-not this spring, we wouldn't be here today recognizing them. But they did do a good job—they didn't blow it. So, they're here and deservedly so. Second, sometimes the lead rabbit needs to eat a carrot before the other rabbits can realize that it *is* a carrot. Believe me, seeing us here today honoring the entire Division of Street Maintenance, the other City departments see this program as the carrot it is. Because, you know, sticks don't always work. Sometimes you need a carrot to get results."

Pamela King whispered to Deacon Wilkens, "I'm thinking the lead rabbit accidentally ate a rotten fish."

Diana Woodard of another television channel then asked a question. "Mayor, if other departments helped out, shouldn't they be recognized? After all, plowing the streets is not their primary role, and it sounds like they really stepped up."

Red exhibited a little frustration. He couldn't believe no one was exulting in his program and its beautiful spinning hubcaps. "No, Diana. The other departments are proud to be part of a team effort. I am sure they are enjoying seeing their sister division getting recognized and are aiming to be the next ones awarded."

Bill Smith whispered to John Nowak, "Enjoy it? I'll bet they're laughing their asses off!" In response to which John laughed out loud, catching Red's attention.

"Nowak, do you have a question?" Red asked.

"Sure, Mayor. If we do a really good job with our community garden, can you get us some of those miniature windmills that *really* spin in the wind? Or maybe we should just walk around with pinwheels while we work in the garden?"

Red laughed back with a little irritation. "Sure, but I hardly think that your garden will measure up."

John continued jousting, "Against what? The stellar job your Parks Department does mowing our neighborhood parks?"

"That's enough. I have a meeting upstairs in a minute that I must tend to. If anyone has any more questions, pass them along through our Public Relations staff, and we will get back to you. Thank you!"

As they started toward City Hall, Pamela King told Deacon Wilkens, "I can't believe he's cutting our funding and still putting those idiotic spinning hubcaps on City vehicles. What a waste!"

Deacon Wilkens said slightly more quietly and with a tone of dignified defiance, "He's deliberately rubbing our nose in it."

Showdown

The CDC delegation entered City Hall, took the elevator to the top floor, and entered the lobby of the Mayor's office. Joan escorted them to a conference room and assured them that Mayor Paley and his staff would be with them shortly. About five minutes later Red Paley entered the room with Roderick, Byron, and Frank in tow. Red had been tempted to leave Frank out of the meeting, but he thought it would be better if Frank witnessed it rather than heard about it secondhand. Plus Red wanted an opportunity to show off his skills at mastering a tough audience.

After everyone had greeted each other, they took their seats around a large conference table, and Red opened the meeting by tossing the initiative to the CDCs. "This is your meeting, so we are here to listen to your concerns."

Deacon Wilkens began. "The group has asked me to informally be the lead spokesperson, Mayor, but I am sure all of us will contribute to the conversation. First, we appreciate the fact that you are able to meet with us on such short notice. Second, I think we can agree that all of us are here because of our love for Westville, particularly its less-well-off people. These are the people the CDCs primarily serve. Third, we know the City has a budget problem, but we believe we are part of the solution, that our work strengthens our community and our economy, that we are part of growing the tax base. We are providers of new housing stock and bulwarks against blight. Contrary to the unfortunate and inaccurate column in today's *Westville Wire & Telegraph*, we are cultivators of people and the neighborhoods in which they live—we are not leaches. We are here to work with you, Mayor, with your team, and with City Council to see if there aren't alternatives to the drastic and painful cuts that were mentioned in Tuesday's briefing.

"As you know, there is a false perception that our productivity is down because of something we either aren't doing or aren't doing well enough. That's simply not true. Our productivity is down solely due to the fact that the City hasn't deployed its HOME funds in about two and a half years. The projects that had already been funded have been built out, and we have more housing units in our pipelines. But we need the subsidies that HOME funds provide so that our lower-income residents can finally become homeowners. To imply otherwise, as Tom Folks did today, is simply not true. Further, many of us believe it was malicious.

"Regardless of that, Mayor, we are here in our capacity as partners with the City. We believe that together we can work out a budget proposal for our organizations that satisfies your needs and still enables us to serve our neighborhoods."

"Thank you, Deacon," Red replied calmly and matter-of-factly. "I too appreciate our partnership. I agree with you that we have HOME dollars that we haven't committed. That is because I really didn't have full confidence in our former Director of Neighborhoods. I believe you, your colleagues, our neighborhood residents, and I all share that opinion. I also agree that the lack of HOME dollars has certainly hurt your productivity." His eyes scanned the room to make sure everyone knew that his comments were directed to the collective group of CDCs. He then proceeded to cast blame elsewhere. "Tom Folks should have checked his facts before finalizing his column."

Red continued. "However, I stand by my belief that the CDCs haven't been that effective. Sure you've constructed and rehabbed hundreds of housing units, but what's changed? Our poverty rate hasn't decreased; in fact it's increased slightly and steadily. If you are a bulwark against blight, you could fool me. The number of homes needing demolition is escalating. All I see are projects that are warehousing poor people. Sure, the construction may be new, but I don't see many people getting a new lease on life. Even if I felt otherwise, I have no choice but to cut your funding. I'm dealing with budget issues that are larger than your problems."

Then, as the CDC directors quietly stuck to their game plan, Deacon Wilkens responded. "Mayor, with all due respect, I don't believe that it is fair to say we are simply building new residential warehouses for people that aren't as well off as us."

He strategically chose not to express his offense at the phrase 'warehousing poor people,' at least not at this time. The Deacon continued: "I've personally seen the joy that a new affordable home brings to a first-time homeowner."

"Yes. But what is it like five or seven years later?" Red interjected. "The homes are frequently not well-maintained; sometimes they've already gone through one or more foreclosures. More often than not, the joy you bring is fleeting. It's replaced by the painful reality of owning and keeping up a home on a shoestring budget. You'd be better off teaching people how to get a job, but I imagine that's a tougher business model." Red made this last point with a slight smirk, his way of poking the CDCs for being too interested in pursuing revenue-generating strategies at the expense of carrying out other important programs.

The CDC Directors' game plan was to eventually segue to Quincy Dewberry as another elder statesman who might appeal to Red's need to cultivate the wealthier, older, white establishment if he planned to mount a serious challenge for the governor's office. Thus Quincy spoke next. "Mayor, if I may, the people of these neighborhoods truly need these CDCs. Are you really going to hurt them?"

Red replied quickly with the lines he had gone over in his mind a million times in anticipation of this very moment in the meeting:

"What I'm doing is keeping cops on the streets. Nobody cries louder for that than the people in the neighborhoods you are talking about. They are the ones most victimized by crime. If you ask them whether their neighborhood CDC is more valuable than additional police protection, they'll vote for the cops every single time. These cuts are giving your people the police they demand, the emergency medical and fire services they use, and the demolitions they've been crying for." Then he went off-script. "You know what? I know your people better than you do. If I go to any street corner in central Westville and tell them I'm laying off cops to appease you, they'll storm your offices.

"So I've got to cut you to fund the other. And I'm not going to pay a political price. Your people demand that we provide these services. Even if they didn't, they don't vote!

"Now, ..." Red paused because he realized he had gone further than he intended. "I've got every confidence that Frank here is going to come up with a plan to get the HOME funds on the street *and* to utilize our limited CDBG funds as efficiently as possible."

Feeling obligated to speak up, Frank said, "Thank you, sir. We'll make it happen."

John Nowak could no longer keep quiet. "It takes money, Mayor. I'm not holding my breath that Frank, try as he may, will come up with much."

"You'll be surprised, Nowak!" Red retorted. Then he continued. "And speaking of efficient and creative new strategies on our end, I think the CDCs need to examine their operations. We have way too many independent organizations for a city our size."

Nowak didn't want to go down that road in front of his coalition members, even though he knew his CDC was likely going to emerge from any consolidation process as a larger entity. Instead, he decided to take another poke at the Mayor. "That's easier said than done. At any rate, speaking of efficiencies, I know one thing. I was surprised that you were wasting more City dollars awarding hubcaps this morning."

Red would have none of it. "That shows how little you know. Workers need something to aspire to, a goal to shoot for. These guys deserved it, and I rewarded them. And one more thing, *John*, half the funding came from the private sector."

Red continued, in the process extending a short, thin olive branch. "Listen, we're willing to listen to any productive ideas you may have. However, we need to make some cuts."

Frank volunteered the fact that HUD's NOFA might offer an opportunity for them to partner with the City on projects such as abating lead-based paint and developing neighborhood redevelopment plans.

With that, the meeting largely concluded, although some inconsequential conversations continued for a few minutes. Afterward, Roderick, Byron, and Frank met in Red's office to debrief the meeting.

Red was particularly upbeat. He felt the meeting had gone particularly well. He had held his line, been firm, and pushed the CDCs. Yet he didn't feel that he had alienated them to the point where they could disrupt his forthcoming, yet-to-be-announced gubernatorial campaign. Still, he was hoping he would be able to figure out a way to throw them a bone.

"Perfect! We scored our points," he said beaming. "I can tell you exactly what they are going to do next. They are going to start lobbying City Council. But we've preempted them. We've got the public-employee unions lined up to back the cuts and save their union jobs. Plus we've got them on the defensive trying to defend their record. They won't make any headway with City Council."

Red continued. "Then they'll be forced to start seriously discussing mergers among themselves. Frank, you come up with something that we can put out there as a new program, something we can fold into a CDC consolidation process so they see some light at the end of the tunnel."

"Yes sir." Frank responded with feigned optimism.

Red continued his roll. "We don't want to crush them completely, but I hope you boys liked my attack—total warfare, scorched earth.

We cut their resources, damaged their community reputation, formed powerful alliances with the public employee unions —I love it. They don't have a chance."

Then Red's mood became more abrupt. "But enough of that. Frank, you've had nearly sixty days. Make something happen!" he said firmly, but not venomously.

With that, the meeting ended, and the trio filed out of the Mayor's office. Frank and Byron agreed to meet late that afternoon to discuss strategy.

CHAPTER 19

At 4:00 that afternoon, Frank Clark and Walter Sage met Byron
Swift in a small conference room within the Mayor's office. Based on
Red's comments earlier in the day, the pressure was mounting to
develop a strategic initiative that would buy the Mayor a little
goodwill with the neighborhoods. Whether it would really work or
not was probably a secondary consideration for Red, although the
three of them, with their closer working relationships with the
neighborhoods, didn't see it that way. Certainly Frank didn't see it
that way. Red had built him up to be some kind of miracle worker—
and for no justifiable reason. There was nothing in Frank's
background as an attorney that would lead someone to charge him
with the duties of assuming a major new position and conceiving a
new program that would reverse Red's standing among neighborhood
residents and the leaders of the organizations serving them. And now
the budget showdown with the CDCs had dramatically turned the heat
up on Frank to deliver something. Red Paley secretly expected smoke
and mirrors. Frank was on the front line, and he earnestly and openly
wanted something effective—he wanted to be an agent of change for
his hometown.

An Idea Emerges

Reviewing the situation, Walter Sage emphasized that he was
responsible for administering a current balance of $3.5 million in
HOME funds, $1.75 million of which came from an earlier allocation
and were at risk of being lost in less than fourteen months. "The easy
thing would be to simply resort to business as usual and free up the

219

money," Walter said. "But I don't think the Mayor views that as sufficient."

"Right," Frank said, "and Michael Casey has about $1.4 million in brownfield funds from US EPA with no real idea on how to use them."

"Yeah," Walter replied, "but the urgent issue is the HOME funds. Fourteen months goes by more quickly than you think, and we can't give this money back to the Feds."

Frank and Byron concurred. "That's true," Byron said. "We'd be skewered, and deservedly so."

"So how do we normally allocate these funds?" Frank asked, partly out of a need to know and partly because he somehow hoped a questioning process would lead them to some blue-sky thinking.

The question had been tacitly directed to Walter as the expert, and he obliged with a concise but thorough answer. "We let developers—usually it's the CDCs—come up with projects that meet the low-income guidelines and need funding from us. Sometimes other not-for-profits and even for-profit corporations have projects as well, particularly large apartment complexes for seniors or people with mental or physical disabilities. If the projects meet the guidelines, we check their financials to make sure they look viable. Right now we have over half a dozen projects in various stages of review that are pretty well baked. They just need us to turn on the spigot and let the money flow like we used to. So we can solve the give-back problem in a hurry if we have to."

With that as a backstop or fallback position, the question-and-answer between Frank and Walter continued as part of the pursuit of something better. "What kinds of projects are in the queue now?" Frank asked.

"Mostly subsidized single-family homes for lower-income households that are being constructed on sites where other homes have been demolished. They can fill in some of the vacant lots the demolitions created. Also, I think we might have a couple of apartment complexes for low-income senior citizens. These are the types of projects we always get."

Frank probed further. "So we are going to construct more single-family housing on lots where single-family housing previously failed?"

"What do you mean?" Walter asked.

Byron responded, "I get it. I think Frank's point is that since the homes are constructed on the sites of previously demolished homes, it's obvious that the neighborhood turned bad for housing, and now people want to simply ignore the market and do the same thing over again."

"That's pretty much what I'm thinking," Frank confirmed. "Just the other day John Nowak was saying that Einstein's definition of insanity was to keep doing the same thing over and over again and expecting a different result. Isn't that what we do if we simply build new homes where the other homes failed?"

"I don't know," Walter replied. "That's what they bring us, and that's what we fund."

"I think we need to do something more. Something that will change the surrounding environment that makes the neighborhood more appealing as a place to buy a house and establish your roots," Frank surmised.

Byron was intrigued. "What would that be? We can't put a shopping mall next-door as an amenity."

Frank thought out loud. "I'm not sure. We need to do something more than just housing. Otherwise, we build homes and simply watch them decay. That's what Red was saying in so many words this morning. We need something to go along with the housing that makes the neighborhood more appealing."

After a split second Frank continued. "Say. Do we ever get proposals to do mixed-use developments along tired Main Street corridors like Elm Street over in the Creekside neighborhood? Maybe rehabbing a three-story building to put retail on the first floor with a couple floors of flats above it?"

"No," replied Walter.

"Why not?" asked Frank.

"That would be a lot more work for everyone, especially the CDC or other developer that has to manage a rental property consisting of residential *and* commercial units. The CDCs like to do a project and then be done with it. They've got their processes down pat. They know how to get the vacant properties from the City's land bank, finance the construction, apply for the low-income housing tax credits, couple the tax credits with HOME funds, build the units, and sell them to people who are simply excited to own their first home. It's pretty much a cookie-cutter process for them."

Frank pushed back. "Yeah, but it's not getting us anywhere. I've been reading Jane Jacobs. She says we need density and a variety of uses. It seems to me that putting mixed-use projects on our old neighborhood commercial corridors, streets like Main, Elm, and Highland Avenue, would help get the level of activity up to a point where people would say 'Something positive seems to be going on here.' These projects would at least put more people on the sidewalks—make it livelier. Right now everything is so damn desolate, the only people living there are the ones that are stuck there."

Byron's interest was piqued. "Okay, Frank. I think you're on to something here, but how do we make that happen? No one wants to do it."

They sat quietly for a few moments, each trying to solve the puzzle that they had laid out for themselves. Then Frank spoke up.

"This probably sounds stupid, but I'm the new guy at this. What would happen if we simply told them this is the type of development we want to fund and that they had better not bring us anything else?"

"How would we do that?" Walter asked.

"I'm thinking of the federal NOFA. HUD uses the NOFA to say 'Here are various programs and here's what you can use the money for.' And of course they provide directions on how to apply for the funds. What if we put a little twist on that? We could say 'Here's what we are interested in seeing as an end product—something that will transform neighborhoods from places to leave to places to come to, stay in, and thrive. And here are the funds that we have available to help you do your project.' To paraphrase the movie *Jerry Maguire*: 'We're showing you the money, now show us the project.' Could we do that?"

Walter replied, "I think we could do that, but I'm not sure what we have to bring to the table. I'm also not sure what kind of response we will get."

Byron was feeling the momentum. "I like it. But Walt has a good point. What *do* we have that we can bring to the table? Especially now with budget cuts?"

Frank's mind was on a roll, and he responded quickly. "I think we have a lot of programs, but we've never integrated them into a proactive, comprehensive, revitalization package. Imagine a worn-out Main Street corridor. We can't create the customers overnight, but what are its redevelopment needs?"

Byron spoke up. "Well, most of the ones I've seen have really pitted-out sidewalks and streets. I think we could commit some capital-improvement funds from the CIP budget."

Frank liked that the team was getting his thought process. "That's a start! Walter, you've got $1.75 million in HOME funds, right?"

"Yes."

"So we can say those are to be used for housing on or immediately adjacent to the corridor that Byron wants to fund. That helps us get people on the sidewalks and potential consumers in the neighborhood."

"We also have a program that can offset some of the cost of the tap fees for new water hookups," volunteered Walter, feeling the synergy. "We could earmark some of those funds for this program."

"Don't forget you've got brownfield funds," said Byron. "Those old buildings need assessments and cleanup."

"You're right!" replied Walter. "Say, we are beginning to marshal some real money here! What's it adding up to?"

Frank thought for a moment. "Just starting with the HOME funds, we have $1.75 million that we might lose, but heck, we can bring the whole $3.5 million to the table for potential funding, right?"

"Yes," replied Walter.

"Then there's the CIP money for sidewalks and potholes, plus the water-tap fee assistance. What are realistic numbers for those?"

"We'd have to check with the Public Service and Water Department, but based on previous projects, I'm guessing $300,000 of CIP and $100,000 for the water taps," volunteered Walter.

"And potentially $1.3 million in brownfield funds," said Byron.

"So now we are at $5.2 million," said Frank. "That should make a difference."

"And get people's attention!" said Byron.

Frank looked at his seasoned veteran. "Walter, you've been around here the longest. Does this idea make any sense to you?"

"Yes," Walter replied enthusiastically. "I don't know how the CDCs will like it, because it changes their funding environment. But I think it is plausible. What do we have to lose?"

"Not much," said Frank. "How about if I rough something out, and we run it past Roderick tomorrow? If he likes it, we can run it up to Red."

"Sounds like a plan!" said Byron. "Say, by the way, I heard it mentioned that Economic Development has about $400,000 in its loan fund. We can always put that on the table."

"Yes! I'll add it in!" said Frank.

"And while we're at it," added Walter, "we have $500,000 in lead-based-paint abatement funds that we can put in the pot."

As they got on the elevator to return to the Department of Neighborhoods, Frank turned to Walter and said, "I've got a feeling that this is going to be either a big success or a colossal failure. It's too bold to fall in the middle."

Walter looked Frank in the eye. "Either way, it's worth a try. If Red wants us to make a difference, this can't be any worse than what we've been doing."

Roderick's Commune

That evening Roderick Campbell stepped out of his townhome at about 7:00 PM and took advantage of the warm evening and the lengthening spring daylight to walk around the Creekside neighborhood he knew so well.

He walked a couple of blocks over to Elm Street and paused to scan up and down the now-desolate commercial corridor. He remembered his childhood and how this street provided a livelihood for so many families and a ladder up for people like him. Over there was the boarded-up building that used to be Elmer's Market, a place that had done more than give him a part-time job as a teenager. It had enabled him to earn supplemental income his mother direly needed in order to raise her family. Had Elmer's not been conveniently located a few blocks away, he never could have taken the time to work, study, and play football.

Just as important—maybe more important—was the way the experience at Elmer's reinforced his developing values of working hard, staying on task, and dealing with others firmly but fairly. He remembered how the senior Elmer Schmidt had told his son to let Roderick work a flexible schedule that would accommodate his studies and his athletics. Roderick hadn't realized it at the time, but he had since wondered whether Mr. Schmidt had seen something in him that was worth nurturing or whether he would have done the same for someone else. In any event, Mr. Schmidt embodied a broader sense of community than what seemed to exist in today's world of isolated shopping centers with their big-box national chains.

He continued his walk down Elm Street past the office of Creekside CDC, the same building where he had opened his first bank account thirty or so years ago. As he walked, Roderick found himself longing, even yearning, for a bygone day when people knew each other—not necessarily intimately, but enough to care and lend a hand like Mr. Schmidt had lent him. He took in the empty buildings on Elm Street and then, as he hung a right on Creek Lane, the vacant lots and homes that dotted the blighted residential area. He interrupted his walk a second time to pause briefly in front of Ella's Styling Salon. Seeing Ella Rickman through the window getting ready to go home for the evening, he gave her a friendly wave and fended off her gestures inviting him inside. He thought of how Ella had done his mother's and sisters' hair, but mostly he thought of how patient Ella had been on those all-too-frequent occasions when they couldn't pay her in full at the time the services were provided. As far as Roderick knew, they had always managed to make good on it somehow.

Roderick saw all the vacant properties, but he also took in the houses that were occupied, particularly the houses where people were trying to keep things up. It struck him how honorable these people were. They didn't have much, but they were determined to do the right things the right way no matter how bad the circumstances were around them.

Roderick followed Creek Lane to Creekside Park. Although he had been walking somewhat randomly, this was the place he wanted to be. Seeing the park empty, he walked over to a picnic table and sat on the top for a spell using the bench as a footstool. The park was a little rougher than it had been when Frank and Pamela viewed it two weeks earlier. It needed mowing, and there was some litter, but all in all it was usable and pretty welcoming, despite the park sign that had once again been converted from "Westville" to "Worstville." And yet the park's invitation to be enjoyed was being ignored by those for whom it was intended—not the gang members and vagrants, but the neighborhood children and their parents.

The emptiness of the park saddened Roderick. This was the Eden to which he would ride his second-hand bike and play, the place where he learned to throw and catch a football and played pickup basketball. It saddened him to think that other children hadn't discovered his former urban oasis. They weren't getting the same enjoyment, athletic competition, and social interaction he got. "They deserve better," Roderick thought to himself.

After a while, the shadows were growing long, and Roderick began walking up the other side of Creek Lane. His thoughts turned to the newly constructed infill houses and rehabbed units Creekside CDC had produced with the City's help. "Some families have better roofs over their heads," Roderick thought to himself, "but there's not an environment of hope. There's not much here now that can reinforce a young person's aspirations. How would I turn out if I were born here now?"

When Roderick was a child, he thought this was the greatest neighborhood in the world. It seemed you could do everything here. It had helped his mother raise a family against incredible odds, and he never wanted to leave it. He stayed here through college, and now, as an adult— and a very successful adult at that—he was still here. But why? Out of some sense of loyalty to his past? There was no objective reason for him to be here. His mother had passed, and his sisters had moved on. Creekside offered nothing of value for him, and his continued presence and investment as a homeowner defied all logic.

"What would it take to bring this back?" Roderick thought. "People are moving out faster than our housing programs can bring them back. There's no reason other than sentiment for the rest of us to choose to stay."

He turned off Elm Street and walked the final two blocks to his home. Walking in the twilight, he absorbed the sounds of the approaching night, of squirrels chattering and crickets chirping. An occasional dog warned him away with a bark. He didn't mind. The sounds of the natural world, urban as they were, took his mind off the problems of *his* world. Arriving home he sat on his front porch, closed his eyes, and drifted off to a more peaceful, slower place.

CHAPTER 20

Frank Clark went home that evening energized by the optimism that came from believing that he may have actually hit upon something that would solve at least part of the Westville urban revitalization riddle. That something, of course, was the notion of a new initiative that would (1) clearly articulate a call for neighborhood development projects that had the potential to create more-vibrant urban nodes that might be the seeds of a broader urban renaissance, and (2) list various funding resources that would be available for qualifying projects. He hoped this new program could drive the CDCs into undertaking comprehensive urban development by drawing upon various funding sources that normally operated in strict programmatic silos. Somewhat worried that the concept was so simple that it might not actually be very effective, he didn't discuss it with Ellen other to say that he had to do a little work after the kids were squared away for the evening.

Around 9:00 he sat at the family computer and began sketching the primary elements of the new program. (Not knowing what to call the program, he referred to it generically as simply a new "Westville Program.")

> The new Westville Program is intended to spur the undertaking of comprehensive urban development projects by coordinating funding opportunities from traditionally disparate programs with the goal of transforming some of Westville's urban neighborhoods

into more complete communities where people truly thrive.

We envision neighborhoods that have sufficient population density to support neighborhood-based businesses and other enterprises that provide the amenities and positive energy that make urban living appealing for a wide range of people.

We envision neighborhoods featuring walkable commercial corridors that offer an attractive alternative to suburban living and wholesome environments for households of all types. Neighborhoods that have active, pedestrian-friendly sidewalks that build and strengthen a sense of community as well as provide a more nurturing developmental and entrepreneurial ecosystem.

The goal of the Westville Program is to generate outstanding projects—not test an organization's technical expertise or proposal draftsmanship.

In consideration of this, and in recognition of the fact that interested development entities may not be fully familiar with the requirements for obtaining and complying with these wide-ranging funding programs, City personnel are available to work with entities on their proposals. Interested parties are strongly encouraged to avail themselves of this opportunity for staff consultation.

Subject to meeting program eligibility and, if applicable, underwriting requirements, the following funds have been identified by the City of Westville as potentially available for projects:

HOME	$3,500,000
Brownfield Assessment	$ 300,000
Brownfield Remediation*	$1,000,000
Capital Improvement Program (CIP)	$ 300,000
Lead-Based Paint Abatement	$ 500,000
Water and Sewer Taps	$ 100,000
Economic Development Loans	$ 400,000
Total:	$6,100,000

*The source is a US EPA Revolving Loan Fund grant which provides for a combination of grants and low-interest loans for environmental remediation.

In addition, projects may qualify for Community Reinvestment Area (CRA) real property tax abatement.

Preliminary proposals are due on or before 4:00 PM, _____, 2000. City staff will work cooperatively with the strongest applicants to further refine their proposed projects.

The City anticipates that some proposals may have multiple development phases that extend over several funding cycles.

The City further contemplates that the strongest proposals will build upon existing momentum in Westville's neighborhoods by leveraging investments in infrastructure and new schools and/or libraries that have recently been completed, are planned, or are under active consideration.

For more information, please contact _____.

At 10:30 PM Frank figured he had enough of it sketched out to share with the team in the morning. He then sent the following email to Dr. Harold Hearst:

Dear Dr. Hearst:

I think I have a program concept that might in some variation be worthy of launching as an urban development initiative. Not knowing what its name will be, I am simply referring to it as the "Westville Program." The idea is to pool various funding sources such as HOME, Brownfields, CIP, Economic Development Loans, etc., and solicit proposals that will access multiple funding sources and be more comprehensive. Hopefully, we will be able to partner with the CDCs and other development entities to come up with some projects that might transform some of our disadvantaged neighborhoods into places where people thrive.

I am attaching a very rough description of the "Westville Program" for your review. Can we meet earlier than next Thursday? I want to run this by you before it goes much further. I will call you in the morning.

Thank you—as always,
Frank

And so Frank went to bed that evening thinking that just maybe they had something cooking.

*****

The next morning Frank Clark arrived at City Hall in good spirits and immediately set to work. First, he printed five copies of the draft he had written the night before with the thought that his initial audience in the following order of vetting was Walter Sage, Byron Swift, Roderick Campbell, and then Mayor Paley. The fifth copy was for him.

Second, he called Dr. Hearst and left a message on his voice mail following up on his email of the previous evening. Then he picked up his copies of the draft Westville Program outline and walked down to Walter's office to start the vetting process. Finding Walter away from his desk, he left a copy on his chair with a sticky note asking him to review it ASAP and then see him.

Frank then circled the office, casually dropping in on his staff to see how they were doing. Arriving back at his desk, he called Byron Swift and arranged to meet with him in an hour. He figured that would be plenty of time to hear back from Walter and tweak the draft if necessary. He then called Joan and arranged for the trio of Walter, Byron, and himself to meet with Roderick at 1:30.

Briefing Roderick

With Walter and Byron both having agreed that the draft outline of the Westville Program was good enough for discussion purposes, the

1:30 meeting with Roderick occurred as scheduled. The three of them had agreed that Byron, as the senior ranking person among them, should open the briefing and let Frank fill in the details. Walter could answer technical questions on any of the HUD funding issues.

Byron began: "We met late yesterday afternoon, Roderick, to strategize on a neighborhood initiative, and I think we've hit on something. Actually, the credit goes to Frank unless, of course, you like it," Byron said with a laugh.

"Really? What is it?" Roderick asked.

Byron continued. "We realized that even though we don't have much in the way of available CDBG funding, we *do* have HOME dollars and brownfield funds. Then, as we thought further, we realized the City also has CIP funds, water-tap funds, lead-abatement funds, and economic-development loan funds. So when you think about it, we actually have quite a bit of money that is not encumbered or even targeted at this time."

Roderick noticeably perked up. "Go on."

"So Frank suggested we put out a call for comprehensive redevelopment proposals and identify these funds as potential resources. One of the things we like best is that we are breaking down silos and seeing if we can get developers to tie these funds together to do something that can really change a neighborhood."

Roderick had been nodding slowly as Byron spoke. "Sounds interesting. How much money are we theoretically putting on the table through this?"

Byron responded slowly for effect. "Six point one *million* dollars," he said, a broad grin slowly forming as he said it.

Roderick let out a low whistle. "That certainly has a nice ring to it." Turning to Walter as the most experienced person in the field, he asked, "Is something like this really doable?"

"We've never done it, but I don't see any reason why we can't. To be honest, I think this could conceivably become a best practice in urban revitalization."

Roderick liked hearing Walter's response and was thinking the same thing. "How so?" he asked to see if Walter and he were considering the same factors.

"First, it breaks down funding silos which should have the effect of amplifying the impact these different programs have by creating synergy. Second, it asks developers to do something much more holistic and transformative than simply the same old same old. It might really generate some good projects," Walter said enthusiastically.

Roderick was encouraged that someone with Walter's knowledge and experience endorsed the concept. "So you are mentioning different funding programs, including brownfields, and saying you want particular types of projects. You aren't talking about putting housing on contaminated factory sites, are you?"

Walter and Byron looked to Frank, deferring to him for that answer. "I don't envision that. I am primarily thinking that some of the commercial buildings along the commercial corridors would need some environmental investigations and maybe a little remediation so that they can be repopulated as mixed-use buildings."

"I see." Roderick thought for a moment. "So what else are you anticipating you will be asking respondents to address or propose in their applications for funding?"

Frank continued. "Well, . . . I think we need more density in order to bring back a little neighborhood retail and other services, which in turn would appeal to people. They would get more than just subsidized housing. They would get a place where they can actually *do* things."

"What kind of density are you talking about?"

"I think we need people on the sidewalks. So having people living above some of the commercial buildings would help. Some of those old lofts and flats are still there, but they need total rehabbing. And maybe a small apartment building here or there could be rehabbed. If we don't get a lot more people, the businesses aren't going to make it."

Roderick thought again, this time longer than the first. "Boy, you are really stepping in it, Frank. Renters and apartments are four-letter words in most neighborhoods." Roderick paused, and the trio thought for sure he was about to shoot their idea down. Then he broke the tension.

"When I was growing up in Creekside, there was a heck of a lot going on, things to do, places to eat and shop. And there were a *ton more people*. It's pretty obvious that neighborhood desertion isn't good for business. Heck, when I was a child, we even had a small motel which all the people of color frequented. They may not have been banned from the major chains, but they sure as hell felt more at home in the Shady Elm.

Then, to the team's relief, Roderick concluded with "Do you have any of this written up so I can review it in more detail?"

"Yes sir." Byron handed one of the draft Westville Program sketches to Roderick.

Roderick glanced at it, and then sizing it up as a concise document, he began reading it out loud—slowly, in order to better gauge how it came across to a new reader or audience.

The Westville Program is intended to spur the undertaking of comprehensive urban development projects by coordinating funding opportunities from traditionally disparate programs with the goal of transforming some of Westville's urban neighborhoods into more complete communities where people truly thrive.

"That's a nice sentence, but it is a heck of a mouthful, particularly where I come from. And I don't know about this last point, 'more complete communities where people truly thrive.' It's great stuff, but way too academic. How about something like this:

The Westville Program coordinates City funds to bring jobs and housing back to our oldest neighborhoods with the goal of creating neighborhoods where our people can live full lives and raise healthy families.

Making quick eye contact with Frank and Walter, Byron sensed their concurrence and said, "I think we can do that."

"Good. Now let's look at this next one."

We envision neighborhoods that have sufficient population density to support neighborhood-based businesses and other enterprises that provide the amenities and positive energy that make urban living appealing for a wide range of people.

"This is okay, but it's the same as the prior one. How is this?"

Recognizing that neighborhood businesses need neighbors, the City of Westville is willing to consider proposals that will increase population density, provided they meet the highest design standards.

Byron agreed without the need to confirm with the group.

"Okay. Here's the third one:

We envision neighborhoods featuring walkable commercial corridors that offer an attractive alternative to suburban living and wholesome environments for households of all types. Neighborhoods that have active, pedestrian-friendly sidewalks that build and strengthen a sense of community as well as provide a more nurturing developmental and entrepreneurial ecosystem.

"I think this comes a little closer than the others, but I don't want to directly take on the suburban lifestyle." He thought for a moment. "How about something like this?

We envision neighborhoods where people can walk to find places to eat, shop, and visit with their neighbors. Neighborhoods that build identity, strength, and entrepreneurship.

This time the group concurred in unison.

"Okay." And then Roderick elevated his gaze from the outline to them. "Really, this is good stuff. I'm just adding a little seasoning to it."

The three of them made it clear that they understood. Frankly, they were relieved and practically overjoyed to have made it this far.

"So . . . here's the next one:

The goal of the Westville Program is to generate outstanding projects—not test an organization's technical expertise or proposal draftsmanship.

In consideration of this, and in recognition of the fact that interested development entities may not be fully familiar with the requirements for obtaining and complying with these wide-ranging funding programs, City personnel are available to work with entities on their proposals. Interested parties are strongly encouraged to avail themselves of this opportunity for staff consultation.

"I think that is good as is. Everyone agree?"

"We're not going to argue with that!" Byron said with a laugh.

"Good." Then Roderick silently read the table of funds and the remainder of the outline to himself. "I think the rest of it looks good. There's only so many ways you can give people the details. The Mayor is up in Harbor Springs spending Memorial Day weekend with the Richardsons, but I am scheduled to call him in about half an hour. I will run it by him and also ask him about the application due date, which you obviously had to leave blank. Of course the due date is necessary only if he likes the program, which I think he will. I'll let you know when I hear from him. Until then, nice job!"

Frank returned to his office a little after 2:00 feeling confident they were on the right track. When he got to his desk, he listened to a voice mail from Dr. Hearst saying he was available to meet at 3:30 that afternoon. Frank immediately returned the call and set up a meeting for 3:30.

Frank then called Michael Casey at Environmental Services and filled him in on the new concept. Michael's brownfield funds were an important funding source, and he deserved the professional courtesy of advance notification. Michael had no objection. He liked the strategy; and, given the short time frame for applying for the program's funding, he would know within a couple of months whether any of the projects were likely to utilize the brownfield money. That would still allow plenty of time to implement a program for expending the balance of the funds.

CHAPTER 21

At 3:30 that afternoon, Frank Clark walked into Dr. Harold Hearst's office. Dr. Hearst was upbeat, almost gleeful. "Congratulations, Frank! I think you've really hit on something here! What a simple approach—simply pool funds and tell people what you would like to see them do to create great places. I'm really amazed we haven't always done this."

"Thank you, Doctor," Frank replied calmly but cheerfully. Dr. Hearst's enthusiasm went a long way towards alleviating his concern that the concept was so simple that it might not be that good. "I really appreciate your help, and I'm glad you think it makes sense."

"I think it makes a lot of sense, but the proof will be in the pudding. I've been thinking about challenges with its rollout and implementation." As Dr. Hearst said this, he walked over to a small round table in his office and motioned Frank to have a seat.

Frank continued the conversation as he sat down. "Good! The Mayor told Roderick Campbell an hour ago that he wants to announce it Wednesday afternoon with a press event followed by a more detailed briefing session for the CDCs and any other interested developers."

Dr. Hearst grimaced slightly. "That's awfully quick, but then again he is under a lot of pressure to do something to counterbalance his proposed budget cuts."

"Yes, I think that's a big part of it. In the meantime, we need to get our own staff up to speed. They're expected to provide technical advice to potential applicants. Proposals are due in six weeks."

Dr. Hearst nodded. "That's a very good part of this program. I am glad you are not testing their knowledge, as you say in the overview. It's a quick deadline, but it looks like the program is designed to have flexibility and work with groups that have some gaps in their proposals."

"Yes," Frank replied. "If they are on the right track, we can continue to work with them to flesh it out."

"Good. I have a couple of thoughts. Would you like to hear them?"

"Definitely," Frank said as he got his pen and paper ready.

"One of the best things is that even though the projects are hopefully going to be relatively ambitious by Westville neighborhood development standards, they should still be off the radar screen of powerful pressure groups like the building trades unions and large businesses that might want the funds for their own projects. There will be conflict regarding which projects get funding and how much the funding will be, but they shouldn't involve any political behemoths that can commandeer the program.

"Of course, there is also a downside to that. The projects that score the best aren't likely to have really powerful allies to help push them through City Council for final approval of funding. That's a potential problem because it is critical to concentrate funds in order to generate a meaningful, catalytic impact. The proponents of projects that don't score well are going to want the City to de-concentrate its neighborhood investments and 'spread the peanut butter thinly over all the bread.' That is exactly what we cannot allow to happen."

Frank looked up from his notepad. "I agree. I've been concerned about that. Some of the smaller groups are not going to survive if they don't get funded through this, so the political heat could be pretty intense."

Dr. Hearst nodded slightly. "Exactly. But strategic mergers among some of the CDCs wouldn't be a bad thing."

"They will definitely have a shotgun-wedding feel to them," Frank observed.

Dr. Hearst nodded. "Yes. But these types of mergers require the surrendering of power from one group to another, and that generally doesn't come about voluntarily."

"That's true," Frank concurred.

Dr. Hearst resumed his thoughts regarding the decision to pool the City's funding programs. "Getting back to this new initiative . . . it is going to be very important to choose only two projects if at all possible."

"I agree. We don't really have that much money, and the projects really need to elevate the areas they focus on."

"Exactly. There's another important consideration I've thought about from time to time over the years. Since we've begun our consultations, I've been thinking more intently about it," Dr. Hearst said with a bit of gravity.

"What's that?" Frank asked with curious anticipation.

"These projects, whatever they turn out to be, will be embedded in what I think of as 'triple weak markets.' First, they will obviously be in weak market neighborhoods. Second, those neighborhoods are further embedded within a city that is a weak market, which is itself embedded within a region that is also a weak market. This broad and deep prevailing weak market is the primary basis for the beggars-can't-be-choosers mass psyche that we talked about last week."

Frank nodded. "I see what you mean. Please continue."

"We've already determined that Westville needs to do really exceptional projects to transform itself into a competitive urban city. The problem is that the private sector doesn't have confidence that the market is strong enough to bear the cost of a really good project. So the City, which has very limited funds, nonetheless has to provide greater subsidies and incentives to bridge the gap between the quality we need and the limited investment that developers are willing to make. If our disadvantaged neighborhoods were located in stronger city and regional markets, developers would be more optimistic about the market and willing to aim higher."

Frank interrupted and finished the thought. "So we need to avoid overextending ourselves in order to provide the deeper financial support the best projects will require."

"Correct. We don't know what projects this initiative is going to generate, but if it works according to plan, the projects will be very broad and aspirational. Westville barely has funding to support two such projects, maybe only one."

Frank smiled wistfully, "And if only two projects get funding, there will be fewer allies as we try to move ahead."

"Yes. Unfortunately, that is the inevitable result. So this is a really good concept, maybe an outstanding concept, but we won't know for sure until we see how it works in reality. At any rate, it's getting late on this beautiful Friday afternoon, and you've had a good week, my friend," Dr. Hearst said with gleaming, broad smile. "I am sure we will have lots to talk about, so keep me in the loop."

"Thank you, Doctor. Have a great holiday weekend!"

"You too Frank—you've earned it!"

As Frank walked to his car, his thoughts alternated between appreciating the beautiful sunny afternoon that promised a fantastic Memorial Day weekend and feeling consternation that the summit of every hill in Westville's revitalization seemed to reveal three more behind it.

That evening he received the customary summary email from Dr. Hearst.

> Frank—As always, it was good talking with you this afternoon. Your funding strategy has tremendous potential, but we have to see how it plays out in the real world. You have an exciting and potentially treacherous journey ahead of you. Whatever you end up calling this new Westville program, it picks winners and losers, and

that is always dangerous. Regardless, you should take great satisfaction in your accomplishments to date. I think the main point from today's session regards triple weak markets:

1. *Westville's disadvantaged neighborhoods are embedded in triple weak markets.* First, the neighborhoods themselves are weak markets that have been losing population. Second, those neighborhoods lie within a city that is a weak market which has been steadily losing population and neighborhood retailers and service providers for decades. Third, the city itself is located in a region that is a weak market whose population has been stagnant during a period of intense national population growth. As a result, developers have little confidence in Westville. When neighborhoods that are losing people are located within cities and regions that are not growing, there is very little reason to optimistically believe that "if we build it, they will come." Consequently, developers tend to aim low; and, as we discussed at our previous session, the community develops a beggars-can't-be-choosers mentality in which caution and acquiescence to cheap development projects are the orders of the day.

CHAPTER 22

An Eventful Holiday Weekend

Although it was Memorial Day weekend, Frank went into the office for a few hours on Saturday morning as was his custom. During that time he caught up on his routine paperwork and, more importantly and interestingly for him, modified the NOFA in accordance with Roderick's direction. He dropped the term NOFA as being too technical and substituted it with simpler "request for proposals" or "RFP" language.

Late that morning, Frank drove home feeling that he had gotten a head start on what promised to be a very busy and eventful holiday-shortened week.

When he got home he glanced at the morning paper, the delivery of which had been delayed for some reason. In it he quickly spotted the following column by Tom Folks:

Community Development Faces Reality Check

> Mayor Paley took a lot of heat recently for making the tough choices that come with the job as mayor. He is seeking approval to cut the funding to outside agencies working in neighborhoods and to bring the impound/tow lot in-house. In doing so he is incurring the wrath of the not-for-profit sector as well as private

249

towing companies. So why did he do this? To preserve City jobs—primarily policemen and firemen.

The neighborhood not-for-profit groups roundly criticize the mayor for proposing cuts to their funding, but what else is he to do? The city jobs that were saved provide critical services to the same distressed neighborhoods and populations the CDCs and social service agencies serve. City Council should support the mayor's recommendations and approve these painful, but necessary, funding cuts.

This is not to say that the not-for-profit agencies do not add value to the neighborhoods and clientele they serve—they do. Nor is this to say that they deserve to have their funding cut—they don't. But hard times make for hard decisions, and there are many not-for-profit organizations that fulfill their missions without any financial support from the city. The community development and social service organizations would be wise to emulate their fellow nonprofits by increasing their efficiency, becoming more relevant to their constituencies, and beefing up their independent fund-raising programs. These are tough times in Westville, and they bring tough decisions. The mayor should be applauded for standing firm and doing his job.

*****

Roderick Campbell began his Memorial Day by brewing a pot of coffee, reading the paper, and processing some routine paperwork. Around 10:00, not wanting to chance the possibility that the Y would be closed for the holiday, he decided to take a jog around the neighborhood. He figured that would also give him an opportunity to take a look at his neighborhood in relationship to the new funding program they were going to propose to Red the following day. He was optimistic that Frank and the crew had hit on something good, but it seemed too simple to be effective. "After all, why wasn't something like this an established practice?" he thought to himself. Not that the idea of doing something like the Westville Program was great, but it did seem pretty good—maybe too good, maybe too easy to be viable.

Jogging the couple of blocks over to Elm Street, he confirmed his feeling that the housing on the block closest to his townhouse was still in pretty good shape. The homes were owner-occupied and well-maintained, with a blend of retirees and working families. On the other hand, when he hit Pine Street, which ran parallel to Elm Street and was only one block removed from it, the environment was noticeably worse. Roderick deviated from his intended route of going straight to Elm Street and instead took the parallel route down Pine.

As he proceeded down Pine, Roderick was puzzled. According to what Byron, Frank, Walter, and he had talked about, it seemed logical that this block would be more stable because it was strategically located next to the shops, banks, and other neighborhood amenities that used to populate Elm Street. The homes looked like they were originally very nice, some even grand. But many of them were in substantial disrepair, several were vacant, and two had been spared from demolition by the concerted efforts of historic preservationists and Creekside CDC. They sat empty and boarded up, waiting for a better day to bring them back to life.

As Roderick pondered this neighborhood devolution, he developed a premise that the "location value" those homes once derived from being adjacent to a thriving commercial corridor was completely reversed when Elm Street deteriorated into a collection of skid-row bars and vacant buildings, and the site of crimes that included muggings, sexual assaults, homicides, and arsons. He even recollected that some of the homes on Pine Street that backed up to the rears of the buildings on Elm Street had sustained damage from fires in the Elm Street buildings. Almost with the flip of a light switch the location had been reversed from appealing to appalling. Many of the buildings had been carved into multiple apartments, several of which had since joined the ranks of abandonment.

Turning right on Creek Road, Roderick tried to imagine the impact a reinvigorated Elm Street might have on Pine Street. It was a tall order to energize the corridor, but maybe doing so *could* bring streets like Pine back from the dead. He could definitely appreciate that they didn't have the resources to tackle more than two or three of these initiatives. "Hell, we might not even have the resources to do one," he said to himself.

Approaching Creekside Park, Roderick could smell charcoal burning. "It'll be good to see someone taking advantage of it for once," he thought to himself. When the park came into view, he saw it was much more than that. Suddenly he recalled that Creekside CDC was having a Memorial Day picnic that day. The park was freshly mowed and trimmed—not nearly as ratty as it had been a few nights earlier. It looked like about a dozen people were in various stages of preparing for the day's festivities. One man with a paintbrush was undoing the "Worstville" vandalism that, as Pam had predicted in her tour with Frank, had recently been done to the park sign. Seeing

Pamela King setting up some tables in the picnic shelter, he slowed his pace and walked up to her.

"Hello, Pamela. It looks like you're going to have quite a party today!" he said with a grin.

Pamela had been too busy to notice Roderick's approach, but she quickly recovered. "Roderick, I'm glad you stopped by. Can you stay for our picnic?"

Despite his introversion and the fact that he had seen his family at baseball and softball tournaments that his nieces and nephews were competing in during the past two days, Roderick was feeling a subconscious desire to congregate with people. "You bet! I've got to clean up a little, but I'll be back in an hour."

"Good! We should have plenty of food coming off the grill by then," Pamela cheerfully replied.

Roderick smiled broadly. "I'll be sure to bring my appetite."

"Yes. And be sure to bring that smile with you. We don't see nearly enough of it," she said, flashing an equally broad smile.

Still smiling, Roderick turned, and as he resumed his morning run, he cut his loop short and made a beeline to his home.

When Roderick returned to the park an hour later, the picnic was in full swing with over a hundred people in attendance. He saw Pamela sitting at a table with a couple of her board members and Ella Rickman. Spotting him, Pamela waved him over. "We've saved you a seat, Roderick. Grab some food and join us!" she said with genuine enthusiasm.

"I'll be honored. Thank you," Roderick replied and headed to the picnic buffet. Walking back to the table with his full plate, he realized it was going to be his turn to be grilled by Pamela and the rest of the table. He knew they weren't going to pass on this opportunity to lobby for a better shake from the City.

After a few minutes of pleasant but mundane chatter about the weather, the food, and the good turnout for the picnic, Roderick asked an innocent question that proved to be the perfect segue for a conversation about the community-building value of Creekside CDC.

"The park sure looks a lot better than it did when I was here a few days ago. Did you get Bill Zawodny's crew to mow it again for you?"

"No," Pamela replied. "We had about a half-dozen volunteers come in on Saturday and mow it. We divided the park into sections and assigned a section to each of them." And then she began her agenda. "That's something Red doesn't seem to understand. Our impact goes way beyond housing."

"I think the Mayor understands more about the role you play than he lets on," Roderick said politely. "Besides, the real villain in this is Congress. They're the ones who cut the Block Grant."

"Yes," Ella Rickman said softly, staying within the boundaries of friendly picnic conversation. "But Red's the one who turned a ten-percent cut from Washington into a thirty-three-percent cut for us. That's just not right."

Roderick remained calm, and chewing his food gave him time to compose his response. Besides, he knew what he was getting into when he agreed to come to the picnic. Plus there was some value in hearing more from their perspective, particularly in the relaxed setting of a picnic. Swallowing his greens, he spoke.

"I concede his approach was a little heavy-handed. . . ."

Pamela interrupted: "Yeah, going to Tom Folks with his side of the story. Boy, he plays that guy like a fiddle."

Roderick nodded slightly and continued. "As I was saying, you can question his methods, but he really didn't have any choice in making the cuts. We all know the public-employee unions weren't going to let him lay off any of their own. Plus he has a good point when he says that the jobs he saved provide valuable services to the neighborhoods."

"That may be true," Ella said, still keeping her voice low and friendly, "but some of those code-enforcement inspectors are real deadbeats."

Roderick showed a trace of a grin. "Every organization, especially one as large as the City, has some employees who are better than others." Then, after taking a sip of his sweet tea, he added, "I think we are going to have some good news for you in a couple of days. We don't have a printing press in the basement of City Hall, but I think you'll see some opportunities for funding that you can get excited about."

"What? Tell us more!" Pamela said eagerly.

Roderick looked at them and, offering a slight smile, said, "I'd like to, but I've already said more than I probably should have. After all, it's the nature of this job that some things have to be kept confidential."

Despite their pleas, Roderick didn't share any more information. Their talk returned to general social conversation, and after about twenty more minutes, Roderick politely excused himself and headed home.

Surprise!

Tuesday began as usual for Roderick. He awoke at 6:00, brewed his morning coffee, shaved and showered, got dressed for work, and opened the daily edition of the *Westville Wire & Telegraph*. As usual, he began by scanning the local news section. Seeing nothing of particular interest, he turned to the editorial page, as was his custom. Then he set his coffee mug down and stared in disbelief.

An op-ed piece signed by Quincy Dewberry and Deacon Wilkens dominated the upper middle and right columns of the page. Titled "The Case for Community-Based Development," it set forth the importance of having community development corporations, governed by boards that included representatives from neighborhood residents and businesses, lead neighborhood redevelopment efforts in partnership with the City. The City's primary roles were to provide big-picture strategic thinking on behalf of the City as a whole, to target special services such as intensified neighborhood police patrols and property maintenance sweeps, and to provide funding—mostly CDBG and HOME dollars that flowed from Washington to the City. It summed up this point with the following provocative statement: "With strong board representation from neighborhood residents and businesses, CDCs practice community-based development, thereby ensuring that neighborhoods are lifted up rather than plowed under." This was an obvious reference to previous urban-renewal programs and Red's recent comment that he could fund hundreds of demolitions with the money that went to CDCs.

The op-ed piece then continued by recognizing the positive community-building work many of the CDCs did, such as providing after-school programs for children, organizing neighborhood cleanups, and promoting Block Watch and other initiatives to prevent and report crimes and suspicious behavior. The authors summed up this point by stating, "In performing these and many other important roles, CDCs ensure that neighborhoods are true communities, not just collections of buildings."

For its third point, the article directly responded to the Mayor's recent criticisms of the CDCs. It admonished the Mayor for focusing solely on housing production and not recognizing the broader community development role CDCs play. Then it tackled the housing production accusations head-on, noting the historical production of the CDCs and directly connecting the drop in the last two years to the City's failure to invest the HOME funds it received from HUD. It closed that point by stating, "It is duplicitous for the Mayor to cut off our lifeblood and then claim we are unproductive."

The op-ed concluded by alerting the readership: "The Mayor's current budget cuts threatened the very viability of the community development system. Community development is more important now than ever, and it requires funding. Without it, most, if not all, of these vital organizations will fail, and their failure will be our failure."

Steaming, Roderick took the paper and drove to work. While the article was signed by Quincy Dewberry and Deacon Wilkens, he knew it was primarily authored by the CDC directors themselves, and he couldn't believe that Pamela didn't give him a heads up at the picnic. When he got to his office, he picked up the phone and called Creekside CDC.

Recognizing Pamela's voice on the other end of the line, he began by saying, "Hello, Pamela, this is Roderick."

"Hello, Roderick," Pamela innocently replied. "I enjoyed talking with you at the picnic yesterday."

"Well, speaking of talking, what's this crap in the paper this morning? Why didn't you let me know?" Roderick's voice wasn't loud, but it clearly revealed his distress and anger at feeling betrayed.

Continuing her game, Pamela calmly replied, "Oh, you mean the op-ed piece?"

"Of course! Why didn't you tell me?" Roderick said sternly.

Pamela had been waiting for this possible moment since yesterday afternoon, and she delivered her lines perfectly. "Well, Roderick, I would have loved to tell you, but you know it's the nature of the job that some things have to be kept confidential."

Roderick was silent for a moment, realizing he'd been had. Then he replied, "Yes, but I think you will be pleasantly surprised by the news *we* are going to share. Thanks to this, my day just got a whole lot worse."

"I understand that, Roderick. But, of course, you understand that the City's new policies are going to make a lot of *us* have bad days—and for a very long time."

"I get your drift," Roderick said recognizing her point. "Still, it wouldn't have done you any harm to tell me. After all, there's no way we could have put the genie back in the bottle."

Pamela remained calm. "Exactly. And had I told you, I would have violated my colleagues' trust, and you wouldn't have derived any practical benefit. So why would I sacrifice my credibility and integrity to give you some useless information?"

Roderick knew he'd lost the debate, but he didn't want to concede that fact. "Maybe. At any rate, if things go the way I think they will, we will be contacting the CDCs about a meeting where we will fill you in on our new program. I'll talk to you then."

With that, the conversation concluded courteously, if not successfully, at least for Roderick. After hanging up the phone, he walked over to Joan's desk and asked her to let him know as soon as the Mayor arrived. They had an 11:00 meeting with him, and Roderick wanted to catch Red and deal with the op-ed piece beforehand if possible. Red was driving in from Harbor Springs, and Roderick figured there was a chance he would have the opportunity to break the news to him.

Unfortunately, Red arrived for their 11:00 meeting at 11:15, so there wasn't an opportunity to talk to him. Fortunately, Red had neither seen the paper nor heard about the op-ed piece.

CHAPTER 23

At 11:15 AM, Roderick, Byron, Frank, and Walter trailed behind Red as he entered his office. Red was jubilant, despite having gotten on the road at 4:00 AM to drive in from Harbor Springs. "Well done, Gentlemen! I understand we have a new neighborhood initiative that we can roll out tomorrow afternoon. That should take the heat off us."

Roderick spoke for the team, staying on topic as he had told them he would. "They've done a really good job, Mayor. I think this program can spur some outstanding neighborhood revitalization—real community building. Breaking down silos between different sources of funding should elevate the quality of the projects we see."

Red continued his roll and took an opportunity to school his team. "What it does, gentlemen, is enable me to announce a new $6 million program at the same time I'm cutting the City's budget. And they say I don't care about neighborhoods!" Red chuckled to himself as he was deriving immense satisfaction from the thought that he was once again outmaneuvering his political opponents. "You know, sometimes I think it's a crime I can't run for a third term."

Red was so caught up in his own success that he didn't realize that everyone else's spirits had just sunk precipitously. Of course, a limited degree of credit went to the others who, not wanting to risk Red's wrath, were doing their best to camouflage their emotions. Frank was particularly struck by the irony of Red's reaction and his hopeful comment to Pamela King just four weeks previously that"maybe we can come up with something so good, Red will jump on it because it's good for the community *and* for his career." That was exactly what was unfolding before his eyes, although it was obvious Red was infinitely more concerned about the *perceived* benefit to the neighborhoods than the *actual* impact it could have.

Roderick tried his best to make the situation more nuanced. "You've definitely outflanked them, sir. To top it off, I'm betting this program wins you a lot of support among some of our neighborhood residents, at least those who live near the winning projects."

Red brushed off Roderick's comments with another laugh. "You guys spend way too much time worrying about people who rarely vote and can't write checks," he scoffed. "As long as I don't lay off police and fire, keep the streets plowed, and pick up the trash, most of them are just going to sleep through every election."

Red thought for a moment and then continued. "One thing you said needs to be taken into consideration. Who knows what that is?" he quizzed the team.

Frank waited for the others, but Roderick wanted to share the floor, and the others were gun-shy. There wasn't much upside to speaking up, so they weren't going to unless specifically addressed. "The downside is that we alienate all the other neighborhoods that aren't selected," Frank volunteered.

"Exactly! And how do we handle that, Frank?" Red asked continuing his quiz.

"I think we can largely ignore it. Nothing terribly exciting has been going on, so how worked up about it can the average resident get? I'm thinking the opposition will be limited to board members,

CDC employees, and a few volunteers. That can't be all that many people. We just need to make sure City Council doesn't over react to a little pressure like they usually do."

"Go to the head of the class!" Red exclaimed. He was excited that Frank was thinking like him, and Frank was equally embarrassed that he had found it so easy to do so.

Red continued his march. "Those spineless jellyfish on City Council cower in fear whenever it gets a little warm in the kitchen. Harry Truman would give all of them the boot. And they're such bird brains they can't distinguish between a mountain and a molehill. So they're going to think the opposition is greater than it is. For their sake we'll have to make sure they talk to and see as many supporters as possible."

Frank remained silent and tacitly ceded the floor to Roderick. "Right, Mayor. We have the plan here if you want to take a look at it before it goes live tomorrow." Roderick held up Frank's latest draft, so that Red could easily see that it was only a page and a half. He knew Red wouldn't have the patience for any serious reading.

Red reluctantly took up his offer. "Oh, all right. I'm glad you guys kept it short for once."

Roderick handed it to Red, who, reading the heading, immediately opened up. "Request for Proposals!" Red exclaimed. "This isn't a goddamn RFP! This is a new game changer. We need to give it a name with some pop!" Then he began musing out loud. "We've got to have 'Westville' and 'Neighborhoods' in the heading. Hmm, . . . if we add an 'I' between them, we have 'WIN.' That will certainly have a good ring to it. What can the 'I' be?"

The group bandied about several words including Innovate, Inspires, Instills, and Involves. Then Walter said, "How about 'Investing in'? Isn't that what we're doing?"

"Bingo!" Red shouted. "That's perfect! *Westville Investing in Neighborhoods.*"

Red then proceeded to glance at the document for a couple of seconds before pronouncing, "I'm sure the rest of this is fine. Set up the press event for tomorrow."

"There's one more thing, Mayor," Roderick said somberly.

"What's that?" Red asked impatiently.

"The CDCs put an op-ed piece in the paper today, signed by Dewberry and Wilkens. They're calling us out pretty badly." Roderick pulled the editorial page out from his folder and handed it to Red.

Red took it from Roderick saying, "That is so like Dewberry to counter with an op-ed. I'm sure it was his idea. Hell, he probably wanted the paper to print a retraction. At any rate, the *Wire & Telegraph* will love a little give-and-take from us on this—it's got to help their readership."

Speed-reading the op-ed, Red handed it back to Roderick with his answer. "This is a bunch of bull. They think they've got a political following? They've got nothing. And when we announce our WIN program tomorrow, they're going to look like ignorant beggars!" And then, looking at all of them, he concluded, "Full steam ahead!"

Rolling out WIN

Wednesday afternoon came, and with it Red's press conference. Red's energy level even exceeded his level during his hubcap announcement of the previous week, because he was very proud of *his* accomplishment—cutting the budget and simultaneously rolling out the WIN program. But first he took a moment to chastise the CDCs for "begging for City funds" and "attacking *me* in a misinformed op-ed piece. For *I* am rolling out a new neighborhood initiative."

In announcing the program, Red made a point of extolling his prowess at "turning lemons into lemonade." He then proclaimed, "This innovative community initiative follows up on our superb employee recognition program." By the time he finished, he had nearly chiseled his own likeness into Mount Rushmore. And then, as usual, after firing off his own version of a twenty-one-gun salute on his behalf, he turned it over to Frank and Byron to handle the technical briefing with the development community.

The technical briefing began immediately following the press conference. In the same council chambers where Frank had announced major budget cuts just eight days earlier, Byron Swift and he were now at the podium describing the Westville Investing in Neighborhoods program. They were joined by Michael Casey to describe the details of how his brownfield funds could be utilized as well as by representatives of Economic Development, Water, and Public Service to describe how their components of the WIN program could be used. Walter Sage was also there, but it was presumed that the developers already knew how to access the HUD programs that were their traditional sources of City funding.

Byron began by welcoming the CDCs and other developers to the meeting. He then described the primary features of the program: the cobbling together of various funding programs and a call for more-comprehensive proposals with the potential to create vibrant neighborhoods of opportunity. He emphasized that proposals that leveraged ongoing positive momentum in neighborhoods, such as new schools, libraries, and other investments, would be more favorably received. "Create synergy with other existing or planned investments and do projects that will attract additional private investment," he said encouragingly. He then gave credit to Frank for thinking of the program and turned the microphone over to him.

Frank emphasized that the City was anticipating that the strongest proposals would utilize collaborations with other agencies, including social-service providers, in order to be more holistic. Frank further stressed that all of the City departments that were making funds available were there to describe how their particular programs worked. More important, Frank noted, the City's personnel were available to provide guidance on how best to tap into various funds. He underlined the point that "this is not a test of your ability to figure out how programs work and write an essay or term paper. This is a quest to conceive excellent urban-redevelopment initiatives. With that in mind, we are here to help."

He then gave a brief overview of the timeline for applying for funding through the WIN program, and then he introduced the representatives from the other funding partners who described the workings of their programs. Following that, the floor was opened up for questions.

Bill Smith of North Towne CDC asked the first question. His organization didn't have strong financial reserves, and his questioning reflected that. "The description of the program you've handed out doesn't say how many projects will be selected, and the Mayor just said in his press conference that there would be *at most* three projects that go forward. Is that correct? If so, what funding can the other CDCs expect to receive?"

Byron replied that the Mayor's information was correct, and then he elaborated slightly. "Given the scope of the projects we are seeking, three is the most I can foresee us funding. It is possible that only two will be funded. I think the Mayor made it clear last week that he expects to see some consolidation among the CDCs. As we look at how we allocate the reduced funding for next year's budget, I think we will expect to see these strategic consolidations take effect."

"In other words, there aren't going to be as many of us going forward," Bill Smith replied.

"Unfortunately, that's probably correct." Byron said flatly.

Pamela King then asked a question. "You aren't giving us much turnaround time for something as expansive as this. Do you think six to seven weeks is sufficient, especially with summer vacations?"

Byron responded to that as well. "We know it's an aggressive timetable, but we are making our staff available to help you. Further, we know that all of you have strategic plans, concepts, even wish lists for projects. We think you can flesh these out pretty quickly. Finally, your proposals don't have to include fully baked projects. We are here to help you get to the next level, which is comprehensive development. As you work with City staff to develop your concepts, we will be available to help you work through the details. This is new territory for all of us, and as we work together, we will be able to get more clarity."

There were a few more questions, including one regarding how close together the various parcels in a larger project had to be in order to be deemed synergistic. Frank replied that there could be no hard-and-fast rule regarding the geography, and that it would be determined on a case-by-case basis. However, the proponent would have to be able to make a convincing argument that the uses of buildings more than a few blocks apart nonetheless mutually benefitted each other and could generate synergy. After about twenty minutes of questioning, the meeting ran out of steam. The CDCs basically needed more time to ingest and process the Westville Investing in Neighborhoods program before probing more deeply.

CHAPTER 24

The rest of the week was fairly uneventful, as if a truce had been declared while people tried to make what they could of Red's budget cuts and the WIN program. Westville City Council was scheduled to vote on the revised budget next week. The CDCs as well as the social-service agencies tried to do a little behind the scenes politicking, but, as Red predicted, the preservation of union jobs easily trumped their efforts. Even the WIN program, which had yet to accomplish a thing, assisted the Council by giving them something to point to with some degree of optimism. While Frank was pleased the program was getting good initial reviews, he was disappointed to hear it used as a rationalization for cutting Block Grant funding to groups that were critical partners in neighborhood revitalization.

On Monday and Tuesday of the following week, Frank was able to take a break from the local shenanigans while Michael Casey and he attended the Great Lakes Brownfields Workshop in Detroit. Hosted by Wayne State University at their midtown Detroit campus, it was jointly sponsored by the United States Environmental Protection Agency and a leading philanthropic foundation. The workshop was for communities that had received or applied for brownfield funds in the past two years. The goal was to elevate performance in that emerging sector of urban redevelopment by sharing best practices and new strategies. Michael's suggestion that Frank attend worked out perfectly. The program had two tracks: a technical track for environmental engineers and a redevelopment track for economic and community developers. Michael attended the first track, and Frank the latter.

After a brief registration and coffee networking session, there was a workshop-wide plenary session in which a speaker from EPA and a speaker from the foundation enthusiastically talked about the general purpose of the conference and the potential for brownfield redevelopment to play a key role in rejuvenating America's urban core. Afterward the workshop broke into its separate tracks for the balance of the morning. Following the redevelopment track, Frank attended two sessions that morning.

The first session was an overview of the enormity of the brownfield problem in the Midwest. The first speaker was a professor of urban studies at Wright State University. He addressed the fact that the abandoned factories that largely resulted from globalization and a realignment of the world's manufacturing base were the primary cause of the brownfield problem, as was urban sprawl, which resulted in a mass outmigration of the urban consumer base and the closure of central-city commercial properties. Other factors such as changing retail trends (primarily the continued evolution of big-box retailers) and obsolete industrial properties were also identified as factors. Many of the industrial sites that were once strategic because of their access to railroad spurs were now obsolete because of their distance from interstate highways. Moreover, any factory that was multistoried was now automatically obsolete.

The second speaker was from US EPA Region 5's headquarters in Chicago. He picked up the baton from the brownfield historian and talked about the immediate impacts of brownfields on America's cities. The speaker went on to note that blight discourages investment, and consequently "blight begets blight." As an example, he pointed to the most recent application for US EPA Brownfield Funds by Toledo, Ohio. Toledo projected that if recent population trends continued, the

2000 Census would reveal that approximately ninety-four percent of Toledo's population loss over the past thirty years occurred in less than half its geographic footprint, which was comprised of distressed Census tracts in which most of its brownfield properties were located. Toledo collectively designated these distressed Census tracts as its "Brownfield Impact Area." Frank made a note to see if Westville's brownfield statistics would be similar.

The second session focused on redevelopment strategies and was kicked off by Lisa Seelbach, Director of Rust Belt Renaissance (RBR), a new initiative in which many major national foundations were collaborating to fund urban-redevelopment strategies for Midwestern rust-belt cities. She began her presentation with a call to arms.

"I want to begin by applauding US EPA and the philanthropic community for sponsoring this workshop. Rust Belt Renaissance is a newly formed collaborative effort by leading foundations to jointly develop new strategies and techniques for urban revitalization in declining markets, provide funding to assist with fielding-testing those ideas in real-world communities, and then provide addition funding to scale-up the most successful strategies and see if they can be replicated in other similar communities and situations. It is my pleasure to be the director of this new initiative, and I am very excited to see that the philanthropic community is recognizing that we need to have more comprehensive development strategies, which includes incorporating brownfield redevelopment into our daily thinking and work regarding community redevelopment.

"Having said that, I am very concerned that out of roughly fifty participants in today's workshop, we only have about fifteen in this room—fifteen of you who are identifying with the community redevelopment side of brownfields. The other thirty-five attendees are engineers and scientists of various types. While fifteen of you is a start, it is not sufficient. As you and I realize, brownfields cannot be viewed simply as technical one-off projects. As our previous speakers noted, brownfields are urban cancers that must be eradicated as part of systemic urban revitalization. We at Rust Belt Renaissance are dedicated to advancing this strategic concept and engraining it in urban policy."

While Lisa Seelbach continued her presentation—addressing the level of funding that was available and how communities could apply for the funds—Frank was thinking "Hurrah! This validates what we are trying to do in Westville!" Since the session was about the size of a senior seminar, he figured he would probably have a chance to speak with Lisa briefly about Westville Investing in Neighborhoods.

After a brief networking lunch, the attendees boarded two buses and took an abridged, ninety-minute tour of some of Detroit's brownfield sites. Although the purpose of the tour was to see the abandoned factories, the view of the neighborhood devastation resulting from disinvestment and its resulting blight was unavoidable and appalling. In some instances, entire residential blocks no longer had a single inhabitable house left standing. It struck Frank that there were virtually no assets in many of the neighborhoods that a reinvigoration effort could center on and build off of. In fact, it was his opinion that many of the areas could honestly be said to be so decimated that they ceased to be neighborhoods at all. For now, any designation of these as "neighborhoods" was purely nostalgic history.

They arrived back at the conference center at 2:00 and once again divided into their two subject-matter cohorts. The afternoon track for the development cohort focused on three real-world brownfield sites that had undergone environmental site assessments and were awaiting redevelopment projects. With fifteen people in the development track, they were able to divide themselves into groups of five and plan out mock redevelopment schemes.

One group was working on a brownfield site that consisted of a fifty-year-old, 700,000-square-foot, former automotive supplier plant sitting on about forty acres near an interstate in Detroit. That group quickly determined that the best redevelopment scheme would be to demolish the outdated building, remediate the entire site, and market it to a developer for either a new industrial plant or distribution center that could capitalize on its location on the interstate highway system.

The second group evaluated a narrow, six-acre parcel that ran along a railroad in the South Side of Chicago. Frank immediately recognized from his reading of Jane Jacobs that although the railroad provided a valuable service, it was a rough "nuisance" border that made it very difficult to build a community nearby. At first the group thought that the need for affordable housing in Chicago might be so great that a subsidized housing project could be located there. However, after trying various schemes to buffer the residences from the railroad, they realized that this concept was not workable. As a result, they defaulted to a linear park that included parallel walking and biking trails and featured indigenous plants to promote environmental sustainability. They were concerned that the site might be a location for illegal dumping but did not have a real solution for how to avoid that possibility.

The third group was charged with redeveloping an early mall in Akron that had been dormant for a couple of years. As usual with malls, once a newer one comes along and has better stores and more sizzle, the older mall becomes tired and obsolete, and this dormant mall was no exception. After struggling for about ten years, it had finally closed. Located in the midst of early suburban neighborhoods, Frank hoped that the site could be redeveloped as an urban village that could feature a vibrant town center that the surrounding single-use residential neighborhoods lacked and dearly needed. Unfortunately, from his perspective, the group he was with couldn't see their way past taking advantage of the vast existing surface parking areas. Consequently, they proposed demolishing the mall and replacing it with a new office park that they believed could provide some employment opportunities for the nearby residents. Frank was disappointed, but as a newcomer to planning activities, he found the exercise interesting nonetheless.

Positive and Potential Reinforcements

During a midafternoon break, Frank found his opportunity to talk to Lisa Seelbach from the RBR program.

Frank politely introduced himself and then complimented Lisa on her opening remarks and the hypothetical planning exercise the group was engaging in. He then gave a thirty-second "elevator speech" on the Westville Investing in Neighborhoods program, which he told her went live last week. He didn't need to ask her for her thoughts on the new program.

"Wow! So you are telling developers you have funds available and this is what you would like to see, this is what would get your attention? I like that. It is very similar to how foundations work. I don't think it's very common for cities to be that prescriptive regarding the comprehensive nature of development projects, but it sounds very promising."

"Thanks. We're kind of going out on a limb with this. Proposals are due in mid-July. If you'd like, I'll keep you in the loop as things progress," Frank said with the hope of building a relationship with a major funder that could also endorse the WIN concept.

"Please do!" Lisa said, clearly expressing her interest in seeing how the WIN program might play out. After a moment's hesitation she continued. "You know, this is the something RBR might want to partner on. I like the way you are bringing all these diverse funding sources to the table."

"Thank you, Lisa. Here's a sheet summarizing the WIN program," Frank said, handing the summary that had been used with last week's rollout. "I will stay in touch."

"Fantastic. Oh, be sure to talk about this with the EPA people while you are here. They will be very interested in this."

This put Frank on cloud nine, and he couldn't wait to share this information with Dr. Hearst and his City team. "Potentially more resources for the WIN program," he thought to himself. "That will be fantastic!"

When he shared the news with Michael Casey at dinner that night, the two of them were in good spirits. It seemed like their new program might actually attract *real* outside funding.

"Maybe," they concluded over a beer, "Westville wouldn't be Worstville forever."

CHAPTER 25

On a rainy morning in a remote corner of a local coffee shop, Dr. Harold Hearst took a sip of his espresso and transitioned the conversation from opening greetings, compliments, and pleasantries to the matter on his mind.

"It turns out we have a mutual interest in our new Director of Neighborhoods," he said with a slight smile.

Dr. Camilla Johnson was pleasantly surprised. "Really? I'm glad to hear that. Frank seems like a nice, competent guy, and I hope he'll do a good job. It's a heck of a transition for him. How do you know him?"

"Yes, he is a good guy," Dr. Hearst replied. "I've met with him several times on the basics of urban revitalization. He has a real acumen for it. He told me you met with him regarding organizational development."

Dr. Johnson sipped her coffee before replying. She wasn't sure how much she should share and thought she would be a little vague until she knew how much Frank had told Dr. Hearst. "That's right. When I heard about his appointment, I thought it might be an opportunity to provide some consulting services similar to what I did with the University. I figured some strategic visioning around the department's goals, accountability, and team-building might be possible. But the conversation took a bit of a twist," she said careful not to disclose too much.

"Yes. He told me that he mentioned that others had cautioned him, and that you picked up on that." Then he added pensively, "I'm worried for him. He's diving into this with great enthusiasm, and he's grasping the concepts. Heck, this Westville Investing in Neighborhoods program that you might have heard about last week is his idea, and it just . . . might . . . work. But Red will throw him and anyone else to the wolves if he needs to. We may need to get ready to help Frank if that happens to him."

Dr. Johnson was relieved to see that Frank had obviously relayed their meeting in some detail to Dr. Hearst. But the fact that Dr. Hearst not only validated her concerns but was worried enough to talk to her was troubling. "He's an honorable man in a dishonorable environment," she said gravely. "I heard about the WIN program; it sounds like a good idea. I hate to say it, but either Red or the system he's in will eventually get him. The question is 'when?'"

Dr. Hearst scanned the room again to make sure they couldn't be overheard. "I don't know. The first milepost I see is in mid-July when the WIN proposals are due. That's when the City has to pick a couple of winners. At that point, the triumphant fanfare turns to hard reality, because picking winners also means that you are implicitly designating the others as losers. There's a lot of money at stake for these organizations, and that could be a triggering event. It will be immediately followed by mergers and dissolutions of the CDCs that are the least solvent. That consolidation stage is a second potential triggering event. Red's embracing the program and milking it for all it's worth, but he's also built up Frank quite a bit as the front man. He could be building him up just to set him up as the fall guy if necessary."

"What do you think we can do to help him?" Dr. Johnson asked worriedly.

"I don't know. Neither of us has the ability to find him a job if it gets that bad. Maybe all we can do is just be there in a supportive role for him."

"Yes. And stand up for him if necessary," Dr. Johnson added.

"Yes. We definitely will need to do that," Dr. Hearst said softly.

Then Dr. Johnson added another thought. "I'm sure we each know some member of City Council. If Frank needs some job protection, we can probably talk to them. It's one thing to cut the program or make him a whipping boy. It's another thing to have him suffer the disgrace of a demotion or worse."

"Good idea," Dr. Hearst replied. "In fact, Camilla, I'm thinking we may want to have a few of those conversations in advance. Red moves awfully quickly, and we may need to ensure that some Council members are ready to defend him immediately if necessary."

They continued chatting for another ten or fifteen minutes while they finished their coffee, but other than agreeing to talk to some Council members, all they could really do is spend more time mulling over the difficulty of the situation. Neither of them, nor any member of Council, was going to be able to throw Frank much of a lifeline if it came to that.

WIN Builds Momentum

During the weeks that transpired between the launching of the Westville Investing in Neighborhoods funding opportunity and the July 17 due date, the WIN Tactical Team, comprised of Byron, Frank, Walter, and Michael, was busy meeting with various CDCs, explaining the City's vision for the program and also answering a multitude of technical questions about eligibility requirements for the various pots of money that comprised the WIN funding.

Over that period of time, the enthusiasm that started among Frank and the team had spread like wildfire to many of the CDCs and other community groups as they began to delve into the WIN program and see the possibilities. Walter Sage came into Frank's office one day just to say, "Hey, Frank, I'm seeing something I've never seen. Some of these groups are moving from competition to cooperation to collaboration. It's really incredible! We've got CDCs and the Westville Metro Library District talking about putting housing within easy walking distance of libraries; we've got the Westville Transit Authority talking to another group about combining a bus transfer station with a childcare facility and a pharmacy. Father Affonso's working on something with John Nowak in Ironton. Pamela King's been asking a lot of questions about economic-development funding for entrepreneurs. I think we are going to get some really good proposals on July 17!"

News of the positive response to the WIN program reached Roderick, and on a Friday afternoon in late June he called Frank into his office. Motioning Frank to have a seat, he said, "Frank, I'm hearing really good things about the response to the WIN program. Are you getting positive signals as well?"

"Yes. It started slowly, but we are receiving very positive signals from most of the CDCs and other nonprofit organizations. Also, the questions they are asking and the requests for technical assistance indicate that they are really working on some unusual collaborations."

Roderick was very pleased to hear this. "Good! So what types of collaborations are you seeing?"

Frank took a deep breath as he quietly ran through some of the better projects in his head. Then he replied, "We've got the library co-locating with an early-childhood-development center and an after-hours tutoring program. I think that's in Abyssinian's district. We've got a small market in Ironton adding a local produce aisle that is going to be supplied in part by some new urban gardens and hoop houses at the Saint Dominic Savio House. Creekside CDC is looking into putting apartments above a thrift store. The Westville Health Alliance may co-locate a clinic with a drugstore, a preschool, and an indoor bus transfer station. Those CDCs and others are also looking at constructing some apartments to beef up the population along at least one commercial corridor in their neighborhoods. The team is pretty pleased with what we are seeing and hearing."

Roderick smiled. "You're certainly a fast learner, Frank. How do you do it?"

It was Frank's turn to smile. "Thanks, Roderick. I've had a lot of help. The staff has been very supportive and willing to give me a chance. But the biggest help has been from Dr. Hearst at the university. We've met several times, and he has been mentoring me. He also told me the best book to read is *The Death and Life of Great American Cities,* which Jane Jacobs wrote in 1960. It's the bible of good urban planning and revitalization."

"Hmm. That name Hearst sounds familiar to me. Where do I know it from?" Roderick inquired.

"He used to be on the Plan Commission. You might have heard it in conjunction with that," Frank surmised.

That refreshed Roderick's memory. "Right! He was pretty controversial as I recall, always speaking out in opposition to projects, even ones that were sure to be approved. I'm not sure if he was ever on the winning side."

"That's him," Frank replied. "I never paid that much attention to the Plan Commission, so I wasn't familiar with him. Based on our conversations, he probably was on the losing end of most decisions. He's a strong proponent of having very high standards for urban revitalization. According to him, we are way too quick to approve projects that ought to be revised or dropped altogether. And he believes we are paying the price for that today. I agree with a lot of what he says."

Roderick thought for a moment. "Yes. I've been thinking about our neighborhoods a lot—particularly in light of our budget cuts. Our problems don't seem to be getting any better."

"I agree," Frank said. "It's a real problem without any simple solutions."

"Yes," Roderick replied, nodding his head as he did so. "This book Dr. Hearst recommended, what's the title again?"

"*The Death and Life of Great American Cities*, by Jane Jacobs."

"Yes. You find it helpful?"

"Definitely! Jane Jacobs is a little long-winded at times, but her points on what it takes to have great vibrant urban neighborhoods are really sound. The four main points are the need for population density; a variety of uses or activities in neighborhoods—not purely offices, not purely residential; short blocks so pedestrians can make their way around more easily; and making sure everything isn't new, expensive construction so that eclectic Mom and Pop establishments that give a neighborhood its unique character can afford to be there. Also, she wrote it forty years ago and, noting the structural failures of various neighborhoods like the South Bronx, accurately predicted the demise of a lot of neighborhoods. So in my mind, that really validates what she says."

Roderick thought for a moment. "That's very interesting," he said. Then he added, "Well, I just wanted to check in and encourage you to keep up the good work. I'm glad you accepted this promotion. Let me know if anything changes."

"Thank you!" Frank said, and he returned to his department.

CHAPTER 26

The next day, a sunny Saturday morning, Frank Clark and Dr. Camilla Johnson sat on the patio of the same neighborhood coffee shop where they had first conferred less than ninety days earlier. To Frank, it seemed like a year or more of activity had transpired. He had learned a good deal about his new department, had dealt fairly successfully with a major funding crisis, and was developing a good understanding of the fundamental principles of good urban revitalization.

However, the purpose of their conversation was not to specifically discuss Frank's transition into his role as the City of Westville's Director of Neighborhoods. Frank had made the time to read *Good to Great* and, as Dr. Johnson had anticipated, found the discussion of Level 5 Leadership particularly interesting.

In Search of Level 5

Dr. Johnson was anxious to hear Frank's thoughts about her favorite book, so it didn't take her long to transition their conversation from vacation plans, the weather, and Frank's enthusiasm for the WIN program to organizational excellence. "So, did you find the discussion of Level 5 Leadership as interesting and provocative as I hoped you would?"

"Yes, I enjoyed it immensely," Frank enthusiastically replied. Thank you for referring me to it. It is unfortunate that Level 5

285

Leadership is so rare. You would think the people who hire CEOs would be more astute."

Dr. Johnson laughed slightly and said, "Yes, but, unfortunately, people frequently mistake braggadocio and rapid action for real leadership ability. Level 5 Leaders are so rarely found at the upper levels of organizations that most of us have never worked for one. I am quite certain I never have."

"I don't believe I ever have either," Frank replied. "I think maybe one or two at least exhibited some of those qualities. I spent a lot of time thinking about the tenet that Level 5 Leaders are aspirational first and foremost for the organization and then for themselves. When I mentioned it to a couple of my friends, they initially misunderstood it to mean that they were aspirational for the organization at the exclusion of their welfare and thought the idea was nonsense."

Dr. Johnson concurred. "Yes, I have had to explain that point from time to time as well. It's not a matter of one at the exclusion of the other. It's a matter of what primarily motivates you."

"It's also interesting that Jim Collins points out that Level 5 Leaders are frequently found in lower levels of organizations or as volunteers," Frank observed. "They not only get passed over by promotion in favor of the ones with the puffed chests, but my experience is they do a lot of the work in the trenches that enables the blowhards to succeed." He then took a sip of his coffee.

Dr. Johnson took the opportunity to explore Frank's current circumstances a bit more thoroughly. "Agreeing that Level 5 Leadership is very rare, what's your assessment of the leadership at the City?"

Frank set his cup down and responded quietly. "It's pretty bad, which is really tragic. After all, public service is where you would expect people to find it more natural to put an organization's interest first. But as far as I can tell, none of the elected officials do that. I think some of the management might. Maybe Roderick does, but I don't know him well enough to make that call."

Dr. Johnson leaned forward, getting to the meat of her interest in the topic. "So . . . I have a theory about Level 5 Leadership in the public sector. I think it is even more important, yet more difficult, to have Level 5 Leadership in government."

Frank was intrigued. "Why is that?" he asked curiously.

Dr. Johnson eagerly replied, but with quiet enthusiasm. (She was well aware of the fact that they were in a public venue, which could make Frank vulnerable in the event they were overheard.)

"In the private sector, the Level 5 Leader puts the company's interest ahead of their personal interest. So there are two dimensions to balancing ambitions and aspirations — the organization and the individual. However, it isn't sufficient for an elected official like Red Paley, for example, to only put the City government's interest as an organization ahead of his own interest. Red Paley has a third dimension that must be balanced if he is to be a Level 5 Leader. He has to put the broader Westville community's interest ahead of the City of Westville government's organizational interest. And of course he has to put his interest behind both of them. Now, sometimes the community and the government's interest are in alignment, and this third dimension to public-sector leadership isn't a problem. But often there are conflicts, and the City government's interest frequently prevails to the detriment, or the perceived detriment, of the community."

Frank leaned back in his chair and took a deep breath. Then, exhaling slowly, he leaned forward. "I hadn't thought of that dimension. It makes a lot of sense. Do you have a couple of examples we can discuss?"

Dr. Johnson smiled. "I'm glad you asked. Actually, one project in particular got me thinking about this a couple of years ago."

"Which one is that?" Frank asked.

"The new State Corrections facility in Westville."

Frank laughed quietly. "Oh, yes, that was pretty controversial!"

"Yes. If you recall, the neighborhood was upset that the jail was going to occupy a portion of parkland and also devalue the surrounding homes. So in their collective mind, constructing a jail there was not good for the community. On the other hand, the elected officials wanted the income-tax revenue the employees at the prison would generate. So from the elected officials' perspective, the prison was a new revenue source that was good for the City government's bottom line—in other words, they were thinking of the organization's welfare, but not necessarily the welfare of the greater community. I suspect that that happens very frequently."

"Yes," Frank replied and then, deciding to pressure-test her theory a little, he continued. "But the greater community has an interest in making sure the City government has sufficient revenue to provide the services they require."

Dr. Johnson nodded. "Yes, and it's possible that if they had done some analysis, they would have concluded that the new revenue and the services it could fund more than offset the negative impact on the community. But do you think they ever seriously pursued that analysis? I don't. I think they saw a chance to grab some revenue for the immediate benefit of the City and coupled it with a ribbon cutting for their personal benefit. The community's greater interest, which ought to be paramount, came in last."

It was Frank's turn to nod. "You are probably right." Then he sighed. "It's going to be a mighty tall order to find elected officials and other leaders who are willing to put their interests third. It reminds me of 'I'm Third,' which was the slogan at the YMCA camp I attended every summer. 'I'm Third,' means God comes first, everyone else comes second, and you come third. Finding people who meet the public-sector Level 5 Leadership equivalent of 'I'm Third' is going to be awfully tough."

Dr. Johnson sighed. "Yes, it is going to be very difficult, and I don't have an answer. Maybe the best we can do is be extremely vigilant citizen watchdogs on behalf of our community."

Frank smiled wryly. "Yes. We need to maintain a permanent vigilance, because our government is inherently flawed—but it's the best we can come up with." Then, laughing, he sarcastically added, "I am so glad you have further illuminated the shadowy world of public service beyond what I've already been experiencing."

After they both enjoyed a slight chuckle at Frank's gallows humor, Frank continued. "You know, Camilla, Westville's political, business, and civic leadership doesn't fare any better when analyzing the other elements of *Good to Great*. In particular, I'm struck by the fact that we fail to recognize—let alone confront—the brutal facts of our reality as a declining rust-belt city. We can't just keep shooting the messengers and pretending the consequences of our weakness—low housing costs, fewer traffic jams, and what not—are actually strengths. And we can't build momentum, to use the book's flywheel analogy[3], when each administration stops the previous administration's programs simply because 'they aren't our programs.' We have incredibly daunting challenges, but I'm hoping the WIN program can enable us to develop a strategy—like the book's hedgehog concept[4]—that we can do well and keep doing, keep improving. At the very least, I hope WIN can begin chipping away a little at our fundamental urban weakness.

"So do I," Dr. Johnson replied. "So do I."

That afternoon as Frank mowed his lawn, his mind wandered as it usually did. He thought about the conversation Dr. Johnson and he had had earlier in the day, as well as Westville's need to become a more compelling urban community. "Geez we have a long way to go," he thought to himself. "This community and its leaders have no idea what it takes to be a great city, no willingness to recognize the

---

[3] Loosely speaking, *Good to Great* identifies the "flywheel" phenomenon as one of the common characteristics of companies that achieved sustained excellence. The "flywheel" refers to the fact that these companies could not point to a singular event where they "threw a switch" and attained greatness. Rather, greatness was gradually attained over time as successful strategies, tactics and behaviors built momentum. For more information see *Good to Great*, Chapter 8.
[4] Another common characteristic of companies that achieved sustained excellence was the use of a "hedgehog concept" – the fanatical implementation of a simple strategy. This is in contrast to a "fox" that unsuccessfully leaps from one strategy to the next. For more information see *Good to Great*, Chapter 5.

fact that we are mediocre, and provide no leadership to build support and guide us there. The gap between what we are in so many dimensions and what we need to be in those same dimensions is enormous. If only we could take Jane Jacobs' planning principles and wed them to Jim Collins' management theories," he mused. "But this community can't be lectured to. It needs to be a softer transition." And then after a mowing a couple of more swaths he thought, "Maybe, just maybe, Westville Investing in Neighborhoods can help gradually weave these dimensions together by serving as a call to arms that focuses resources around a sustained strategy that gives the community and its leaders something to rally around." And then he had just one more solitary thought. "Maybe."

Initial Success

The WIN momentum continued, with added fuel provided by a positive column by Tom Folks, and on July 17 the City received six proposals. To the City leaders' pleasant surprise, several of the proposals involved collaboration among two or more CDCs—a bellwether of future consolidation that would be necessary given the overall HUD cuts. Three of the proposals for the lead entities were Ironton CDC, Creekside CDC, and the Abyssinian Progress Association, because they were by far the strongest. They were able to knit new housing with other neighborhood amenities in ways that offered the possibility of jump-starting the rebirth of their respective neighborhoods.

The WIN Tactical Team ranked the proposals and forwarded them to Red and Roderick. Frank also called Lisa Seelbach at the RBR collaborative and kept her in the loop. She was very pleased by the initial response and requested that Frank continue to keep her apprised of their progress with WIN. Frank was quietly ecstatic. It seemed to him that everything was falling into place.

CHAPTER 27

When Red Paley rolled out the WIN program with much fanfare on May 31 he intended to draw attention to it, and particularly himself. The resulting publicity gave him a shot in the arm, and he was very pleased by what he had managed to pull off. He really had managed to combine budget cuts with an exciting new initiative just as he had bragged about when reviewing the concept with Roderick, Byron, and Frank. One person who took note of the program, and more importantly, its accompanying funding was Leonard Malinowski.

Leonard Malinowski had been born and raised in the eastern European ethnic neighborhoods that populated Westville's north end. He started in the plumbing trades and worked as a journeyman for fifteen years. Then in the mid-1970s he bought a plumbing supply company that was a victim of the economic recession. Figuring there was more money to be made supplying the job than doing the job, and that there was always going to be a demand for plumbing, he placed his bet on going into business for himself. "Besides," he reasoned, "I can always go back to being a plumber and make a good living if I have to."

Leonard proved to be a good businessman, and he now was a self-made millionaire owning investment properties in Westville and Florida. But one of his investments hadn't panned out yet, and it was time to change that.

Leonard had purchased the Western Vista Hotel six years ago while it was in financial receivership. The hotel had struggled almost since the day it had opened in 1975. It was intended to work synergistically with the newly constructed River City Convention Center. Together, those buildings would be the showpiece of a rejuvenated downtown. The convention center struggled as did the hotel. Whether the hotel's losses were the result of bad management, bad location, a weak convention business, or other circumstances was of little consequence to Leonard. In his mind the hotel—like his first venture with the plumbing supplier—would be a good investment if the price were low enough. In a sense he used the same logic as when he purchased the plumbing supply company: "There must always be a certain threshold level of demand for downtown real estate which supports prices at a certain level below which there is never a long-term drop." But this time, the depressed market for the hotel was lasting much longer than he had imagined possible.

Leonard had operated the hotel at a loss for two years and then closed it down altogether. Now the burden of maintaining and paying taxes on a vacant property combined with the embarrassment of being well-known as the owner of a major downtown failure to prompt him into action. When Leonard saw Red Paley's announcement of the WIN program and all the funding that accompanied it in the *Westville Wire & Telegraph* he exclaimed, "Bingo!"

During the weeks that followed, Leonard Malinowski quietly met with his bank and retained an architect to put together a plan for completely overhauling his hotel. While his team was working on that, he secretly met with the Director of the River City Convention Center and convinced him to update a renovation plan that, due to a lack of funding, had been sitting on a shelf for five years. In mid-July, with his project and its financing needs pretty well roughed out, he made his first overt move.

Despite his reservations concerning Red's temperament, Leonard Malinowski had supported Red Paley's initial campaign for Mayor, but he had seen too much during Red's first three years as Mayor to support his reelection bid. Leonard believed in working hard - and playing hard - and he had no patience for Red's endless parade of sideshows and erratic policy changes. This led Leonard to support Red's Republican opponent when Red ran for a second term with the unfortunate result that he was now a political outsider. Consequently, Leonard had to begin building his political coalition by drawing on his ties with the County's leadership before meeting with Red. Leonard was able to do this and gain the County's modest financial support, conditioned on the City in turn making a major commitment to invest in *its* downtown. To do this, Leonard would have to rely on some old friends for support – who he had no doubt would come through for him.

*****

And so it came to be that on July 31, two weeks after the WIN proposals were submitted, Red Paley walked into Lonnegan's at 4:45. He had spent a good part of the afternoon with a chip on his shoulder—ever since 1:30 when he got the call from the leadership of the building trades unions summoning him to this meeting for the purpose of discussing a confidential major development project that they wanted him to support. The unions had played a major role in enabling him to win his reelection, and he knew he owed them every possible political favor.

Red also knew all too well that "support" meant money – something he didn't have in great supply. Financial support of whatever this new project was would have to come at the expense of his programs, and this was the root cause of the chip on Red's shoulder. Red was in his fifth year as Mayor, and he was becoming increasingly frustrated by the fact that he didn't have a chance to advance *his* agenda (for his own self-serving reasons). He was convinced that the WIN program could validate him as a political genius, but he sensed that whatever the unions were about to ask him for would nix that opportunity. He regarded himself, with some degree of validity, as a master navigator of political waters, but it was increasingly frustrating to him that he never had the opportunity to steer his ship of state in calm seas. Every time he turned around, another storm was brewing, whether it was Bobby Turkel making promises he couldn't keep, the Feds cutting his funding, the budget crisis worsening, the community development sector rebelling, or now, the building trades apparently about to call in their political markers.

Even Red, the great political admiral, was no match for the storms that were rocking his ship. "Just once," he thought to himself, "it would be nice to be in real control. Here I am the Mayor, and I am forever buffeted by forces outside my reach." What Red hadn't realized was that he was trapped within the confines of a systemically dysfunctional political biosphere that was probably beyond *any* politician's ability to control. And now that dysfunctional biosphere was careening out of control and carrying him along with it.

The 5:00 crowd at Lonnegan's hadn't arrived yet, and catching sight of Joe slicing some lemons and limes at the far end of the iconic wooden bar, Red quickly walked over to him. "Upstairs?" he asked, nodding toward the back stairway that led to the Oak Room.

"Yes, Red," Joe replied.

"Thanks. I'll take a double. I think I'm going to be pretty thirsty this evening."

"You got it, boss!" Then, handing Red a double Jameson on the rocks, Joe added, "By the way, Bonnie should be here soon. She'll be covering the room."

Red smiled and took a sip of his whiskey before slowly heading up the stairs. Bonnie was a busty strawberry blonde—an institution at Lonnegan's. She began working there before she was of legal age, and now in her early forties she could still turn heads. "Things always go down better with Bonnie," Red thought to himself as he continued walking up the stairway. No matter how bad the message he was about to receive, the whiskey and scenery would ease the pain.

Red reached the door of the legendary Oak Room, a private drinking den that was rumored to be the site of many an infamous evening. Rarely open, the Oak Room was reserved for use by Lonnegan's best customers at a premium price. By Red's own count, even he—a regular of substantial stature—had been in the room only about a dozen times.

The Best Laid Plans

Red entered the room slightly ahead of schedule and found the three ranking leaders of the Building Trades Unions sitting at the vintage marble-inlaid poker table, enjoying cigars and whiskey. The room was about 25´ x 40´, and the table was about fifteen feet from the door. A massive stone fireplace dominated the far wall. Along the

298 | Ford Preston Weber

wall to the immediate right of the table on a built-in dry bar sat a bottle of Jameson Irish Whiskey Special Reserve 12, a sterling silver bucket of ice, a tall pitcher of ice water, and a bowl of hard-boiled eggs.

Quickly taking the room in, and knowing his three hosts well, Red immediately tried to exude an aura of calm confidence as he walked toward the trio. "Gentlemen, how good it is to see you! Especially here in the Oak Room! Hopefully, you've arranged to have Bonnie keep us hydrated!" He then quickly shook hands with Billy Riley, President of the Building Trades; Stan Paulsen, First Vice President of the Building Trades; and Tony D'Antonio, Business Manager of the Building Trades.

Red then sat down in the unoccupied chair at the table opposite Billy Riley and took a sip from his glass. Billy Riley exhaled the smoke from his Macanudo and began talking. "Red, we're glad you could join us on short notice. This is an important occasion, and we arranged for this room, and for Bonnie," he added dryly, "in appreciation of this occasion. After all, we all share your fondness for Bonnie. I believe she comes on duty in a couple of minutes. Until then, being thirsty men, we were able to impose upon Joe for a bottle and the other provisions you see."

Red continued to maintain levity. "Looks like you've thought of everything. I'm certainly not disappointed." For a man about to have the heat turned up, he was very good at maintaining a relaxed, confident appearance.

Just then the door opened, and Leonard Malinowski walked in.

"Don't tell me you're part of this," Red said sharply.

"Relax, Red. We're on the same team now. I think you're going to like what we have in mind," Leonard replied. His voice reflected strength but also a degree of affinity. This was a meeting to build bridges, not walls.

Billy Riley jumped in. "Lenny's right, Red. This is a new day, and we have a proposition for you that's a real winner. It'll springboard you to the Governor's office." As Billy spoke, Leonard walked over to the dry bar and poured himself a drink.

Red smiled. "Billy, you certainly know how to get my attention, and I'll give you a fair shake. I've always appreciated your help—in fact you're damn near indispensable." Turning to Leonard he said, "Lenny, I'll keep an open mind. But you fucked me over and damn near cost me the election, so you're going to have to earn your way back in."

Leonard replied calmly and kept his distance at the dry bar, not wishing to elevate Red's emotions. "I understand, Red. But you'll like this. As Billy said, this is going to bring you to the doorstep of the governor's office."

Red tried to play it as coyly as he could given his well-known aspirations. "I appreciate your interest gentlemen, but the governor's race is almost three years away. And as you know, I haven't declared my intention to run."

It was Billy Riley's turn to smile. "Right, Red, but we can all read a map. You're term-limited as Mayor, and a gubernatorial run is the next move, the logical way to top off your career." Taking another pull on his cigar, he stroked Red's ego a little. "And if you're not actively considering a run, we'd like to encourage you. Wouldn't we, gentlemen?"

Stan Paulsen and Tony D'Antonio nodded in agreement, and Stan quickly added, "We'd love to see you in charge, Red! You understand where the working man comes from."

In acknowledgment of Stan's testimonial, Red took a healthy swig of his whiskey and slowly let it trickle down his throat so that he could savor every drop. As he did so, Leonard walked over from the dry bar and reinforced his allies' sentiments. "Red, I really do think we can put together a deal here that builds momentum for the Statehouse. We can get this done!"

Leonard would be a powerful backer for his campaign, but Red didn't want to appear too eager to let him back into the fold. Pretending to be somewhat disinterested and glancing at the nearly empty glass he was holding he said, "You say Bonnie will be here soon?"

Billy Riley laughed, "Yes, Red, she'll be here. But, as noted, we are well stocked in the meantime." Nodding toward the dry bar, he added, "Please help yourself. That's what it's there for."

"So I see," Red replied with a brief nod toward Leonard. "But we might as well give Bonnie a chance to earn her pay." His confident smile and relaxed demeanor masked his anxiety. "What the hell do these guys have in mind?" he thought to himself.

Red then continued. "So while it's just us boys, what's on your mind that is worthy of all this?" He released a little nervous energy by walking over to the dry bar and studying its contents.

Billy responded on behalf of his team. "I don't need to tell you that things have been slow since we built the truck plant. I've got people who've had a couple of lean years, and I need to get them work. The project at the old Edison brownfield site isn't moving forward, so we are in a real bind. Fortunately, Leonard has a project that will invest $30 million in downtown, generating about three hundred construction jobs. In addition, it will preserve twenty permanent jobs and create another sixty or so. And best for you, it will really get downtown humming again, just like the old days.

Red played along as he returned to his seat at the table. "How can I say no to that? What is it?"

Billy Riley nodded to Leonard, his cue to talk about the project.

"Red, I've put together a development team that will revamp the River City Convention Center and completely rehab the Western Vista Hotel. It can't miss, and all we are asking the City to do is put in some CDBG and HOME funds, pass some of that brownfield funding through to us, and provide a HUD 108 Loan. It's all federal funding; we aren't tapping your general fund at all. It's a lot higher profile than trying to revive a ghetto or two."

Red drained the last of his Jameson and took in a little ice as well, which he slowly sucked as he stood and made his way back to the provisions on the dry bar. He needed to buy a little time and therefore didn't wait for Bonnie to arrive. Red painstakingly added ice from the bucket, carefully using the tongs rather than his hands, and then poured a short glass - he wanted to save plenty of room for Bonnie's services. While doing all this, he slowly formulated his response. He had no practical way of saying anything but yes, but he wanted it to appear as difficult as possible so Leonard and the union leadership would fully appreciate the sacrifice he was making for them. He didn't care for Leonard's remark about saving ghettoes, but he didn't take it personally – WIN was just for show and political gain.

Having organized his thoughts, he walked back to the table and took his seat. "Gentlemen, this is a strong project, and I would love to do this. As you know, we have very limited funds and a Westville Investing in Neighborhoods program that has generated some strong proposals, and for which we have pledged funding. You're asking me to fund your project and pull the rug out from under WIN. That is a tall order."

Knowing he had more pull with Red than Leonard, Billy Riley responded, in the process brushing off Red's concerns. "Well, Red, if you want to tap the general fund, those dollars are just as green to us, but you've made it clear the general fund is in trouble now *and* for the foreseeable future. We've already thought it through for you so that you will be well armed with the facts you need to build public support, of course." Bill Riley was careful to make it clear that Red had no choice but to do as they directed without being so blunt as to directly mandate it. "The WIN dollars really need to be redirected to this project."

Red got the point and did not want a conflict with the unions. After a pause he replied. "I might be able to pull this off, but I need your help. How do I keep from being crucified by the neighborhood groups?"

Billy Riley set his glass of whiskey down and he leaned forward. "The neighborhood groups aren't going to love you no matter what you do. Sure, they like the WIN program, but they aren't going to embrace you. There's too much history there, and even with WIN you are still cutting their funding. They aren't going to rally around your gubernatorial campaign. On the other hand, you've always been our guy. We've put a lot of money into your campaigns, and we can continue to do that. We need to regain the Governor's office, and we've got a big war chest. I'm sure Leonard can stir up plenty of support from the business community as well." He paused for a moment during which time the thought was not lost on Red that Billy Riley's union war chest could be directed towards another candidate if he didn't go along.

"This isn't that big a sacrifice for the City, Red. We need an infusion of HOME and CDBG funds for a couple of years. Those funds get replenished annually. The HUD 108 Loan really just requires the City's guarantee and maybe two years of payments. After that, the project cash flows on its own. Plus I forgot to tell you that we are putting in $6 million of our own money. So we've got skin in this too."

Red looked pensive, and Stan quickly added, "We need the brownfield funds to assess the asbestos in the hotel and help with the cost of abating it. For a building of its age, it's supposedly not as bad as most. The upside of doing this is you can spend this money, and then go to US EPA and show them that you've used the funds and need more. In the meantime, just tell the neighborhoods they have to wait a couple of years. They can use the time to better plan their projects."

Leonard then spoke up. It was only proper that he, as the owner of the hotel, emphasize the redevelopment plan's financial soundness. "We've gone over the financial projections very thoroughly Red. This project will pay for itself after a couple of years and be a huge boost to downtown."

Before Red could answer there were two taps on the door, and Bonnie entered wearing tailored black slacks and a red, low-cut top. The men flirted with her and dutifully ordered a round of double whiskeys, not that they needed any arm twisting, while deliberately ignoring the nearly full bottle of Jameson on the bar.

Bonnie left, closing the door behind her. Red continued: "This comes with a big price for me to pay in the neighborhoods. Can I count on you – all of you - now and in 2002?"

All of them, including Leonard, answered enthusiastically and without hesitation. Billy Riley added, "Trust me. You'll be thanking us for this one."

Red was skeptical of that, but they had him cornered, and there was no sense in raining on the parade. Raising his glass, he said, "Here's to the River City and the Western Vista Hotel!"

They enjoyed their toast, and then there were two knocks again on the door. Bonnie walked in bearing her tray laden with five double Jamesons on the rocks.

"Here you are boys—five fine Irish whiskeys for five handsome gentlemen. Five of a kind wins every time!" Her beaming smile cheered them all, and Red, continuing the charade that he was the "man in charge," raised his glass. "Here's to the best part of the night, gentlemen—Bonnie!"

The others responded with cries of "Here! Here!" and "For sure!" The glasses were quickly emptied and another round was called for.

"Of course!" Bonnie said with a knowing gleam, and she vanished to retrieve five more Jamesons.

Upon her departure Red said, "Men, you know I am always glad to help, but I want you to understand I am going to get a lot of blowback for announcing the WIN program and then leaving it on life support while I plow funds into downtown."

"We understand, Red," Billy Riley said. The others all nodded their heads in agreement.

Red took note and continued. "I know. I just want to make sure I'm clear. This isn't just about campaign money. I need your rank and file, especially those who are residents of Westville, to stand up and champion this. And Lenny, I need you to get the business community engaged."

Billy quickly replied, "We can make that happen. Stan and Tony, we've got the people, right?"

Tony quickly replied, "Yes! We can pack the public meetings and the City Council hearings. Our people will turn out in droves for this."

Not to be outdone, Leonard upped the ante. "The entire business community will back it. We'll get the Chamber, utility companies, banks, everyone." He was also glad that Red referred to him as "Lenny," a good indication he was back in Red's fold.

Red was encouraged. "Good! It will get loud, and it won't be pretty. There's one more thing I need, and I think it will be a big help to this project."

There was a brief period of silence. Leonard and the others tacitly deferred to Billy Riley. Billy took a pull on his cigar while he puzzled over Red's last statement. He hadn't expected this additional request, especially when he figured they called all the shots. "What would that be?" he asked flatly.

"Gentlemen, we need to add someone to our team. Someone who can spar with the CDCs on our behalf, who can take our battle to the enemy, so to speak. And let's face it: we are of the wrong complexion to pull that off." Red paused for dramatic effect. It was apparent to him that they were intrigued by his line of thought and probably had shifted from being predisposed to reject his request to being predisposed to grant it. "It just so happens that I owe a bit of a favor to someone who needs a break and could do exactly this. And, better yet, he would probably love the opportunity to screw the CDCs. Gentlemen, we need Bobby Turkel."

"Holy shit!" Billy Riley was stunned. "You know, this sounds crazy, Red, but I think you're right. I've gotta believe Jive Turkey Turkel would love to mess those guys up."

"He'd do it in a heartbeat," Red said. "He's been unemployed for a couple months, and he's probably getting a little nervous. But don't get chintzy with him. He deserves a good deal for carrying our laundry. I'll bet he'll do it for a $100 an hour, maybe a bit more."

Billy Riley liked it. Turning to his right he asked, "Lenny, I think between you and us, we can swing that, right?"

"Sure, Billy." Leonard replied. "If you guys think Turkel is the right guy to seal the deal."

"There's no doubt!" Red replied. "Bobby can handle those guys. He knows how to play them."

"All right," Billy replied. "I think we're in."

Red couldn't believe his good fortune. To be sure, one huge problem had popped up, but now at least another problem was about to go away. Seizing the opportunity to seal the deal, he continued, "News of this is going to break loose really fast. I've got Bobby's number here. How about if I give him a call and tell him to join us? We can nail it down now."

"Go for it!" Billy Riley replied.

Red popped his mobile phone out. "I'm not too good at this thing, but let me give it a try." After a few seconds he was able to reach Bobby.

"Hello, Bobby, this is Red. I've got a hell of a deal for you."

There was a brief silence while Bobby responded. Then, "Good! I'm in a meeting at Lonnegan's. How quick can you be here?" And then another pause. "Twenty minutes will work. Listen, we are upstairs in the Oak Room. Do you know where that is?" Another pause. "Really? Well, you are in for one hell of a treat. If you see Bonnie, she can help you find us. We'll see you in twenty minutes— just come as you are."

The call ended, and Leonard chimed in, "This is good, Red. For you, for us, *and* for Westville. We can sell this message. Bobby is just a little insurance for us."

"Good!" Red replied. Looking at his empty glass, he said, "Geez, Bonnie should be back by now." As if on cue, there were two knocks on the door, and Bonnie stepped in with another tray of Jamesons just like the first.

"Here you are, gentlemen!" Bonnie said with another smile that filled the room.

As Bonnie distributed the drinks, Red spoke up. "Say, Bonnie, Bobby Turkel is going to join us in about fifteen minutes. Can you send him up when he gets here? He's never been in the Oak Room."

"Sure, Red. Everybody knows Bobby. Best-dressed man in the house."

"Good! And by the way, have Joe get a double Jack and soda ready for him."

"Don't worry. I'll be sure he doesn't come up here unarmed," she said with a twinkle.

The five men engaged in general chatter and nursed their drinks for about fifteen minutes when Red suddenly looked at his watch. Seeing that it was approaching quarter to six, he said, "Say, I'd better go down and wait for Bobby. I bet Bonnie's getting pretty busy with the after-work crowd."

"Sure thing, Red," Stan replied. "We'll try to save some Jameson for you," triggering a laugh from everyone.

Bobby's Comeback

Red carefully negotiated the stairway and located Bonnie picking up an order at the bar. He let her know he would escort Bobby to the Oak Room and collected the drink he had ordered on Bobby's behalf. Just then he spotted Bobby coming through the entrance. Red gave him a wave, and Bobby came on over.

Extending his hand, Red said, "Bobby, how the hell are you?"

As they shook hands, Bobby replied, "Not too bad, Red. What's up?"

"I told you I'd take care of you, and now I am. Leonard Malinowski is upstairs with Billy Riley and a couple of his top guns from the Building Trades. We've been having some drinks and cigars. They've got a big project, and I told them they need you on their team. I think they can pay you $125 an hour."

"That works for me," Bobby said with a smile.

Red then handed Bobby his drink. "I almost forgot about this," he said smiling. "There's more good news to this—you get to tangle with the CDCs."

"I'll drink to that," Bobby said raising his glass and then doing exactly that.

"Good! Let's go up. Play dumb like I haven't really told you anything much. Just remember to play up the fight with the CDCs like it's going to be brutal. That's where they need you and have to pay your freight."

"You got it!" Bobby replied, and they went up the stairs.

They entered the room, and Red introduced Bobby to the gang. After a few minutes of idle chatter, Leonard took the lead and brought up the evening's business.

"I have a big project that I'm working on, Bobby. Red and the building trades are on board. To give Red full credit, he thinks you'd be a valuable addition to our team, so if this sounds good to you, we'd like to talk turkey in a minute. But before I get ahead of myself, I thought I'd fill you in on what we are doing."

"I'm all ears," Bobby replied.

Leonard proceeded. "I think we all can agree that downtown needs a shot in the arm. When I was young, it was the place to shop, have dinner and drinks, and take in a show. Most of that is gone now. Certainly all the stores are gone. I want to bring it back.

"I have put together a redevelopment plan for the River City Convention Center and the Western Vista Hotel. If we can get people visiting here, staying downtown, and spending money, we will be moving in the right direction. How's that sound so far?"

"I like it," said Bobby. "How do I fit in?"

Leonard puffed on his Macanudo before responding. Bobby used the opportunity to take a swallow of his drink.

"We need the City to defer some of the neighborhood spending that was laid out in the WIN program. You're familiar with that, right?" Bobby nodded, and Leonard continued: "Well, we need to move that money downtown. We're anticipating a firestorm from the CDCs and other neighborhood groups. You know the terrain better than we do. We need you to take on the CDCs and help us convince City Council that this is a good thing."

"It's going to be a real dogfight, Mr. Malinowski," Bobby replied, following Red's advice. "The CDCs feel like they got screwed with the first round of budget cuts a couple of months ago. Now they're going to scream bloody murder! But I think it's the right thing to do. It'll be tough, but I think we can get there."

"Good!" Leonard was pleased. With a wink, he continued, "I hate to mix business with pleasure, but that's exactly what we're doing here. So what does it take to get your consulting services?"

Bobby continued on Red's tack. "I've been asking $150 an hour or $750 for a day. But for this project, seeing as I believe in the cause and it's right here in my own backyard, I can do it for $125 an hour plus expenses."

"That's a bargain price," Red said. It was a good bluff. Getting Bobby a little extra money at their expense was making him feel a little better about being steamrolled by Malinowski and Riley.

"All right," Leonard replied. He wasn't about to quibble over a mere pittance. "I think we can do that."

Billy Riley then spoke up. "Why don't you stop by our office tomorrow, Bobby? We can put it in writing." Looking at Tony D'Antonio, he said, "Tony, draft something up."

"Sounds like a deal!" Bobby said, and they all shook hands.

With the hour beginning to grow late, the gathering began to break up. They said their goodbyes to Bonnie, and Tony settled the bill. Leonard Malinowski and Billy Riley were happy to seal their deal with Red, and Red was making the best of an unfortunate situation. He was happy to at least have solved his problem with Bobby; stuck it to Leonard and Billy a bit on the fee; and, best of all, hopefully sewn up their political support for his yet to be announced gubernatorial campaign. Bobby Turkel was more than happy to get a good consulting gig that would also allow him to exact a little revenge on the neighborhood groups. Happiest of all was probably Bonnie, who got a week's worth of tips for making a few trips up the stairs and practicing the art of flirtation.

CHAPTER 28

It was 8:00 that night and Byron Swift was getting out of his car at Lonnegan's. As he did, he could see Red, Billy Riley, and three other men exiting the building in an obviously good and whiskey-lubricated mood which, coupled with his desire to evade a conversation with Red, enabled him to slip through the door undetected. Byron took a seat at the bar and waited for a former colleague of his at the University of Westville to arrive. He ordered a drink and then spied Bobby Turkel coming out of the men's room. Bobby saw him and came over.

"Hey, Byron, how are you?" he said flashing a big semi-inebriated smile.

"I'm doing well, Bobby, but it looks like you're doing better? What's up?"

"Some pretty crazy shit, man. We are going to do a big project downtown with the Convention Center and the Western Vista Hotel, and *I'm* going to be in charge of public relations."

"Congratulations! That sounds great. I'm glad you've got a good gig." Byron was being his usual polite and gracious self, always glad for others' success. That was one reason he was so popular, as Red had noticed.

Bobby, however, didn't have any of Byron's capacity for understatement or graciousness. "That's not all of it, man. We're taking the WIN money and putting it toward the project. I get to stick it to all the neighborhood groups that think I'm nothing but a bleeping jive turkey—and I get paid to do it!"

Suddenly, there was perfect equilibrium between the two of them, for Byron felt as low as Bobby felt high.

"You're kidding me! Red's not backing away from the WIN program!" Byron protested.

Bobby smiled. "He sure is, brother. Red and I just got done meeting upstairs with the Building Trades. They're the ones pushing this, and there's no way Red can say no to them. Oh, they're going to put some lipstick on the pig and say WIN is just being deferred a year while the top-scoring projects can do some more planning and predevelopment work, but the serious coin is gone.

"Sorry to wreck your night, but I'd better be running along. I've got some business to take care of." And with that, Bobby Turkel and his personal hurricane walked out of Lonnegan's.

Byron Swift couldn't believe it. He threw down his drink, barely tasting it as it went down the pipe, and decided to forego meeting his tardy friend. Settling up his bill, he asked Joe to pass along his apologies, but he had to tend to an emergency at work. He went to his car and departed what he regarded as a crime scene.

Ten minutes later, Roderick Campbell answered the knock on his front door to see Byron Swift standing on his porch. He knew this had to be serious. He invited Byron in and listened in stoical disbelief as Byron excitedly conveyed what Bobby had told him. Roderick asked a couple of questions and satisfied himself that this was, unfortunately, likely to be true. Right now, his job was to calm Byron and keep a lid on the situation.

"Listen." he said calmly and seriously. "This may be true, but it might not be true. In either event, we can't do anything until Red tells us what is going on. He's the Mayor, and it's his news to break. Plus he's pretty clever [he actually meant conniving, but was being tactful], and he may have a trick up his sleeve we don't know about. Let's pretend we don't know anything, and do business as usual until he tells us otherwise. I don't see any other options."

Byron concurred, and Roderick thanked him for the information and wished him a good evening. Roderick closed the door, turned the lock, walked into his kitchen, and slammed his fist on the wall as he exclaimed "Shit!" in frustration.

The next morning, Roderick arrived at the office and placed a phone call setting up a late afternoon meeting. Uncharacteristically, Red was barely in the office that day, and Roderick didn't hear anything from him regarding the WIN program or a major downtown project. At 4:00 Roderick left for his meeting.

*****

Roderick would have needed a telescope to see Red Paley, because that afternoon the flagship of Westville's fleet—replete with shiny chrome spinning hubcaps—turned down a private lane in one of Westville's plushest, old-money suburbs. It pulled into the circular drive of a stately manor, and Red Paley walked up to the front door carrying a small floral arrangement.

The ring of the bell was quickly answered by a distinguished-looking man in his mid-sixties.

"Hello, Red. How are you?" he said warmly.

"I'm fine, Willie," Red said feigning enthusiasm. "Thank you for meeting with me on such short notice." Then, extending the floral arrangement, he continued. "I got these for Susie. Martha and I want to thank her again for her gracious hospitality when you hosted us in Harbor Springs over Memorial Day weekend."

Wilfred Richardson took the flowers from Red and said appreciatively, "That's not necessary, Red. We enjoy having Martha and you visit us. But I know Susie will love these. Let's set them in the kitchen. She's playing tennis at the club this afternoon and won't be back for a while. We can sit out on the veranda; we should be able to find a comfortable spot in the shade."

They walked into the kitchen. Wilfred put the flowers on the kitchen island and continued talking. "What can I get you to drink?"

Even though he had no intention of going into City Hall that afternoon, Red was feeling the effects of the previous evening at Lonnegan's. Consequently, he responded with "Just an ice water, Willie. Thank you."

Wilfred smiled. "An ice water it is. I'll do the same."

A minute later Red Paley and Wilfred Richardson were sitting in the shade on the back veranda enjoying a lovely view of the garden that was in full bloom.

"That's Susie's pride and joy," Wilfred said, gesturing toward the garden. "I have nothing to do with it. But tell me, what's on your mind?"

Red took a deep breath and began. "I've had to make a major policy change, Willie, and I want you to hear about it before it goes public," Red said sadly.

"I appreciate that, Red." Wilfred's tone was strangely matter-of-fact, lacking the degree of empathy Red had expected and hoped for.

Red continued his depressive narrative. "Leonard Malinowski, Billy Riley and a couple of other top people in the building trades met me at Lonnegan's last night. They really put the screws to me to back a project for them. As a result, I've got to bail on the WIN program for at least a couple of years so that I can redirect those funds to a complete overhaul of the Convention Center and the Western Vista Hotel."

Wilfred nodded. "Go on."

Red sighed and continued. "I played up the WIN program as a 'game changer,' and now I'm rolling it back before I fully rolled it out. I'm going to be the laughing stock of the city, and the neighborhood development organizations are going to crucify me. This might seriously damage my chances in the gubernatorial campaign." Then he stressed his main reason for being there: "Willie, as a friend and major ally, I thought you should know."

Wilfred could plainly see Red's angst; however, he decided practicality had to rule the day. "It's time for Red to get a dose of *Realpolitik*," he thought to himself.

"Thank you for letting me know, Red. But this doesn't bother me at all. The neighborhood groups don't have any political clout. Heck, you demonstrated that yourself when you steamrolled them with the budget cuts. Plus the gubernatorial election is two years away. You've got plenty of time to put WIN in the distant past. Redeveloping the convention center and the hotel will help you do it."

"I suppose you're right," Red said quietly, still evidencing concern over his plight.

"I'm sure I am," Wilfred said somewhat arrogantly. "I've done business with Leonard for years in Florida. He's a shrewd businessman." Then his tone became extremely serious. "You've got a bigger problem than the neighborhood groups."

"What's that?" Red asked with alarm.

"I heard Frank Clark speak to the Funding Committee of the Westville Community Foundation a couple of weeks ago. He's very passionate about revitalizing our neighborhoods, and particularly about the WIN program. He said his dream is to see a day when the word 'Worstville' is never spoken again."

"Good for him! I hate that term, 'Worstville!'" Red said, regaining his energy. "He should be excited about WIN—it was his idea." Then he added with a bit of a smirk, "I get to take the credit, but he thought it up." Then, returning to his current predicament, his tone dampened. "Of course, now I'll be taking the blame for killing the program."

Wilfred Richardson was by nature an impatient man, and he was in no mood to tolerate Red's continuing soliloquy of self-pity. "Quit worrying about WIN!" he said sternly. "The problem is Frank Clark. He's an idealist trying to save Westville. The only thing wrong with Westville is people like Frank Clark who go around talking us down. Every city has its slums and ghettoes. Fighting that is an exercise in futility. It's impossible to resuscitate those neighborhoods. They've been comatose too long! We don't need Frank's type of unfettered idealism. That stuff died in the '60s. Frank Clark's got to be reined in—if that's even possible to do. We can't *afford* to have him going around talking about what could have been, what should have been."

Red Paley stared blankly at his biggest political supporter and confidant like a deer caught in the headlights of a semi-truck. While Red sat in his fog, Wilfred proceeded to elevate the state of alert even further. "He's an uncontrolled zealot, Red. But it might get even worse. If he starts converting people to his way of thinking, he becomes a *missionary*. That is intolerable. The *mere possibility* of it happening is intolerable."

Still reeling from Wilfred's dire warning, Red was incapable of thinking strategically. The best he could offer was a fallback to his most elementary thoughts about men and their traditional responsibilities. "He's got a family to support. I think he will fall in line. If not, I suppose I can always transfer him back to Law," he said meekly.

Wilfred thought for a moment. He had already dismissed the notion of Frank falling in line. The risks were too great to gamble on that. "Good God, do I have to think of everything," he thought to himself. Then Wilfred began speaking very deliberately, expressing his thoughts as he organized them in his mind. "No, the Law Department won't work. If he becomes a cancer, you need him out of City Hall, far from City Hall. He needs to be in one of your field operations." Then he added, "But you can't make him a martyr. He needs to have a good position, a good title—but with no role in community and economic-development policy."

Red recovered slightly. It was easy for him to trace the route Wilfred was mapping out for him. Following the bread crumbs he said, "We've got the Department of Public Utilities or the Department of Public Service. Both of them have substantial facilities that are far from City Hall. I could declare "mission accomplished" with respect to developing a new neighborhood strategy. After all, my public position is that I am just deferring its implementation for right now. Maybe I could make him a Deputy Director in one of those departments, task him with developing similar innovative programs, and send a signal that he is being groomed for promotion?"

"There you go, Red! That's using your noggin!" Wilfred was pleased that he had once again prevailed on Red to be pragmatic.

Red thought for a moment. He still wasn't completely sold on the idea of transferring Frank to another department. In addition to thinking that Frank might not follow the party line, he knew he had to be politically astute about the timing of such a move in the event it proved necessary to execute it. "Frank may like the idea of being in charge of strategic innovation at another department. But Willie, I can't move him until after City Council approves the reallocation of funding to the downtown project. It will raise too many questions." And then he added a caveat. "Unless, of course, he goes completely off the reservation."

Wilfred considered what Red said and quickly concurred. "You're right. It will be better if we wait, assuming his actions afford us that opportunity. Otherwise, he *will* likely become a martyr, which is exactly what we don't want."

CHAPTER 29

At 4:15 PM that same afternoon, Roderick Campbell and Father Affonso were sitting on the screened-in porch at the Saint Dominic Savio House. The house, located on eight acres in central Westville, served troubled youth. As the men chatted, they could see half a dozen of the youth doing gardening, yard work and other chores. They were out of hearing distance, so their presence did not impede the serious conversation that was taking place.

"I want to thank you again, Father, for taking the time to meet with me."

"I am glad to do so, Roderick. I must confess I was a little surprised when you said you wanted time to talk about some personal matters. Since you are not a member of the Church, why me and not someone else?"

Roderick offered a slight smile. "If you're asking why you and not one of my brethren, so to speak, let's just say that sometimes it's better to get a little distance from home."

"I understand. Be assured I will keep our conversation as confidential and privileged as any conversation I would have with my most devout parishioner."

"Thank you, Father."

Father Affonso took a sip of his iced tea. "Where would you like to begin?"

Roderick Conflicted

Roderick talked very slowly and in a low voice. He had gone over this in his head, but it still didn't come that easily. He cleared his throat, took a sip of his iced tea, and began.

"I don't know how much you know about my upbringing, but all my life I've had to work hard and be the responsible one. I played a major role in raising my sisters, and I still help them out now and then. Nothing major, but if they need help with my nieces' and nephews' tuition bills or something like that, I'm there if they need me."

Father Affonso nodded but didn't interrupt.

"And it has been much the same way in my professional career. I've worked my way up as a darn good manager, always making sure people are in alignment, doing what they're supposed to do, and doing it right. I've come a pretty good distance, and yet lately I've had this feeling that maybe I'm really not accomplishing anything much, and it's been causing me to lose some sleep."

"Hmm. I must admit this is an even bigger surprise than the first. You're the bastion of the City. Everyone knows Red is a high-energy politician, but those of us who *really know,* know that *you* are the operation. If Red's the fancy body of the sports car, you are the engine, suspension, you name it. So you don't think being all of that is making an impact?"

"I know it helps. I try to keep the Mayor on track, and I know people appreciate having trash picked up, roads paved and plowed, and safety forces that respond. But I was skimming through some Steven Covey material the other day, and it occurred to me that my role is almost entirely about making sure things are done right, which is what managers do, and not much at all about determining what ought to be done, which is what leaders do. And there's a void there in the City. Red just isn't that good at developing strategies that are going to turn Westville around and take us to the next level."

Father Affonso took a sip of his tea and held it in his mouth, swishing it around as if wanting to taste every droplet before swallowing. Finally he spoke. "I hadn't thought of it that way. I guess we've both had to learn how to work in hierarchies. So efficiently providing basic services isn't doing enough to help people like the youth working in the field over there and so many others?"

"No. We need to reinvent our community. We've lost 70,000 people over the past thirty years while our country has added what, 150 million? We are leading in all of the wrong categories: poverty rate, school dropouts, unwed pregnancies, mortality rates, you name it. I can't help imagining what it would be like for all of our people if Westville were on a true upswing. We should be creating a vibrant urban core and knitting our great institutions together, but we aren't. It seems like all of our best assets are simply castles with moats around them. And the peasants aren't faring too well."

Roderick continued. "I know this sounds kind of crass, but there is one other thing that occurs to me as a result of dealing with budget cuts. When it comes to any city's finances, there are only two kinds of neighborhoods: those that generate more tax revenue than they demand in public services and those that demand more in public services than they generate in tax revenue. Neighborhoods that pay for themselves and neighborhoods that do not."

Father Affonso leaned forward. "So there are neighborhoods that contribute to the City's financial well-being and neighborhoods that subtract from it." He thought for a moment and continued. "That's very interesting. Asset neighborhoods and liability neighborhoods, I suppose."

Roderick nodded. "Of course, we are only speaking about their financial impact on the City budget. A neighborhood that isn't a net contributor to the City's bottom line may still have many outstanding characteristics and be home to wonderful, hardworking people. But I'm obligated to balance the City's budget and meet increasing needs with decreasing resources, and it just strikes me that we have too few neighborhoods that operate at a profit to subsidize the neighborhoods that operate at a loss. And the federal funds to fight poverty, blight, etc., are too limited and facing continuous cuts. They aren't sufficient to offset our liabilities."

"I see. I imagine that we could also say there are some neighborhoods that provide nurturing environments for people and those that do not. But getting back to your point, you think Westville has to develop a strategy to convert some of its liability neighborhoods into asset neighborhoods?"

"Yes. Just providing efficient services doesn't do that. We need to make some investments that change their character. These new *asset neighborhoods* would be stronger economically and much more likely to be places where people could get ahead. I grew up in Creekside. It was a lot better then. I don't know for sure, but I'm guessing it was either an asset neighborhood or close to being one. I don't think I'd be anything more than another gang member if I grew up there today."

Father Affonso nodded. "I'd like to say, 'I doubt that,' Roderick, but sadly, you are probably right. We point to the small percentage of young people and immigrants who succeed against enormous odds in adverse environments and we say, 'See it can be done if you work hard enough and keep your nose clean.' In effect we use the rare exceptions of success as evidence to rationalize our opinion that we don't need to be more engaged in changing our community. As if one successful student is proof that a teacher is proficient regardless of whether another twenty students are failing. What we ought to be doing is creating nurturing environments where people are expected to flourish, and for the most part *do* flourish."

Then Father Affonso added, "But returning to your situation, you're frustrated because we aren't doing this? We aren't creating stronger neighborhoods?"

"Yes. Not only are we not doing it, but we've never even recognized the need to do it. Everyone says they love Westville, but, like a parent who doesn't want to admit their child has a problem, they don't love it enough to recognize and admit its weaknesses, let alone its fatal flaws. They gloss over its faults and don't fight to make it better. In fact, they frequently take the consequences of its weaknesses, like a lack of rush hour traffic gridlock, and convert them into strengths. The Westville Investing in Neighborhoods program is our best chance to begin reversing our decline."

Father Affonso responded somberly. "The parent who recognizes and admits a child has a problem has an obligation to get involved. I believe, and I am guessing that you do as well, that people who recognize the same situation in the community have a moral or ethical obligation to get involved. Like the uninvolved or under-involved parent, the community's current 'so called leaders' might not want to acknowledge the seriousness of a problem that would in turn demand their serious attention."

Then, with more enthusiasm, he added with a smile, "With respect to WIN, I really like the concept. We are partnering with Ironton CDC on a proposal."

Roderick concurred, but with less enthusiasm. "I haven't seen it, but Frank tells me it's one of the best we received."

Father Affonso nodded slightly. "So if we have the WIN program going, aren't we starting to do the things you just said we need to do?" he asked curiously.

Roderick sighed. "Yes, but WIN's in trouble. Any day now the Mayor is almost certainly going to announce that it is being deferred in favor of redeveloping the Convention Center and Western Vista Hotel. The building trade unions are really pushing it, and it is virtually impossible to overcome their political power."

Father Affonso didn't let this disappointing news about the prospects for his program's proposed partnership with Ironton affect the demeanor of his pastoral role. "Is the convention center project viable?" he asked calmly.

"I don't think so. It'll make an initial splash and create a lot of buzz. But in the end it will have little positive impact, and it will need perpetual subsidies just to stay afloat. Worse yet, I am sure that these subsidies will redirect funds that could have gone to our neighborhoods. On the other hand, the strongest neighborhood projects responding to the WIN program are more practical, and should make sustainable community contributions once they are fully developed.

Roderick continued. "So the result is that we are likely opting for an ill-conceived convention center project that seriously worsens our perpetual budget crisis and discarding a couple of well-conceived neighborhood projects that would eventually help us financially. They would be modest incremental improvements to our neighborhoods, but improvements that nonetheless would at least be positive first steps."

It was Father Affonso's turn to sigh softly. "And there's nothing you can do to encourage Red to change his mind, is there?" said Father Affonso in a tone of resignation.

Roderick shook his head slightly. "No. There's too much political and financial clout behind it."

Father Affonso took another sip of his iced tea. "What are you going to do?"

Roderick was a bit lost but not despondent. "I can't afford to walk away. But I also know I have to have more impact in the community, more impact on people's lives. I don't know what to do. That's why I'm here."

Father Affonso took another long swishing sip of his iced tea. "I can't tell you what to do. You will have to pray and do your own soul-searching. But I can share a couple of thoughts that might help you. First, you will eventually have to do something that reflects your higher calling to serve humanity. If you don't, it will eat away at your soul. Eventually, you won't be the man you want to be. You probably won't be as good a man as you are today. The calling that goes unanswered has a way of doing that to a person."

Father Affonso continued. "You have responsibilities to yourself and your sisters, nieces, and nephews. So there are practical reasons to continue your current path. Maybe there are strategic reasons as well. If you wait, a better opportunity to take action may emerge. But you can't wait forever. The unanswered call will continue to eat at you. The Lord does not want us to bury our talents in the sand or hide our light under a bushel basket." Then he paused a moment to make sure what he had said had an opportunity to soak in. "I don't have any doubt you will step forward when you feel the time is right. And when you do feel that it might be time to do so, do not be afraid. For the Gospels also tell us that the same Heavenly Father who provides for the birds of the air will surely provide for you."

Roderick nodded his head. "Thank you Father. I greatly appreciate your wisdom and guidance."

"You are very welcome. The work we do is difficult enough under the best of circumstances. It is a shame we have to also deal with this ethos of mendacious self-enrichment." He took a sip of his tea, and, sensing that Roderick and he had exhausted the topic for now, he continued. "Now, how about if we bow our heads in prayer? Then if you have time, I will show you around the Saint Dominic Savio House. I think when you see what our young people are doing you will feel a bit better. We will both feel a bit better."

After the prayer and tour, Roderick felt a great sensation of affirmation. He knew he had been carrying a heavy burden, but it took the lifting of it, however temporary, by Father Affonso for him to realize just how heavy a burden it had been. He had already made up his mind as to his need to develop a different course of action, but he now felt more reinforcement, clarity, and inner peace than before. For those things, Roderick would be eternally grateful to Father Affonso.

CHAPTER 30

The following morning Frank was sitting outside the Mayor's office. He had been summoned to meet with him about the WIN program. Joan came around the corner with Roderick trailing her and said, "The Mayor will see you now, Mr. Clark."

As Frank stood and began walking toward the Mayor's office, Roderick said, "Good morning, Frank." Then he whispered, "Keep your cool. You aren't going to like this." Frank followed Roderick into the Mayor's office. Red was sitting at his desk. Roderick, being in the lead, sat opposite the Mayor's desk in the chair farthest from the door. Frank sat to his immediate left. Red began speaking very tersely and calmly.

"Frank, you've done a good job with Westville Investing in Neighborhoods, but we're saving it for another day. Fortunately, a major opportunity has emerged that will transform downtown—really put it on the map. As you know, we don't have many resources, so we are going all-in on this project. It's big; it's going to be great for Westville."

Frank tried to play along. "That sounds tremendous, Mayor! What is it?"

"We're going to revamp the River City Convention Center and Western Vista Hotel. The project will invest about $30 million. It's going to create construction jobs and help us retain the jobs in the Convention Center and the hotel. Both of those are buried in red ink.

The hotel has been closed for several years and now the Convention Center is in danger of closing."

Frank remained unemotional. "$30 million is a big investment. Where's the money coming from?"

"The building trades are investing $6 million of their funds. We are putting in some direct CDBG funding to help pay for some of the site work, ripping out some old siding, mechanical systems, flooring, and stuff like that. We'll put in a HUD 108 loan[5] as well. We'll also invest some HOME funds. All told, we are looking at $500,000 of CDBG each of the next two years, a $4.5 million HUD 108 loan, and $2.5 million of HOME funds. We are a big player, $8 million or so total. Come to think of it, that doesn't even include our brownfield funds. The project has some asbestos contamination they can help us deal with."

Remembering Dr. Hearst's admonition about the power of the building trades and their disregard of good urban planning practices, Frank cringed at the thought that the building trades were pushing it, but he continued to remain even-keeled. "That's a big project, sir. How does it qualify for HOME funding? Is there an affordable housing residential component?"

"Yes. The hotel will have two floors of affordable apartments in addition to six floors of hotel rooms. Naturally, the affordable apartments will be on the lower floors, just above the lobby and dining and meeting facilities."

---

[5] HUD 108 Loans are a program by which cities can borrow money from the United States Department of Housing and Urban Development (HUD) to fund eligible urban redevelopment projects and pledge future Community Development Block Grant (CDBG) funds as a loan repayment source.

Frank continued to draw out the details. "The CDBG funding, sir. . . I take it that it will have to come out of the pool that would normally be allocated to the not-for-profit sector?"

Red continued enthusiastically laying out the details. "Yes, I'll be walking the plank if I cut the social-service agencies any more. They are pros at pulling on people's heartstrings. So the cut will be to the funds normally allocated to the CDCs. But of course if our revenues recover, we may not have to redirect so much of our CDBG to pay for City staff. And this project has a lot of promise—it could revive our downtown economic engine and tax base."

"About the HUD 108 loan, sir. . . the way that program works our annual CDBG allocation guarantees the repayment of that loan. Just to be sure, I imagine that would come out of the not-for-profit CDC pool as well?"

Red quickly replied, "Yes. How much is that Roderick?"

Roderick likewise responded quickly. "It looks like the loan repayment is about $450,000 a year for fifteen years, Mayor. We'll have Walter verify it."

Red continued: "The good news is that the repayment kicks in only if the project can't pay for it. Leonard Malinowski is pretty shrewd, so I don't think that is likely," Red said with false optimism. "Of course, he backed the wrong horse last year." He then continued on the topic, "But you can see, Frank, there simply aren't enough resources to go around. WIN will have to be tabled for at least a year."

Frank probed a little farther. "Sir, will the convention center have shops and restaurants that open onto the street and serve the general public?"

"How would I know," replied Red. "I haven't seen any pictures, and I don't see what difference it makes. It's a goddam convention center, and we're doing it."

"So we're investing all this money in a project we don't know anything about?" Frank asked incredulously.

Red's tone sharpened. "We do know about it. We know it's a $30 million project that is creating jobs downtown – that's good enough for me."

Frank toned his manner down a little and continued calmly probing. "What's the hotel owner investing in the project?"

"How should I know? He bought the building, and I'm sure he's lost his shirt," Red retorted.

The project made no sense at all to Frank, and he decided to try a little reasoning with the Mayor. "Sir, this is the equivalent of doing major surgery on a person. This is like downtown is getting a heart transplant, and we need to know more about how the project knits in to the surrounding area. According to Jane Jacobs, these big projects don't usually result in a more vibrant community – especially if the convention center is just a large imposing structure where people simply attend special events. In that case it would actually harm the surrounding area by creating a giant bland, boring tumor. There simply aren't any shortcuts to creating a compelling, nurturing, and vibrant urban core."

Red looked at Frank in dismay. "What the hell are you talking about? Who the hell are you talking about?" he asked with growing impatience, irritated by Frank's unwillingness to simply salute and say 'Yes sir.'

"Jane Jacobs is the leading thinker in urban planning, sir. She wrote a classic book forty years ago that I recently read. It's helped me immensely as I've transitioned into my neighborhood role."

"Well I don't have time to read some book by whoever it is you're talking about. This ship is sailing, sailor. You need to man your post!"

Frank continued calmly but resolutely advocating for WIN and the neighborhood impact it would have. "I realize the money is spoken for, sir, but we had some good proposals and really serious funding interest from the Rust Belt Renaissance Consortium. They are very excited about our WIN program, and I think they are ready to come here with some serious funding to see if this can really work. They've been talking confidentially about a $1 million grant, maybe more over a series of years."

"It'll have to wait until next year." Red's voice was growing stern. He had tried to soft-pedal the changes to Frank, but despite the promising start, it wasn't turning out to be as smooth as he had hoped.

"Our money won't be there next year either. It's committed to the second installment of $500,000 of CDBG funding for the Convention Center. Plus we will almost certainly be making the $450,000 payment on the HUD loan for only God knows how long, because this project isn't going make a profit. Does anyone think people are beating down the door to have their convention in a place people refer to as Worstville?"

Red stood up and shouted in anger: "Don't ever say Worstville again! If you do, I'll fire your ass on the spot!" Then he calmed down slightly, sat down and testily continued. "WIN has to wait. And believe me: the Rust Belt Renaissance or whatever they call themselves isn't coming to Westville. Those national foundations never have and never will. They are obsessed with Detroit and Gary."

Roderick felt it was time for him to interject himself before either Frank or Red went too far. "Frank, this project is on the train, and it has left the station. We may be able to do a scaled-back version of WIN; but downtown is king, and it's got political support. We've got a project for it, and the HUD and brownfield funds are all we have available."

Frank was dejected, but he got in one more jab for the neighborhoods. "I'm sorry Mayor, but this is our chance to create some vibrant neighborhoods that could eventually reverse Westville's decline – neighborhoods that can change our urban character. The foundations *are* tired of pouring money down the drain in Detroit – they've told me that. Westville's a perfect proving ground for evaluating new strategies. This is more than a missed opportunity for funding. This is a chance to form a strategic partnership that we are going to let lie stillborn at our feet. We are blowing a golden opportunity to bring in national resources and make a real difference."

"What part of 'I've made up my mind' don't you understand?" Red asked sternly. "This is not open to debate."

"But Mayor, I thought we just wanted force the CDCs to consolidate. I think this is going to be the death of all of them. How are we going to rebuild our neighborhoods without them?"

Red feeling tired and stressed from the past two days' developments, and with Wilfred Richardson's warning still ringing in his ears, snapped. He stood once again, pointed at the door and shouted, "Out of here! And don't come back until you're ready to fall in line!"

Frank quietly got up and began leaving the office. Roderick gave Red a knowing look that signaled "I'll take care of it from here" and left the office as well.

Talking Frank off the Ledge

When they were barely outside Red's office, Roderick briskly walked up behind Frank and said, "Frank, come here for a minute." When Frank hesitated, Roderick shot him a look that made it clear that it was an order, not a request. Frank walked into Roderick's office and dutifully sat down opposite Roderick's desk. Roderick closed the door tightly behind him. The crisp sound of it latching shut resonated throughout the quiet office. Roderick sat behind his desk and began.

"What the fuck do you think you are doing?" he asked. Frank remained silent, figuring Roderick was speaking rhetorically and had more to say, which he was and did. "This downtown project is a done deal. There are forces greater than us behind it. Forces that are greater than Red. Red's not asking your opinion; he's telling you what he's doing. What we are doing. You don't engage Red like that. You can't afford to go off half-cocked lecturing him and saying, 'he's blown it.' You've got a wife and family to support. So you've got to suck it up and fall in line. You can't play the martyr."

"I know," Frank said quietly. "But the community—"

"You don't work for the community. None of us do." [Roderick couldn't believe he was saying that, but it was unfortunately true.] "We work for the man who occupies the office down the hall, the man who gave you the best job of your career. He's the only one who works for the people, and there was an election last November where they just rehired him for four more years. You need to get that through your thick skull. And, while you're at it, transfer some of that thickness from your skull to your skin."

Frank resigned himself to the situation, "I know, Roderick. I appreciate my job and what you are doing for me now. I'm just frustrated because this project is going to tank. Even if it doesn't tank, it's not going to help Westville become a place where people choose to be. All my life I've seen Westville get kicked around and be the butt of jokes. Most of my high school classmates are long gone, same with my wife's classmates. For the most part the only ones who stuck around had family businesses that they wanted to eventually run. I thought I could help Westville begin to change. Boy, was I ever wrong."

Roderick thought for a moment, searching for a way to be tactfully supportive. Finally he said, "Listen, we are glad to have you on the team, Frank. If we weren't, Red would have fired you—and then probably asked you to come back a few days later. Someday things will get better. I've got to believe that. Who knows, maybe Red *will* become governor and send some state resources our way. Or maybe the next Mayor will be better. In the meantime, keep your head low and be careful what you say. We don't need any negativity finding its way back to Red."

"Thanks, Roderick. I appreciate it."

Then Roderick paid Frank the highest compliment of all. "Listen, I know you are down right now. But for what it's worth, Frank, you are making a difference. Red actually thought about cutting the social-service agencies, but they have powerful boards, much more powerful than the CDCs. And, for what it's worth, you have broadened my perspective on public service and leadership. Thanks to you I've even read *The Death and Life of Great American Cities*. I am sure you have positively affected others as well. We care for you, so be careful."

Frank was visibly touched by Roderick's comment. "Thank you," he said softly. After a momentary pause, he added, "Since you've read the book you know where I'm coming from."

"Yes," Roderick replied. "And you still have to toe the line – just as I am."

Frank nodded and then sadly added, "You realize the CDCs are going to fold."

"I was afraid of that. Are you sure?" Roderick asked.

"Well, I was trying to do the math as the Mayor was rattling off the numbers. A couple of months ago we cut the amount of money we put into the community organizations from $3 million to $2 million. If we split that evenly between the community development corporations and the social-service providers, we have $1 million for each pool of agencies. The Mayor just said we are putting in $500,000 a year in CDBG for the first two years. We also have to guarantee the annual repayments on the $4.5 million HUD 108 loan, which must be about $450,000 a year or so. That adds up to $950,000. The Mayor says all of that has to come from the CDC pool, so it is essentially spoken for. There is nothing left to help offset their operating costs or to subsidize projects that might generate some development income for them. Even the HOME funds that could have been a source of housing profits for them are being chewed up to a large extent."

"Damn," Roderick said under his breath.

"Yeah. Two months ago we were talking about groups consolidating and becoming more efficient. Now it's not a matter of culling the herd and performing better. It's a matter of extinction."

And with that, Franklin Jefferson Clark got up and quietly went down to his office to tackle what he hoped would be the more routine items of his job.

No sooner had Frank sat down at his desk than Ann, his executive assistant walked into his office holding a phone-message slip. "You look like you could use some good news! I've got some for you."

Frank looked up. "Thanks, Ann. You're right. I could definitely use a pick-me-up."

Ann was puzzled, because she assumed the morning meeting with the Mayor was to simply update him on the WIN program. "Why? What happened?" she asked.

Frank lowered his voice because the door was open. "The Mayor is announcing that the WIN program is being deferred for a year or two so that the funds can be redirected to the Convention Center and hotel."

"You're kidding me," Ann said controlling her volume despite her shock.

"Nope. From the looks of things, he'll announce it today, maybe before noon. Anyway, it takes so much CDBG, HOME, and Brownfield funding that WIN is going to be comatose for at least a year, maybe two or three. To be honest, it's probably dead. What's more, I don't think any of the CDCs can weather the funding drought."

"You must be devastated."

"I've been better, that's for sure," Frank said dryly. "So what is your good news?"

"While you were in the Mayor's office, you got a call from a woman planning a national urban revitalization conference in Philadelphia. I've got her name and number here. She was referred to you by Lisa Seelbach. She wants you to be part of a panel presentation on best practices in urban redevelopment," Ann said with a smile.

"Best practices?" Frank said raising his voice slightly. "Tell her 'This is Worstville. We don't have any best practices in Worstville.'" Then, catching himself, he quickly added, "Give me the message anyway. I'll call her. I guess I can at least go on the panel and give them some advice." As he said it, he forced a small smile. As a leader, Frank was supposed to stay positive, but that was the best he could do for now.

Then Frank added, "It just occurred to me, but can you ask Walter to call his team together? I want to break the news to them before they hear about it from the media. Don't tell Walter what's going on, just that he should convene his crew. I'll join them in the conference room in a couple of minutes. The inspectors are all in the field, and they'll just have to hear about it secondhand."

Frank quickly called Joan in the Mayor's office, and five minutes later he was in the department's large conference room with Walter Sage and about fifteen housing specialists and program monitors. These were the departmental staff who primarily oversaw the City's funding for housing projects and who monitored the community organizations' use of the HUD funds that the City awarded them. They were the ones closest to the department's community building mission and the ones most affected by funding strategies such as the WIN program.

Frank began slowly and calmly.

"I think you deserve to hear some news before it hits the media. I know this is going to be very difficult for you to do, but I need you to keep it confidential. You need to hear this because it impacts your work, and you deserve to know it ahead of time. This morning the Mayor called Roderick and me into his office and informed me that there is a change of direction in the WIN program. I just confirmed with Joan that he is holding a press conference at 11:00 to announce that he is deferring the WIN program in favor of another project. Since this is highly confidential, I don't think I should be the one to tell you what that project is. However, I will say that it is large enough to basically use up all the funding we had pooled for WIN. So right now, the Mayor's position is that the highest-scoring WIN projects will get some predevelopment and other planning money, but no major funding is available this year.

"As you know, we all thought Westville Investing in Neighborhoods had the potential to really have a major impact. I don't think I have to tell you how I feel about this, but I've got my orders, and we're just going to have to do the best we can. So I think our message when we are asked is that the program's launch is simply deferred until the next HUD funding cycle. We will rank the projects that have been submitted and see if there are some planning funds to further develop the best concepts. But no big money hits the streets right now."

Walter was the first to respond, "Thanks, Frank. We appreciate the heads-up. I think all of us know how you feel without you having to tell us. We'll do what we can."

Terri, a senior housing analyst with almost as much seniority as Walter, would have none of it. "I don't believe this! You told us four months ago how you were dedicated to making Westville better. All you've done since then is gut our funding! I smell a rat!"

Walter interceded on Frank's behalf. "That's out of line, Terri. Do you think Frank thought up WIN just to have it taken away? Get real."

The room fell silent, and Frank replied. "When the announcement is made, I think you will be able to connect the dots for yourselves. There are powerful forces at work. Frankly, I'm not sure whether the

Mayor really likes this. But it is what it is, and I don't think the Mayor's going to be persuaded to change his mind. I'm sure we will have plenty of time to discuss it after the news has broken. For now . . . I've given you some confidential information. Whether you respect me or not, please keep it confidential until the press conference. Thank you."

And with that, Frank got up and quietly left the room.

CHAPTER 31

Roderick took a sip of his soda and looked directly at Pamela for several quiet seconds. Growing impatient, Pamela repeated the question, this time more sternly. "Roderick, what are you going to do to keep this from being the end of nonprofit community development in Westville?"

Roderick exhaled slowly and replied. "Red's made up his mind. Or maybe his mind was made up for him; that's probably more accurate. At any rate, there's nothing I can do." Then, after a brief pause, he somewhat rhetorically added the hopeless question, "Is it really that bleak?"

"Yes." Pam's reply was stern and unhesitating. "There is no way the economics can work. It was going to be hard enough to make ends meet when he announced the initial cuts. Then we thought the WIN program would give some of us a chance to survive if we carried out some mergers and consolidations. But now with WIN dead and Red diving headfirst into the downtown project, there is simply no hope. That project's CDBG expenditures along with its HUD 108 loan repayments are going to bleed the pot dry. Surely you know that."

Roderick replied, slowly stirring his drink as he did. "I know. Frank said as much, and then Walter Sage crunched the numbers for us. Any CDC that is going to survive would probably need to have three years' worth of operating reserves in the bank in order to make it, and who has that? Even if you did, there's no guarantee things will be any better three years from now. In all likelihood, the HUD 108 repayments are going to be a long-term drain on our funds, and the City's budget problems are only going to worsen."

Pamela's tone turned from sternness to dumbfounded despair. "Don't they realize they need us? At least some of us? Who's going to be on the ground in these neighborhoods working to make things happen and maintain some cohesiveness if we go away? Things are going to fall apart, and the deterioration will accelerate." Continuing after a brief pause, she added, "The whole thing is so phony. The Convention Center and hotel were modern when they opened twenty-five years ago, and they failed then. You can bring them up-to-date and they will still fail, because nothing around them has improved. Hell, nothing else anywhere here has improved. Westville is still Worstville—only more so.

Roderick's eyes quickly searched the room. Carmen's was doing its usual good lunch business this Friday, but there was enough commotion that Roderick was sure their conversation was private. "*They* don't care, and *they* are too powerful. Red has more stature than most politicians here, especially coming off his reelection just ten months ago. But even he can't stand up to them."

Pamela leaned in and said quietly and pleadingly, "What are *we* to do?"

Just then their server delivered their lunches. Roderick took a bite of his sandwich and thought as he chewed it slowly. "I don't know, Pam. Is there any chance a concerted fund-raising campaign would work? Maybe the community would rally around the cause."

Pamela had already wrestled with that option and quickly replied. "No, there's *nothing* for them to rally around. We are bare of projects without the WIN program. Simply keeping us afloat until there's a better day is hardly an inspiring cause. If WIN were truly viable, we could fund-raise like hell around that. But WIN's a ghost and soon we will be too."

Stymied in his efforts to find a practical solution, Roderick lapsed into talking about its impact on his team. "Our morale is pretty low. Even Frank blew up a couple of days ago when Red broke the news to him. And he's usually pretty even-keeled."

Pam responded empathetically. "He must be devastated. He had a great idea, and now they've managed to snatch defeat from the jaws of victory."

"Yeah. I had to talk him off the ledge a bit. He's made a real difference in many ways, but we'll probably lose him before too long. Who wants to be on the crew of the *Titanic*?"

Pam nodded. "We're our own worst enemy. As Pogo said, 'We have met the enemy and he is us.'"

Roderick amplified Pamela's thinking. "We aren't just the enemy. I heard someone mention brain drain the other day and say that 'Westville has a habit of eating its own.' That is starting to get awfully real."

"That's certainly a nice image at lunchtime," Pamela replied gloomily.

"I'm sorry." Then he continued: "I know it's not much of a consolation, but speaking of losing people, at least you are marketable, Pam."

"I know. But I can't work in my chosen field here. This is a wasteland when it comes to community development." She stared at her food for a moment and added, "The problem with being Worstville is there is no bottom to the abyss. Who knows how much further we will sink?"

Roderick offered up a bit of macabre humor. "I know. It seems like the elected officials and the power brokers are always racing to the bottom instead of reaching for the stars. And every time you think it can't get any worse, you find out the bottom is lower than you thought. Look what they did to Byron."

"What was that?" Pamela asked innocently.

"Red and the University traded him like he was a piece of meat. Red convinced the University to more or less terminate him, while he simultaneously created a place for Byron in the City. They acted like the guy was just a used car to be bought and sold. President Carter and he worked it all out before they even talked to Byron about it. When I told Red that Byron may have hopes, dreams, and career aspirations, he looked at me like I was from a different planet."

"That's unbelievable," Pamela replied, both stunned and outraged.

"It sucks," Roderick said quietly. Then he quickly glanced around the room and continued speaking. "There's something people might not understand about those of us who are dealing with this crap at the City. No matter where you work, you get upset when something stupid or flat-out wrong occurs at your workplace. It might be an incompetent manager or owner, a bad policy, employee favoritism, whatever. When those things happen at the City, we share all of those emotions just like any other worker in any other job. But we also have one more dimension they don't have. We have the anger and frustration of being a citizen and seeing our government do something stupid or wrong. And unless it's illegal, we have to carry out their decisions—we have to be abettors in their crimes against the community—when we are told to do that. So we suffer the pain on two planes: as an employee *and* as a citizen. And believe me, it hurts. It hurts a ton. But I don't make the rules. I try to influence Red and nudge him along." Then his pace slowed dramatically. "But *I don't make the rules.* And this time, I don't think he does either. I'm no great fan of Red, but this whole place is screwed up, and even he can't control it. So I have to go about my job knowing that you and others are about to suffer, knowing it's bad policy, and execute it nonetheless. And somehow I have to find a way to live with that.

Then Roderick offered another thought. "You know, it's a miracle all those power brokers calling the shots don't have beards, because in order to shave, you have to be able to look yourself in the mirror. I don't know how any of them can bring themselves to do that."

Pamela spoke quietly. "I know it hurts, Roderick. You've got all this authority, and yet in a way you don't. In a way, I suppose Red doesn't have as much authority as he thought he had either – not that it would make any difference to those of us in the neighborhoods, and not that we care about Red. To some extent all of us are victims of a system that is larger than us."

Roderick looked at her and quietly said, "You're right." Then he grimaced and added, "It's systemic, and I don't know how we change it. I've got management power, but I don't have strategic leadership power. Even then, it's hard to know what the right things are to do in the midst of this mess. The problems are just so vast and complex."

They continued their lunch in relative silence. When they had finished, Roderick picked up the check and promised to let Pamela know if he had any ideas or good news. Pamela thanked him and walked to her car knowing she was unlikely to hear anything. They both knew there wasn't going to be any good news in Worstville for a long time.

CHAPTER 32

The community outrage was so loud following Red's announcement that the CDCs called a community meeting for the following week that Red felt compelled to attend. The community meeting regarding the proposed cuts to the WIN program was held in the theatrical auditorium at Creekside High School. Creekside was chosen for its central location and the availability of its auditorium, which, with comfortable seating and a raised stage, was well-suited for a public meeting. As the Executive Director of Creekside CDC, Pamela King had the honor of convening the meeting, but in her brief opening comments she made it clear this was a meeting for all neighborhoods. She then noted that she had the honor and privilege of introducing the Honorable Charles "Red" Paley and then turned the program over to him. Knowing it was going to be a tense evening that could potentially trap her between her constituency and a major funder, she was glad to be able to exit the stage and immerse herself in the large crowd of about four hundred fifty residents. Some of the residents held signs expressing their support of WIN and opposition to the downtown project. Two such signs read, "Killing WIN is a SIN!" and "Red Paley – Worst Mayor of Worstville!"

Red walked up to the podium from his seat in the front row to address an audience as he had countless times before. Only this time there was no warm applause. In fact there was no applause of any type, not even the cold polite applause a mayor would normally receive—simply stone-cold silence. The virulent signs and lack of applause bothered Red, but he didn't let on. Red was an experience politician, and he knew tonight wasn't going to turn out well. For him, it would be about damage control. He began almost as if giving a mundane college lecture.

"I want to begin by thanking you for having me here so that I can hear from you. I want the benefit of your experiences, your thoughts, your opinions. And so I am especially thankful to each and every one of you for taking the time to be here yourselves. Active citizen participation is the key to our democracy.

"We have two microphones set up near the front of each aisle so that everyone can hear you speak, particularly me, because my hearing isn't what it used to be," he said with a smile, hoping to elicit a laugh that would help thaw the crowd. Getting nothing, he continued. "To set the table a bit, let me just say that a lot has been written and said about the River City Convention Center and Western Vista Hotel reinvestment project, what is now being called River City Vista, and I want to make sure you have the benefit of the correct facts."

Red now began speaking very seriously and deliberately with careful emphasis on his points. "First, River City Vista is about jobs—construction jobs *and* permanent jobs. Jobs for people in our neighborhoods who are just asking for a chance to get ahead.

"Second, River City Vista is going to put people back in downtown. It's been asleep a long time, and we're waking it up! We are going to have a place we can all enjoy, because while we each live in separate neighborhoods, downtown is the *one* neighborhood we *all* share. It is *our* neighborhood, the one neighborhood we can support without picking winners and losers." He paused briefly in the hope that people would think that the neighborhood projects being brought forth under Westville Investing in Neighborhoods did indeed require the selecting of winners and losers. With a little luck, the neighborhood groups would once again fracture into their separate factions.

Continuing, Red added, "So that's why I'm pushing River City Vista. It creates jobs and enlivens the one place we all have in common. All of us win when downtown wins. My third point is this: Westville Investing in Neighborhoods isn't dead. We get a new round of federal funds next year, and some of those funds will go toward the projects we select this year. During the next year, those projects can do more planning, which I know they will benefit from given the quickness with which we undertook the WIN process. They will really be ready to take off the following year when we receive new federal funds.

"So that's what I wanted to say, and with that, I'm all ears. Thank you!"

Upon hearing Red's invitation a young African American woman walked up to the microphone in the left aisle, bringing two grade-school-age boys with her. She began her comments.

"Mayor, I've got my children with me tonight, because we need neighborhoods they can grow up in. I'm on the citizens committee for Creekside CDC, because this neighborhood is important to me and my family. To be honest, we were skeptical when the WIN program was announced, but we worked hard on our proposal because, you know, what else are we supposed to do? Turns out the more we worked, the more we liked what we were putting together, and the whole WIN idea of taking one plus one and getting something more than two made sense. Mayor, we really began to believe this was going to work, and now we hear you doing this downtown thing—

again. To us, it's the same old same old, some big downtown project pushing us aside.

"Now, you can say what you want about downtown being everyone's neighborhood, but my family is *here,* not there. My boys aren't getting anything out of some downtown hotel. What they're getting and what we're getting is the back of your hand, a slap in the face." Then she took her seat to a loud round of applause from the crowd.

Next up at the right microphone was an older gentleman dressed in a slightly worn charcoal gray suit. He began his comments.

"Mayor, my name's Ernest Tucker. I'm seventy-two years old, lived in Westville all my life except for serving in Korea and visiting family down South as often as I can. I've served my country in combat and paid my taxes. Now, with all due respect, sir, I don't see where this helps us. I remember when our streets were good. They aren't so good anymore—no sir. I remember when our houses and yards were kept up. Well, they aren't so kept up anymore, sir. There's a few of us keeping things up, but now there's way more demolitions, vacant lots, and disrepair than not. There's more bad than good, so you tell me how taking money from my neighborhood and spending it downtown is good for me or any of us."

Red took up the challenge with a patronizing, paternalistic tone. "Thank you, Mr. Tucker. I'm glad to tell you why this is good for you and good for everyone in this room. It's about jobs, sir. We've got a couple hundred good construction jobs, jobs where young men can put real food on the table and take care of their families. And we've got permanent jobs in the River City Vista, jobs this community needs. And I feel the need to repeat this: the WIN program is not dead. The top two or three WIN projects will be selected so that they can do planning and prep work knowing that they will be funded next year."

Mr. Tucker replied, "If I may, Mayor, you go down South, you see all the fine buildings that were built by black labor—black *slave* labor. But you come up here, and what do we get? Nuthin. Oh there's lots of good construction jobs, but not for us. We get to haul away the demolition debris and bring back dirt and fill material, unskilled jobs that anyone can do and that don't pay as well. The real jobs, the jobs where you can live like you're someone, those don't go to us. You look around any jobsite, and you'll see lots of plumbers, electricians, masons, carpenters, welders, and pipe fitters. But they sure as heck don't look like me.

"Now the Bible tells me that I've got to help my neighbor. But I need two strong arms to do that. One to take care of me, and one to extend to help him. These jobs you're talking about, sir—whether they are construction jobs or hotel jobs—they don't give us two strong arms. They don't even pay enough to give us one strong arm."

Mr. Tucker sat down to an even louder round of applause, and an older woman stepped up to the left microphone. "Mayor, I was just going to listen tonight, but when I saw that young woman before me talking about her two boys, I had to speak up. I'm a mother, a grandmother, and a great-grandmother. I'm here for her boys, for my young ones, and for all the children in this neighborhood.

"We need help now, Mr. Mayor. Not next year, this year. We've waited long enough. As Dr. Martin Luther King Jr. said in his letter from the Birmingham jail, 'Privileged groups seldom give up their privileges voluntarily.' He also said that those in power always somehow seem to think that the oppressed ought to be more patient, that the timing *just isn't right*. Well, looking around this crowded auditorium, you can see that we are not privileged people. You can see that our neighborhoods are not privileged places. Compared to us, your downtown project is a project for privileged, powerful people in a downtown that mostly serves *them* and is privileged over *our* neighborhoods. And now you're telling us that we need to wait, that we need to be patient. No sir. We won't be quiet, we won't wait. We have waited way too long already.

"Those two boys who are here and all our children need help *now*. They don't have good schools. If it weren't for us in this room, they'd have no hope. Each night I pray to the good Lord that we will make it through this, but it's a tough battle that keeps getting tougher. We need the City's help *now*."

She sat down to another ovation, and Red felt compelled to respond. He sensed an opening through which he could at least partially escape. "Thank you, ma'am. I couldn't agree with you more that education is the way to get ahead, and Westville Public Schools has let your family down. In fact, WPS has let everyone down. Here they are investing hundreds of millions of dollars in new schools, and they aren't doing nearly enough to ensure that minorities are getting opportunities as contractors and employees. Unfortunately, they don't answer to me."

Then a young man standing at the right microphone quickly retorted, "No, but *you* answer to *us*!" which brought a loud roar from the crowd, triggering Red's full retaliation.

"Let me tell you something. You tell me you are law-abiding, taxpaying citizens, which you are. But the taxes your neighborhoods pay amount to peanuts. We pour way more money into all of your neighborhoods than you generate in taxes. So you can lecture me all you want, but the City is already giving you more than your fair share. So I'm investing in downtown, because it pays for itself *and* for neighborhoods like yours. And if you want to threaten me about how I work for you, just remember this—I work for the entire City, and you folks don't get out and vote. So you can talk all you want, but I'm doing the right thing, and I'm not backing down."

Red's night did not get any better as the meeting wore on. About a half-dozen more people took their turns at the microphones, all expressing their disagreement with Red in various levels of amplification. Two even questioned the Mayor's motivation for cutting a deal for the downtown.

Then Bobby Turkel, the hired gun, stepped up to bat wearing a dapper three-piece suit. "I don't understand why everyone's getting so dramatic," he said incredulously. "Everyone here is acting as if the CDCs are miracle workers changing the world. Well, I sure don't see any evidence of that. They do good work to be sure—when they actually do something—but what has really changed? Things still get worse or at best tread water. Now you're all excited 'cause the money is going downtown. I say, 'Why not try something new?'

"And I'm sure you're all going to say that downtown isn't something new, but it is. In the last four years, the only thing the City has supported downtown is one condo project, and the support for that was just some demolition and site clearing. There weren't any huge subsidies for the developers.

"One last thing. Everyone here is saying downtown isn't your neighborhood, that you don't go there much. This project is helping change that. It includes HOME funds for some affordable housing units in the Western Vista Hotel. So here's a chance for people like us here in this room to have an opportunity to live downtown. I think that's good. Downtown living isn't for everyone—we all know that—but it's nice to have options. So let's all calm down and give it a chance."

Bobby changed the tenor of the meeting for the few moments he spoke, but only for those few moments. When he sat down to only the faintest of polite applause, three more people proceeded to pick up where the previous speakers had left off. After the third speaker spoke, Red, seeing about eight more lining up for a chance to voice their opinions, spoke up.

"I am very pleased at the turnout tonight, and, believe me, I have heard you. Now I'm not changing my plans, but I *am* going to redouble my efforts to find funding for the WIN program. It will be even bigger next year. I can promise you that. Unfortunately, it's 8:00 now, and I'm late to another meeting. Mr. Byron Swift, my Senior Director of Strategy, is going to step up here and continue the meeting. Thank you and have a good evening."

With that, Red Paley abruptly exited the stage without any applause and to a slight murmur of jeers and various unflattering comments. He walked straight to the parking lot and got in his car, cussing to himself. Ten minutes later, he walked through the door of Lonnegan's for a prearranged debriefing with Billy Riley, who had been quietly sitting in the far back of the auditorium and took Red's departure as his cue to do the same. An hour later they were joined by Bobby Turkel, who in the meantime had remained at the high school for the duration of the public meeting.

Meanwhile, back at the high school, Byron Swift, who had been left in the dark about Red's planned exodus and rendezvous, walked up to the stage and continued the meeting for another forty-five minutes, all the while seething inside. Of course throughout that time there were no favorable comments from the neighborhood residents. Only the hired gun, Bobby Turkel, had spoken in favor of Red's River City Vista plan. Inadvertently, Red had enabled the creation of a promising new neighborhood initiative and had trumpeted it only to now be pressured into snuffing it out before it drew its first breath. And he was paying a price for that in the neighborhoods.

When Frank and Byron returned to their respective homes that night, each expressed his disappointments to his wife. Both men were very impressed by the community's articulate opposition but were despondent that the odds of reversing the downtown venture nonetheless seemed insurmountable. In addition, Byron was very bitter that Red had put him on the spot, and he vowed to get even "somehow, someday with that goddamn manipulator." A year earlier he was riding the peak of popularity as the Assistant Athletic Director who had transitioned to the City and helped Red Paley win a second term as Mayor of Westville. Now he was soiled by Red's apparent war on neighborhoods.

"I still remember that morning in President Carter's office when Red said, 'Don't worry, the buck stops with me.' Yeah right!" he said with burning sarcasm. "He'll get his due payback someday!"

Frank recounted the evening's events to Ellen and expressed his empathy for Byron's plight. "I'll bet Byron goes back to college athletics," he told her. "He's been shafted by Red." Ellen concurred, and then Frank somberly told her that he was going to start quietly looking for another job. "I've had the rug pulled out from under me twice in sixty days. I have to move on," he quietly but resolutely stated. When Ellen suggested that he could go back to the Law Department, Frank replied that he had been on the cutting edge of City policy for four months and didn't think he could go back to being the lawyer draftsman writing up the agreements for other people's errant programs and projects. That job just wasn't proactive enough for him. Ellen quietly agreed.

Then Frank continued on a different dimension. "I've been thinking about it a lot lately. The City leadership's most important job is to turn Westville around, to take it to a higher level. But they don't try to do that at all. They just try to advance their political careers. To them, it's all about winning an election or obtaining an influential office. They're like actors who think winning the audition is all that matters. For these people it's never about how to use the authority that comes with those positions to change things. It's never about making a positive difference. Hell, they refuse to acknowledge that anything here is fundamentally wrong. I suppose buying into that type of group thinking enables them to rationalize the fact that they are abdicating their fundamental duty to transform Worstville to Bestville, or at least Pretty-Goodville."

Frank continued and Ellen patiently let him vent. "And instead of working with an engaged public, they just want the public to acquiesce as they do whatever is politically expedient. It may not be a crime, but their failure to strive to reverse Westville's descent and get us on the right path *is* criminal. They act more like *Westvillains* than Westvillians. Looking back on my experience in the Law Department, we spent a lot of effort helping fundamentally unethical, unprincipled people comply with the law. If we weren't actual abettors, we were certainly enablers."

"Honey, I know you're upset, but don't you think that's a little over the top?" Ellen replied.

Frank didn't have to think long before replying. He had already tried to internally balance his thinking on the topic. "Some of them are worse than others. Some of them blatantly exploit the situation to their advantage and are always conniving ways to get ahead. Some of them are just going along with the flow, but that still means they are culpable. None of them approach their role as elected officials from the perspective that 'something is seriously wrong here, and we need to dramatically change it.' So I think it's a fair appraisal of them collectively. And I suppose we, as the City's administrators and employees, have no choice but to carry out orders, but *we* are the ones who end up implementing all this crap they come up with."

Then Frank despondently added, "This is the biggest go-along-to-get-along community imaginable. It's like high school—everyone wants to be part of the in-crowd. Nobody is willing to say, 'Look, the Emperor has no clothes.' Not exactly something to be proud of or get inspired about."

In contrast to Byron and Frank, Roderick Campbell lingered in Creekside following the conclusion of the community meeting. First he chatted with various attendees who wanted to continue expressing their opposition to the River City Vista project and generally vent their frustrations regarding the City. Doing so took some of the heat off Byron and Frank. He shared their frustrations and was worried that the two of them would soon leave the team. Roderick hadn't known Frank before he came to the City. As a former athlete at the University of Westville, Roderick was remotely acquainted with Byron through his role in the Athletic Department, but in only a year and a half for Byron and slightly less for Frank, each of them had become key players. He had had low expectations for Byron, but had come to regard him as a valuable contributor. And Frank of course had blown the roof off. Now he was sure both of them would start looking for other opportunities. Further, he was getting burned-out from the ordeal of managing a rudderless, unprincipled Mayor who was failing to make a real impact on the City as well as struggling with failing to fulfill a higher purpose as he had confided in Father Afonso.

Thinking that it would help him clear his head, Roderick drifted off from the last exiting residents and began slowly walking through the halls of his alma mater. It had changed little over the past thirty years, except for a few upgrades in technology. The tiled floors, wood paneling, and translucent glass transoms were still there. As each turn down a hallway brought back new memories, he took unexpectedly great pleasure in gradually indulging in sentimental nostalgia. Among his reflections, it occurred to him that he enjoyed his self-tour just as he had his springtime neighborhood walk, and that he should take more time to emotionally connect with his roots. Subconsciously, it did him good to take his mind off the current neighborhood conflict, the community meeting that had just concluded, and the morale of his top people.

The Conspirators Strategize

Meanwhile, Bobby Turkel caught up with Red Paley and Billy Riley. Leonard Malinowski had opted to avoid the community meeting thinking he, as the owner of the hotel, might become a lightning rod. They were sitting in the back room at Lonnegan's, ironically in the same booth where Red and Roderick had met six months earlier when Roderick was trying to contain the spinning-hubcap fallout. Billy started the conversation. Turning to Bobby he said, "Red and I were saying before you arrived that it was pretty rough in there tonight."

Bobby readily agreed. "It was tougher than I expected. They had a lot of people, they were upset, and they were coherent. I figured one or two of those three things would happen, but I didn't expect all three of them. We've got to do a lot of work between now and Council's vote next Tuesday." Then, recognizing his role as the hired gun, he confidently added, "But I know we will get it done."

Not to be outdone by Bobby's optimism, Red chimed in. "We will make them run for the hills before this is over. Billy, you've got City Council wrapped up. We just need to have your people there in force, sitting as a bloc and stepping up to the microphone talking about jobs, jobs, jobs."

Red took a drink and continued. "As I said at the meeting, the message is simple: first, this is about jobs; second, downtown is everyone's neighborhood; third, the WIN program is just being given a little more time to percolate. Hell, I started it, and I have the right to stop it!" he said loudly and firmly, as if saying this forcefully enough would somehow make it true. Red was determined that he wouldn't be trapped by something of his own creation. Then he mused, "If only Frank Clark hadn't been so good at coming up with something. He's turning into my Frankenstein."

Bobby interjected. "He's come to think of himself as the great white savior of the CDCs. No offense, Red, but I'm looking forward to shooting him down."

Red and Bobby's comments got Billy's attention. "Do you have him under control, Red? We don't need any loose cannons out there."

Red nodded. "I'm pretty sure he's back on the reservation. He was pretty upset, but Frank, Byron, Walter, all those guys, they have families and they need their jobs. I think he'll keep quiet. Besides, I can't very well claim that the WIN program is alive and then kick him in the ass." Then he added, "But if I have to, I will. You can count on that."

Then Bobby spoke up, more calmly and thoughtfully this time. "Roderick's single, Red. Will he toe the line?"

Red looked at Bobby as if he had just landed in a UFO. "Are you a total idiot? Roderick is the most stable guy I've ever seen. He's got a great job that he'll never jeopardize. Plus he helps his nieces and nephews from time to time. He may be single, but he's a family man through and through." Red stirred his drink for a second and added somberly, "He'll be in line. We can count on that—we have to count on that."

Then Red picked up his glass of Jameson on the rocks and held it in front of his eyes as if it were a large magnifying glass. "Funny thing about a glass of whiskey.. . . you can see partially through it, but not all the way." Then he took a healthy swallow and set it down.

Billy Riley didn't care for that turn in the conversation. "We'll have our people there, and they'll be there early. You can count on that!" he said, bringing them back to the matter at hand.

"Right," Red replied. "Council is at 4:00. Have some of them there at 3:00 to save seats. Sit in the front ten rows to the right of the main aisle if possible. I want your people looking the Council members in the eye when they take the roll-call vote. I'm sure Lenny will have the business community there as well. They won't be able to say no."

With that, the conspirators finished their drinks and called it a night.

CHAPTER 33

When Red got home, his wife Martha was fast asleep. He put his dog on a leash, and together they took a long walk through the neighborhood so that Red could compose his thoughts. He knew they would prevail at the Council meeting next week; that wasn't what was bothering him. Tonight was the roughest public meeting he'd ever attended. "The people are really pissed off at me," he thought to himself. I'll have to try to find some additional resources to save the WIN program, but how? Damn, Frank—you did your job too well." Then he thought of a possible solution. "I'll call that Rust Belt Renaissance initiative," he thought to himself. "They can make an announcement to fund WIN that will save the day."

At 8:30 the next morning, Red called Frank. "Hello, Frank. This is Red. Following up on last night's meeting, I'd like to call that gal at the RBR and line up some funding commitments. Can you give me her contact info?"

"I can give you her info, Mayor; but she called me last week to see how our program was coming along. She remembered that our proposals were due in mid-July. I gave her an update on your decision to defer the program. She's very concerned and doesn't think they can fund us, sir. They need a bigger commitment from the City to do that."

"What?!" Red was shocked, and anger sizzled through the wires. "You gave her the wrong message. We're still committed. We are just

369

deferring the main kickoff. I'll set her straight. Give me her name and number."

Frank willingly complied, and thirty seconds later Red was on the phone with the receptionist at the RBR initiative.

"Lisa Seelbach, please. This is Red Paley, Mayor of Westville calling."

"I'll ring her, sir."

In a moment, Lisa answered. "This is Lisa Seelbach. May I help you?"

Red awkwardly blended an aura of authoritative formality with a little semi-charming icebreaking. "Yes. This is Charles Paley. I'm the Mayor of Westville. You probably know me as Red Paley [as if *everyone* had heard of him]. How are you on this beautiful morning?"

"I'm fine, Mayor. How are you?"

"I'm great! I have a lot of really good things going on here, which I believe my employee Frank Clark has talked to you about," Red said, hoping that referring to Frank as a mere employee would make it easier for him to explain that Frank had conveyed inaccurate information.

"Yes sir. We were very interested in the WIN program. When Frank first shared it with me, I could see that it was an innovative concept that might make a difference in Westville's neighborhoods. I'm sorry to hear it's not going forward." Lisa's tone was very steady and professional. Fortunately for Red, she couldn't see him cringe at the continued reference to Frank.

Red dropped his authoritative formality and substituted some sugary condescension in its place. "Oh no, it *is* going forward. I just got off the phone with Frank Clark [using his full name was another attempt at establishing some distance as opposed to the informal "Frank"] and straightened him out on that. It's complicated, but I'll try to explain it to you. These projects that were submitted in response to WIN are pretty ambitious. That's a good thing, but the problem is they are very complicated—lots of brownfield studies and cleanups, marketing analyses, working with various community groups, planning and zoning, all that type of stuff. You might not be familiar with what it takes to do these projects, but do you follow me?

Lisa overlooked the insult. "This could be a good one," she thought to herself. Maintaining her professional demeanor, she replied, "Yes sir. Please continue."

Relieved, Red proceeded. "So they need to bake a little longer before they ripen. In the meantime, we've got a project ready to go downtown that needs these funds now. It's going to create jobs and really generate some energy that will radiate throughout the entire City, instead of just helping one or two little neighborhoods. So, in the meantime, the WIN projects can spend another year planning their work, lining their ducks in a row, that kind of stuff. I'll tell you, Lisa, it's really fortunate how all of this is coming together."

Lisa had been bullshitted by potential funding recipients before, but she was especially enjoying listening to the Mayor of Westville try to convince her that defunding the project and putting it on hold for twelve months was an essential part of implementing it. She almost wished she were in Westville to witness it in person. Rolling her eyes, she said, "So I see. You are going to put the projects through an intense predevelopment stage?"

"Yes! That's it exactly!" Red couldn't conceal his relief that she was apparently getting his drift.

Lisa continued matter-of-factly. "I see. That's very interesting. It's always good to see a project be well-planned. How much support are you giving the leading project teams to do their predevelopment work?"

Red looked at the WIN summary sheet in front of him and enthusiastically replied, "We've got $3.5 million of HOME funds. $2.5 million is going to the downtown project, but that leaves $1 million for the WIN projects. Hmm . . . I don't know if those can be used for much planning. Then we have over $300,000 in brownfield assessment dollars. No wait, those are going to the downtown project for asbestos and other environmental studies. Let me see, we've got $1 million in brownfield cleanup dollars. No, those are going for the abatement of the asbestos, but we will be applying to EPA for more funds as soon as these get spent."

Red suddenly realized he wasn't doing himself any favors by talking about funds that were being redirected from WIN to the downtown project. Changing directions, he continued. "At any rate, these WIN projects are important priorities, and we will make sure they get funding. That's why I'm calling you, Lisa."

Lisa continued enjoying listening to Red as he rolled towards a total train wreck. "How so, Mayor?"

"Don't you see? We need you to fund these projects to carry them over for a year or so while we are doing the downtown project. Then we will reload and get them going in full gear!"

Lisa continued playing it straight. "That could work in some circumstances, Mayor. But I don't see the City making a big enough commitment for us to step in now. We might have committed $3 million over three years for the WIN project, but not when it is no longer the City's main priority. The best I can see is about $25,000 a piece for maybe three projects to do some planning—and that's not a sure thing. Frankly, Westville isn't evidencing a strong commitment to the program. We are here to assist communities. We aren't the lead driver of projects. We can't jump in while you are pulling out."

"I'll tell you what," Red frantically replied with one last Hail Mary pass. "I've got about $40,000 left in my Mayor's Discretionary Fund. This means so much to me that I'll throw it in. It means saying no to a lot of orphans, mind you, but that shows how committed I am to the WIN program."

Lisa nearly laughed outloud at Red's dramatic orphan bull shit ploy, but she managed to remain calm but firm. "I'm sorry. That's not nearly enough to demonstrate your commitment. Besides, I certainly don't want the headline to read that we are depriving needy orphans."

Red continued playing his losing hand. "But you need to work with me on this," he pleaded.

Lisa's toned became slightly more firm as she replied, "With all due respect, Mayor, I would like to work with you, but I don't *have* to work with you. We have many communities that need our services. I appreciate that you are desperately offering to add your discretionary funds to the WIN project, but it is simply not sufficient."

That struck a nerve with Red, and he quickly replied, "I am not desperate. I'm just trying to be creative. Work with me on this."

Lisa's tone was unchanged. "I'm sorry, Mayor. You are *not* sufficiently committed."

"But you don't understand," Red protested. "We are *still* committed. We just have a downtown project that has to come first."

"You have a downtown project that has become your number one priority," Lisa calmly but firmly replied. "In fact, it sounds like it is your *only* priority. When the WIN program is a true priority as evidenced by real funding commitments, *and* when the City is assuming its proper leading role, we will be glad to talk. Thank you, Mayor."

And so the conversation concluded, and Red realized he wouldn't be able to do anything more than fake his way through the continuing debate about the future of the WIN program.

Red Paley sat at his desk for a few moments and then began pacing around his office. He needed to regain the public initiative, and, like water flowing downhill, he wasn't going to let the first impediment dam him up. "I need a response to last night's meeting," he thought to himself. Finding money for WIN would have been the best solution, but it was apparent that wasn't going to happen, at least not anytime soon. "Those people kept attacking me," he said to himself. "Worst Mayor of Worstville, like hell!" he said a little more loudly. And then, much more loudly, "I've got it!"

Joan heard the Mayor's exclamation and ran into the office. "Are you all right, Mayor?" she asked with concern.

"I've never been better!" Red replied. "Tell Roderick, Byron, and Frank I want to see them right away!"

Within a few minutes the team had hurriedly assembled in Red's office. Red was standing, and he told them to be seated. He then began to address them.

"I don't think you can soar with the eagles if you don't think of yourself as an eagle. A turkey can't soar with the eagles. A pigeon can't soar with the eagles. A turkey or a pigeon would simply watch the eagles soaring and say, 'I'm a turkey or 'I'm a pigeon'—I can't do that.' But if you feel good about yourself and strive, you just might be able to soar with the eagles."

Roderick, Byron, and Frank silently stared at the Mayor with expressionless faces. No one had a clue where Red's narrative was heading.

"Now I've been thinking a lot about the crowd at last night's meeting. There were a lot of references to 'Worstville' on the signs they were holding. I also noticed many acts of vandalism in the neighborhood on the way to and from the meeting. Many signs and buildings have been defaced by 'Worstville' references. One vacant building at the corner of Elm and 22nd streets had 'Welcome to Worstville' painted in large letters on an entire wall for the whole world to see.

"I don't recall any of the speakers using the term 'Worstville,' but they certainly spoke negatively about our community." And then, looking very directly at the three of them he said, "*Our* community, *your* community. Now I don't know how you feel about that, but I don't like it. I don't like it when someone criticizes my hometown. Why, it's like someone criticizing a member of your family!"

"The people at last night's meeting don't have any self-esteem. They don't realize how good Westville is. They're all caught up in 'Worstville.' They are forgetting how affordable home prices are here and how easy it is to drive around without traffic jams. They don't realize Westville should be soaring with the eagles. That's what River City Vista is all about—having a downtown that lets us soar with the eagles.

"So I'm officially declaring war on 'Worstville.' 'Worstville' is the ten-ton anchor holding us down. We can't take our rightful place as a leading city while we are weighted down by the baggage of 'Worstville.'

Byron, being the most impulsive of the three, and still upset about having to unexpectedly stand in front of a hostile crowd the night before, excitedly blurted out, "So does that mean you are restoring the WIN program, Mayor?"

Red was dumbfounded. "*What?*" he asked.

Byron continued with a little less enthusiasm and confidence. "I thought if you were declaring war on 'Worstville,' you must be funding the WIN program in order to tackle the neighborhood problems. You know, slum and blight and all that," he said sheepishly.

"Hell, no! I just told you the River City Vista is about soaring with the eagles," Red said disgustedly. "Is this so difficult for you to follow?"

"No sir," Byron replied meekly.

"Good! Like I said, I am declaring war on 'Worstville.' From now on, that word is banned in City Hall. Any employee using it will be subject to discipline. Further, we are going to have our graffiti team go around and obliterate all references to 'Worstville.'

Then, turning to Frank, he added, "Frank, I want your code enforcement inspectors to alert me as to the most visible and heinous uses of 'Worstville' on buildings, trees, signs, wherever."

Still stinging from his bruising from last week's outburst from the Mayor, Frank agreed to do so, despite his reservations about the ban on free speech and the likelihood that the City's graffiti team would be trespassing on private property. Fortunately, Roderick gingerly raised a couple of concerns.

"Mayor, the graffiti team is active only one day a week. The rest of the time they man the roadkill truck."

Even Red had never heard of the 'roadkill truck.' "What the hell is the road kill truck?" he asked.

Roderick calmly explained. "It drives around the city and picks up dead animals and car parts that are in the right-of-way. You'd be amazed at how many possums, raccoons, tail pipes, and mufflers they collect. The roadkill team doesn't get any publicity, but those things

378 | Ford Preston Weber

don't disappear all by themselves. The *Wire & Telegraph* wanted to have a reporter ride along a couple of months ago, but I vetoed it. I couldn't see any favorable publicity coming out of that article. Next thing you'd know, some whacko group would be calling for animal funerals."

Red smiled at Roderick's sense of humor and continued. "Well, change their priorities. Have them do graffiti four days a week and roadkill one day. The carcasses and car parts can wait."

Roderick concurred. "I'll change their schedule, sir. But it's the summer season, and the stench from those rotting animals is going to generate complaints."

Red nodded. "Maybe so, but I can deal with that."

Roderick added an additional cautionary point. "Sir, you may want to check with the Law Director. As much as I hate to consider it, banning 'Worstville' may have freedom of speech implications.

Red paused for a moment. He hadn't considered the possibility that people would have a Constitutional right to use 'Worstville.' "All right. Let's get Karen's input. But I'm going to go ahead in either event. If they sue us, so be it."

Karen's legal advice was that Red could only ban the use of "Worstville" as it related to the employees' job duties. As private citizens, they were allowed to voice their opinions and use the term freely. Red proceeded to call a press conference that afternoon at which he announced his "Declaration of War on 'Worstville.'" Notwithstanding Red's intentions as relating only to the use of the word "Worstville," many people in Westville's disadvantaged neighborhoods viewed the declaration of war as being directed at *them*. When Pamela King heard about it on the evening news, she thought to herself, "How symbolic. Red's already been raging war on us. He might as well go ahead and make it official." After a pause she thought, "I wonder how Roderick is dealing with *this*."

A Noon Tete-a-Tete at the Kielbasa Kastle

The Kielbasa Kastle was a legendary restaurant embedded in Westville's historically Eastern European neighborhoods that populated the near north end. Poles, Hungarians, and Czechs couldn't agree on a parish, but they all loved the Kastle's Old World decor and generous servings of homemade sausages, soups, potato salad, pickles, and pastries—all of which were frequently washed down with steins and pints. "Sausage and suds!" was the frequent rallying cry at quitting time and on weekends. Numerous union halls were nearby, so it was a natural locale for sorting out the working-man's issues of the day. On the day following the community meeting at Creekside High School, an entrepreneur and a power broker were going to find it to be a useful meeting place as well.

Leonard Malinowski needed to gauge whether the media's portrayal of the community meeting as a major public relations fiasco for the Mayor was accurate—and, if so, whether his River City Vista redevelopment project was in jeopardy. Sitting in a booth at the Kielbasa Kastle shortly after noon, Leonard stopped poking at his sausage platter and bluntly moved the conversation to the matter he and his lunch companion had come to discuss.

"So, the media makes it sound like last night was a real cluster fuck. You were there. How bad was it?"

"It was pretty ugly, Lenny, but we can control the damage. The neighborhood groups can gain a lot of sympathy but nothing more. They don't have any political pull, and the politicians know that."

"Are you sure?" Leonard asked worriedly. "Have you talked with Red? What does he think?"

Billy Riley took a sip of his cola and responded confidently. "Red and I debriefed following the meeting. Bobby Turkel joined us as well. We've got it under control. When City Council meets you will have the business community there in force, and I will have my boys. City Council knows who butters their bread."

Leonard still wasn't satisfied. "Are you positive? I've got business dealings with Wilfred Richardson. In fact, I cut a deal with him to buy a one-third interest in the hotel a month ago as a bit of a political insurance policy. He owns whatever portion of Red you don't. I can have Richardson call Red and make sure he doesn't cave."

"That's not necessary," Billy said with even greater confidence. "Red is standing tall. He's not going to let a bunch of neighborhood groups and rabble rousers push him around. He got reelected without their help, so he doesn't owe them a thing. Even if he did, he knows as well as anyone else that they don't carry much weight. More important, his next move is for the statehouse. He knows he needs us if he is going to mount a gubernatorial campaign. Believe me, he's locked-down on this."

Leonard breathed deeply and exhaled, a smile forming as he did. "You're right," he said light-heartedly. "Without us, particularly you, he won't be able to *mount anything*. Of course, if that occurred, his wife could sleep more soundly."

They both laughed at Leonard's joke, and Billy assured him things were a bit less tidy than preferred, but very much under control. "Trust me, Lenny. We've got this sewn up. Our union membership and their families are going to pack City Hall. There's no way City Council is voting against them."

Leonard nodded in agreement. "Good! Now I can really enjoy my lunch!" With that, they devoured their lunches and departed the Kielbasa Kastle in good spirits.

CHAPTER 34

That afternoon Frank met again with Dr. Hearst, who had been gone for much of the summer and hadn't talked with Frank since the WIN program was conceived in late May. After departing on such a high note with the release of the WIN program, they never imagined that the reunion of mentor and student would occur under such bleak circumstances.

"I never saw this coming. You must be devastated," said Dr. Hearst. As with their last meeting, they were at the small conference table in Dr. Hearst's office. It seemed to Frank that the switch to the conference table mirrored the more collegial nature of their relationship, a growing sense of being positive collaborators rather than a professor lecturing a pupil from behind the desk.

Frank looked at Dr. Hearst. "I'm still a bit shell-shocked," he said somberly. "Ironically, the same time the Mayor was giving me the news, my assistant was on the phone with an organizer of a conference who was asking if I would speak on a panel regarding best practices in urban redevelopment." Then, lowering his voice even further he added, "Confidentially, Ellen and I have agreed that I need to begin looking for another position. I was excited about the opportunity to make a difference. I can't make a difference here."

"I agree," Dr. Hearst said without hesitation. He took a drink of water and asked the question that had been weighing on his mind. "Do you think your job is in any immediate jeopardy?"

Frank sighed slightly. "I don't know. I got a little loud with the Mayor last week when he broke the news to me. Roderick had to calm me down and sort of tell me the facts of life."

Dr. Hearst nodded. "I don't blame you. I've taken the liberty of talking to a couple of Council members, and I'm sure others either have or will. They hold you in very high regard. Of course, Red isn't noted for consulting with Council, but I think Council will do what they can if it comes to that." Then he smiled a bit to take some of the edge off his cautionary advice. "In the meantime, keep your head down and don't do anything that could aggravate the situation."

Frank nodded and assured Dr. Hearst that he would do so.

Then Dr. Hearst returned to the larger dynamic.

"I'm still amazed that this happened. I never saw it coming. I thought for sure that the WIN neighborhood projects would be under the radar screen of big developers and the building trades. Consequently, the conflicts would be among the winners and losers, the neighborhoods and groups that scored well and those that didn't. As I recall, that's where we thought the challenges lay."

Frank concurred. "That's what the Mayor thought as well. He figured the groups that didn't get funded would be upset, but he discounted their political clout. I'm sure he was banking on this panning out."

Dr. Hearst nodded and continued. "Instead, the City unwittingly laid out all the potential economic development funding when it launched WIN, and the big boys came in and snatched it. They didn't usurp control of the WIN evaluation process—they stole the whole goddamn program."

"Yes, and Red keeps saying the WIN program is simply being deferred. But that's a joke. The River City Vista project is going to consume almost every dime we have. The CDCs will probably fold. There's no way this is simply a postponement of WIN."

Dr. Hearst shrugged his shoulders. "You're right, Frank. But you can't say that."

"I know," said Frank softly. "Oh, here's another thing. No one can say 'Worstville' either. Red's banning the use of it in City Hall and pledging to wipe out all of the graffiti that uses it. He doesn't care if his policy is overturned in court."

Dr. Hearst stroked his chin for a moment and then expressed a thought. "So he's going to censor the expression of the problem instead of addressing it. That's typical." Then he continued. "You know, the Mayor saying that WIN is simply being deferred works to your advantage if you play along."

"How's that?" Frank asked.

"Because it occurs to me that his contention that WIN is still a good and viable program loses all of what little credibility it has if he does anything to you—the architect of the program—that looks like a demotion or other form of punishment. After all, if WIN is still alive, you have answered his challenge to deliver an innovative initiative. For what 'crime' could he now plausibly punish you?"

Frank perked up a bit. "I guess that's true. So I will go with the flow, and look for another opportunity, I guess."

Dr. Hearst smiled wryly. "Yes. You have to look out for yourself and your family. The people in authority here don't like to make waves, nor do they like people who make waves. And now you have to play their game for your own survival."

Frank nodded and then suddenly frowned.

"What's wrong?" Dr. Hearst responded.

Frank shook his head slightly and began. "I was just thinking of what Dr. Johnson told me. This is going to be yet another blow to my credibility. My department won't have any confidence in me."

"I see," said Dr. Hearst. "Well, Camilla certainly saw the writing on the wall, didn't she?"

"Yes," Frank replied. "At least I was forewarned."

With a wink, Dr. Hearst commented, "That's small consolation, but true." You know, it's strange how this city – being so dependent on manufacturing -- was so badly damaged by foreign competition in the seventies and eighties and yet doesn't see the need to become more competitive as a community. We really haven't learned anything from the past, and we are damned to experience the catastrophic impact of competition again. Only this time it will be less a trade war between industries and more a struggle between entire communities where the winners offer a quality of life that generates a deep talent pool and sparks collaborative innovation. The dull communities will lose that contest."

Then, feeling a need to further mentor Frank, Dr. Hearst added gravely, "Mendacity permeates the politics and leadership of this town, and unfortunately you are going to have to swim in it for a while until you can land somewhere else. It's toxic, but as long as you remember it's toxic and aren't in it too long, you'll be all right."

Frank smiled slightly. "What are you thinking?" Dr. Hearst inquired.

"Oh, I was just thinking that what you said was pretty ironic."

"What's that?" Dr. Hearst asked curiously.

"That it's hard to *mend a city* in the midst of all this *mendacity,*" Frank replied.

Dr. Hearst laughed slightly. "Yes, I guess that is a bit ironic."

With that bit of dark humor, Frank summoned some positive energy and warmly thanked Dr. Hearst again for all he had done to help him.

"You're welcome, Frank. I have enjoyed it very much as well. By the way, if you can be careful of what you say, you should speak at the conference. It is good exposure for you as well as good experience."

"Thank you. I'm glad you think so. I have accepted their offer. I'm going to work on it at home, because I want to start at full throttle—I think that may be therapeutic—and then sanitize it. If you don't mind, I'd like to run it by you before I finalize it."

Dr. Hearst smiled. "I'm looking forward to it, Frank."

As Frank started to leave the office, he paused and turned to Dr. Hearst. "You know, I guess you and the others were right when you warned me that Red might simply be using me. I wanted to make a difference here, and I've slowly reached the conclusion that I can't. No matter how much I don't want to reach that conclusion, I feel that's the true reality. Do you think homicide detectives ever have moments when the facts in a complicated case inevitably point them to a suspect they wish was innocent?"

"I'm sure they do," Dr. Hearst replied. "Remember when O.J. Simpson was fleeing in the white Bronco? I kept wishing he was innocent. But the facts led to the inevitable conclusion that he committed a double homicide, despite the jury's verdict."

"Yes, I felt the same way," Frank said somberly. "And now I feel the same about my hometown," he added sadly.

"And if you ever go public with your case, Inspector Clark," Dr. Hearst warned, "this community will never convict itself. The Westville jury doesn't *want* to acknowledge the facts and *won't* acknowledge the facts. Even though they have witnessed it, even though they are themselves the victims to varying degrees, they will not return a guilty verdict. Instead, they will point the finger at you and at people like me who think like you."

Some Thoughts from Frank

After dinner that evening Frank sat down at the same family computer where a mere seventy-five days earlier he had enthusiastically drafted the first iteration of the program that eventually became Westville Investing in Neighborhoods. Now he bitterly and sadly began expressing his disappointing "lessons learned", trying his best to temper his emotions and avoid being too cynical. After an hour, he had drafted the outline below.

Views from the Basement:

Perspectives on Transforming Weak Market Cities

It is critical that weak market cities focus on long-term, transformational, holistic neighborhood revitalization, not merely incremental redevelopment.

1. This is because weak market cities have experienced such a high degree of urban flight and its accompanying disinvestment that they require comprehensive revitalization. The plight of these neighborhoods is so bad that mere incremental improvements will not reverse their decline any more than a Band-Aid will heal the wound of an amputee.

2. Furthermore, these devastated neighborhoods have few assets to build upon and little positive momentum to flow with. In short, there is little of value to which an incremental improvement can be tethered.

3. It is extremely difficult for weak market cities to garner the necessary resources for successful transformative development.

The gulf that separates the current status of these cities from what it takes to become places where people thrive and want to be is extremely wide. Bridging this gulf requires enormous capital, both financial and human.

Most weak market cities have systemic budget problems and are forced to meet the needs of concentrated populations of disadvantaged residents while simultaneously providing essential municipal services. Balancing these needs in an environment of perpetual budget crises leaves very little funding for strategic urban revitalization.

The enormity of the task and the limitations of resources are compounded by the requirement that transformative urban revitalization must be strategic. This necessitates the concentrating of substantial resources on narrowly defined target areas in order to have a great enough impact to potentially be transformational. In many cities, such resources simply do not exist.

Weak market cities need to deploy limited resources with the goal of generating as much synergy as possible. At the risk of sounding trite, one plus one *really does* have to add up to something greater than two. For instance, federal housing funds shouldn't simply be invested in an isolated affordable housing complex or in a collection of scattered site residences that are mindlessly strewn across a city's geography. These housing units and the neighborhood investments they represent should be deployed strategically to repopulate emaciated commercial corridors and the neighborhoods most immediately adjacent to them. In this way, a city can fulfill HUD's affordable housing mandate *and* stimulate a more vibrant urban core. Ideally, other amenities and service providers such as libraries, schools, grocers, and healthcare facilities will also either be nearby or choose to locate nearby.

The Westville Investing in Neighborhoods (WIN) program is an attempt to meet the requirements set forth in items one through three, above. Looking at the three requirements in reverse order, WIN:

> First, attempted to generate synergy by specifically stating that the program intended to "spur job creation and housing redevelopment in our oldest neighborhoods with the goal of creating communities where our people can live full lives and raise healthy families." And, further, that "we envision neighborhoods where people can walk to find places to eat, shop, and visit with their neighbors. Neighborhoods that build identity, strength, and entrepreneurship." In other words, WIN attempted to create stronger, functional, vibrant urban neighborhoods.

Second, garnered resources for the initiative by creatively aggregating funding sources that traditionally operated in silos.

Third, promoted the formulation of long-term comprehensive and holistic proposals that had the potential to be transformative by encouraging applicants to forge broad partnerships and swim downstream with positive momentum already existing in their neighborhoods. Specifically, the WIN program stated: "The City further contemplates that the strongest proposals will build upon existing momentum in Westville's neighborhoods by leveraging investments in infrastructure and new schools and/or libraries that have been recently completed, are planned, or are under active consideration." With respect to the anticipation that these would be long-term projects, the WIN Program also specifically noted: "The City anticipates that some proposals may have multiple development phases that extend over several funding cycles."

WIN succeeded in generating several broad-based and potentially transformative proposals that broke down silos among both funding programs *and* among organizations and institutions. Examples of collaboration include:

- A library co-locating with an early childhood development center and an after-hours tutoring program.

- A small market in the Ironton neighborhood adding a local produce aisle that would be supplied in part by new gardens and hoop houses at the Saint Dominic Savio House, which ministers to troubled youth.

- A CDC in the Creekside neighborhood that would rehab a vacant building by constructing apartments above a new thrift store.

- The Westville Health Alliance considered co-locating a clinic with a drugstore, a preschool, and an indoor bus transfer station.

- Two of the CDCs in the project areas mentioned above were also going to construct some apartments to beef up the population along at least one commercial corridor in their neighborhoods.

Unfortunately, WIN has been deferred due to other calls on our limited resources. This underscores the financial and political pressures weak market cities are contending with.

Lessons Learned:

It is very difficult to marshal political support when focusing resources on narrow target areas. Focusing resources requires that a few prioritized neighborhoods receive vastly disproportionately high levels of city funding at the expense of the great majority of neighborhoods. This may result in the non-prioritized neighborhoods, being far and away the majority of the city, choosing to block the program from going forward.

As noted above, WIN required the majority of Westville's disadvantaged neighborhoods to accept a reduction in their *pro rata* funding for the benefit of the prioritized project areas, most likely over a multiyear period. Asking the majority to subsidize the few is not politically sustainable. **Therefore, WIN's ultimate success was predicated on attracting external resources, most likely from the federal government and philanthropy.** Given the City's decision to defer funding for the program, it is unlikely that those external resources will be obtained.

The WIN program was created very quickly in response to Westville's financial predicament. This didn't afford the necessary time to convene a public engagement process. This is unfortunate in many respects, not least of which is the fact that WIN did not have the opportunity to gain a public mandate. Whether a public mandate born out of a community engagement process would have been sufficient to fend off the deferment of the WIN program is open to speculation, but it certainly would have helped.

Revitalizing cities requires broad and deep leadership from the entire community. Political, business, civic, philanthropic, and institutional leaders must be willing to advance the community's best interests. We need an extension of what Jim Collins calls Level 5 Leadership in which leaders are first and foremost aspirational for the community, then for their organizations, and finally for themselves. Despite the fact that we are *all in this together*, we are not *all working together*. As a consequence, we have not succeeded.

Ultimately, we get the quality of government that we are willing to work for. It is incumbent upon all of us, as governing citizens, to be vigilant watchdogs ensuring that our government acts strategically in our best interests. If we fail to work hard and do our part, we do so at our peril.

CHAPTER 35

On Sunday morning, just three days before City Council was to take action on the fate of the WIN program, Red woke and eagerly went to his front door stoop to retrieve the morning paper. Red's self-proclaimed declaration of war on "Worstville" had generated a fair amount of criticism from opponents who primarily objected to either the diversion of city resources from other graffiti and blight-abatement issues or to what they perceived to be a self-serving assault on free speech that was going to be accompanied in some instances by a trampling of individual property rights. In response to this, Red had personally authored an open letter that the *Wire & Telegraph* promised to print that day. Opening the editorial page, Red smiled upon seeing his letter prominently published. With a self-satisfied smile, he quickly read it:

War on "Worstville"

I am writing this open letter to my fellow Westvillians in response to the unwarranted, and in many instances malicious, criticism to which I have been subjected in the brief time that has elapsed since I took the unprecedented action of declaring war on Worstville. These unjust and largely politically-motivated attacks have compelled me to state my case thusly.

First, I am sure most of you agree with the action I have taken, and I want to assure you that I am not going to reverse my decision.

Second, I am waging war on Worstville because that is what I as your leader am supposed to do. That is, I am charged as your mayor with protecting your health and welfare. When I see something that jeopardizes your wellbeing, I have a duty to act; which is what I have done.

Now some people are asking "How does the word Worstville threaten my health and welfare?" The answer is simple. Worstville demeans our community and debases our self-esteem. We should be soaring with eagles, but we don't – not because we can't, but because we don't think we can. Yes we have our blemishes like any community, but we belong among the elite cities in our great country; and Worstville is the little voice inside our heads that says we can't do what other cities do.

Worstville stigmatizes many of our worst neighborhoods, in the process stigmatizing the entire community. We have been branded with Worstville to our detriment. I say, "Worstville has to go!" My opponents say Worstville is a form of political speech. I don't buy it. If they are right, where is the Worstville political party? Where is the Worstville political platform? They don't exist because Worstville is a simple grunt that only Neanderthals, usually armed with spray cans use – a grunt that only losers and vandals use.

I say Westville is for winners. That is why I will do everything in my power to eliminate Worstville. Because doing so is a duty I owe to each and every one of you.

So I am stamping out Worstville because that is what holds Westville back – Worstville and all the Worstville apostles. Those ignorant naysayers and critics are dragging us down, and they must be silenced. I am asking each of you as true Westvillians to join with me and express your support for this – our crusade for *our* city.

Hon. Charles "Red" Paley
Mayor

Red's spirits diminished slightly when he read the following, which was printed directly below his letter.

Note from the Westville Wire & Telegraph Editorial Board: We do not support Mr. Paley's ban on the use of Worstville. We do not endorse or condone vandalism, but Mr. Paley's ban of Worstville appears to extend in some instances to its expression on private property. When in doubt, we will always defend the First Amendment and the right to freely express one's thoughts. Further, we pointedly disagree with Mr. Paley's opinion that Worstville is nothing more than an unintelligible "grunt" uttered by "Neanderthals," and along with many residents of Westville's older neighborhoods we take great offense at his statement. We firmly believe that Worstville can have political and artistic value as an expression of anguish and outrage. One need look no further than Edvard Munch's famous painting *The Scream* to comprehend this. Nonetheless, in the interest of fostering the free exchange of ideas we have afforded Mr. Paley an opportunity to freely express *his* reasons for assaulting *your* freedom.

Then Red's eye caught the following lead editorial.

Neighborhood Flip-Flop

Last November following Mayor Paley's reelection to a second term we editorialized that "given Mr. Paley's penchant for moving up the political ladder, we are not optimistic that Westville's prosperity, rather than winning the Governor's office, is his top priority." Recent events cause us to suspect that our concerns have been born out.

Mayor Paley's announcement that he is abandoning his Westville Investing in Neighborhoods (WIN) program before it even gets off the ground is both puzzling and troubling. Let us review this disconcerting chain of events. In a span of ten weeks the Mayor first announced that he was slashing the funding for community development agencies, in the process translating a 10% cut in HUD funding into a staggering 33% cut to them. Two weeks thereafter he announced the innovative WIN program which promised to partially offset the damaging budget cuts he imposed by effectively focusing a wide range of potential redevelopment resources on strategic opportunities. This program has been enthusiastically received by the neighborhood organizations and the broader community, and deservedly so. Then, as the prospects for a successful WIN program reached the crescendo point, he has now—despite his protests to the contrary—apparently killed it via summary execution.

Why would the Mayor terminate what appeared to be his best chance to revitalize disadvantaged neighborhoods and establish a credible track record of successful and innovative community development? And why would he pour gasoline on his personal conflagration by assaulting the First Amendment and our core American values with his ban on the use of the term *Worstville*? Well, it's not difficult to connect the dots, and that's why we are troubled. The Mayor has shifted his support to River City Vista, an ill-conceived convention center/hotel project being pushed on him by the property owner, building trades unions, business community, and other downtown vested interests. The financial ramifications of this project do more than terminate the WIN program. They likely eradicate Westville's entire population of community development corporations (CDCs); the very organizations that are in the front line of combating the conditions that give rise to the use of the term *Worstville*. The Mayor has simultaneously delivered a below-the-belt sucker punch to the City's community revitalization partners and assaulted the First

402 | Ford Preston Weber

Amendment in return for *what* from the property owner, labor, and the business community? Support for his not-so-secret gubernatorial campaign? Maybe some other perk or opportunity?

The people deserve to know the rest of this story. Why should Westville trade a WIN for a loss? City Council should be very wary of burying Westville's neighborhoods *and* the City Treasury, which will surely be the results should they support what we believe will be the River City Vista Disaster.

This editorial ruined Red's Sunday. It caused him to spend most of the day calling Leonard Malinowski, Billy Riley, leadership of the Chamber of Commerce; the CEO of Westville Central Hospital; and other downtown stakeholders to make sure they would steadfastly and vocally support the project. He received assurances from all of them that they would continue vocalizing their support for River City Vista, but he made one more call, followed by a 4:30 trip to Lonnegan's.

It not being football season, Lonnegan's was virtually empty on this Sunday afternoon. Red arrived to find Tom Folks sitting alone at the far end of the bar drinking a pint of Harp Lager, as was his custom. He quickly approached him.

Red greeted Tom with false enthusiasm—other than the fact he was glad to be at the bar. "Tommy, my boy, how are you?"

"I'm doing all right, Red. You're looking pretty chipper despite the latest developments," Tom responded with a smile.

"Your publisher is fucking me as usual," Red replied. Then, catching the bartender's attention he called out, "Set me up with a double!"

It being a Sunday and, as noted, not football season, Joe O'Neil was not on duty that afternoon, and the young bartender in training was not familiar with Red's drinking preferences or with Red for that matter. Naturally, this, coupled with the stress Red was under, was not a good set of circumstances.

"Well, sir, I'd be glad to help you, but I don't know what that is," the young man replied in a rich Irish accent.

Red was a bit miffed but not terribly irritated by the rookie's lack of knowledge. "Young man, that's no problem. I always drink Jameson on the rocks. And Joe as well as everyone else behind this bar gives me a healthy pour."

The bartender, trying his hand at a little server's humor, responded with "Well, that's what they all say, sir. I'll do my best, but Mr. Lonnegan keeps tabs on me."

Despite the bartender's telltale accent, Red was growing a bit more perturbed because he was getting the sense that the bartender had no idea *who he was.* And few things are more irritating to a professional politician than to be unrecognized in their own community, even by an obviously new arrival. "Trust me. All the Lonnegans take care of me just fine," he said faking a faint smile with a stern tone.

The bartender approached him with his drink, an average-sized double. "And why is that?" he innocently inquired.

Tom Folks could sense the gradually heightening tension, but before he could proactively intervene, Red exploded.

"Because I'm the goddamn Mayor, you fucking moron!"

Fortunately, only six people were there to witness the Mayor's exclamation as it reverberated throughout the bar.

The bartender practically wet his pants and begged for mercy. "I'm sorry, sir. I had no idea. I've just moved here from Cork, and the Lonnegans have been kind enough to give me a job to add to the Irish flair, so to speak. Please don't hold it against me. I didn't mean anything. Honestly, I didn't!"

Red sympathized with the young man's plight. That plus the facts that he was a fellow Irishman and had no independent stature caused him to quickly reverse course. After all, this man meant no harm and could be serving beer and whiskey to hundreds of voters.

Improvising his best Irish accent Red replied, "That's all right, lad. Just remember that Red Paley likes his Jameson on the heavy side." Then, raising his glass he added, "Welcome to Westville," and took a healthy swig. "What's your name, sonny?"

"Danny Whalen, sir," the bartender said, eternally grateful for the reprieve.

"All right. From now on it's Danny Boy for you! I look forward to seeing you many times again. Bring us another round in a couple of minutes."

And with that, Red turned his attention to Tom Folks and the matter at hand. "I need your help, Tom. City Council has no backbone. Everyone tells me Council is going to stand firm except for Stivek and Givens, but I don't trust the lot. They're a bunch of possums. I understand Stivek and Givens; the best WIN projects are in their districts. But I need your help with the rest of them. They could use a boost from you."

Tom took a drink of his Harp. It bought him time to think before he delivered his message. "I'd love to do that, Red, but I can't. We both know the River City Vista project is a loser." Red got ready to interrupt, but Tom continued. "Now, I agree with the prognosis that Council will back it. But I don't think it's a good project. I backed your WIN program, as you know. As I recall, you were riding pretty high after that. And I really went out on a limb by suggesting that the editorial board support your war on 'Worstville.' That one made me the whipping boy of the entire staff at the paper – including the publisher. But while I can't write in favor of River City Vista, I *can* promise you I won't write against it—unless ordered by my boss to do so, of course. But I can't write a column in support. I just can't."

Red's shoulders sagged. He polished off his drink and discreetly signaled Danny Boy that they were ready for another round. And then the combination of alcohol and emotional fatigue got the better of him: Red Paley dropped his guard. He began slowly and softly. "I can't blame you, Tom. I'm as pissed off as anyone about this, off the record, mind you."

"Of course," Tom replied. "I'm not wearing my reporter's hat today. Hey," he said with a chuckle, "I'm off on Sundays."

Red laughed. "Damn right you are!" Then he continued. "You know, I made the right decision cutting the funding for the non-profit agencies a couple of months ago. Yeah, I wouldn't mind seeing some of those loudmouths have their organizations dissolve and lose their bully pulpits, but the real point is it would be politically impossible to lay off cops and other City personnel. But I've got to hand it to Frank. I thought this WIN program could be the real deal. It could give me some chits *and* placate the neighborhoods. But man, you never get a chance in this town. Sometimes I feel like Muhammad Ali going up against a five-foot punk with an Uzi."

Tom Folks smiled slightly in response to Red's analogy. Then he sympathetically replied. "You're right, Red. But I'm sure you will come out okay. And listen, no hard feelings. I just can't go against my publisher and my editor on this one." With that, Red Paley and Tom Folks slowly enjoyed their beverages and calmly discussed the upcoming college and pro football seasons.

***

Meanwhile and elsewhere, Roderick, Byron, and Frank intentionally avoided any discussion of the *Westville Wire & Telegraph's* editorial. Each of them supported the WIN program and knew the others did as well. Adhering to an unwritten code, they kept their mouths shut to make sure they were not openly disloyal to Red. In part, they were also quiet because they also didn't relish the thought of working with Red following such a major defeat—if that turned out to be the case. They were wise enough to keep their thoughts to themselves and await the vote which was just two days away.

On the other hand, some of the CDCs took the editorial as an indication that they might be able to gain a victory after all. Quincy Dewberry had been neutered by the Chamber of Commerce's public support of the downtown project, but Deacon Wilkens was cautiously optimistic and encouraged his congregation to contact City Council and make their opinions heard.

Pamela King had been terribly despondent, but the editorial gave her new hope. She arranged to meet John Nowak at Carmen's to get his thoughts on the latest turn of events in the hope that he shared her optimism. Their CDCs had the two highest-scoring projects and the most at stake. Unfortunately, John gave her no encouragement. He was convinced that the forces in favor of the River City Vista project were too strong to be overcome.

"I hope I'm wrong," he told her, "but there's too much money behind this. The paper's endorsement couldn't carry the mayoral race, and I don't think it can turn the tide here. Too many people in our service territories don't vote. That's what enabled Red to ram the budget cuts down our throats. And many of those who do vote either don't read the paper or think it has little credibility. To them it's still *The Waste of Time*."

Pam's enthusiasm shrank. "John, I hope to God it's not true. We can't survive if this goes through. I've got two wonderful, dedicated staff members—you know them—who I'll have to let go. We will be out of business, and no one will serve our neighborhood."

John was equally downhearted. "Believe me, I know, Pam. I'm in the same boat. I just think the reality is that we are sunk. I'll be there Tuesday for sure. But I'm planning on drowning my sorrows, not celebrating, afterward."

408 | Ford Preston Weber

Pamela sighed. "As much as I hate to admit it, I think you're right. But for once I hope you're wrong." Then she added, "I've been thinking of that column Tom Folks wrote a couple months ago when he questioned whether we were leaders or leaches. I think we are going to see the real parasites in action on Tuesday."

John looked at her and said, "You're right." Then he continued philosophically. "They truly are parasites living off of Westville as they pursue their own selfish aims. It seems to me that Westville is part living organism and part corpse. I wonder what they will do when Westville no longer has enough meat to support them. I can imagine them picking at the bones."

"Ugh!" Pamela exclaimed. "First Roderick and now you. Why must you use such graphic metaphors?"

"I'm sorry," John said with a slight laugh. "Tell me, what did Roderick say that was so crude?"

Pamela willingly obliged. "We were having lunch here on Friday, and he told me someone had recently told him that Westville's problem is it eats its young. Believe me that went well with my soup and sandwich."

John smiled. "Yes, I guess that wouldn't be a pleasant thought, however accurate it may be. John thought for a moment and then added, "It's interesting that Roderick would repeat such a negative thought, whether he agrees with it or not." Then, moving on he added, "Well, one thing's for sure. We will see the whole array of leeches and vultures in full force at Tuesday's Council meeting."

CHAPTER 36

On Tuesday, August 15, 2000, the Westville City Council chambers were packed with a standing-room-only crowd. True to his commitment, Billy Riley's union members had arrived early and taken seats down front. Noting the positive impact children had made at the Creekside community meeting, Billy had instructed several of them to bring their families. Leonard Malinowski had also delivered on his end of the bargain; the business community was well represented. The neighborhoods and CDCs also had strong contingents present. They would have been even stronger, but City Council members had already clued them in as to their probable votes. It was clear that the die had already been cast, and the River City Convention Center and Western Vista Hotel were going to carry the day.

The meeting was called to order shortly after 4:00 PM. City Council conducted some routine business for about twenty minutes before turning their attention to the River City Vista project. They began by calling on the executive director of the Convention and Visitors Bureau and on Leonard Malinowski to present on the redevelopment plan and financial impact of their proposal. Each of them talked about how this would be a top-of-the-line project, which was essential if the River City Convention Center and Western Vista Hotel were to reverse their losses. The manager of the Convention Center noted that the City and County subsidized it to the tune of about $400,000 per year. The only way to reverse this he said rather unartfully, "was to double down and invest more money in the center and the hotel so that they would be competitive with other convention

409

sites." This drew some snickers from the opposition, who pointed out rather loudly that a gambling analogy was certainly appropriate for this long-shot project. They were followed by the Board Chair of the Chamber of Commerce who spoke about how the project would rejuvenate downtown and enhance Westville's prestige in the regional business community. He was followed by the President of Westville Central Hospital. She emphasized that the River City Vista project was only eight blocks from their hospital and would help stabilize the neighborhood.

Following that, the City Council called on the forty or so members of the public who had signed up to speak on the issue. Of the forty people who spoke, about thirty were strongly in favor of the project. They were predominantly members of the building trades and talked mainly about the importance of having good jobs, the fact that downtown was a community-wide asset, and of course, almost to a person, the fact that they were born and raised in Westville or the surrounding area.

The ten or so people who spoke in opposition to the project were interspersed in the speaking lineup, so it seemed that there would be three in favor and then one opposed, and so forth. The opponents asked Council to take note of the Creekside community meeting and reiterated that the WIN program had given them a new sense of hope, but that they now felt the City was breaking its promise to help the neighborhoods. The opponents further accused the City of making a long-term commitment to subsidize a bad project in exchange for a lot of short-term union construction jobs and a handful of long-term, minimum-wage jobs. They pointed out the obvious fact that this hardly created a path to prosperity. John Nowak spoke for all of the Community Development Corporations as a bloc and delivered the ominous forecast that this program likely meant that all twelve of the CDCs would be forced to fold.

The high point of the whole anticlimactic affair was when one of the speakers opposed to the project stated that it would "perpetuate the decline of Worstville." This elicited the wrath of the President of Council, who interjected that he proposed that Westville hold an annual "Bestville Celebration," perhaps commencing on the same date as the ribbon cutting for the River City Vista project. In typical Westville behavior, numerous Council members quickly piped up in sycophantic support of the Council President's *brilliant* idea.

After two hours of taking community testimony, the City Council members took turns speaking on the project. As if reading from the same script, almost every member started by saying that both WIN and River City Vista were great projects, and they wished they could fund them both. This inevitably segued into talking about the importance of both neighborhoods and the downtown. Then there was a third and final section to their speeches during which the Council members chastised the Mayor for announcing WIN and then deferring it; expressed their "sincere hope" that the CDCs would continue to be viable and do valuable work; stated their "serious reservations" about the financial viability of the downtown project; and then pronounced that they would be voting in favor of it anyway. In characteristic Council fashion, they did everything they could to state their opposition to River City Vista before voting in favor of it, as if somehow stating all the negatives about a project insulated them from the fact that they nonetheless voted for it. As Joe Schwartz had told Frank, they already had their political exit strategies lined up.

It took about an hour for the Council members to stroke the community activists, chastise the Mayor, cover their political asses, and then cave under the development pressure. During this time, to Council's disappointment, almost no one left the chambers. This left them to cast their votes in front of constituents they were permanently alienating. Only two members had spoken in favor of the WIN program. They were the Council members who represented the neighborhoods in which the two highest-scoring WIN proposals were located. They spoke so apologetically about not being able to vote for both projects that it was clear they were more interested in not alienating Billy Riley than they were in persuading any of their colleagues to vote for WIN. As Roderick sat in the Council chambers, he remained outwardly stoical, but he was seething inside. "This is par for the course," he thought. "Even the two Council members who ought to be fighting for the WIN program don't care enough about the neighborhoods they supposedly represent to put any of their personal collateral at stake."

At about 7:30 PM the vote was finally taken and the inevitable occurred. By a 10-to-2 vote, City Council supported the downtown plan.

Frank hadn't attended the meeting; nobody wanted him to be a potential lightning rod or media interviewee. He stayed in his office and listened on the City's internal audio system as the City Council members abdicated their leadership responsibilities. Frank thought, "It's exactly like Joe Schwartz told me it would be. They are trying to simultaneously support it and yet distance themselves from it. What cowards!"

Red also stayed in his office and listened to it on the City's internal audio system. He had no desire to suffer through the Council meeting in person and was still available to appear and cast the tie-breaking vote if necessary, his only legislative function as Mayor.

Only Roderick and Byron attended the meeting on behalf of the administration. When the meeting adjourned, Roderick and Byron slipped out through the Council members' exit, but not before Pamela King caught Roderick's eye and gave him a look of total despair and disappointment. "What do we do now?" was written all over her face. Roderick subtly echoed her frustration with a slight shrug of his own and then quickly exited. He couldn't be seen consorting with the enemy on the field of battle.

Meanwhile, John Nowak overheard one of his supporters say that Westville needed a change of leadership. "Leadership?" John replied. "All Westville has is *leadershit*."

CHAPTER 37

Following the adjournment of the City Council meeting, Byron went straight to his car and drove home. He was still steaming about the reversal of WIN and the continued lessening of his popularity. He was being used – exploited – by Red, and he didn't like it one damn bit. His wife, Dinah, tired of hearing him vent about it one more time, tried to put the reversal on WIN in perspective.

"Remember, honey," she said calmly, "what they say about politics."

"What's that?" Byron replied.

"Politics, my dear, is the art of the possible. Is it possible that WIN is just too ambitious?"

Byron thought for a moment and then replied. "I come from the world of big-time athletics where we believe in setting stretch goals. That way if we fall short, we may still accomplish something significant. In reversing WIN the City aimed so low, it hit its target – and in the process we've blown our foot off."

Dinah was forced to concede the point. "I guess you're right. Lately, you've been so upset and stressed out over this. I'd just like to have the old Byron back—at least for a visit," she said with a smile and gave him a short kiss.

Byron got her point and returned her affection with a longer kiss. "I'll try to go find him for you, honey. It may take a little while, but I think he's still here somewhere." He paused and then continued. "It's just that I feel like I got on the wrong train when I came to the City. It's like the *Seinfeld* episode where Jerry and George got in the chauffeured car at the airport only to slowly find out it was being driven by neo-Nazis. My career used to be going in the right direction. I don't know where it's going now, but it's pretty scary."

*****

Like Byron, Frank was in no mood to stick around City Hall. He lingered briefly in the office to allow time for the crowd to dissipate before riding down the sixteen floors in the elevator and then slipping quietly out the back of the building. He successfully evaded the public, the politicians, and the media.

When he arrived home, he briefly filled Ellen in on the carnage he had predictably witnessed. In doing so, he primarily highlighted what Joe Schwartz, Pamela King, and Dr. Hearst had told him:

First, the politicians – even those whose districts would benefit most from implementing the WIN program -- would try to play the issue both ways before inevitably siding with the politically powerful unions, developers, and business community.

Second, there would be no acknowledgment of anything wrong in 'Worstville.' (They both had a cynical chuckle at the idea that there would be a 'Bestville Day.')

Third, the proponents of the project would have no difficulty adding the business community to their coalition and overwhelming

City Council. No one was going to seriously contest their proposal – or more precisely, their muscle.

Later that evening, Frank returned to the same family computer where he had first enthusiastically put the WIN program to words, only to then express his bitter and sad 'lessons learned.' He sat down for the third time, but now with the purpose of updating his resume as the first step in self-imposing his professional exile from Westville.

*****

Unlike Byron and Frank, Roderick went to his office following the City Council meeting and tried to get some work done. Red poked his head in Roderick's doorway and said, "Well, we did it, young man! Now we can put this mess behind us and watch downtown really blossom!"

"Yes sir," Roderick replied, feigning enthusiasm.

Red continued out of the office, and Roderick stared at the paperwork on his desk. After trying to concentrate on an item, then exchanging it for a second and then a third, he realized he wasn't going to get anything done. His mind, or maybe his heart and soul, weren't going to let him, not tonight.

Coming Up Short

Meanwhile, Red continued to Lonnegan's for a victory drink with Billy Riley, Bobby Turkel, Leonard Malinowski, and some of the other masterminds and supporters of the River City Vista project. Red was standing at the bar with a Jameson in his hand as usual when someone came up from behind him and put a hand on his shoulder. Wheeling around, Red came face-to-face with Wilfred Richardson.

"Willie! I didn't expect to see you here, tonight. This isn't usually your cup of tea," Red said, happy to see his benefactor.

"I wanted to be here, Red, to show my appreciation. You took some arrows on this one, and I'm going to make some money as a result."

"How's that, Willie?" Red asked, puzzled.

"I'm partnering with Leonard on the project," Wilfred said plainly.

"What?" Red was incredulous.

"I bought a one-third interest in the River City Vista Hotel from Leonard. He thought he might need my help getting the funding approved if things got too rough. My investment was a little political insurance for him. And on my end, I can sell my interest back to him anytime in the next five years for a guaranteed profit of not less than fifty percent. I'll be doing that sometime next year in all likelihood. It was a great deal for both of us. In fact, I wouldn't be surprised if Leonard flips the property once it has been completely renovated."

Red was floored, not because the man who had reinforced his decision to abandon his boldest neighborhood program was actually benefitting financially from the decision—that was part of the game. But Red felt his friendship had been betrayed, that he should have been informed that Wilfred's advice was self-serving. After all, he had gone out of his way to personally advise Wilfred of his change of direction and its political consequences. And here Wilfred was giving him self-serving advice without coming clean about it.

"Why didn't you tell me? Don't you trust me?" Red asked, amazed he had been left in the dark.

Wilfred condescendingly sloughed off Red's shock. "Of course I trust you, Red. This all came about in the last month. When we talked a couple of weeks ago, I thought it would be better for you, for your own protection, not to know that your pal and major donor had an ownership interest. That way you could play it straight up. You know, I gave you plausible deniability. Hell, I gave you true deniability. Besides, I honestly believe what I told you. WIN was a pipe dream; it's foolish to think we can revitalize those places. You can't make something from nothing. Come on, let me buy you a drink. Your glass is getting light."

Red willingly had another drink and resumed a celebratory demeanor, but he wasn't happy. He had been played by Wilfred, and it didn't sit easy with him. Red was feeling the pain of being diminished and disrespected by his own friend and ally. For the next hour he heard Billy Riley bragging about securing eighteen months of construction work for his people. "Big deal, they will be unemployed again after that," Red thought. He heard Bobby Turkel boasting about getting a measure of revenge with the neighborhood development groups. "Well, now he's back to being jobless and looking for his next gig," Red said to himself. He heard Leonard Malinowski and Wilfred Richardson counting the money they were going to make on the River City Vista project, to which his rationalization was "Maybe they can funnel some of that into my gubernatorial campaign." All the while, he felt his pocket had been picked—not just of the funding for

WIN but also of political goodwill. In sum, Red's self-esteem had suffered a mighty blow.

When all the hoopla had ended and the bar had largely emptied, Red sat in self-absorbed solitude slowly finishing his last Jameson and running through the thoughts that were troubling him. Once again he found himself damning Frank Clark for coming up with a potentially game-changing program. He longed for the simple pre-WIN days—a mere seventy-five days ago —when all he had to do was focus on providing safety forces, maintaining streets, and picking up trash. The good old days, when all he had to do was say there wasn't enough money to go around and that he wasn't to blame for that predicament.

As Red thought it through, he tried to make the most of the situation—that he had achieved a victory that day. But even if he had won a victory, it was an empty victory. Hell, for all he knew it was a Pyrrhic victory. Sure, he was pretty confident he had sewn up the support of the building trades for his next campaign, but at a high cost. The neighborhood groups in Westville would be nipping at his heels as he focused his sights on becoming Governor. Plus, he had to swallow his pride and help Leonard who had deserted him during the last campaign. To make matters worse, he couldn't help believing that Wilfred Richardson could have at least tried to stall the River City Vista project for a year. That would have bought him time to begin executing WIN, maybe bring in some major grants from foundations, and give *him* a brilliant victory to celebrate.

The cocktail of turmoil that was causing Red such angst was further fueled as his thoughts returned to where they were when he confided in Tom Folks two days earlier. Ever since the public meeting at Creekside High School, it had slowly dawned on Red that the WIN program wasn't just about him making a big splash. WIN *wasn't* just about a great political magician imposing budget cuts and simultaneously pulling a neighborhood development rabbit out of his hat. At first he was primarily upset that the building trades were calling in their chits and taking over the helm of his "mayoralship," in the process causing him the political embarrassment of reversing course with the WIN program. "Hell, don't I even get a victory lap," Red thought to himself. But it had increasingly occurred to Red, further intensified by his conversation with Lisa Seelbach, that the WIN program could have been the type of bold policy move that would have enabled him to differentiate himself from the other gubernatorial candidates regardless of whether WIN succeeded in revitalizing any neighborhoods. WIN could have bolstered the side of his political resume that emphasized his support of the community good. Further, gaining funding from national foundations would have served as an independent endorsement of the program – *his* program. That would have been a big feather in his cap as he ran state-wide regardless of whether WIN actually succeeded in revitalizing any neighborhoods. If it failed, those chickens wouldn't come home to roost until later. As of now he was just another politician and a damn good one at that, or so he had always thought. But it would be a great advantage to be known as a damn good politician who makes a difference, and he just wasn't there.

Making matters worse, Red's leadership capability was suddenly vulnerable to criticism that as mayor he couldn't even take the first steps in implementing his own "mega" program. And now, further reflecting on how Wilfred had played him, or at least had taken him for granted, he had doubts about just how good a politician he really was. Suddenly he was a little less confident of his prospects for being elected governor.

Sitting in isolation on his bar stool, Red Paley was a rudderless admiral. The self-absorbed career politician now had a slightly broader and much more dismal perspective. His sheen was fading.

Joe O'Neil finished washing the stack of highballs and pints and walked down to Red's end of the bar. "Care for another, boss?" he asked.

"No," Red quietly replied. Then for the second time in three days, the Red Paley facade was lowered. The short-term successes of others had come at his expense. The great navigator had been out-maneuvered, and he was tired of pretending that *any part* of it benefitted him. Red's insecurities fueled his worries. As Red's insecurities grew they pushed his inflated ego aside, revealing the obvious reality that if Willie and the others could work their schemes behind *his* back, they could work them behind *anyone's* back. And if they could do that, he had no intrinsic value to them. Any Mayor - any Governor – would suit them just fine. "What's to keep the building trades or Willie from backing someone else at the drop of a hat?" he wondered.

Red Paley looked up at his friendly bartender and in a melancholy tone inquired, "Tell me, Joe. Winning's supposed to feel good, isn't it?"

"Yes sir, Mayor!" Joe replied enthusiastically.

"Hmm. Somehow tonight just doesn't feel that good. Why do you think that is, Joe?" Red asked wistfully.

"I don't know Mayor. Maybe you're just a bit under the weather," Joe suggested maintaining his upbeat demeanor. Then he went about wiping down a nearby portion of the bar in preparation for closing.

Red looked past Joe and studied his image in the mirror behind the bar. For the first time he didn't hold the person he saw in much regard. Where he once saw the Grand Mayor of Westville and Future Governor, he now saw vulnerability and mediocrity. He stroked his cheeks and chin, feeling the stubble that had grown since his morning shave. "Hmm, I wonder how I'd look in a beard. Maybe I should try growing one," he thought. Then he stared at the remainder of his drink before polishing it off. "'A bit under,' I think that's true," Red thought out loud. Then, speaking slightly louder so that Joe could hear him clearly, he said, "Yes, I'm a bit under. Thank you, Joe."

And with that Red Paley, narcissistic, pathetic, and consumed by self-pity, called it a night.

Lamentations

Unlike Red Paley, there was no part of Roderick J. Campbell that longed for the pre-WIN days or blamed Frank Clark. He was troubled to be sure, but he wasn't going to blame Frank for aspiring to find a better way of doing things. Roderick's thoughts launched him into a mental soliloquy. "WIN was worth a real try. It was a chance to begin reversing Westville's direction and do something for the people. And there's Red Paley—the self-proclaimed great admiral of the City and political navigator—and he can't even plot a new course. That gutless sonofabitch!"

It was about 8:30 when Roderick returned to his townhome, still ranting about Red to himself, and took some leftovers out of the fridge. He put them on the kitchen counter and let them sit. Even at this hour dinner would have to wait until *he* was ready.

Roderick walked over to his sound system, stopping first to look at a picture of his family that had been taken about seven years ago at the wedding of one his cousins. His mother succumbed to cancer two years later, and it was the best picture he had of his mother, sisters, nieces, nephews, and himself. His mother used to call him "Joey." She was the only one who ever called him that. She would say, "You're going to do something great someday Joey. I know you are." He then focused for a moment on his sister Kendra, whom he had recently learned was going to have a biopsy in the coming week.

Then Roderick's eye quickly scanned some of his favorite books on the shelf: the church Bible he grew up with; a history of the American civil rights movement; and a few biographies of leaders such as Martin Luther King Jr., Mahatma Gandhi, Malcolm X, and Abraham Lincoln. Last, he scanned his favorite books on personal improvement and organizational development by writers such as Stephen Covey, Patrick Lencioni, and Jim Collins. A new book on urban planning, *The Death and Life of Great American Cities*, had recently taken up residence there. Collectively, the contents of these shelves kept him centered on his duty to God, family, society, and the City—in that order.

Roderick thought about the events of the past few weeks. Previously his life had always appeared very clear and linear to him – simple and neatly structured. As he reflected, it occurred to him that his life had largely been about furthering the aims of others: starting with his mother; then his teachers, coaches, and professors; followed by a succession of bosses, most recently Mayor Red Paley. Now things were changing dramatically.

The world Roderick had always seen was no longer so clear and straight-forward. What had been in focus just days ago was now blurred. Everything from his conversations with Fr. Affonso, Frank, Pam, and Byron, and his engagement with the community; to his reflective walks and meditations revealed a world turned upside down. What had been linear now had infinite dimensions and complexity. It seemed to Roderick that every element of this chaotic world was challenging and tormenting him. He needed to adapt, to respond in ways that would be more fulfilling. His relationship with the world he now saw had to be redefined.

Suddenly the man who was the epitome of self-disciplined service was paralyzed by internal conflict. It seemed eerily ironic to him that he who was always able to remain steady and calm was now so perplexed. He had endured many challenges in his life, but the challenges he now confronted were the most daunting to date. "Do I have what it takes?" he thought to himself. Then he sighed, selected a CD, and proceeded to sit back in his favorite chair, where his music usually transported him to his inner refuge, a peaceful place of beauty, harmony, and clarity.

Whether Roderick's choice of music this night was intended to take him somewhere else or to simply invite the possibility of a different journey, the weight of Westville's predicaments and his personal challenges combined with the music to do exactly those things. Roderick listened as a dulcet saxophone introduced Marvin Gaye's voice soulfully singing about war, death, brutality, and injustice, challenging us to see "what's going on."

Roderick accepted the challenge and thought of the people who were hoping Westville could be better and were striving to make it so.

He thought of the Westville that could be and should be, the Westville that was and the Westville that wasn't. The music hit him like a river nearing flood stage, and he let its current sweep his thoughts deep into his soul. He soon found himself gently wiping tears from his eyes. He thought about his role, what he had done and maybe should have done, and what he hadn't. What kind of man he could be and should be, the man he was, and the man he hadn't yet become. He thought of what Father Affonso had said about how an unheeded calling would burden his soul. His city, his people needed more from him, and he hadn't given it. Worse yet, he wasn't sure he ever would. And then the dam that had held his emotions at bay for so long broke, and Roderick wept.

After a few minutes, Roderick composed himself and walked down the hallway and into his home office. Sitting at his desk with the music still playing, he began putting to paper the key thoughts that had been growing in his mind and torturing his soul during the past few weeks. After about twenty minutes, satisfied that he at least had a solid first draft, Roderick smiled softly and exhaled, in the process releasing an enormous burden that had been weighing him down. He then neatly folded the paper and put it in his desk drawer. And then Roderick Joseph Campbell pushed himself back from his desk, stood up, and, stepping more lightly on a new path in his life's journey, returned to his kitchen where he was now finally able to enjoy his dinner.

Appendix A
The Living City
Dr. Harold Hearst, Ph.D.

Logic dictates that anything that is essentially comprised of living organisms must be viewed as itself being alive or at least having many life-like qualities. Would anyone think of a crowd attending a sporting event or a line outside a theatre as being anything but alive? And so it is that we need to begin thinking of cities themselves, as the ultimate sociological association of living beings, the "Human Realm" if you will, as being much more than the bricks and mortar of buildings and public infrastructure, the "Built Realm." In fact, the Built Realm in its essence exists solely to serve and support the Human Realm. Urban planning, development and redevelopment must place more emphasis on cities as incredibly complex dynamic life-like organisms if we are going to see cities achieve their full potential as sustainable communities where people truly thrive.

The concept that cities are alive or life-like should not be difficult to accept. After all, cities are often described in terms of human characteristics such as "friendly," "hard-working," "dull," and "energetic" among others. Chicago and New Orleans have justifiably earned the respective tag lines "The City of Broad Shoulders" and "The Big Easy." No one contends that New York is not "The City that never Sleeps." Clearly, we intuitively believe that cities have animate characteristics.

There are also objective reasons for approaching urban issues from the perspective that cities are alive or life-like. Both individual living organisms and the collective Human Realm that occupies cities are dependent on sophisticated inter-dependent systems for their health and survival. For example, humans have respiratory, digestive,

427

428 | Ford Preston Weber

circulatory, nervous, and reproductive systems to name just a few.

circulatory, nervous, and reproductive systems to name just a few. Cities have sewer, water, and transportation systems; power grids; and communication networks among others – and these systems exist solely to benefit the collective population of living human beings comprising the city's Human Realm just as the human body's individual systems exist solely to support the human organism. None of these systems has any reason to exist in its own right. Each exists solely to support a greater entity, and the performance of each of these respective systems is vital to the health of individuals and of the populations they comprise.

Moreover, the inter-dependency of these systems and networks means that adverse conditions in one system frequently have far-reaching impacts across multiple systems. Just as medical conditions such as high blood pressure and diabetes result in multiple health issues that extend beyond the confines of the circulatory and digestive systems, the consequences of poorly performing city systems have dramatic and far-reaching consequences. For example, it is well known and fully accepted that real estate development tends to follow the development of infrastructure, particularly in a growing market. Retail centers, distribution facilities, hospitals and major manufacturers all want to be well-served by the interstate highway system and other major arteries as well as other public utilities such as water, sewer, gas and electric, and communications.

Clearly strong, well-connected infrastructure systems play a critical role in forging strong communities in the same way that biological systems are essential for individual people to thrive.

Similarly, urban diseases such as slums and blight spread through city districts much like malignant cancers spread through bodies. Blight discourages investment in nearby properties, and in so doing 'blight begets blight' with the same destructive impacts on neighborhoods as multiplying and dividing cancer cells have on living beings.

Just in case this concept needs more support, let me point out that populations of wild animals – as well as humans – migrate to more nurturing, safer physical environments. Herds of herbivores (followed by those that prey on them) migrate to more fertile grasslands and deeper water holes. In a similar manner, people move to neighborhoods that offer a better opportunity to survive and prosper. Access to better job prospects, school systems, healthcare, basic services, located within the confines of a safe and well maintained Built Realm are primary factors in determining whether community grows or shrivels. And whereas that environment in the United States has recently been embedded in a suburban, automobile-dominated environment, growing numbers of young people, empty nesters, and immigrants are finding walkable, dense, vibrant, urban domains much more appealing – if not mandatory. For many people, these are the equivalent of David's verdant pastures.

This leads us to an additional factor of utmost importance that adds to the difficulty of planning great urban places. Regardless of whether we are thinking of animals or plants, the biological and botanical systems that support living organisms have already been seamlessly incorporated into the lives they serve. The same is not true for the man-made Built Realm. Cities need to incorporate essential elements of infrastructure and services into communities that focus primarily on the Human Realm in which the experiences of residents and pedestrians are of paramount importance. We need to focus on creating places where people want to *live* or spend substantial amounts of time, not on places that drivers can rapidly commute *through*.

With these life-like qualities of cities in mind (and paying heed to the conflict between creating places to be as opposed to places to motor through), urban planning and revitalization needs to be approached in a manner very much akin to the practice of holistic medicine. Projects cannot be viewed in vacuous isolation but as potential changes to complex inter-connected systems that often have far-reaching, unanticipated, unintended consequences. Sometimes these consequences produce pleasant surprises, but in the vast majority of instances they do the exact opposite. We need to consciously recognize that the development of urban property isn't just a financial transaction involving the conveyance of property and a capital investment. The construction of a new water line isn't just an extension of public infrastructure. A new school isn't just a place for educating our youth. A new shopping center isn't just a place to purchase goods and services. All of these investments have radiating impacts on walkability, connectivity, sense of place, density, diversity of uses, demographic inclusiveness, and a multitude of other factors impacting the degree to which the Built Realm supports, furthers, and enriches the Human Realm - the Human Experience - which are either positive, negative, or a combination of both.

Further, failure to recognize this "holistic medicine" nature of planning and development makes it impossible to adhere to Hippocrates' admonition to "first do no harm." Consequently, investments in urban areas usually fail to live up to their potential to be catalytic, and in fact have major negative consequences. As Jane Jacobs pointed out in *The Death and Life of Great American Cities,* no amount of money will revive a community if it is spent doing the wrong thing. In fact, she emphasized that large sums of money invested in the wrong things (or the right things but done wrongly) produces cataclysmic results. Equally important, when projects do attain catalytic stature, they usually do so accidentally rather than intentionally; which generally results in a failure to recognize and appreciate the reasons for their broader contributions and a missed opportunity to attempt to replicate those successes with future projects. Unanticipated consequences, whether favorable or unfavorable, should be analyzed so that we can better learn from our experiences.

As an added caution, the rule to "first do no harm" is particularly important when one is tinkering with a part of a community that is functioning well. This is because the downside of causing unintentional damage to a neighborhood that is thriving or at least satisfactorily functioning is much greater than when a project is launched in an area that is under-performing. When an area is not meeting the needs of people – when it is not sufficiently supporting the Human Realm, the risks of undertaking a project that will result in unintended negative consequences are much lower because there is not as much down side exposure. Consequently, there is more opportunity to boldly, but intelligently and prudently, experiment when undertaking projects in weak markets. Of course intelligent experimentation requires an understanding that that is in fact what you *are* doing, and having an "anything goes" development mentality is not the same as experimenting intelligently and greatly increases the risks of failure without generating nearly as much valuable feedback. Conversely, this admonition is not a universal excuse to avoid taking action in high-performing neighborhoods by relying on the axiom that "if it ain't broke, don't fix it."

And so I conclude this brief essay by asking my colleagues to focus more of their energies and vast intellects on evaluating projects not singularly but as parts of a much greater whole and with a perspective that focuses almost exclusively on the immediate impacts on the residents, pedestrians, employees, and patrons of the neighborhoods in which they are situated.

Appendix B
Dr. Harold Hearst's Collective Email Bullets

1. *Cities need to be vibrant in order to be successful—vacancy and dullness are the primary enemies of any urban neighborhood.*

2. *Two of the four essential requirements for a vibrant neighborhood are population density and a variety of primary uses (e.g., housing, retail, offices, restaurants, institutions, etc.).*

3. *Single-purpose neighborhoods and districts such as housing-only neighborhoods and government/judicial complexes are fatally dull.*

4. *The best urban neighborhoods and districts can be enjoyed aimlessly. They don't require an agenda of things to do.*

5. *Providing better city services and beefing up safety forces can help a declining city slow its population exodus, but they are not sufficient to enable a city to **replenish** its population. Doing that requires the development of vibrant neighborhoods that offer an appealing quality of life to people who have the wherewithal to choose where they are going to live.*

6. *Urban projects need to be designed and planned by people who have three qualities/characteristics.* First, they must have a basic knowledge of how great urban areas function for the benefit of people (how the Built Realm

433

best furthers the Human Realm). Second, they must have an urban mindset. Suburban thinkers can't design and plan great urban places, because they simply aren't capable of sufficiently adapting their thought patterns to urban environments. Third, the designers and planners must have a passion for urban living. They must design places as if they themselves might actually live in them or utilize them, and they must view the potential spaces from the perspectives of a diverse range of people who may live in or utilize them. Too often, powerful executives who might have good intentions drive projects forward that simply don't create great urban places. In most instances, these executives lack all three of these characteristics.

7. *Weak market cities such as Westville need to concentrate limited resources on narrow target areas through pilot redevelopment projects in order to have enough impact to be transformational. This is very difficult because the elected officials prefer to spread resources evenly across the city, and the neighborhoods that are not prioritized generally oppose such a strategy.*

8. *The transformation of weak market cities such as Westville takes a very long period of time, because as weak markets they do not experience high levels of private investment. As a result, neighborhoods tend to be relatively stagnant and slowly but steadily continue to age and devolve. On the other hand, the best urban growth comes about gradually and organically through urban evolution. In that way development that furthers a healthy people-oriented community slowly but steadily reinforces itself.*

9. *Weak market cities frequently don't focus enough on reinventing themselves as vibrant urban places (building a tap for the in-flow of new people), because the majority of the population has suffered financially due to globalization and innovation and simply wants the city to efficiently and effectively provide good basic services. Plus there aren't many successful projects that advocates for reinvention can point to in support of their plans.*

10. *No matter how bad the status quo is, there are those who benefit from it and resist change.*

11. *Weak market neighborhoods and cities need to do exceptionally high quality projects in order to elevate their overall quality of life and create a community where people thrive.* You don't improve from average to good by simply doing more of what got you there, just like a C student doesn't raise his or her grade to a B without earning mostly A grades.

12. *No amount of tweaking can make right that which is fundamentally wrong.* There are some buildings, roads, and other proposed uses of land that are simply critically flawed and need to be dropped or terminated altogether— not just modified to mollify. As Jane Jacobs pointed out, capital investment in the wrong project actually does more harm than good, and major capital projects that are erroneously carried out can be cataclysmic.

13. *To love a city, you must be willing to fight for good development and against bad development.* Cities in a way

are like infants: they are defenseless. Now, cities do have some resiliency just like children. And, like children, strong and healthy cities are more resilient than weak cities, just as strong and healthy children are more resilient to afflictions than sickly and malnourished children. So just as to love a child is to nurture and protect it, so it is with loving a city. Therefore, to love a city, you must be willing to fight for good development and against bad development.

14. *The predicament for weak market neighborhoods and cities is "How do you do 'A' quality work when the developers believe the market can only bear the cost of 'C' quality work?"* The solution is to use strategic subsidies to 'prime' the market until such time as the market becomes strong enough to support high quality projects. This need for project subsidies usually leads to serious conflict in weak market cities because they are confronting a wide range of increasing needs and costs while simultaneously having fewer financial resources with which to address them. The funds that are necessary to bridge the quality gap for projects in weak markets are also direly needed to solve numerous other problems. The result can be an epic conflict over the "revitalization bucket" – how to fix the leaks while also generating a flow of water through the tap.

15. *Westville's disadvantaged neighborhoods are embedded in triple weak markets.* First, the neighborhoods themselves are weak markets that have been losing population and amenities. Second, those neighborhoods lie within a city that is a weak market which has been steadily

losing population and neighborhood retailers and service providers for decades. Third, the City itself is located in a region that is a weak market whose population has been stagnant during a period of intense national population growth. As a result, developers have little confidence in Westville. When neighborhoods that are losing people are located within cities and regions that are not growing, there is very little reason to optimistically believe that "if we build it, they will come." Consequently, developers tend to aim low, and the community develops a beggars-can't-be-choosers mentality in which caution and acquiescence to cheap development proposals are the orders of the day.

Appendix C
Westville Investing in Neighborhoods
Office of the Mayor
The Honorable Charles Paley
City of Westville

The City of Westville is coordinating City funds to spur job creation and housing redevelopment in our oldest neighborhoods with the goal of creating communities where our people can live full lives and raise healthy families.

Recognizing that neighborhood businesses need neighbors, the City of Westville is willing to consider proposals that will increase population density provided they meet high design standards.

We envision neighborhoods where people can walk to find places to eat, shop, and visit with their neighbors. Neighborhoods that build identity, strength, community, and entrepreneurship.

The goal of this program is to generate outstanding projects—not test an organization's technical expertise or proposal draftsmanship.

In consideration of this goal, and in recognition of the fact that interested development entities may not be fully familiar with the requirements for obtaining and complying with these wide-ranging funding programs, City personnel are available to work with entities on their proposals. Interested parties are strongly encouraged to avail themselves of this opportunity for staff consultation.

Subject to meeting program eligibility and, if applicable, underwriting requirements, the following funds have been identified by the City of Westville as potentially available for projects:

HOME	$3,500,000
Brownfield Assessment	$ 300,000
Brownfield Remediation*	$1,000,000
Capital Improvement Program (CIP)	$ 300,000
Lead-Based Paint Abatement	$ 500,000
Water and Sewer Taps	$ 100,000
Economic Development Loans	$ 400,000
Total:	$6,100,000

*Source is a US EPA Revolving Loan Fund grant which provides for a combination of grants and low-interest loans for environmental remediation.

In addition, projects may qualify for Community Reinvestment Area (CRA) real property tax abatement.

Preliminary proposals are due in the Department of Neighborhoods on or before 4:00 PM, July 17, 2000. City staff will work cooperatively with the strongest applicants to further refine their proposed projects.

The City anticipates that some proposals may have multiple development phases that extend over several funding cycles.

The City further contemplates that the strongest proposals will build upon existing momentum in Westville's neighborhoods by leveraging investments in infrastructure and new schools and/or libraries that have recently been completed, are planned, or are under active consideration.

For more information, please contact Byron Swift, Senior Director of Strategy, Office of the Mayor.

Appendix D
List of Characters

Name	Job Title or Role
Charles "Red" Paley	Mayor of Westville
Roderick Campbell	Chief of Staff
Karen Jones	Director of Law
Byron Swift	Senior Director of Strategy
Chief McNally	Chief of Police
Bill Zawodny	Director, Department of Public Service
Wilfred Richardson	Wealthy political supporter of Red Paley
Tom Folks	Reporter for *Westville Wire & Telegraph*
Valeria Rodriguez	Director of Human Resources
Art Hill	Director of Finance
Joan	Mayor's Executive Assistant
Franklin "Frank" Jefferson Clark	Attorney; Director of Neighborhoods
Father Affonso	Director, St. Dominic Savio House
Joe O'Neil	Bartender at Lonnegan's
Quincy Dewberry	Chair, University of Westville Board of Regents
Dr. Janice Carter	President, University of Westville
Mayor Pickett	Mayor of Greenfield
Pierce	Janice Carter's Executive Assistant
Bobby "Jive Turkey" Turkel	Former Director of Neighborhoods
Ellen Clark	Frank Clark's wife

443

Kayleigh	Intern, Mayor's Office
Joe Schwartz	Senior Attorney, Law Department
Walter Sage	Senior Administrator, HUD Programming, Westville
Aisha	Former Administrative Assistant for Bobby Turkel
Dr. Harold Hearst	Chair of Planning Department, University of Westville
Dr. Camilla Johnson	Private consultant on organizational development
Pamela King	Executive Director, Creekside CDC
Ella Rickman	Owner of Ella's Styling Salon in Creekside
Michael Casey	Manager, Environmental Services
John Nowak	Executive Director, Ironton CDC
Bill Smith	Executive Director, North Towne CDC
Deacon Wilkens	Abyssinian Baptist Church
Lisa Seelbach	Program Director, Rust Belt Renaissance
Billy Riley	Pres. Building Trades Union
Stan Paulsen	First V. P. Building Trades Union
Tony D'Antonio	Business Manager, Building Trades Union
Ann	Executive Assistant, Neighborhoods
Leonard Malinowski	Owner, Western Vista Hotel

Worstville Timeline of Events

Charles "Red" Paley elected to first term as Mayor	November 1995
Bobby Turkel hired as Director of Neighborhoods	March 1996
Roderick Campbell hired as Chief of Staff	February 1997
Midterm elections: Bobby and Red's scheme	November 1997
Frank Clark joins City as Senior Attorney	August 1999
Byron Swift hired as Senior Director of Strategy	Late April 1999
Charles "Red" Paley elected to second term as Mayor	November 1999
"Hot caliente"/spinning hubcaps Staff Meeting	January 2000 (four months in)
Frank Clark hired as Director of Neighborhoods; Bobby Turkel fired	Early April 2000
Frank's first two meetings with Dr. Harold Hearst and first meeting with Dr. Camilla Johnson	April 2000
Meetings with Michael Casey and with Pamela King, respectively	Early May 2000
"Catastropher" staff meeting	Early May 2000
Roderick confirms budget deficit	Mid-May 2000
HUD budget cut announced	Same day-mid-May 2000
First budget meeting with Red	Mid-May 2000
Second budget meeting with Red	Late May 2000
Frank's third meeting with Dr. Hearst	Mid-May 2000
HUD briefing session with CDCs	Tuesday, May 23,

	2000
Frank laments the first blow to his credibility	Tuesday, May 23, 2000
Red awards first Hubcap Prize	Thursday, May 25, 2000
Red lashes out at CDCs	Thursday, May 25, 2000
Westville Investing in Neighborhoods (WIN) idea is hatched	Thursday, May 25, 2000
Roderick takes neighborhood walk in Creekside	Thursday, May 25, 2000
Frank, Byron, and Walter vet WIN with Roderick; Frank's fourth meeting with Dr. Hearst	Friday, May 26, 2000
Roderick attends Creekside Memorial Day picnic	Memorial Day, May 29, 2000
Briefing Red on WIN and "WIN" Name Adopted	Tuesday, May 30, 2000
WIN is published	Wednesday, May 31, 2000
Dr. Hearst meets with Dr. Johnson	Early June 2000
Brownfields Workshop in Detroit	Mid-June 2000
Rust Belt Renaissance expresses interest in WIN	Mid-June 2000
Drs. Hearst and Johnson have coffee together	Mid-June 2000
Frank reads Collins's *Good to Great* and has coffee with Dr. Johnson	Late June
WIN proposals submitted	Monday, July 17, 2000
Building Trades Union meets with Red	Monday, July 31, 2000
Byron meets with Roderick	Monday, July 31, 2000

Roderick meets with Fr. Affonso; Red meets with Wilfred Richardson	Tuesday, August 1, 2000
Red meets with Roderick and Frank	Wednesday, August 2, 2000
Red announces River City Vista project and defers WIN	Wednesday, August 2, 2000
Roderick and Pamela have lunch together	Friday, August 4, 2000
Community meeting at Creekside High School	Wednesday, August 9, 2000
Leonard and Billy have lunch at Kielbasa Kastle	Thursday, August 10, 2000
Red calls Lisa Seelbach at RBR; Frank's 5th meeting with Dr. Hearst	Thursday, August 10, 2000
City Council votes for River City Vista, deferring WIN ramp-up	Tuesday, August 15, 2000

ABOUT THE AUTHOR

Ford Weber practiced law for fourteen years before transitioning his career to the field of economic and community development in 2001. He has worked extensively in Ohio and Virginia and attained Certified Economic Developer (CEcD) status from the International Economic Development Council (IEDC) in 2010.

35155885R00252

Made in the USA
Middletown, DE
02 February 2019